USURPERS

A NOVEL OF THE LATE ROMAN EMPIRE

EMBERS OF EMPIRE
VOL. II

Q. V. HUNTER

Eyes and Ears Editions
130 E. 63rd St. Suite 6F
New York, New York,
USA 10065-7334
Copyright 2013 Q. V. Hunter

ISBN 978-2-9700889-2-9

Q. V. Hunter has asserted the right under the Copyright,
Design and Patents Act, 1988, to be identified as the author
of this work

1. Hunter, Q. V. 2. Constantius II 3. Magnentius 4. The
Battle of Mursa Major 5. Late Rome 6. Gaul
7. The Roman Empire 8. Roman Emperors 9. Action and
Adventure 10. Espionage
I Title

TO P, OUR ROCK

ALSO BY Q. V. HUNTER

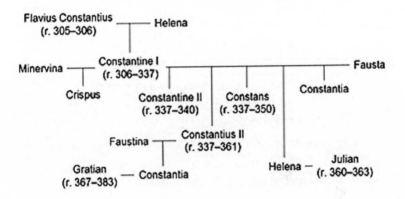

THE CONSTANTINE FAMILY

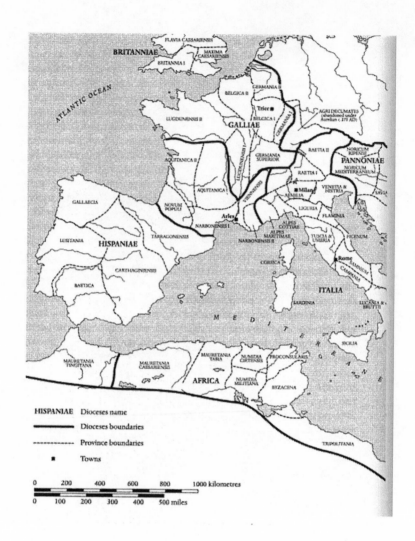

BRITANNIAE

FLAVIA CASSARIENSIS

MAXIMA
CAESARIENSIS

BRITANNIA I

ATLANTIC OCEAN

GERMANIA II

BELGICA II

Trier ■

GALLIAE

BELGICA I

GERMANIA SUPERIOR

LUGDUNENSIS II

AGRI DECUMATES
(abandoned under
Aurelian c. 275 AD)

RAETIA II

NORICUM
RIPENSE

PANNONIAE

NORICUM
MEDITERRANEUM

AQUITANICA II

RAETIA I

AQUITANICA I

VENETIA &
ISTRIA

SAVIA

Milan ■

AEMILIA

GALLAECIA

NOVUM
POPULI

LIGURIA

FLAMINIA

Arles ●

NARBONENSIS I

PICENUM

LUSITANIA

TARRACONENSIS

HISPANIAE

ALPES
COTTIAE

ALPES
MARITIMAE

NARBONENSIS II

TUSCIA &
UMBRIA

CORSICA

SAMNIUM

Rome ■

CAMPANIA

CARTHAGINIENSIS

BAETICA

ITALIA

SARDINIA

LUCANIA &
BRUTTII

M E D I T E R R A N E A N

SICILIA

MAURETANIA
TINGITANA

MAURETANIA
CAESARIENSIS

MAURETANIA
TABIA

NUMIDIA
CIRTENSIS

PROCONSULARIS

AFRICA

NUMIDIA
MILITIANA

BYZACENA

HISPANIAE   Dioceses name

──────   Dioceses boundaries

----------   Province boundaries

■   Towns

0   200   400   600   800   1000 kilometres

0   100   200   300   400   500 miles

TRIPOLITANIA

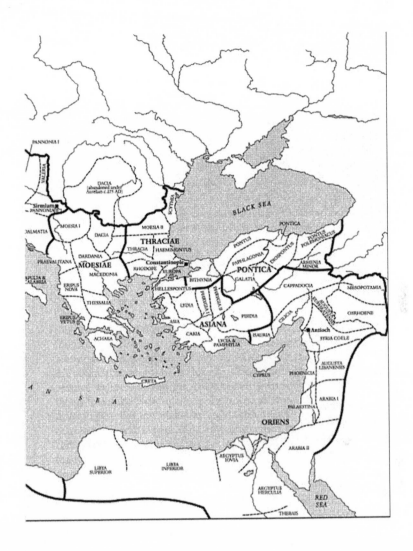

PANNONIA I

VALERIA

Sirmium
PANNONIA II

DALMATIA

DACIA
(abandoned under
Aurelian c. 275 AD)

SCYTHIA

BLACK SEA

PONTICA

PONTUS
POLEMONIACUS

MOESIA I

DACIA

MOESIA II

PRAEVALITANA

DARDANIA

MOESIAE

MACEDONIA

THRACIAE

THRACIA HAEMIMONTUS

RHODOPE EUROPA

Constantinople

PONTUS

PAPHLAGONIA

PONTICA

DIOSPONTUS

ARMENIA
MINOR

EPIRUS
NOVA

APULIA &
CALABRIA

THESSALIA

BITHYNIA

HELLESPONTUS

GALATIA

CAPPADOCIA

MESOPOTAMIA

OSRHOENE

EPIRUS
VETUS

ACHAEA

LYDIA

ASIA

ASIANA

CARIA

PISIDIA

ISAURIA

CILICIA

Antioch

SYRIA COELE

LYCIA &
PAMPHYLIA

CRETA

N
E
A
N

S E A

CYPRUS

PHOENICIA

AUGUSTA
LIBANENSIS

ARABIA I

PALAESTINA

ORIENS

LIBYA
SUPERIOR

LIBYA
INFERIOR

AEGYPTUS
IOVIA

ARABIA II

AEGYPTUS
HERCULIA

RED
SEA

THEBAIS

Table of Contents

CHAPTER 1, CONSTANS' HUNTERS

We had all heard Gaiso was a legendary hunter but I'd seen nothing like his bloodlust before, on or off the battlefield. The joy of the chase carried him faster and farther than the rest of our party. I leaned low in my saddle, dodging branches and jumping fallen logs, but I couldn't catch up with this officer, no matter how hard I galloped after him.

The dogs' baying signaled our prey was escaping us, slipping out of sight somewhere ahead and below. The animal was hiding from us farther down in the untracked valley. They say that the boar is the animal of death—nocturnal, solitary and dark—to be hunted as the year itself comes to a close. And true to his legend, this bristly beast was leading us as deep as he could to his lonely, hellish lair far away from the day's open skies and carefree laughter.

I raced forward to where Gaiso had stopped at last. He was fixing the dogs' position and he glanced back at me with a grin to confirm that of all the hunters who'd set out with us that morning, at least I still kept up. It was an expression sharing his sporting greed for the slaughter. If I was a low-ranked *agens* enjoying a morning's break from my duties, just a bored messenger boy relieved to be riding free and hard for a change, Gaiso was no longer a mere senior officer on horseback. He'd become one with the maddened canine pack.

'We can't wait for the others,' he said. 'We'll lose him.'

Gaiso gave his horse a sharp kick and the animal sidestepped down the densely forested slope. Horse and rider sank into the gold and red foliage and out of my view. I spurred my own mount to track his. It took the others some two or three minutes to catch up. Too careful of their horses' safety to tackle the steep descent through a carpet of slippery leaves, they reined in at the ledge above and watched me disappear.

The darkness shading the forest floor chilled my humid brow. My eyes couldn't adjust. I rode between the trees, feeling the bark brush my elbows and the hooves sink deep into the leaves. My own panting mixed with my horse's sweaty snorts. I heard the dogs' baying ahead. The exhilaration of the impending kill filled my pounding heart.

This was a dangerous happiness. I checked my weapon, remembering the boar hunters' warning: kill the powerful pig with a first and expert thrust—or it will drag you down by your spear to your death.

More than a dozen of us had set out this morning, trotting past the Imperial Mint, through the crowded streets of *tabernae* and bathhouses, under the dark stone arches of Treverorum's main gate, past the amphitheater and onwards to the river. But once across the bridge, Lieutenant Commander Gaiso showed us all up.

The Emperor Constans had set out with us, along with his bodyguard of handpicked German archers, his favored prisoners-of-war. But Gaiso led the hunting party at such a clip that he had quickly put a clear distance between the keenest among us and the Emperor's party.

Then Gaiso had opened a second gap between the serious hunters and the two of us, with me dashing hard behind him towards the densest part of the surrounding forest.

The feeling of charging behind Gaiso's heroic silhouette had turned dreamlike and timeless. I reveled in the autumn sun painting the fiery treetops, the pounding of the horse's flanks beneath my saddle and the pack dogs' barking. This was what real men were doing—not hanging about foyers and corridors, sorting messages, checking road papers, and collecting trivial gossip. This was what a young man like myself was made for.

The dream-like sensation turned to confusion. Had I lost Gaiso? No, I spotted his stallion's flanks disappearing around a rock formation where the valley narrow into a bottleneck. We two still followed the dogs' call, thrashing through leaves and ground cover.

Now I'd lost him again, but I kept riding with one ear cocked for his hunting cry. He would signal for the Emperor Constans to advance and finish off the beast. Preening and smirking, Constans would bear the prize home of course, but to the rest of us, the visiting officer Gaiso would be the hero of the day.

Now a different kind of howling came at my back. Released from their leashes, half a dozen catch dogs descended from the ledge above the valley and whipped past me with pointed ears pressed flat against their hard little skulls. It was time for them to take over from the bay dogs. Their snarling through bared fangs triggered an excitement throbbing in my own temples.

I must be near, I thought. In answer, I heard the boar itself, a chilling sound.

At last I made out the dark forms of Gaiso and our quarry in the distance, just as the bay dogs backed off to let the catch dogs sink their teeth into the boar's ears and pin it fast to the ground for the kill.

Reckless, I closed the last fifty feet at a gallop, branches lashing my face. I caught up with Gaiso whose arm stretched out to me in warning. The boar writhed only a few feet from us, squealing and yanking his head. The catch dogs sank their teeth even deeper. The hounds finally flipped the pig off its feet, exposing its yellowish underbelly for a lethal thrust—the privilege of the Emperor.

But Constans was nowhere to be seen. Six dogs fought to keep the boar pinned down, a mountain of bristles, muscle, fat, and savage tusks framing mean black eyes.

'Signal the Emperor!' Gaiso yelled and glared at me. The signaler was nowhere to be seen. Gaiso raised a frustrated howl of his own, drowning out the dogs and boar, in the direction of the ledge above. We heard the hunting cornet blown—once, twice—and waited, checking our anxious horses from rearing. The boar threw off one of the dogs and nearly bit the leg off another. The dogs doubled up again and pulled the boar back off

3

its feet, their legs braced hard to keep hold of all sides of its grotesque head.

'Get that bastard Constans here!' Gaiso shouted. 'This is his hunt! Where is he?'

The horn blew a second round but no horses appeared in the valley. After another five minutes of this mayhem, with no emperor or bodyguard in sight, Gaiso screamed, 'Find him!'

But it was too late for me to fetch the stragglers in our party back up on the ledge. The boar had tossed off three of the dogs and scrambled back to his feet. He dragged them dee^pper into a cleft between the rocks. In a minute, he might squeeze through some secret exit behind the stones, leaving even the most determined dogs behind.

We were within seconds of losing him.

Gaiso couldn't hold himself back any longer. He was aiming from a bad angle, but he reared back and flung himself forward in the saddle. He shot his spearhead at the boar's heart. Instead his weapon caught fast in the neck. He held on, his horse stepping backwards in panic. The boar's squealing pierced my eardrums. I pulled my horse over to the side of Gaiso's, reined back and launched my own spear, praying for a better hit. My spearhead scored off the bony skull and bounced, clanking against the rocks. I stayed in my saddle, too terrified of the lashing tails, teeth and tusks to dismount for it.

The boar was winning but Gaiso wouldn't give in. His grip on the spear tightened, his face muscles contorted, and his teeth clenched as he yanked again and again, but the spear wouldn't come free. There was no thought of the Emperor now. The boar stood fast, jerking back towards the rock cleft, using hundreds of pounds fuelled by pain and power. The pointed hooves on its stiff little legs made the most of their purchase in the soft forest earth.

And then, with one ferocious yank, the great hog had unseated Gaiso and dragged him flat onto the ground. The only thing slowing his attack on Gaiso's upper leg was his struggle to fling off the last catch dog. Before I could dismount to fight him off, the boar had managed to sink his teeth into Gaiso's upper thigh. I sprang out of my saddle and taking hold of that last catch dog's wide leather collar for leverage, I sank my dagger between the boar's ears. The short blade glided right off the bone. The animal lifted his head in anger, a lethal tusk just missing my arm. I took lower aim and thrust the blade again, deeper into the lower throat muscles, again and again and again.

It felt like stabbing wood, rock or iron—not flesh. I kept my eyes fixed on the bristling hide resisting my knife and then finally, glistening with blood. The boar's squealing and the pack's howling filled my ears. My breast filled with a passion for killing until I felt Gaiso grab my arm.

Gaiso said, 'Stop. Now. Stop.' His leg was free. The huge boar lay next to him, warm but dead. The dogs dropped their heads and circled around us in a silence filled by forest birds.

I gasped and bent over, relief flooding my limbs. I dropped my bloody dagger on the dirt.

'Well done,' he said. 'Name?'

'Marcus Gregorianus Numidianus.' I took off my Pannonian felt cap.

He took in my olive skin, dark hair and brown eyes. 'Auxiliary soldier?'

'*Agens in Rebus, Circitor Upper Class*, just promoted up from rider to receiver for the postal service, attached to Treverorum a few weeks ago.'

'Well, bravo, mail boy. Your kind of courage is wasted sorting memos!' He ran his fingers through hair stringy with sweat. 'How I love a good hunt! Will you look at that thing? My biggest ever, I think.' He rose and limped over to pat the boar's greasy head as if it were a fallen comrade-in-arms.

'I've seen that kind of wound fester on the battlefield, Lieutenant Commander. Can you ride?'

'He pierced me, but didn't tear out any flesh.'

'It's bleeding hard. Stay put.'

He grimaced. 'I should bind it up before riding all the way back.'

'You need a medic to disinfect it with acetum. I'll leave you my drink.'

Gaiso laughed through his pain and emptied my wineskin in one greedy glug. 'Hurry back before Constans gets here. He might feel cheated of his trophy and finish me off instead.'

I searched the blazing treetops for my bearings. It was midday, hard to find my direction but for the chaotic path of trampled greenery behind us. I picked up the reins of my horse and waved back from my saddle at Gaiso grinning in his agony there on the dank earth.

'Get going! Boar's meat goes off faster than anything!' he shouted after me.

It wasn't hard to navigate back up the dense slope and reach the abandoned ledge. The others must have decided to search out a safer descent or given up. So there was nothing for it but to head all the way back alone. Ahead of me there was a wide stretch of open brush, then a woodland of young trees that circled the capital like a second wall built by nature to match the impressive fortifications of Roman engineers.

At a fast gallop I reached the edge of these trees. I looked for the path cutting straight back to Treverorum, but there was no obvious trail. My horse slowed and sniffed the air, as if he sensed something wrong. Boar? Bear? I wasn't frightened but I was skilled at fighting men, not four-legged enemies.

I rode him at a walking pace as we threaded our way between the tree trunks. Only now I noticed a torn piece of trousers flapping against my naked shin. My horse had also suffered scattered nicks that were oozing blood across his forelegs and barrel between my knees. My hands were smeared with rusty crusts of the boar's blood.

But what were a few grazes? I almost wished the cost had been higher. It had been like something out of the tales I'd read as a slave of ten to the old blind Senator in the Manlius house back in Roma. I'd thrilled to Homer's heroes hunting the boar that ravaged Calydonia, a beast so monstrous only a band of Argonauts could destroy it. Or there was the youthful Odysseus, gored in the leg by a boar. His hunting scar was the only thing his elderly nurse Eurycleia recognized when the warrior finally returned to his wife Penelope still waiting for him in Ithaca.

I was exhausted but heartily glad of the adventure. I'd enjoyed a whole day out in the fresh air unclouded by the incense and intrigue that floated through the Treverorum Palace corridors. If there were any really important secrets for me to report, they stayed well above my head so far. I was too lowly to answer directly to Constans or his sister, and too bored to make much of my new assignment. I was an *agens* at the bottom of the pecking order, a hierarchy that grew more rigid by the week. I wondered constantly about the people I'd left behind for this new life of menial routine and secrecy.

I missed soldiering, even as a slave-bodyguard to a master who'd fathered me, denied me as his son, and only freed me under duress. But if there were more days like this one, with a hearty veteran like Gaiso to follow, I'd put up with the tedium of delivering messages and memorizing empty conversations.

After twenty minutes of slow going, I spotted a wider path rutted by wheels and hooves. I jerked the horse's bit to the right. He stopped testing the moldy leaves with petulant steps and started a confident canter along the moist track. We continued on serenaded by birds darting around the leafy forest roof. I thought I heard laughter for an instant, but my horse's hooves pounded the trail, so I dismissed it. I hurried him, knowing Gaiso's wait must seem endless. Any minute we should emerge from the woods in sight of the Porta Nigra's powerful black arches.

I heard that odd laughter again, unmistakable this time, followed by strange sighs and short grunts. I reined in my horse to listen, but heard only the birds. Then an eerie little squeal reminded me of the ferocious pig lying next to Gaiso deep in the valley. I hurried onward and ignored another series of odd sounds, some animal defending its young or in rut. But there was that sound like laughter again, first tittering, then harsh and mocking, and this time much closer ahead on my trail.

Through the trees, I glimpsed a flash of rich purple. I slowed the horse again to a walk. I heard strange cheers and a cry that set me leaning back in my saddle.

If these were beasts, they were not four-legged.

The trail now slanted up a small slope towards the sun. I didn't remember this as part of our outward race towards the hunt and figured I was stumbling on a peasant village or private farm. If only it were so.

My horse crested the hillock and halted at the edge of a glade or I should say a sort of circular room of grass, boulders and brush, patchworked with black shadows and bright patches of sun. Some half dozen or more naked German prisoners of war sprawled on the grass or lazed with their backs against boulders. Their bronzed forearms and calves looked much darker than usual when seen next to the pink skin of their backs and haunches.

Some of their bodies were striped with vicious purple scars, yet all these men were youthful beauties, spared from harsher slavery by a blond boy emperor not yet thirty himself. But according to rumors around the Palace, their debasement was no less a prison.

The Germans didn't notice me at first. They'd just started up a drinking song in their rough dialect, drowning out the sound of my horse breaking the brush of the clearing. Two of them lay side by side facing each other on a cloak spread across the grass. They tossed dice. I stared, astonished to see the embroidered imperial crest, with gold bands hemming its purple fabric, used as a casual picnic blanket.

The gamblers looked up. 'What's this?' He addressed me in a coarse Latin.

'Covered in blood. A refreshing sight! Join the party, messenger!'

They leered at me with eyes reddened by drink. My horse's nostrils flared. Now I was noticed by the whole group, except for two men busy at the far edge of the glade making noises fit for a brothel. The man face down beneath his partner looked up and met my horrified gaze. For a glazed second, through his mix of pleasure and humiliation, his eyes locked on mine. Another German stood by the couple, waiting for his turn.

Love between men did not offend any Roman, but enslavement of any kind reminded me of my own past. Now I saw with my own eyes that the Emperor of the Western Empire had become no more than a slave addicted to the abuse of our Empire's enslaved.

Cheeks burning, I turned my horse as quickly as I could and retreated into the shadows of the forest again, retracing my way back to the wide path and taking another turning to the town.

Confusion flooded my mind. All these weeks since arriving in Treverorum, I'd worked to get noticed, be promoted, and earn a real assignment. I'd hoped to be transferred back to the Castra for better training and to be posted closer to my boyhood home. I'd wished that the *magister* who'd overseen me from an untried slave-bodyguard through my liberating army mission to a freedman ranked among the *agentes in rebus* would do more than ask me to open mail and listen at keyholes.

I'd been posted to the court in Treverorum to spy out any reasons for rumored discontent or disgust. I was supposed to dig up the roots of low morale roiling the military professionals across the north and west of the Empire.

Today I'd stumbled on why the treasonous comments of generals and war veterans worried ears in influential offices and book-lined studies. Now I understood why, from court to court, burly fighting men called the Emperor Constans' engagement to Olympias, the daughter of a praetorian prefect, a longstanding farce.

Some of these unhappy soldiers were old enough to remember service under the fearless Constantine. They had been trained to defend their Empire, to the death if necessary. Instead they found themselves answering to Constantine's effeminate and spendthrift youngest son—who repelled their sense of honor and purpose even as he in turn scorned their medals and their courage.

It wasn't affection between two men that revolted them. It was Constans' physical and emotional prostration to the profit and ridicule of the enemy. He made a mockery of Roman valor and service.

The images of the morning stayed frozen in my memory, like stone figures carved a rich man's coffin, one side depicting a vivid boar hunt, the other a scene of debauchery. A coffin for an empire as well?

I'd seen enough in the glade for my first proper report to the spymaster Apodemius at our *schola*'s headquarters, the Castra Peregrina in Roma. Unfortunately, the sovereign Constans had seen *me*. He might be more inclined to sport with a German archer than a vicious boar, but the Emperor wasn't stupid.

It was hard to know how Constans had slipped from the most promising of the Constantine sons to the least. Almost immediately after his father's death—even before he'd come of age—Constans had carried off a resounding victory over invading Sarmatians in 337.

His eldest brother, Constantine II, had died in 340 underestimating his youngest brother's strength. He had tried to snatch Constans' share of the Empire and failed. It was a conflict that loomed large in my personal history because Constantine II had died in an ambush of Illyrians led by my own ex-master under the walls of Aquileia. Commander Atticus Manlius Gregorius had watched from the banks of the Alsa River as his victorious cavalrymen tossed Constantine II's body into flowing waters.

It was a victory that the winner Constans didn't see in person. True to form as a killer by proxy, he had lingered back in Dacia while Commander Gregorius finished the job. Nobody had to tell me that Constans let others fight his battles for him—against boar or brother.

Now the golden-haired Emperor, only twenty-six years old, ruled Gallia, Britannia, Italia, Hispania and Roman Africa, though actual ruling lost out to banqueting. He was indeed not stupid but reports of his cruelty filtered down to my *agens* post. The Emperor knew exactly what my account would mean if it reached his remaining brother Constantius II, now fighting a real battle against Persia along the Empire's eastern border.

But I couldn't worry about that right now. As I galloped the final mile towards the capital's Porta Nigra, I concentrated on getting aid as fast as I could back to Gaiso. The sentries saw me racing towards them. A signal went up and a few of our original hunting party assembled under the arches, waiting for my news.

I summoned the nursing Gaiso needed and pushed concerns about my report on Constans to the back of my mind—but it wouldn't stay in retreat. The degree of debasement and risk to the Empire was bound to be as explosive as Greek fire and just as dangerous to my career. I was trained to serve the Empire, not my own safety. How should I word such a dispatch? How should I portray the degradation of the one man appointed to defend the new Christian Church against pagan critics in Roma? How could I do my job without being accused of treason myself?

And with an entire Western Empire at stake, would I be allowed to file the report at all?

Chapter 2, Constantia's Desire

Gaiso's thigh, bound firmly with boiled rags soaked in acetum, was still inflamed and tender that evening. His rising fever worried everyone in the palace. Dinner for the staff was perfunctory and subdued—the usual harvest-season smoked game and nut-crusted preserves in honey these northerners like. Their bread was dark and indigestible. I would have given a month's wages for a succulent fig or some fresh sea catch drizzled with lemon juice. But we ate better than anyone else in this prefecture, thanks to the Emperor's demands.

I picked at my food, listening to the conversation around me as ordered, but I was also mulling over thoughts darker than any of the careless banter. I quit the meal as soon as was polite and slipped back to my small first-story room overlooking the inner and outer palace courtyards, with my postal cubicle at the arch linking the two.

No doubt Gaiso's imperial hosts and the higher-ranked of our hunting party were right now digesting a final course in the Emperor's private dining room. They would be talking about the hunt late into the evening.

In the palace's outer courtyard, a couple of cooks with arms like anvils prepared the heavy beast. They had lashed it with ropes and spikes to a spit for skinning and defatting. Scabby waifs scrambled for bristles and scraps of hide tossed their way. Some disrespectful joker had tied a length of purple ribbon around its gargantuan neck.

By tomorrow's midday meal, there would be roasted boar meat for a ceremonial tasting. I wasn't tempted. This particular creature was a hoary old specimen, famed among the locals for its thick hide, aggressive personality and canny evasions of all previous expeditions. I could still smell its musky fecal stench on my hands.

Treverorum boasted the largest baths north of the Alps, but I was too tired to push through its streets crowded with off-hours wool merchants, arms-dealers and imperial paper-pushers adding to the common throng gawking at the monster pig on display.

I washed and scraped myself clean using water in my basin like an army man. I bolted my oak door, snuffed out my bronze oil lamps and retired to my narrow bed. The autumn sun was barely down and the banquet below my window not yet over, but I hated the shrinking hours and chilly nights of the north.

On festive evenings like these, no one would miss the Numidian *agens*. Most of my duties fell in the morning hours—receiving and registering the post and sorting the messages, as well as reading them in secret and making copies as necessary. I skimmed through accounts from the local mint. I kept an eye on army dispatches informing the Emperor of skirmishes along the Rhenus River and I shook my head at religious appeals calling for Constans to settle theological questions.

Was the new Christ really part-God or merely God-like? It boiled down in Greek to a single letter, 'i.' The Christian bishops' tedious debate made me yawn.

I tried to doze, but tonight half my brain feared a footstep outside my locked door. The other half recalled a warm desert night in Numidia Militaris when I held the runaway servant girl Kahina in my arms. I forgot for a few hours my assignment to spy on the fanatic religious outlaws she had joined. I had saved her from martyrdom and unknowingly saved my unborn child, only to lose them both to none other than my former master and unacknowledged father.

I loved all three—especially the unseen child—but secrecy, resentment, jealousy and most of all, my own ambition kept me at arm's length. My son would be better off raised as a legitimate heir to the House of Manlius, not a freedman's bastard. Kahina had protested she could never love her betrothed, but I knew her mettle. She would honor the bravery and name of Commander Atticus Manlius Gregorius, despite his disfiguring, crippling wounds.

She had no idea she was marrying not only my former master but also my natural father. He had no idea his legitimate heir by Kahina was actually his own illegitimate grandson. I knew he was my father, but when he tried to evade his promise to free me, I'd broken away from him in bitterness. I was too proud to ask him to confess the truth. I would let him live with his conscience, as the rebuffed, discarded owner of an ungrateful slave and unacknowledged son.

I was the only person who knew every one of these secrets that bound the four of us together. I kept them buried in my heart. I gambled everything I cared about now on proving an ex-slave could rise in station to become a trusted imperial agent.

I heard a swish of robes passing my door but no footsteps—or at least, no honest feet shod in respectable leather. I didn't trust men who wore brocade slippers or jeweled sandals in this climate—and there were a lot of them around every corner and corridor of this brand new capital.

I drifted off at last, to the comforting sensation of a reliable horse to ride and no spying eyes watching my every move . . .

Then I woke up. This time those were indeed solid boots striding up to my door. Someone gave it a sharp, single knock.

'Numidianus, you're wanted!'

I pulled my tunic shirt back on and found an aged porter in heavy wool layers waiting outside, coughing up phlegm.

'The *Augusta* Constantia has a message to dispatch to the East. Go pick it up.'

I shook my head. 'I'm not authorized to enter the imperial suite. Tell her maid to bring it down to me in the main reception hall. I'll register it for tomorrow morning's bag to Mediolanum.'

He was a wily old coot, familiar with the goings-on in the regal residential wings. He gave me an unpleasant wink with a rheumy eye. 'Sorry, friend. She asked for "the Numidian". And as far as I can see, you're the only damned African between here

15

and the Circus latrines.' He leaned on my doorframe and wiggled his eyebrows.

'It sounds wrong to me. Check with Eusebius. He never sleeps.'

One didn't cross Eusebius in this palace. The eunuch was the *praepositus sacri cubiculi*, senior chamberlain of the imperial quarters, the 'man' who led the silk slipper cohort. Needless to say, we hadn't had eunuchs back in the army, but I'd seen immediately that where Eusebius was concerned, rank or office didn't matter.

What Eusebius lacked in masculinity, he made up in guile. He was smart, observant and powerful. In many, he inspired fear. I tried to forgive it in his case because he'd lost the essentials of manhood, either through a misfortune of birth or some unlucky encounter with the Fates.

'Eusebius is busy.' The old man waggled his eyebrows again.

'He's always busy—'

'She asked for you, she wants *you*.'

'Inform the Lord Chamberlain anyway. I'm coming.'

Anyone in imperial service learns quickly that state artists tend to flatter their subject matter. I'd seen the Augusta's features in both marble and paint, but only once in the flesh. She was crossing the threshold of the inner courtyard to clamber into a litter festooned with swags and gilt.

The two Emperors' sister had all the ingredients for beauty—a slender figure, black hair fixed in three or four rows of curls piled high at the front of her brow over the same large eyes and neat nose of her younger brother Constans.

She was lucky. She could have inherited the heavy, upturned chin and hooked nose that gave busts of Constantius II the aspect of a crab's claw.

I had also noticed a piercing glint to those dark-lashed eyes and a mean set to the rouged lips that wasn't alluring.

Error or not, my summons to her rooms tonight gave me a better chance to check the Constantine female line up close.

I straightened myself up, but had no time to don full armor. On the way to the imperial bedrooms, I passed the winter *triclinium*, where the raucous diners were still at it on their cushioned couches. I continued into less familiar corridors and announced myself. Two of Constantia's ladies escorted me into a shadowy marble foyer to wait.

The sculptor's art, no matter how accurate the line and scale, also misses out on smell and sound. Lamps and braziers gave off light and warmth, but my nose sensed the *Augusta* before I saw her. A whiff of jasmine conjured up my Mediterranean childhood.

From the approaching jangle of bracelets, belts and earrings, I knew she must be nearby, even before she emerged from behind a filigreed screen.

Back in Roma, my mistress Lady Laetitia once confided to me that if we men put on helmets, breastplates and leg guards for battle, the ladies of the Empire arm themselves with their finest jewelry in defense.

If so, the *Augusta* was wearing full battle gear tonight. She wrapped her person in a carapace of gold collars, bracelets and even a leather belt studded with light blue topazes, golden amber, garnets and green emeralds. Yes, she'd braced herself into a female version of imperial armor but I doubt she intended to give the first impression that I actually got—that of a tired, drawn creature shackled in overpriced chains and handcuffs.

There were hollow circles under her eyes, underscored by the Belgican fashion in heavy eye-makeup. She smiled with small, very white teeth.

'Did I disturb your rest, Numidianus?'

'I'm honored. You have a message for me to dispatch?'

'For the *Augustus* on the Persian front. A *private* message.'

I nodded my head. 'All imperial messages are secure, *Augusta*.'

She smiled to herself. 'Aren't you surprised I asked for you?'

'As you please, *Augusta*.'

'There are other messengers on duty, aren't there?'

I bowed my head and waited. Questions from above tended to be rhetorical. Years of early slavery in a patrician household had taught me to listen and observe.

From underneath lowered lids, I took in the lurid decor of her private rooms—walls warmed with fur hangings tied with gilt ropes, a folding table strewn with delicate unguent flasks and at least one silver-handled whip. Her window curtains were sewn from flaming orange brocade held in by gold braid fastened with pheasant feathers. Her personal dining couch was upholstered in the black and white stripes of an animal I didn't even recognize.

The whole effect was more feral than imperial.

'My message isn't quite finished,' she called to me. 'Follow me while I add a few more words.'

I trailed her into an adjoining chamber dominated by a wooden bed ornamented with ivory carvings and pink-belled seashells. She sat down in her sloped chair at a makeup table and resumed writing.

'It's a comfortable room, but not as nice as my suite in Mediolanum. I'm always cold here,' she pouted.

'As you say, *Augusta*, Mediolanum is much warmer.'

'Goodness knows, no one needs an *augusta* near any damned Rhenus defense line. That's what I'm writing my beloved brother. Do you like my mural? I commissioned it.'

A painting behind her bedstead depicted an orgy scene. Satyrs cavorted with nubile half-dressed women, offering them grapes, goblets, and far more personal assets.

'Charming, *Augusta*.'

'Oh, look at it more closely. Use that lamplight if you wish. You may kneel on my bed—it won't break, even under a young man's strong pressure.'

Across the polished expanse of mosaic tiles, she tossed a friendly smile over her shoulder and added, 'It's been tested.'

I realized she was proud of her lovely, straight teeth. Then she licked her rouged lips, as if she'd detected my admiration, and went back to finishing her letter.

I stayed well clear of the embroidered bedclothes and kept my eyes fixed on the dogs painted in the lower corner. They reminded me of the hunting dogs closing in on Gaiso's doomed boar.

'I'm not close to my little brother, but I hold the *Dominus* Constantius very dear. You guarantee that this will remain private?' She warmed her sealing wax over a flickering flame.

'Your letter?'

'Yes, of course my letter.' She gave a low chuckle. 'What did you think I meant?'

'Yes, of course, *Augusta*.'

Her voice took on a taunting edge. 'How can you guarantee my letter will even leave these walls?'

'I assure you—'

'You can assure me because you're the "nobody" who reads everything that goes in and out of this palace.' She threw her head back and laughed through those bright, sharp teeth. 'Am I right?'

Before I could answer, she sauntered over and gave my shoulder a light tap with her letter. 'You see, Eusebius tells me everything. He's my eyes and ears, on every floor and in *every* corner of this palace. He reports to me. He's my spy.'

'I'm new here. I've got much to learn from the chief of the *cubicularii*.' It was true. No one was in a better position to know court secrets than the eunuchs who tended the imperial bedchambers.

She rounded the end of her bed and backed me up against the mural. Her tight black curls smelled of jasmine oil and something else that might have been civet essence.

'How fast will my letter travel from this freezing dump?'

'By twenty-four hour relay to Mediolanum in four and a half days via Augusta Raurica and Brigantium, then eastwards for fifteen days through Sirmium to Constantinopolis and then to the battle front.'

'I trust you, Numidianus.' She pressed her letter on my chest with a hand laden with rings.

'Oh, what's this?' Her sharp fingernails feeling through my shirt, she took the measure of my amulet, an oversized *bulla* from the old Senator Manlius.

I extracted it from her tight grasp with care. 'A sentimental trifle.'

'You're a grown man but still wear a child's ornament?' She tilted her face to one side and tested a playful wink. 'What if I asked for it as a present?'

'It's a worthless clump of bronze-covered pottery. Nevertheless, I promised someone to never give it up, even in manhood.' I slid the letter out from under her fingers and gave her a formal nod. She didn't accept my gesture that the order of business at her bedside was complete.

'Do you like games?' she purred. Close up, I saw not only circles under her eyes, but creases collecting the black kohl into feathery lines. The widowed *Augusta* was something just under thirty, I guessed. That made her some seven or eight years older than myself.

'I enjoy sport, like any man, *Augusta*. I enjoyed hunting with Lieutenant Commander Gaiso this morning.'

'My younger brother has claimed all the credit. He always does.' She took a deep breath but didn't move even an inch away. 'Do you like indoor games as well?'

'I prefer sports in fresh air.'

She took it in good humor. 'My late husband, the General Hannibalianus taught me games of all kinds. I miss him.'

'King of kings and Ruler of the Pontic people, yes, I have heard that the late Constantine had a good friend in your husband—or should I say uncle?'

'But Hannibalianus was supposed to rise farther. He failed. We never do beat the Persians, do we? And so I never got to be Queen of the Pontic people.' She sighed as she played with one of the heavy necklaces adorning her scrawny neck. 'Then Hannibalianus died . . . prematurely.'

'Yes, your entire family suffered sad losses.'

She chuckled. 'You *are* diplomatic as well as efficient. You call those murders "sad losses"? We Constantines love to play games. We're a family with a peculiar pastime. We stick together until we kill each other.'

'Not very sporting, *Augusta*,' I slid free of her shadowy presence and bowed my head again to end the interview.

'Oh, you're wrong, *Agens*. The sport lies in guessing when and who.'

She wandered around the room for a moment with an exaggerated flip of rustling hips until she found a length of silk cord lying on one of her side tables. She wound it around her wrist and sauntered back around the bed. I confirmed with a quick glance around the suite what my instinct had already whispered. Her maidservants had retreated. The *Augusta* and I were alone.

'Hannibalianus told me that in battle, sometimes pain and excitement become one, so that you can't tell whether you're dying or in ecstasy. He said wounds come to mean nothing in the heat of combat, with the crush of men and their blood and sweat on all sides, the roars and screams as body presses upon body . . .'

'Thank you, *Augusta*.' I bowed again, lower, and made for the arch to the outer foyer, but she stopped my progress halfway by looping her golden cord around my waist and catching the tasseled end. She drew my hips close to hers.

'There's a rumor around this palace that you were a boy slave in the Manlius household in Roma and earned your manumission by bravery in the field.'

'The Empire found a use for me and rewarded me.'

'You were quite right to fight for your freedom. I hear the Manlius clan is played out, finished, like that whole malarial city.' She toyed with her cord, chafing my back as she pulled on one end, then the other, back and forth. 'Do you look for a better future here in Treverorum?'

'I hope to advance in rank, *Augusta*.'

'It might be easier than you think—all those ranks and classifications—the *agentes* act as if they were the cavalry! That's so boring. There might be a more interesting use for your training.'

I said nothing and tucked her letter under my tunic.

'I hear you *agentes* learn to ride very hard and fast.'

'Yes, *Augusta*.'

'That you go for days and nights without sleep.'

'We rest a little between stages, *Augusta*.'

'You train to go long distances without ... ever ... ' She pulled the cord tighter and whispered in my ear, 'stopping.'

'We're trained to serve.'

'You could serve in so many easier ways.' She let the cord go a little slack. 'Slaves can't say no, but then there's no pleasure, is there? For real excitement, there has to be willingness and freedom and sometimes a little pain.' She jerked the cord tighter around me again. 'Excitement mixed with pain or ...' Her dark eyes narrowed as she added, 'just ... pain.'

Her breath, coming now in tiny pants, told me hunting was her sport, too. She was as expert as Gaiso in her way. I felt cornered, even without the bay dogs harrying me.

My stubborn silence triggered that spark of cruelty in her eyes. 'Did you ever meet one of the palace clerks here, a Gaul named Dax?'

Ah, here came her catch dog.

I swallowed before answering, 'A palace *clerk*? There's a cripple near the gate they call Dax.'

I'd seen the mutilated barbarian, both legs atrophied and twisted backwards underneath him as he begged for coins. We passed him every day as we rode in and out of town.

'He used to be a playmate of mine, she whispered, 'before his accident.'

I heard a swish of thick robes. By the gods' intervention, perhaps her maid was back in the room.

A strange, high voice broke in. 'It's late, *Augusta*. As the saying goes, a messenger detained is a message delayed.'

Cocooned in silver-embroidered maroon brocade, the eunuch Eusebius stood in the dark archway between the outer chamber and the foyer. I'd forgotten I'd asked the palace runner to inform him. I was more than ever aware of the Constantia's silken belt. The eunuch could be a dangerous witness if something was misconstrued. Already his protruding eyes bulged out at us standing side by side next to the bed.

'I'm so sorry to disturb you,' he bowed, 'but I feared there was some mistake. Surely an *augusta*'s messages aren't meant for the collection of an *agens*, especially a mere *circitor*.'

The cutting cord slackened its bite. She sighed. 'You're right, Eusebius, as always. I mustn't keep Numidianus. He seems tired from the hunt.'

She tossed her head to dismiss me. I strode past Eusebius holding a low and grateful bow. As I closed the outside door, I heard the whip of golden cord slapping on marble.

Her letter to Constantius was sealed tight, its wax resting still warm on my bare skin and the heat of her breath still burning my ear.

CHAPTER 3, 'THE CHAIN'

—MORNING, TREVERORUM—

I felt suspended, like some Subura slumdweller waiting for their cloddish neighbor's other sandal to drop on the floor overhead. Only in this case, my surroundings were luxurious and the other fellow wore hand-stitched embroidered slippers.

Eusebius was patient and clever. He didn't summon me until well after dawn—only a short 'autumn hour' or so before the outgoing rider was to ride south with the morning's dispatches. I still carried Constantia's letter on me, intending to add it to the post at the last and safest possible minute.

'Your first time to my office, Numidianus? Take a seat.' He patted his fawn-colored hair flat down on his skull with a pudgy hand. His boiled-egg eyes bulged at me in welcome.

'Thank you, Eusebius.'

He had a spacious room decorated in a refined, classical style—unexpected in such a vulgar, modern palace of garish mosaics and clashing draperies. I stood on the same black and white tiles I recalled from the Manlius vestibule back home in Roma. Eusebius had filled his shelves with expensive new papyrus *codices* with spines embossed in gold—no old-fashioned scrolls for him.

Behind his sleek desk hung a colored map of the Roman world stretching from the Persian border in the East across Thrace and Illyricum to Italia, south to Egypt and Roman Africa, and all the way up to the barrier built by Hadrian to mark off Roman territory from the Celts'. This was no working sketch, no military guide, folded and refolded, muddied or blood-smeared. It hung in an ornate frame, as pristine as a painting.

It was all very elegant, but the eunuch could not resist a touch of his native East. Wisps of overpowering incense floated from a burner hanging on a chain near the doorway.

I couldn't help gagging.

'Sorry, but I can't bear the stink of that thing roasting below.'

'I doubt the animal will taste any better than it smells.'

'Still, the man who kills such a beast is bound to be seen as heroic.' His eyes flared wide at me with meaning.

'Gaiso would have waited for the Emperor, but the boar would not postpone his own death.'

The eunuch smiled at my evasion. I could see he enjoyed playing games.

'Numidianus, I'm a great admirer of your *schola*. You *agentes* are efficient and nothing if not discreet. But I prefer to be open-handed in a court with so many interests.' He slid a silver pitcher of diluted wine across his desk. I demurred.

'Oh, take a sip. You're a man in need of friends, Numidianus. I want to be one of them.' He patted his stomach and belched. 'I ate too much last night. I always eat too much up here. It's the cold. It piques the appetite.' For all that talk of cold and the padding of his robes, his pale brow glistened with sweat.

'Freedmen like myself mustn't get above themselves. I make friends slowly, Eusebius.'

'So, start with me. We might begin by sharing the contents of the *Augusta* Constantia's letter?'

I shrugged, wondering how much diplomacy would help me this morning. 'As you say, I'm new. So I follow regulations, *to the letter*. No post is shared, in principle, with anyone but the recipient or his secretary—today, tomorrow or next week. If you're setting me a test, I fully intend to pass. You can rely on me to keep the section of the post and road service under my direction honest.'

'Ah,' he shook his head, 'an *agens* fresh as a green apple from his upgrade course. Well, let me make it easier for you then, just to save us time.' He rang a silver bell sitting on his desk. A slave came through a small door in the corner of the room, obscured by a folding screen. He laid a platter of dark bread slices spread with honey and smoked fish paste on the desk. Eusebius offered me a taste. I wasn't hungry but I took a slice. A mouth full of fish paste can't leak secrets.

'First, last night the *Augusta* told you I was her spy.'

I raised an eyebrow and kept on chewing.

'I'm not her spy, though it's easy enough to fool that woman. Officially, I report to the Emperor Constantius on what she and the Little Emperor do on their various escapades around the courts of the West.'

'I wondered why you were here and not near Constantius himself. You say, *officially* you report to him, but—?'

'Yes,' he smiled, 'But I investigate what I want and whomever I want, and so far have kept the best tidbits to myself.' He took a slice of bread and gobbled it down. 'I advise you to do the same, particularly since the recent hunting outing. You never know when a little dirt can come in handy.' He pulled a bit of grayish fish meat from his teeth and wiped his lips with a gold-trimmed linen napkin.

'Second, the *Augusta* probably told you she disliked the Emperor Constans and preferred our senior Lord in the East.'

'I didn't inquire.'

'If she even implied it, she lied. She despises poor Constans, true, but she fears their older brother to the point of terror. After all, after the old Constantine died, Constantius killed her husband along with most of their other relatives—hardly an act of Christian, brotherly love.'

'She seems a lonely woman.'

'My, you're observant.'

'Eusebius, I'm going to have to leave you now for my rounds.' His fish paste was oily and bitter. I rose from my chair.

'Show me her letter.'

I cocked my head as if I'd heard someone call me and headed for the door.

Eusebius tossed aside his bread slice and waved me farewell. 'It's all right. I can guess the contents. "Dear Esteemed Brother, Eternal glory to your reign, *et cetera, et cetera*, success and victory against the Persians follow your every step, *et cetera*, and get me out of here and give me a court of my own somewhere warm." Something along those lines?'

He was accurate to the last comma but I wasn't going to tell him that. 'Eusebius, you have misunderstood my simple message to you. I serve the Empire.'

'So you think like all new-made barbarians. You men of fresh blood amuse me. You revere the club you've just joined and elevate it into some kind of priestly calling. You think you serve the Empire, but listen to me. You serve a vain and short-sighted man in *Apodemius*.'

I stopped short, my hand frozen around the door handle. Few men bandied around the name of the discreet, arthritic traveller who recruited unlikely agents from all corners of the vast imperial network of cities and towns. Apodemius answered only to the *Magister Officiorum* of the whole Roman Empire. No eunuch—no matter how well positioned—could equal the old man's reach. If I owed any personal thanks for giving me a new life after cutting myself off from army and ex-master, it was to Apodemius as well as the retired *agens* who recruited me, his friend Leontus Longus Flavius of Theveste.

I wasn't about to discuss those two cherished mentors with a half-man like Eusebius.

'I'm sure we'll be friends, Eusebius, and I'm listening to you very carefully indeed. But don't expect a new recruit to do anything but deliver the mail.'

He lifted his bulky body with surprising grace and on moist, small feet, padded up to his map on the wall. 'Apodemius has all the old cities as well as the rich export towns of Africa covered well, but he's short of men on the ground here in the new north and in the fleshpots of the Eastern territories.'

'I wouldn't know.'

'But I bet you're here to find out what you can. There are things he wants to know, things he *needs* to know. He and I could work together.'

'For the sake of the Empire?'

'Oh, stop prattling about the Empire! Can't you see the deep cracks running through it? The divisions? You've seen our Emperor Constans! Is he a leader of men? And even a real man like Constantius is losing the East to Shapur! You can't mend such cracks. Just be careful not to step into one yourself!'

'I'm very careful.'

'You'd better be. Any information about the Emperor's special recreation in the forest will be traced back to you. You may find yourself trapped by "The Chain." And then you'll be begging for my friendship.'

I wanted to escape the stifling air of his office. Even through his curtained window the smell of roasting boar mixed with the perfumes and turned my stomach. The sun was well up now. The outgoing rider would be leaving soon for Divodurum, with or without the *Augusta*'s appeal in his sack.

But I needed to know what Eusebius was threatening me with. '*The Chain*? That sounds like a scary tale told to children.'

Eusebius gestured me back from the door to join him at the window. 'You may look down on me as unnatural, but I can assure you that Catena is more of a monster than I. Look, he's down there now, waiting to intercept you.'

Eusebius drew the curtain and shifted aside a shutter of thick opaque glass that insulated his window. He pointed towards the outer courtyard beyond.

Wreaths of smoke rose up off crackling fat dripping over the spit. Through a greasy cloud wafting to and fro, I saw the two cooks at work. They turned the beast evenly around and around as it spat back at them and they carved the boar meat off the haunches as it browned.

The smoke shifted. Now I was able to make out the hearty Gaiso leaning on a makeshift crutch and chatting to a bull of a man in full armor. This stranger's face, even seen from a high angle, was disconcerting. Each feature of it was made well

29

enough, but didn't match the other elements. His high-arched nose was too small and pointed a beak for his broad, thick jaw. His black eyes slanted downwards, one larger than other and set closer to the black eyebrows. His mouth was too small for a man. The overall effect was of someone who'd borrowed his identity from various passers-by.

'Paulus Catena,' Eusebius murmured. 'He's nicknamed "The Chain" because he enjoys dragging people by chains to their death, but also because if he can't find evidence against you, he'll forge a chain to bring you down, link by link and lie by lie.'

'What is he?'

'He claims to come from Hispania with antecedents from Dacia, though I detect hints of Persian ancestry in his taste for interrogation techniques that are, shall we say, unusual?' Eusebius' eyes bulged suggestively. 'Some say he started out as a wine steward at the imperial tables and then got himself appointed as a notary.'

'Who gives him orders now?'

'Constans. You tread on the edge of a razor, my African friend. Constans doesn't want to hear that his foibles are on the tongue of every merchant from Constantinopolis to Sirmium. Within an hour of your rushing back from the hunt, the Emperor had asked Catena who you were. By nightfall, Catena's flunky had asked me. Now both imperial siblings are watching you. Constantia tested you last night, in her own way, to see if you were working for me, or Catena, or really just a simple messenger with strong thighs.'

'A simple messenger. Thank you for the snack.'

I bowed to Eusebius and left his office, allowing myself no more chance of falling for his delaying tactics. His reference to the *Augusta* had reminded me of my duties. I ran from corridor to stairs out the palace entrance to archway, racing against the clock to pass Constantia's letter to our service rider. Breathless, I reached our cubicle through which the palace traffic passed and found the rider pitching saddlebags of court paperwork bound for Mediolanum and Roma out of a pushcart and onto his horse.

'Numidianus? Someone's asking for you,' the rider said, stuffing the *Augusta*'s letter into his chest satchel and gesturing in Catena's direction. We ran through the mail register one last time, I initialed it, and he was ready to go.

'Oh, sorry, I nearly forgot. Here's a message for you collected at the Brigantium station.'

'Thanks.' I took my letter and turned with a sigh of relief at a delicate task finally off my hands. I immediately bumped into the hairy bulk of Paulus Catena.

'You enjoyed the hunt, Gaiso tells me.' He patted my shoulder. 'Congratulations for your kill—and discretion in letting others take the credit.'

'I only finished it off. I'm relieved to see Gaiso back on his feet.' I examined the Hispaniard's piercing gaze and his day's growth of black stubble.

'Last night the Emperor asked me who you were.'

'I'm honored.'

'Really? Don't be.' Catena's black eyebrows were level with my own but tall as I am, his bulk outweighed mine by an easy twenty pounds of brawn. If Constantia acted like the exposed, bruised heart of the Constans court and Eusebius its heartless brains, I might have just met its muscles.

'You saw too much in the forest, I hear. But perhaps a Roman slave-boy thinks nothing of such pastimes? Had a bit of the rough yourself, I imagine.'

I didn't answer him. He slugged me on the back like a soldier in camp. 'Nothing for a southerner like you to mention, surely? Only provincial rubes would be caught telling tales.'

'You insinuate too much—Catena, isn't it? I carry messages. I don't write them.' I cinched the heavy sack of documents that had just arrived a little tighter and slung it over my back. 'You're a notary? Get busy and bring on the paperwork,' I joked.

'Oh, come on, it's pretty juicy stuff, isn't it . . . but of course, of course, you're not shocked. You're a good-looking man. Perhaps you yourself were someone's *delicatus* back in Roma? How could you avoid it? Roma's more decadent than ever, I hear. Still so pagan, so corrupt.'

I laughed along but kept walking toward the Palace. He wasn't satisfied.

'No wonder nobody visits Roma anymore. Not even emperors bother with the place. There's nothing there but arrogant old senators making speeches to themselves while we defend them. They disgust any decent official.'

'So, don't go to Roma.' I kept walking.

'Isn't that where everything is rotten?' he taunted me.

'Not entirely,' I said, stopping to face him. 'I was raised in a patrician Roman household. I know their old-fashioned ways, good and bad. But I also know that customs of affection between an adult citizen and his favored youth have very well defined limits. Certain indignities are restricted to slaves. The rule in a good family is that a citizen youth grows up and moves on to women, experienced but . . . intact. Even as a slave, I was never used in that way.'

'Sure, sure. Just presses and caresses for the toffs.' He adjusted the heavy green wool cloak that protected him from the chill. He wore armor with leather padding over a woolen tunic and northern trousers. There were hobs on his thick boot soles that left dents in the fine courtyard gravel. I hated to think what they did to the mosaic tiles indoors.

'Only slaves have no choice but to endure that—' Catena pointed to the boar, run through from ass to mouth by the spit. 'Take the cut meat inside now for saucing,' he shouted at the cooks, then turned back to me. 'So the male getting a spike up his ass must be a slave by definition, not a master, right?'

'By tradition, but it's none of my business. Maybe customs change.'

'You're about to find out. Yesterday, you earned yourself a rich opportunity, messenger-boy. And you're not even blond. Constans invites you to join his happy band of prisoners.'

'Even the Emperor has to clear it with my *schola* in Roma to have me transferred upstairs, Catena, And now I've got mail to deliver.' I switched the sack of dispatches from one shoulder to the other, missing his jumbled face by an inch or less.

The ingratiating little grin disappeared. 'Maybe you don't appreciate your new duties. Maybe your tastes run the other way. I hear stories about you and the *Augusta*,' he said, marching right alongside of me.

'Not true,' I barked back, retreating towards the back entrance of the palace. He lunged and grabbed my arm in a vice.

'Not true *now*.' He shook his head, 'but the stories Paulus Catena hears have a way of coming true, sooner or later.'

'What do you want from me?' I rounded on him, fed up.

'Your tongue on a spit, if you talk.'

He gave up when I turned the far corner of the main palace. I dropped the mail sack and heaved a sigh of relief. No one took notice of me as I crouched on my haunches to catch my breath. I thought of the cripple Dax, a former 'friend' of Constantia's and now perceived the hand of Catena at work. Then I remembered that I carried one particular piece of paper that couldn't wait. It might contain news of my child or his mother, the Lady Kahina. It might be a note of encouragement from Dr Ari, the Greek slave who doctored the Legio Augusta III back in Numidia Militaris.

What I didn't expect was to find nothing more than an unbleached scrap of paper. It had been ripped off the corner of a much-used page defaced by many erasures and now scrawled only with the image of a small mouse—an *apodemus*.

It was a code that meant I was to leave at once for our headquarters in Roma. Either I was in a little trouble with Apodemius or I was in *big* trouble, but I didn't care.

Either way, I was escaping Treverorum just in time.

Chapter 4, The Homecoming

—THE TAVERN AT THE PORTA AURELIA—

'They finished St Peter's when I was six, so why did I spot a construction scaffolding over the roof as I rode into town?' I joked to Verus.

The old steward of the Manlius House had come out to the northwestern city gates where I waited for my formal clearance to enter the ancient capital. This security check was a bore for any *agens*, but the city's regulations imposed on our *schola* gave me a chance to enjoy a good drink—or three—with my trusted old friend. He arrived at the Tavern of the Seven Sages with a bowed swagger, hands weathered by age, but eyes still sharp enough to spot me in the crowd.

'Building companies!' he said, winking. 'Remember when the Senator tried to put in a private bath for the Lady Laetitia during her illness? Those workers always promise to finish your project during one consulship, but before you know it, you're hailing two new men rising to the top, but the scaffolding around your extension shows no sign of coming down.' Verus polished off his third cup. 'I needed that, boy. Is there time for another?'

I wanted to know everything I could about Kahina and the child, and if there was any news of the Commander Gregorius, reposted from North Africa to the Legio VI Herculiani, originally based in Pannonia, but now patrolling eastern Gallia.

But I hid my curiosity from Verus who had been the stern-faced *dispensator* of the townhouse in its bustling heyday. He had terrified the staff when I was a boy, but mellowed into an affable doyen of back alley gossip. I noticed today that his conversation flapped, like a rag snagged on a branch in a high wind, unable to detach itself from his favorite irritant—Clodius.

Clodius was the son of Lady Letitia's sister, moved into the Manlius house for official adoption as the Senator's heir. Yet the adoption had never gone through and Clodius still hungered for legal instatement with an avidity that embarrassed any onlooker.

'He got Lady Kahina to sell off half the staff for "budgetary reasons" and now *I'm* supposed to answer the gate! Me! Demoted to *ostiarius*!'

'Where did the profits from the sales go?'

'Oh, she keeps a tight fist on most of that, though she didn't like to see some of the good maids and the under-cook go to the dealer.'

'It must be hard for the Lady Kahina to hold down management of the house when Clodius has been in place for so long.'

'And now, he's going on and on about the deed box, as if there was any call for him to know about deeds,' Verus scoffed. '*Look in the cellar, Verus, find me the archive boxes, Verus, search the Senator's library while he's at his bath, Verus.* Find the deeds? Find the key to the deed box?'

Verus popped half a hard-boiled egg with anchovies into his mouth and went on, 'Marcus, I ain't no intrigant behind the Lady Kahina's back! I tell'im, if you want to see the deeds to the oyster beds or the honey farms or them herds up in Gallia, you just ask the Senator for'em.'

'And why doesn't he?'

'Clodius doesn't dare, but I know that boy is counting on selling off the Via dei Vigili apartment in Ostia behind the old man's back sooner or later to pay off his gambling debts. Already, Roma's plastered with that slimy creep's IOU's.'

'A little respect, Verus, just a little. This tavern has very small cups, but very big ears.' The fact that I had to shout this caution into the old servant's hairy ear to be heard over the *taberna*'s midday uproar made my admonition less than convincing.

'I.O.U.'s! Signed Manlius, all over town! It's a disgrace! He has no right to sign that name!'

'I heard you. Does Clodius ever read to the Senator? He could put the old man in a good mood and ask him then.' Reading the Greats of Latin and Greek literature out loud been my job, as well as my pleasure, my escape. In the end, it also gave me my treasured education as a young slave assigned to the blind elder sheltered in his back room, a *tablinum* squeezed under the eaves and lined with books.

'Read, to the old man? All Clodius reads is the betting sheets from the Circus and the odds on gladiators. The rest is Greek to him, ha!'

'The mistress?'

'Ah, she's a lovely girl, she is, but her tutor tells me she ain't no scholar—at least not yet.'

I smiled. I hadn't loved Kahina, briefly but passionately, for her erudition. 'What does the Senator say?'

'He invites Clodius up to his rooms, but Clodius is always "out on business".'

'Gambling?'

'At least that would be halfway honest. No, the latest game for wastrels like his lot, you see, is to haunt the courtyards of old men, sucking up in case one of 'em pops it and puts you in his will. It's practically the municipal sport these days.'

'Clodius should enlist in the army and win over Gregorius with a little real time in the field.'

'Well, the army certainly made a man out a scrawny bookworm like you. But Clodius? Oh, no, he'd rather gussy up every morning to hang on the coattails of that childless widower, the ex-Consul Picenus. Clodius *claims*,' Verus watered his garrulous tongue a little, '*claims*, mind you, that Consul Picenus favors him for a legacy. I caught that sneak decanting some of the Senator's best vintage into a jug to haul over to that Consul's salon as a festival gift. I reported it to the lady. She and I changed the locks on the wine cellar the next day. So Clodius takes candies to sweeten the gossip he imports from the street, but Picenus should be mighty careful. I wouldn't bet that those candies ain't poisoned.'

37

'The lady's well?' I kept my eyes trained on a flirtatious cook scraping scales off a fish ordered for someone's lunch. Verus could be as canny as a slum concierge on commission.

'She's fine, fine. Now, tell me. What's it like up in the Land of the Treveri? Subdued the hairy barbarians, have we? Got any trophies for your old friend Verus? A moustache comb? A golden *fibula*?'

'You're still living in the last century, old man. Treverorum has more baths, libraries, amphitheaters and fancy villas than you could count. It's cleaner than Roma, that's for sure, and their white wine is better than this piss.'

Somebody cleared his throat next to our table and his spit just missed my boot.

'But it's cold up there, right? And no real history, like us? No place is like good ol' Roma, is it?' The old man actually hugged his barnacled self for reassurance. 'And you won't catch me calling that new town out East the "New Roma," no matter what ol' Constantine built hisself out there.'

A gatekeeper signaled me from the crowded doorway. My clearance paper travelled overhead from hand to hand to our table. I dared one last casual question, shouted while paying my tab, as if it were only a courteous afterthought. 'Is the little boy walking yet?'

Verus shrugged. 'Not that I've heard, but how would I know? He's down in Setia with his wet nurse, Lavinia. Got a bit of a chest thing last spring and couldn't throw it off. The Commander panicked when he heard and ordered him out of the city. Only son, last chance for the Manlius line, well, you can imagine the fuss over just a little cough. Smiley little runt. Got his mother's skin, glossy as honey, he is.'

A little runt, sickly, tended by a strange nurse? My whole future, exiled out to the overgrown and neglected Manlius vines, even as autumn set in?

But Verus didn't catch the shadow that crossed my face. 'Right, off we go, Marcus. What was the Lady Laetty always gabbing about with her Christian girlfriends? Some Prodigal

Son, that's you all right, the prodigal slave all tarted up now, a real freedman, you are . . .'

We entered 'good ol Roma' . . . so fetid with sewage and the crush of people, I covered my nostrils as I followed Verus. Despite his age, he was hopping along the narrow sidewalk raised out of the muck for pedestrians, dodging awnings in which the jobless slept off their morning drink, and fending off stray dogs with his walking stick like the native he was. But on all sides, I noticed the refuse of Roma's dominions—idle, garrulous, fractious immigrants of all kinds living on the welfare state—a testament in color and costume to the width and breadth of an impossibly large empire.

Roma the city was nothing more than a teeming leftover now, hardly even a ceremonial capital, long-abandoned by emperors for the brisk and modern Mediolanum. Fifty years ago, Emperor Diocletian had fled the place in horror, cutting his visit to his 'licentious' Roman subjects insultingly short by weeks.

But still the foreigners flooded in, layer upon layer of hungry mouths and empty hopes. This discarded metropolis, overflowing with beggars, rubbish, clogged alleys, sparkling fountains, imposing statues, crowded *insulae* and crumbling monuments, was my home. The old townhouse that greeted me now as I marched up the lane on the Esquiline hill beckoned the child slave inside with remembered love. Huge fig branches rounded both corners of our front walls, like the arms of a defiant Roman mother facing off some Celtic invaders of old. Soggy fig leaves blanketed the stones under a sky of heavy clouds threatening more rain. I had once swung from those branches until Verus scolded me to come down and do my chores. An imposing and ancient tree was an object of veneration in a Roman neighborhood, not a child's gymnasium.

We went through the gates and entered the dank *fauces*. The storeroom was locked up and the fountain in the atrium silent.

'The house is so dark, Verus.'

'That's the mistress, saving on oil. She keeps a tight little book, that missus.'

'If I didn't know my way by heart, I'd stumble.'

'Come into my room, boy, and I'll light a lamp or two and we'll scavenge up some snack before—'

'Ah, the slave-boy hero!'

Through the dim lights, I saw my old playmate and rival, the near-heir, leaning against stained columns in the rear of the peristyle garden beyond.

'Hello, Clodius. How are you?'

'Don't you mean, Clodius *Domine*? Oh, that's right. You're a freedman now, thanks to some secret mission in the African desert . . . suicide martyrs . . . heretical priests of death. Ooooo,' he waved his manicured hand and gave a mock shiver. 'I heard all about it, over and over, whenever Uncle Gregorius reached the bottom of the wine bottle. Congrats.' He extended his hand for the first time in two decades to me, although we'd roughhoused and kicked each other enough in the alley off the kitchen door.

'Who wouldn't have tried? I speak the dialect and it was a few weeks' worth of discomfort for a lifetime's liberation. That doesn't make me a hero.'

'I heard you had the shit whipped off your back so you could pretend you were a runaway. Can I see the scars?'

'Later, Clodius,' Verus piped up, 'Hero or not, he's hungry now. I'm taking him into the kitchen for a cold sausage or two.'

'Go ahead to the kitchen, Verus, and dig out your sausages. First, I want a word with Marcus, here. That's a good old fart. Listen . . .' Clodius threw one arm over my shoulder and turned me in the direction of the reception rooms. We entered the familiar winter dining room, now covered in protective sheets. How many years had I stood at attendance in this *triclinium*? How many evenings had I gamboled and preened as a child-jester for my master and his military mates on winter leave?

Now it was obvious that, with the master of the house serving in Gallia, Kahina did no regular entertaining on her own.

40

'Marcus, I wanted to ask you an awkward question.'

'Awkward? What could be awkward between two men who used to have pissing contests all over the vegetable garden?'

'I always won,' Clodius chuckled.

I lifted an ironic brow.

'You let me win?'

'I was a slave. I also had to let you beat me and blame me for every broken vase or stolen cake in the house. Want a piss-off now?'

'Ha! No, listen.' Clodius lowered his voice. I noticed his shaving was sloppy and his bath scent stale. 'When you were a little brat, did you ever see the deeds? You know, the property files and rent receipts on the farms and apartments?'

'There's a problem? A lawsuit?'

'No, no, more a matter of accounting.' His shifting eyes avoided my inquiring look.

'Aren't the rents and foodstuffs coming in?'

'Yes, though I suspect the managers are taking too big a cut. Obviously the new matron hasn't a clue. We need to get a handle on what's happening with the estate overall. You don't know where they might be?'

I was thinking by the way Clodius lowered his voice that Kahina must be somewhere in the house right now. What would she say, what would she do, when she saw me? After so many years, did any of that one night's passion remain in her soft breast now?

Clodius fingered the tight curls his barber had set, row over row, around his high forehead. For an instant, he resembled his late Aunt Laetty. Her memory aroused sympathy in me. He might feel humiliated to be asking me about Manlius family business but I cared more than he imagined. He had no idea that for the sake of my child, the deeds' whereabouts were now my business too.

In fact, I was more Manlius that he. I suddenly stood straighter, reminding myself again that I carried a thin strain of old Roman blood, even if it was mixed with my Numidian mother's stock and a Gallic dilution via the Commander's mother, the Senator's second, noble provincial wife.

The deeds' disappearance would be no joke for my son if he reached manhood only to find them traded away by Clodius. They had to be found—and protected.

'They're locked up somewhere, I suppose. Why don't you ask the Senator?'

'Well, I would, old pal, but I'm afraid you'll find him a bit . . . lost in time?' Clodius wiggled his fingers into the dusty afternoon shadows. 'Here and then, not here—if you know what I mean.'

'I'm sorry to hear that.' This news worried me indeed, as the Senator was not only the head of the house, but its moral conscience, its dynastic memory and its practical safeguard against the spendthrift Clodius. The Senator had been a sharp judge of character in his prime, whether castigating a corrupt official on the floor of the Senate or raising a disapproving eyebrow as he passed the nursery. There were no doubt good reasons he had always dragged his feet at making Clodius' adoption official.

'Almost gaga,' Clodius said. 'So you see, it's really up to me, Marcus, the responsibilities for all this estate—caretaking, rent collecting, equipment upkeep, harvest hiring . . . Uncle Atticus is never here, gallivanting from border to border with his army pals. Come on, you must have seen them. Or maybe your poor mum? Sewing and scrubbing away every day? Under some bed? Behind a storage chest?'

'Well, I do recall a metal box, bound in iron bands, with a small padlock—'

'That's the baby! Locked with an ancient ring-key that Laetitia said was too small for even her finger, so she wore it on her belt. Then she got sick and mislaid it.'

'Did she? All I remember are the jeweled crucifixes she wore after she converted. Anyway, the Senator must have had a copy of the key.'

He sighed and was about to let me go to supper. I'd had enough of his perfumed anxiety.

'Wait, Marcus.'

'Hm?'

'You know the old man's library, or you used to. Full of first editions, is it?'

I smiled. 'Nothing but. However, even an elderly blind man can guard his own study, Clodius. And the Manlius name is inscribed on each scroll and codex. As long as he's alive, those books will have to stay upstairs—just in case you were thinking of taking up . . . reading.'

I had my snack of cheap wine, salad and liver sausage with Verus, all the while my ears cocked for the sound of Kahina's light footsteps passing the servant's quarters or kitchen. I had no right to announce myself to her without the attendance of a maid or some other concession to her privacy and reputation, what with the Commander so far away. I wondered what her social standing really was. She was installed in the venerable bosom of such a famous clan, but short on the training and education her predecessor had enjoyed as the social queen of our aristocratic neighborhood.

And the house itself now occupied my thoughts. The old cook had retired early. A sullen teenage slave fumbled and banged the bowls and ladles with a comment to Verus that she'd already cleaned up the main meal. My mother's narrow sleeping pallet was gone and our tiny room off the kitchen now housed old cushions and summer garden fixtures.

'I'll go up and say hello to the Senator now.'

Verus nodded. His sad expression echoed the troubling warning from Clodius.

When I reached the top of the stairs, I hesitated outside his door, overcome as always by memories. Every morning of my childhood, it had been my job to first sweep these steps and then knock promptly to begin reading to him. When I was ten or so, he had still enjoyed partial sight. He could see the walls stroked with sunlight but couldn't make out the motes of dust dancing through the air. He could keep an eye on the small slave on a long hard bench built right into the side of the wall, cushioned only by a worn rug. He would stretch a large text across my bony brown knees and remind me where to pick up from where we'd left off the previous day.

The Senator's great frustration had been that as soon as he tried to find the letters right under his nose, they disappeared. Sometimes he worked his way along the shelves, his head tilted to one side to read by the margins of his sight, but by the time I was thirteen and could select the books myself, he'd lost even that much vision.

'Senator?' I knocked three times.

'Who's there? Why are you growling, Kahina?'

'It's Marcus, Senator. Home from Treverorum.'

'Marcus? What's a child doing up in the wilds of Belgica?'

I entered and found him still lying on his couch, finishing a nap. He turned his whitened eyes towards the door. 'Come here, boy, and let me lay my hands on you.'

I knelt beside the moldy old couch, smelling of camphor, wine and old-man-mildew. His toenails needed clipping. He'd lost a lot of weight. The tentative fingers tapping along my forehead and face could have been drifting feathers.

'But you're not Marcus!' he cried. 'Marcus is my slave boy, not old enough to shave.'

I pulled back and choked out, 'I *am* Marcus, that same boy, now over twenty-two and freed by special service under the Commander's command. I've been stationed at the new capital on the Mosella River as an *agens*.'

He struggled to rise from his couch and flailed around for a bell on his table to call for help. He seemed frightened by this intruder in his private sanctum.

'I've come to pay respects to you and your new daughter-in-law.'

He cast his gaze to the left and right, as if hoping someone else in the room would correct me or upbraid me for insolence. 'My boy Marcus? Where's *he*?'

'He's *here*, Senator. I am he.'

'I don't know your voice. Clodius must be playing some damned trick. I heard his footsteps downstairs. I know he's in the house. Send him up here at once.'

I let out a frustrated sigh. 'Clodius will come up, Senator, if you insist, but only to empty your shelves and cart your whole library off to Soren, the Book Dealer.'

He grinned a wily, almost toothless agreement. 'Oh, Soren would love to get hold of my collection. He's just waiting for me to—did you say *Clodius* frequents Soren?'

'Yes, Senator, but as a potential seller, not a buyer.'

'I would *die* to protect my library.' He pounded a bony fist on his couch and a pouf of dust hit my nose. 'But what use are all my books anyway, when there's no one to read to me?'

'The Lady Kahina?'

'Oh, she tries. Her pronunciation is coming along but . . . I'm not complaining, mind you! The virtue of that girl speaks for itself. Roman women are so frivolous these days, so immoral. You know, Tacitus was right when he praised the virtue of German tribal women. I took a noble Gallo-Roman for a second wife and I'm not sorry my son found a good Numidian bride.'

'Yes, she is virtuous, Senator.'

'Of course, I would have liked a grandson by Laetty. Laetty was a true Roman aristocrat, a good girl—perhaps a little too good when she joined that Christian cult?' He chuckled, 'But this one's given us a legal heir at last! That Clodius can go to the dogs!'

His laugh turned little odd, but the smile seemed genuine. 'But reading, young man, we were talking about reading, weren't we? It's the Greek I miss. My Homer . . . You see, there was a little boy here, clever little tyke he was, who held a special place in the house. Very special . . . This was his bench, right here.' The old man stumbled to the side of his study and patted the low bench from which I read every day. 'He was my slave and I taught him to read. He had a good pair of eyes and a wonderful memory.'

'Senator Manlius, I *am* that boy.' My voice cracked with frustration.

'No, no, no.' He chuckled. 'Our Marcus was very skinny and shy. His little voice had hardly changed when he joined my son in the field. They came back, though, once, but my poor Atticus was mutilated. You know, sometimes, I'm thankful I can't see.'

'I carried the Commander to safety myself.'

'So you met our young Marcus, too, in the field?'

I sat back on my haunches, defeated. I moved over to the wall and rested, sitting on that narrow platform plastered right along with the walls, which were covered with fading murals. It was still covered with a worn-out rug. This had been my perch, when I too still too short in the legs to take a real chair. Now my knees were around my ears.

I laid my face in my hands and sighed, 'Would you like some wine, Senator?'

'Yes, but not too strong.'

I helped the Senator off the couch to the chair where he had once listened to my lines and guided his hand to the cup.

'Homer?' I took down the familiar volume and found a favorite verse where the Trojan hero Aeneas is outmatched by Achilles, yet is fated to survive their deadly bout and thrive as the founder of Roma:

'But come, let us ourselves get him away from death, for fear the son of Kronos may be angered if now Achilles kills this man. It is destined that he shall be the survivor, that the generation of Dardanos shall not die . . .'

I had read for some five minutes before I stopped to quench my own thirst. I poured some water and then turned back to the Senator, fearing he'd fallen sound asleep without warning, the way the old sometimes do.

Instead, I saw his sightless eyes streaming with tears.

'Don't stop, please. It is you, child,' he said with a sob. 'You've come back to us. Thank God. Oh, Marcus, I've become such an old fool.' He pulled his worn old tunic across his face in shame at his tears.

'Here, Senator. Put your fingers around this and know me for the boy I was.' I reached for his hand and placed it under my collar around the superstitious talisman, the clump of ill-wrought bronze-dipped pottery on a cord that he'd once begged me never to lose or discard.

'It's come through battle and danger. A boy's thing, but even as a man, I wear it always for protection and loyalty to this house.'

'Never lose it,' he whispered. 'Tradition is the key to everything.' To him, name, family and tradition formed the bedrock of life, even in this crumbling house of dust, smothered kitchen fires and dried-up fountains.

'You're back now.' He cocked his head and listened for a minute. In the distance we heard a vendor's evening sales cry echoing down in the alley off the kitchen door, but otherwise, I wondered why he looked so wary. 'I have to talk to you, Marcus. Is there someone on the stairs?'

'I don't think so, Senator.'

'Listen, there's something I must tell you. It's hard to explain so late, but you're old enough to know—'

Did the Senator know, too, that I was the bastard child of his son and the sorrowful Numidian servant who had languished unloved in the back room for so long?

He was interrupted by a short knock on the door. Someone *had* climbed the stairs, but very softly. 'Senator? Are you awake? May I enter?'

Kahina's accent—that little whistling 's,' and the funny way we Numidians pronounced the 'l'—hit me like a desert breeze off the Aurès Mountains. It was the sound of my mother's accent. Kahina's 'Shenator?' betrayed her as the North African-born servant girl she'd once been.

She looked at the Senator and then saw me leaning against the wall. The door swung open the rest of the way by itself as she scowled at the surprise.

'I see you have a visitor, Father, Marcus Gregorianus Numidianus.'

'Oh, no fancy titles for my young friend here, Kahina. I knew this young man when he was the cleaning lady's whelp, the slave Marcus, and nothing more, right?' The frail man pulled on my arm to steady himself and then leaned on his neglected reading table. He stared at the air in her direction. For my part, my gaze was as intense as the beam of the Alexandria lighthouse.

How she'd changed!

Motherhood had robbed her of that vulnerable slim figure, once so light that suicide cultists had borne her on their shoulders as if she'd been no heavier than a sacrificial lamb.

Now she wore fine-gauge layers of linen and soft wool against Roma's November winds. I knew how Africans suffered north of the Central Sea. The wintry rains and humid fevers had finally killed off my sad mother. Kahina's usual belt, which I remembered as a sort of rope back in the Circumcellions' camp, had been replaced by an item in the latest Germanic fashion— gold filigree studded with blue and amber stones. She gripped the ends of her dark blue *stola* as if that simple length of expensive weave could guard her from any renewals of my love.

I detested her new hairstyle—these tight cylinders of hair piled into a headdress that bobbed forward as she approached me. In Numidia, her long hair had hung loose and softly dusted by the desert. Now it looked shiny and lacquered into place.

Marriage to my natural father and former master had turned her into a Roman matron—statuesque, respectable, and dignified.

'I've found the Senator in good health, Lady Kahina. We've been reading together.'

'He will have enjoyed that, I'm sure. But he must be tired now. Your dinner will be sent up soon, Father. It's stewed baby lamb with grapes.'

'Soft enough to mash?'

'If we cook it any softer, it'll become soup.'

'Thank you, child. I'll have a rest now.'

He stepped, hand over hand, past the table and felt for his couch. Kahina and I stretched him out. I took care not to touch her but it was hard to be so close to her again.

We left the Senator and descended in pregnant silence down the few short steps to the atrium.

'You'll forgive me if I don't ask you to stay with us, Marcus?'

'You're majestic, Kahina. Like something carved in marble—beautiful and smooth, but cold.'

'It wouldn't be appropriate, even if Clodius were dining in, which of course, he's not.'

'I'm so happy for the boy. And for you, of course. You look so noble dressed like that.'

'My thoughts are more noble now, too. The Senator is very careful about my reputation, you see. He's determined that all the nicest families receive me.' She pulled her shawl tighter.

'I'm sure they find you charming.'

'I've been invited to salons by the ladies of all five princely clans—the Aemilii, Claudii, Cornelii, Fabii, and Valerii and—' she ticked them off her ringed fingers and I stopped her, grabbing her hand in mine.

'I *understand*, Kahina. It's all right. I'm bunking at the Castra Peregrina with the other *agens* in training. I'm not hounding you on purpose. I was summoned here. But I couldn't come to my home city and not visit where I grew up.'

'Oh, I see.' Her stony expression relaxed one degree.

'Kahina, it will be all right between us. We made our decision. I don't regret it . . . do you?'

Her eyelids fluttered nervously. 'Of course not. I have everything I hoped for, and something more, Marcus.'

I feared the truth, but had to hear it. I'd felt the change in her the moment her cool eyes and unsmiling lips faced me in the study.

'Back in Numidia, that day you said you were leaving, I called the Commander a monster. I found his injuries fearful, even repellant. I hated my family for offering me up like that and I hated Leo for introducing my parents to the Commander. So I ran away. I had fallen in love with you in the Circumcellion camp. You were so young, handsome and . . . whole.'

'We were both frightened. Those weeks among the Circumcellions were a strange time for both of us. We were surrounded by death so we grabbed at life. But in the end, we owe Leo a lot. He knew the Commander would give you a wonderful new life here and he knew that I would try to make a good *agens*.'

'Yes, Leo was right in the end. The point I'm trying to make is that I've come to respect Atticus and . . . to love him, Marcus.'

'Where is he now, exactly?'

'Serving as best he can with the Herculiani. He's away for months at a time. It's not easy, but I imitate his fortitude. He loves me very much, Marcus. To him, the child is a miracle from Jove. But I'm afraid. Our honor and safety rest on the Senator.'

'Not for much longer, I'm afraid.'

'Marcus?'

'Kahina, the boy's future is everything to both of us. I can't love you now as I did then, but I will protect you and—' I broke off. I'm sure my expression was laughable.

'What is it?'

'I forgot to ask. What's the sprog's name?'

She laughed and then named the very man who had changed both our lives for the better. 'Leo. We named him after Leo.'

I had never seen a Roman die more nobly than Leontus Longus Flavius. If my son grew up as brave as that, I'd be satisfied.

'I'll try to protect you and Leo for as long as I can, but that means trying to stay in Roma. As an *agentes in rebus* my fate is not my own but I promise I'll try.'

She nodded and extended her hand to me. This time it was not as rigid as marble. I nodded my good-bye.

Outside the gate, I leaned against the fig tree, taking it all in—the feeble Senator, my sickly child, the greedy Clodius and Kahina's stoic pride. For many minutes, I wept hot silent tears. Then I pulled myself together and headed off to report for duty.

CHAPTER 5, THE CURIOUS ONES

—THE CASTRA PEREGRINA, ROMA—

I headed off for the echoing barracks of the Castra Peregrina on the Caelian Hill. The Castra was originally built to house non-Roman auxiliary troops, the *peregrini*, before it was given over to the *frumentarii* for their headquarters. But the hated *frumentarii* dragged the imperial messenger and road service into such disrepute for corruption and skullduggery that Emperor Diocletian disbanded them in disgrace.

Not that a single citizen was fooled when a few years later, the *agentes* set up shop in the same sprawling stone compound. Even though we were more honest and professional than the despised *frumentarii*, the stigma of underhand dealings stuck to our cloak hems like caked mud.

Agentes weren't admired like generals or trusted like senators. We certainly weren't idolized like gladiators. Nobody scribbled our names in celebratory graffiti, if only because whatever we did in pursuit of duty, we stayed discreet.

We were also exempt from state prosecution. An *agens* of Roma had a license to do, well, do whatever he saw fit. As a result, we were *feared*. As we departed from offices or garrisons, people hissed our nickname, the *curiosi*, behind our backs.

Generally, *agentes* were too busy to worry about such insults. The state expected us to courier dispatches and escort officials, to monitor roads and cargo, to inspect traffic warrants, and double-check customs records.

When the Emperor issued a decree, we followed up to make sure it was enforced. From time to time, we had to arrest people—or worse. We were those faceless, nameless men who escorted disgraced officials into exile.

But it wasn't always self-effacing work. I had heard of an *agens* who once served as ambassador to the Persian court of Shapur II, the Great.

The fact he never returned alive wasn't the point.

The point was that everybody in the Dominate counted on the *agentes*, even when they whispered that we answered only to our own dark hearts.

They were wrong about that. Independent and aloof, we served an ideal of empire that most people no longer tried to live up to. I answered only to Apodemius and he answered only to the Master of Offices. I was proud to be an *agens*, if only a *circitor* still near the bottom of five ranks. In my youthful, boastful heart, I liked to see myself as a classical hero, singled out by the gods for a destiny greater than my birth.

But then my feet touched ground and I recalled I'd been a slave, recruited from a border patrol camp in North Africa, and chosen not by the gods but by a former *agens*-turned-oil trader, Leo. I'd survived a suicide mission intact and won my freedom and a chance—my only chance—for a life. The gods were indifferent, though I clung to my childish amulet hoping they'd remember me from time to time.

I started service as an *eques*. For nine months I ferried dispatch bags from Aquileia through the Pannonian capital of Siscia to Sirmium, the gateway to the Eastern Empire. Then I rode the route all the way back. I got used to the long, lonely hours in the saddle. We Numidians have horses in our blood. Even if my origins lay closer to humble mules than thundering stallions, I'd held my grip and concentration for weeks on end.

Time and again, I recorded early deliveries. At every stopover *mansio* on my route, I arrived sober, always grabbed the best horse and spare for myself, and tipped the stable slaves with an open hand.

Then I'd been promoted to the express service and allowed to wear the signal feather in my leather *petanus*. My ambition matched my speed.

Finally, I got a summons to Roma. There Apodemius told me in a five-minute midnight meeting to shift my sleeping roll up to Treverorum and handle internal distribution in the palace.

The old man had added, 'Numidianus, this time it's not just about mail. I want to know everything you hear up there, *especially* insults, jokes and rumors—no matter how outlandish. All messages to me in code from now on.'

That was the first occasion I had been authorized to use code.

As I walked through the city now, I wondered if this time some juicy tales about the Emperor Constans and that inquisitive eunuch Eusebius might earn me more than a brief juice break with our *schola's* master. Or would I get just a curt command to turn on a *nummus* and head off to the Persian front or the wilds of western Hispania?

This time I didn't want to leave Roma. I had new worries at home.

A thunderstorm clattered above and then discharged buckets on my weary head. Within a minute, I was drenched. I could have been forgiven for sheltering in a tavern, but I was anxious to get bedded down. Even weighed down by my pack, I made good progress walking east from the Manlius House— only because the pounding rain swished and eddied over the tops of gutters and washed the streets clean of beggars, bazaar stalls and delivery carts.

I got to the Castra gates in time to get assigned a tiny cell. I cleaned out some mouse droppings and the last guy's fruit peelings from under the cot. Finally, I headed to the dining hall to eat.

The room was crammed full of noisy men. Some of them were bronzed black by service in Egypt and Mauritania. Others were pale and coughing hard from service in the north, riding messages to garrisons in north Britannia or ships bobbing next to Londinium on the Thamesis River.

'Back from Treverorum'?' one man hailed me with a broad smile. I didn't ask his name and he didn't want to know mine. Sometimes it was better that way. You never knew when you might run across one of our *schola* wearing the guise of a complete stranger or comporting himself in some inexplicable way for a secret reason. It was easier to keep a straight face on mission if you weren't pals.

Still, we were all colleagues. I was grabbed in jest by my sword belt and yanked down on a bench to devour my grub with a band of hard-drinking customs inspectors reporting in from Aquitania.

'. . . It's the wine traffic that'll keep us there once the tin and lead are played out,' one was saying across the table.

'Decent stuff?' I asked.

'The reds are unbeatable. The Treasury should tax more for them.'

'Much action from the Celts?'

My dinner companion's ruddy good health said more about inspecting vineyard accounts than manning palisades. 'It's a mix. There are nine tribes speaking a gabble of dialects, but more Iberian than Celt. They're all right. Pretty settled down now. It's a soft assignment in a mild climate, nothing like it. I hope I'm not getting transferred now . . .'

After the filling meal, I laid out my cloak and riding trousers to dry near a warming brazier. Then I washed, dove under an army blanket and closed my eyes. The dice games in the corridor under the flickering sconces outside my door were like a familiar lullaby. I had spent my boyhood napping outside a patrician family's dining room and my teens listening to soldiers' campfire chat in the field. Wherever you were, there were always some guys who never went to bed.

I fell asleep within seconds, a useful talent for a rider.

A sharp rapping on my door woke me up. 'Marcus Gregorianus Numidianus! Meet-up with the boss!' It was Caius, a page-slave of about ten, who darted between our low-slung buildings like a child's wooden wagon on a pull string.

I combed my hair and recovered my trousers and my working satchel. This time there was no secret mouse summons. I ran to the main building through the drizzle thinking that this was the second time I had a debriefing with Apodemius well after into the night. I had first met him in a sunny North African villa but perhaps he did his routine work only after bedtime. Another fellow was leaving the darkened exit of the main reception room. As I passed him in the shadows, he murmured, 'His joints are acting up. Don't expect any laurels.'

I took a deep breath and went up to the old man's study.

'Hello, come in, Numidianus. Got your seals? Pass them over.'

Apodemius was sitting in his padded chair with his bare feet soaking in a bucket of steaming, scented water. I glanced around the study lit by the flames of a couple oil-lamps. All around me I saw paper—rolls stored in cubicles, neat towers on the old stone floor, stacks on his desk and scraps of it pinned to a large, map painted and fixed to a cork backing.

A marble bust of an elderly man stared at me from the shadowy windowsill. For the life of us, not a single *agens* had been able to find out who that man was. We joked among us that this Venerable was no doubt the most successful *agens* of all time—totally anonymous for all eternity.

There were a few other items peculiar to the old man—a *latrunculi* game board with black and white pieces set in an unfinished game, various ointments and unguents on a shelf near his couch and a cage of spoiled mice, the *apodemi* that reminded us all of his secret signature.

As he dried off his knobby feet, I opened my satchel and brought out copies of the official seals that had passed through my hands in Treverorum.

As trained in the Castra workshops, I'd taken a mold of each seal impression using a special white clay. Then I had refashioned duplicate seal dies from the imprints using a plaster mixed with fine-ground lead. This meant that I could melt down the wax of anyone's seal, read and copy his letter, and re-secure it without being caught. It was standard procedure, but this was my first time passing on my handicraft. I felt nervous watching Apodemius glance through my handwritten labels as I lined them up.

'The Emperor Constans. The Lord Chamberlain Eusebius. The notary known as Paulus Catena and . . .' I laid the last seal down with the emphasis my discreet cleverness had earned, 'the *Augusta* Constantia.'

'Good, good.' He waved them from his thoughts. 'Now, I've read your reports on the mint's production. I thought your observations on barbarian relations with the state markets up there not *entirely* laughable. I also note that Commander Gaiso was due for a visit. He interests me. Report.'

I chose my words with care. I stuck to the facts but omitted nothing that might be useful. While I regaled him with the excitement of the boar hunt and the Lieutenant Commander's athletic skill, Apodemius massaged his swollen ankles with camphor lotion. I would have bet my best tunic that nothing I said interested him. I stopped at one point, sure that it was all pointless nonsense.

'Go on, go on, I'm listening.' He lifted himself onto his stiff legs and limped back and forth between the cluttered corners of his cramped room. The needlework cushion on which his pointy old pelvis often rested was faded beyond recognition. Under years of his restlessness, the stitching of his leather chair had burst. Clumps of sheepskin stuffing poked through. I felt embarrassed, as if I'd caught sight of an old man's hairless flanks in the public latrine, his greying undercloth flopping around his ankles.

I tried not to think of Eusebius right now in his smart and fragrant offices up in Treverorum. I plowed on with my report. 'And when I was racing back to get help, that's when I stumbled on this startling scene of—' I hesitated.

'The Emperor buggering his Germanic archers.'

'Well, yes . . . but no, actually, not quite, *Magister*.'

A slight hesitation in his pacing betrayed a sliver of interest.

'You see, *Magister*,' I hesitated, 'there *was* buggering, but it was the prisoner-of-war doing the—'

'Witnesses?' His voice turned sharp.

'The other prisoners, *Magister*. Laughing, making sport of him. Of course, I don't speak Germanic, but if you'll excuse the expression, the Emperor seemed the butt of their jokes.'

'No, no, boy, *witnesses*. I meant *Romans*, of course.'

'There were no Romans *there*, in the forest. But the eunuch Eusebius knows what I saw. So does that notary, Paulus Catena. Eusebius warned me Catena might act to protect Constans from this report to you by framing me with some crime to shut me up. Already he had arranged for me to join the Emperor's playmates like a prisoner myself.'

'I'm not surprised. Does Catena have anything on you?'

I thought momentarily of Constantia's overpowering perfume, but answered, 'Nothing, *Magister*.'

Apodemius flipped over a timer on his desk and the sand started to run down again. He rattled his bucket at me with a white, knobby hand and settled back down into his chair. I fetched a fresh pot of boiled water from his discreet, deaf attendant standing watch at the door outside. The steaming water hit the medical concoction in the bucket with a hiss.

'Numidianus, tell me something I don't know.' He sighed with pleasure as his feet plunged back into the water.

'The *Augusta* wants to escape Treverorum. She mailed an appeal to Constantius.'

'Nothing new.'

I tried again. 'Eusebius asked all about you.'

This amused him. 'Well, that's hardly news, but tell me the gist, Numidianus. We haven't got all night. There's a man in from Vindabona waiting outside.'

'Eusebius says you could use his help up north. He wants to share information with you—your network of *agentes* for his web of eunuchs. He claims he reports to Constantia, officially spies for Constantius on Constantia, and *unofficially*, keeps the best secrets for his own trade. He says the Empire isn't worth holding together and it's every man for himself.'

'Well, it's certainly Eusebius for Eusebius. His property holdings would embarrass Crassus.' For the first time this evening, Apodemius looked straight into my eyes through the flickering shadows with a smile. 'You know what they say about the Lord Chamberlain Eusebius? That Constantius II enjoys *some* influence over him.' His smile faded in an instant. 'But no matter how powerful Eusebius grows, I wouldn't trade secrets with that vile, immoral spider for all the gold in Constantinopolis.'

'I didn't doubt it, *Magister.*'

'Is that all? Leave the seals with me. I'll have my secretaries check them for changes against the others in stock and copied if necessary.' He pulled his woolen cloak tighter around his shoulders and waving me away, hunched over his bucket and his thoughts.

I'd committed something worse than skimming customs tax or lying in lust with a senior *agens'* wife.

I had bored him. I had failed to make any impression.

'You told me to keep my ears open, but—' I hesitated before trying one last thing, even though it seemed no more than a joke, 'I *saw* something strange. The boar we killed was staked through for skinning and roasting in the courtyard. I saw that some joker had tied a purple ribbon around its neck.'

'Dear gods! Lieutenant-Commander Gaiso saw this?'

'*Gaiso*? I don't know. He was down in the courtyard the next morning talking to Catena.'

'Try to remember! It's important! Did *Gaiso* see the ribbon?'

I couldn't recall if the ribbon had still been there when Gaiso and Catena stood talking. I couldn't recall which way the hunter had been facing. I had failed.

'Did Eusebius see the ribbon?'

'The boar was under his window the whole time.'

'Has Gaiso left the Treverorum?'

'Not yet, I think. His wound will delay his return to service for another week at least.'

Apodemius told me to step outside and instruct the *agens* from Belgica to go to bed. I returned to find him hunched over a pile of reports, muttering to himself. 'Yes, a ribbon, something about a ribbon. Here it is. A ribbon tacked to a brothel door.

And there was something else. Where is it? A purple ribbon dumped on a pile of kitchen compost.' He riffled and sorted through paper of all thickness and scents, sent in from all corners of his network. 'A purple ribbon festooning an idiot's cap in Comum . . .'

I waited, watching the sand course down into the lower glass of his clock. Suddenly Apodemius looked up. 'Come over here, son. No, bring the stool. This isn't the army.'

I sat opposite him now, on the other side of his desk. For an ex-slave, this was heady stuff indeed. He wasn't bored any longer.

'You need more training, Numidianus. A month or more here, then you'll be ready. It's dangerous but you're worth risking.'

Was that a compliment or was I deemed expendable?

'Thank you, *Magister*. I think.' I didn't like the sound of this nor the silence that followed as Apodemius studied yet another coded report and scratched at the scabby, sun-blotched pate gleaming through his rumpled white hair in the lamplight.

'What training have you completed? I haven't time to look it up.'

I ticked off my courses. 'Seventy-two-Hour Riding certificate, Wrestling Rank, eight, Seal Molding and Invisible Writing, Basic Code Breaking, Sword Award ten out of ten *with merit—*'

'Yes, I recall you were a bit of a boaster. You had a good memory, too, for literature, if I recall.'

'Greek and Latin, *Magister*.'

'Done your Long Document Memory Training?'

'Not yet.' It didn't sound like fun.

'Silent Assassination Skills? Disguises and Dialects? Arrest Procedure?'

'I was hoping to move from circuit supervisor up to Customs, *Magister*.'

He laughed. 'Hah! All you new boys want Customs, as if I didn't know that's where the money hides. Quick money, early retirement.' His canny blue eyes narrowed. 'I'm not wasting your talents on Customs, *ever*.'

'Please, I need to stay around Roma. There are family concerns and temporary problems that need to be sorted out. The security of the Manlius estate is at risk.'

'I see.' His hands stopped shuffling papers and he heaved a sigh. 'I thought I might attach a strong young fighter like you to a pivotal surveillance posting. You could continue to keep an eye on your new friend, Gaiso.'

He must mean he wanted to send me back to Treverorum.

'I'd prefer Customs, really.'

'Really?'

I nodded.

'That's too bad. I see, I see. Well, you're not my slave. I learned long ago that men don't work well in an unsuitable post but I pride myself on fitting the man to the job.'

I sat, silent and sad, but determined.

'Well, Numidianus, more training won't hurt you in any event, so start tomorrow on those courses I just mentioned. If you're set on staying in Roma for Customs, add the Accounting Course, too. You can skip Disguises and Dialects.'

'Thank you, Apodemius.'

He hobbled around his desk and escorted me to the door. We had been together well over half an hour. I'd disappointed him and even rebuffed an exciting assignment, so why was he being so courteous?

He hesitated before excusing me. 'Tell me, Numidianus, how would you say that man Eusebius sees the world?'

'A marketplace for trading secrets?'

'Indeed, but I think he sees a spider's web stretching from Antiochia to Londinium. His Empire looks fragile and porous and he warns you of cracks, but secretly he thinks it's resilient and sticky enough for his purposes. And he wants whatever sticks to it for himself.'

'Is he right?'

'No, Numidianus. The Empire is fragile and porous. It's a piece of fine but aging linen, like this robe of mine, a seamless fabric with the sheen of age. But it's worn, my boy, worn with use and tension. It may fray without warning, if we're not careful. We saved it a hundred years ago, by sheer force of will. We must save it now.' He laid a distended hand on my shoulder.

'I'll keep that in mind, *Magister*, and do my best.'

'If Customs Collectors can save the Empire, Numidianus, which I very much doubt.'

ΨΨΨ

The next morning I registered for Accounting and Long Document Memory Training. The first course was well above my number skills. I was set long problems to calculate after dinner, which meant I missed the rounds of Knucklebones or Lucky Six that made the Castra such a pleasant place off-duty.

Long Document Training was easy for me at first, because our instructor set texts I'd read as a child to the Senator. After receiving a few marks of one hundred percent on the satirical poems of Juvenal and tedious passages from Sallust, he twigged that I was a bit of a ringer, despite my Numidian ex-slave dossier. By the end of the week, he'd dredged up some turgid arguments from the Council of Nicea to test my ability to recite by heart a passage I'd only read through once. Then he tested my ability to read it upside down and regurgitate it word perfect.

Silent Assassination Skills started up after two weeks of Accounting. I was desperate to get out of the Castra library. If I was de-enrolled from the Assassination class, I was ready to argue that a Customs Officer might need to assassinate a recalcitrant taxpayer when you least expected it. I turned up for that class, fully armed and five minutes early.

There was one other student waiting, in northern trousers, loose-tailed tunic shirt, a wide leather over-tunic and felt cap. He was smooth-cheeked, short and young. I didn't know they enlisted such squirts into our *schola*.

He didn't like my expression. 'I thought the point of this class was to look unarmed and harmless,' he said, pointing to my *spatha*.

I ignored him, ready to offer a little self-assertion in the form of a clout or punch if he got above himself.

'Mind if I try out your sword?' He reached for my scabbard.

I stared down at his face to tell him to piss off.

He was a she.

'My name is Roxana.' Her grip was like a vice pressing my palm. 'I'm what they call around here a Special.'

'You're what we call around here a girl,' I retorted.

The other three students showed up—one my own age from Rhaetia who cracked his knuckles as he chatted, a thuggish-looking rider from Pannonia and a tall, thin man so stooped, I wasn't surprised to learn that he was not trying to join Customs Accounting but to get transferred out of it by any means he could.

We filed into the room. I was in trouble from the beginning.

'Numidianus. Drop your weapons. In this room, we only fight dirty.' The nearly naked instructor waited, hands on his hips, at the end of the long, tiled exercise room. I left my blades at the door. As I approached him, he dropped to one knee and adjusted one of his boots.

The next thing I knew I was on my back with a wire wrapped around my neck and cutting into my flesh. With one deft pull of the wire's end, my head might be rolling across the floor.

He unwrapped the garrote and helped me to my feet. I realized it was his bootlace, reinforced from within. He wound and tucked the lethal string around his formidable wrist.

'Tomorrow I want you each to return to class with a disguised ligature of some kind—a chain, rope, scarf, wire or fishing line—anything that could strangle a person and be hidden on your person without detection. You don't get into this class with less than Wrestling Five. Anyone out?'

That got rid of the Accountant. So now there were only four students. We paired up to practice strangleholds. I pulled short straw and got Roxana, which was a bit of a joke unless I planned on strangling Constantia during our next bedroom encounter.

Before I knew it, Roxana had me on the floor. I was panting, purple-faced and gurgling between the strangling cords of her underwear belt.

'Very good, Roxana,' the instructor smiled. 'Numidianus, stop trying to remove the cord and kick her feet out of under her . . . Numidianus? Roxana, release him!'

If this was how Roxana 'practiced' strangling, I resolved to partner with the evil-looking Pannonian in Poisons Class.

CHAPTER 6, CALL IT 'CHRIST MASS'

—THE CASTRA PEREGRINA—

By early December, I'd mastered the basics of accounting and even obtained the highest marks of the season for memorizing half a dozen pages by some bishop named Athanasius.

I hardly understood a word of it.

A week's classes in Arrest Procedure wasn't hard, just a lot of rigmarole about titles, legal rights, hierarchies and displays of respect, depending on the alleged crime and position of the unlucky felon. We practiced 'resisted arrest,' 'arrest before judicial suicide,' arrest after interrogation,' and 'arrest of high-ranked females.' We took turns announcing our arrests in ever more stentorian tones meant to intimidate the accused out of all hope of escape. The hardest part of that class was keeping a straight face.

From what I heard, tax dodgers and crooked customs collectors didn't try to commit suicide very often. If you were lucky, they offered you a cut on the side to look the other way. I was sorry to see the Arrest Procedure course come to an end.

I kept fit in the gymnasium by wrestling with the knuckle-cracking Julius and lifting weights with the Pannonian. Other men grunted and wrestled around us from dawn to dinner.

Roxana was 'special' indeed, the only female I saw in the barracks who wasn't a cook or a girlfriend. She kept to herself during our free periods. She went running on the outdoor track in her exercise halter and short trousers, even as the Roman weather turned nasty. She used her room basin for washing or visited the women's baths in town.

Late some evenings, she swam length after length in our pool by herself. We men were on our honor not to peep at her lithe limbs stroking the heated water each night, her chestnut hair trailing almost to her waist. She was a graceful animal, her dark nipples taut as she swam, her undertunic clinging to her stomach and hips as she lifted herself out to rest, prone and panting, on the stone floor.

I knew this, of course, because I peeped.

She was watching me, too. The barracks were full of *agentes*. But when you took a good look at them, most of the men in our *schola* were better suited than I to spying on others, precisely because they were the kind of men nobody noticed.

Some looked slow and overweight. They were the watchful kind that Apodemius posted to process paperwork at provincial crossways of the *Cursus Publicus* or to linger in taverns listening to the gossip of the day. Nobody linked them to an intelligence service.

Some were lean, quick riders, real veterans of the saddle, made of nothing but sinew and backs folded forward by years riding express. They looked like dried meat hung on hooks in the smoking house.

Some, like our friend the accountant, were talented at numbers and fated to ferret out any imperial cheats by auditing the praetorian records, prefecture by prefecture. Our accountant was not only round-shouldered, but also shortsighted. No Apollo there.

I grew happier by the day as I checked off the competition for Roxana's favor. Too short here, a bit cross-eyed there, bald or bow-legged, lisping or limping, my eyes cancelled one man after another from the ranks of her potential suitors.

It took my mind off my troubles. When I got a night off, I'd sit with Verus in a greasy *popina* near the Porta Esquilina at the foot of our hill.

'Clodius has got some of the books off to that book dealer Soren in the Vicus Sandalarius, he did, before Lady Kahina asked him where he got so much money for gambling. It was a real to-do, I can tell you.'

'What did the Senator say?'

'You don't think I'd upset him? The books disappeared while he was on the potty bowl in the little room at the back. But he suspects something, because now he keeps that filthy thing right next to him in his study. Won't let anybody but me empty it.'

'Lucky you.'

Verus sat up straight. 'I'm honored and don't you mock.'

I steered my questions away from Kahina and the child but the two of them never left my thoughts. 'When does Gregorius get back? The patrol season is over. The whole army should be in winter quarters until spring.'

Verus could smell this was information I wanted, so he waited until I'd bought him a fresh drink.

'Well, that's the thing.' He lifted his eyebrows and nodded like a sage.

'Well?'

'The young missus hasn't had word for weeks and weeks. Our warrior Gregorius was never one for love letters, as Lady Laetitia well knew, but this is a pretty long no-sign-of-life, even from the Commander. He was always home by Solis Day.'

'I remember. He never missed it.' The Roman festival of *Dies Natalis Solis Invicti*, the birth of the Sun Deity, came every December. Extra torches and lamps brightened the neighborhood. Banquet tables groaned with expensive treats in every house on the Esquiline Hill. As a favored boy-pet, I stole my best nibbles from the *Solis* feast tables.

Verus frowned. 'You don't think he's hurt again?'

'Then we'd get word for certain.'

Verus nodded. 'Yes, that's right. Wouldn't we?'

It was odd. I knew I had to stick close to Roma now, more than ever. My training upgrade would finish in another week and a half, but I would insist that Apodemius keep me here. I'd explain that my suspicions that the Manlius estate could be dismantled were turning to sad realities under our very noses.

First the rest of the books would go. Then Clodius would uncover the deeds. More than two hundred years' worth of family acquisitions and prudent management would disappear over his signature.

I had promised Kahina to protect her and our boy. I had to accept any job, no matter how boring, to keep my sights on Clodius. Some day Gregorius would thank me, even if Apodemius didn't.

Roxana and I had a week of Poisons training to finish. I had prepared a truth serum based on the herb I'd seen used in the army to relieve pain. *Herba Apollinaris* always loosened men's tongues, but an overdose could kill.

Roxana arrived late for class. For a change, she was wearing female dress. She fiddled a little with the *fibula* pinning down one fold of the outer tunic over the shoulder of her under tunic. She carried no poison vial or bottle and there was no waist pouch hanging off her belt.

'Forget your homework?'

'Search me.' Her eyes were playful. Suddenly I wanted to kiss her right there next to the gymnasium entrance. Instead, I took up her challenge. I ran my hands up and down her hips, then around her firm buttocks and down her shoulders to her wrists.

'Nothing there,' I said.

'You're not finished,' she teased.

I took a breath and resumed my slow, delicious search, running my palms up and down her back and finally, slowly, from her neck, over her upturned breasts and under their weight to her waist and even below.

'Nothing . . . much.'

We went into class. When it was my turn, I explained my poison—how I'd seen it used on the battlefield by Dr Ari, the Greek medical slave and how I had once witnessed a fatal overdose. Nobody was much impressed. Distracted by the memory of Roxana's warm breath brushing my shoulder, I barely passed the oral exam on antidotes.

Roxana was the last to be tested. She slowly walked up to the instructor, a wily ex-spice merchant from Carthago. She reached into her hair and took out a small, bent hairpin. She was about to press its two points into the teacher's neck, but he stopped her with one strong fist and laughed.

'I don't need a demonstration, just an explanation, my dear,' he said. 'But before you describe your poison, I should point out that your victim would see what you were doing too far in advance. We all did, didn't we, gentlemen?'

'Yes, *Magister*.' She gave a discouraged shrug and lifting both arms, replaced the ornament. We all admired the thick coils of her hair. Her outer tunic shifted off her shoulder and she adjusted that unreliable *fibula*. Then before the teacher realized, she had moved on him again. He yelped and stared down at his forearm to see two ugly red welts rise up off his white skin.

Her *fibula* dropped on the floor. She bent down and recovered her deadly accessory.

'I'm sorry if I hurt you, *Magister*. I diluted the venom, of course. If I'd used the full strength, you'd be dead by nightfall,' she said, with bright eyes. 'You did promise that we'd be graded on technique as well as composition.'

Sometimes Roxana scared even me, but not enough to forget the promise I'd seen before class in those thick-lashed brown eyes.

That night, I lay on my cot, listening as usual to the richer *agentes* lose their money and laugh it off. I couldn't sleep. How could I stop Clodius from denuding the townhouse of Manlius treasures? Too much was sitting there for the taking—imported rugs, statues, silver tableware, carved furniture and worst of all, the beloved books collected by one Manlius after another, reaching back to the days of the Republic. How could Clodius do it?

A knock at my door stopped my restless tossing. 'Come in,' I mumbled. No doubt one of the gamblers, full of wine, hoped to borrow a *centenionalis* or two off me. But I sat up, prepared to warn him that I was low on bronze that week.

Roxana stood in the doorway, her figure untouched by motherhood or care, her muscles taut and shining with some kind of oil under the corridor's lamplight. Her hair was still wet from her swim and pinned high onto her head but there was no lacquer or false fashion about it. Golden earrings twinkled at me as I borrowed the flame of her lamp to re-ignite the one next to my bed.

'I hope those hairpins aren't poisoned,' I said.

'Just in case,' she answered, 'here they go.' She pulled her hair loose and shook her head, sending brown waves tumbling down to her waist.

She dropped her shift and came to me. I saw she was depilated in the Eastern style and perfumed with oil between her thighs. I got off the cot and she stretched out in the very warm contours I left in the thin mattress. I slipped one leg over the cot and placed one knee next to her thigh. I ran my fingers along her slippery skin and realized that the perfumed oil came, not from a bottle, but from her own excitement.

As I said, sometimes Roxana scared me, but that night of rocking, sighing and moving inside her strong and sleek body wasn't one of those times.

I fell into an ecstasy balanced between abandon and control, astonished at her supple skill and unfettered passion. After twenty minutes of her encouraging sighs and mounting gasps, even I had nothing left and finally gave in to a release that left me limp.

Sated, she moved off and sat on one end of the cot. I lay on my back, with my eyes closed, but opened them in time so as not to miss the sight of her pulling her shift back over her head. She stood up and checked the corridor for stray *agentes* or strangers through a crack in the door. She was the only female recruit, but she wasn't the only woman smuggled into a cell. Our barracks were jammed with healthy, normal men—unlike those ghettos down in the Subura slums of forswearing Christian cultists.

'You're wonderful, Roxana.' I could not take my eyes off the soft rosy-olive curve of her hip visible under the thin linen.

'I'm supposed to be,' she said. 'A Special has to take certain courses in skills the ordinary *agentes* never master.'

I stared at her and gulped. 'Surely what just happened was more than a training exercise.'

'It was pleasant enough. More enjoyable than swimming regulation lengths to keep slim or learning how to poison a lady's face cream.'

'Roxana! You can't fool me!' I laughed and jumped up to hold her tight. I brushed her forehead with kisses and reached through her shift to play a bit with her bottom. I'd had many women in the houses, from Lambaesa to Lugdunum. I knew a woman's cries of true contentment from false. Men like me heard both.

'We'll each have new assignments soon, but mine are different from yours. If I cannot fool every man I meet, I'll soon be nothing but a lovely corpse,' she said. 'Goodnight, Marcus. Let's hope we can practice together again, very soon.'

⚔⚔⚔

I dreaded the moment I had to recite my private worries to Apodemius yet again. I heard the little page Caius summon other *agentes* one by one for midnight meetings with the white-haired boss over in the main building. When the old man gave his decision, men obeyed without protest. Sometimes they didn't even show up for breakfast the next morning. Sometimes they just swept their things out and with a smile or frown, paid off their gambling debts, left a letter or two for posting, waved the rest of us a business-like farewell, and disappeared.

Yet it was now the third week of December and Apodemius hadn't called me in. More often than not, as my acquaintances took off for new postings in distant parts of the Empire, I found myself eating alone.

There was one jolly night when those of us left behind decided to turn up in disguises for a little feast. I came in a *retiarius* getup, complete with trident and net, rented for a pretty price from a shop that sold the used kit of dead gladiators. Everybody got a little drunk that night. We

71

composed a spontaneous funeral ode to Florian, an unlucky recruit who had died during training.

I drank and sang along with the best of them. I was happy to recall some of my favorite poems learned at the Senator's knee and even a few learned in the Manlius kitchen, like that limerick, 'There was an old Roman named Nero, considered by some as their hero ...' but I kept one eye on the door. I hoped for a visit from Roxana, but she skipped the party altogether.

Finally after eleven that night, I caught sight of her returning from the swimming pool. Her face looked distracted and troubled. I slipped away without hailing her. Now that classes were ended, she seemed to have forgotten me.

I dragged my bloodstained net to my cell and threw the rusty trident in a corner. The celebration had left me a bit sulky, what with all the toasts and boasts of fellows soon to be moving on. Everyone but me had his assignment for the coming year.

An old bronze mirror hung on the wall. When I saw my wavering reflection, I felt ridiculous. The new year promised me nothing but more customs, accounting and tax training. The only 'relief' would be depressing meetings with Verus to review the decline of our house. Still dressed in my costume, I flung myself down on my cot.

Just then Caius knocked on my door. I peeked out and saw him nod. He didn't have to say anything.

'Do I have time to change?'

The little slave gave my costume a scathing look up and down. 'Nope. He's working by minutes, not hours. He already turned the timer. Technically, your meeting is already in session and you are late.'

I dashed across the moonlit paving to the main building, my garish cloak flying behind me in a vermilion streak.

'Reporting, *Magister*.'

Apodemius was wearing a heavy felt bed cloak over his shoulders and soft boots of sheepskin on his suffering feet. The room was ablaze with oil lamps. Clearly he intended to work through the night. I saw some hard cheese and a stack of flatbreads on a sideboard next to a large pitcher of wine keeping warm over a low flame.

He raised a stern eyebrow at my getup. 'Hungry? You seemed dressed for the kill.'

'No, *Magister*. There's been a sort of party—'

'How's the Customs training coming along?'

'Fine, *Magister*. Fine.'

'Still want to stay within reach of Roma?'

'Yes, of course.'

'That's too bad. I had hoped to see more initiative from you, after your little adventure with the Circumcellions. You did well then.'

And not now.

'Thank you, but as I explained there are troubles in the Manlius house that are worsening in the Commander's absence. I owe it to my old master to save what's left.'

'Troubles in the Manlius house,' he mumbled to himself. 'You have no idea.' He broke off a chunk of cheese and dropped a piece into the cage for his sleepy mice.

I stood there, waiting. He had not offered me a stool.

'I had an assignment for you, Numidianus, a sensitive one, even a dangerous one.' He sighed. 'I should have entrusted it weeks ago to a more experienced agent.'

He pulled his cloak tighter. His room was indeed cold at this hour. The men firing the hypocaust steam system that kept the building's walls and floors nice and warm had retired for the night. Working while the stone building cooled down couldn't be good for the old man's joints. And when did he sleep?

Suddenly he spoke up. 'Numidianus, did you see any other signs of disrespect to the Emperor Constans up in Treverorum?'

'No, Apodemius.'

'And yet rumors reach me here.' He paused. 'Are you *sure* I cannot persuade you to leave Roma?'

'I've promised to protect my former's master's family.'

'You had no right to make such a promise. You were sworn to serve the Empire.'

This meeting threatened an outcome worse than a boring career in Customs. My divided loyalties meant I was about to be dismissed from the *schola*. This was why Apodemius had delayed our meeting for so long. He'd been hoping I would use the extra weeks to straighten out any Manlius headaches and free myself for some garrison on the Upper Rhenus or desert postal hub out East.

I took a deep breath and concentrated on my little Leo, for whom everything must be protected. I fought back a perverse curiosity as to what chance at glory I'd just missed out on. I was almost grateful that for discretion's sake, Apodemius would never discuss one man's mission with another—especially a fool who was refusing a good career he'd fought hard for only two years before.

But Apodemius didn't sack me yet. First, he had to wring me dry of any last information he might need.

'So, to whom do you swear your loyalty?'

I thought hard—of the Senator, the Commander, Kahina, my son and the old Leo buried far across the Great Sea—a Roman buried deep into the sand of an empire frayed and fragmented beyond recognition.

'To the Empire,' I said.

'Yes,' he said slowly, 'And?'

'To the Empire and all its citizens?'

'Precisely. We're the eyes, ears and conscience of all of its citizens, even the lowliest. Do you understand what I'm saying?'

It was a lecture even a stubborn Numidian-born mule like myself couldn't misinterpret. The Empire wasn't the noble families and their crumbling Senate, the arrogant commanders, the decadent Emperors' courts in Constantinopolis, Sirmium, Treverorum and Mediolanum filled with ambitious officials, not to mention one miserable and vicious imperial sister.

The Constantines wore purple—but their Empire wore leather, fur, homespun cotton, hemp, wool and linen. The Empire spoke dialects of Latin so garbled and twisted now that old Marcus Tullius Cicero wouldn't have understood a single syllable.

The Empire was *us*. Our loyalty was to an idea that embraced everyone.

Apodemius came over to me. He stood there, a head shorter and a brain smarter. 'Did Gaiso say anything about disgruntled soldiers?'

'No, *Magister*.'

'Has the Commander Gregorius written home of any discontent among his men?'

'Not that I know of, *Magister*.'

'When's he due back?'

'The household still hasn't heard.'

Apodemius shook his head, confused. He crossed the room and stood in front of that large map on the wall behind his desk. With his finger he traced the stations linking Treverorum to Mediolanum.

'Did anyone up there mention a General Magnentius?'

'No, *Magister*.'

I waited with a heart torn and miserable. I wished Apodemius would just finish me off with a clean dismissal.

But he kept on almost talking, more to himself than to me. He ran his fingers over the black lines running across his parchment map. 'It can't be true. It can't be right. Constans *saved* Magnentius from a rebellion in the protectorates. But then, he would never expect it coming from the Herculiani.'

'The Herculiani?' I asked. 'Commander Gregorius is with the Herculiani.'

He started, as if he'd forgotten I was still there. 'Yes, I know, Numidianus. That legion is the nest of many rumors.'

'Please explain this to me.'

Apodemius dismissed me with a wave of his hand. 'Certainly not to an accountant in Customs. You can go now.'

'No! I'll take the mission, whatever it is. I hate Customs Training. Send me on this mission, *please*.'

Apodemius rested his pained hips on the edge of his desk. 'Even if it means forgetting your distractions at the Manlius townhouse?'

'The Manlius House is a pillar of the Empire. What have the Herculiani done?'

'You may be in time to save him, Numidianus. He has bound himself to a powerful man, a man who means well, but who may trip over his own ideals and pull us all into an abyss.'

'I'm ready, *Magister.*'

He pulled his cloak tighter around his shoulders. 'I thought so. Good.'

A bell tower in the distance rang out midnight. A mouse woke up and skittered around the cage.

Apodemius cocked an ear as it chimed. 'Ah, the beginning of another working day.' He chuckled as he picked a memo off the top of his towering pile of paperwork and waved it at me. 'It seems I'm under orders to wish everyone I greet today a "Festive Christ Mass".'

'I beg your pardon?'

He read, with the faint sarcasm of any proper pagan for Constantine's 'official' cult, "Pope Julius"—and what a politician he is, eh?—"decrees that henceforth, on every December 25, the people shall celebrate the Nativity of our Lord, Jesus Christ, rather than the Roman festival of *Dies Natalis Solis Invicti,* the Birthday of the Unconquered Sun. They shall refrain from all labors, and attend Mass in their churches to give thanks to the one and only truly God for the Gift of his Son" *et cetera, et cetera.*'

He tossed the memo back onto the pile. 'Well, that's the gist of it but we'll ignore the "refrain from labor" bit. Now, back to work. You're to wait in Lugdunum only as long as it takes to ascertain the likely rendezvous of this General Magnentius with the Secretary of the Emperor's Private Revenues, one Marcellinus.'

'What does this Marcellinus actually do, *Magister?*'

'His office collects the rents of state properties and if necessary, seizes and redistributes properties that were confiscated by or falls to the state for lack of heirs. He supervises the sale of state property and makes cash payments from the imperial treasury.'

'That's real power. But why must I watch him?'

'Because dark waters are roiling, boy. The problem is, I can't determine where the waves will break. Perhaps our *Augusta* Constantia is plotting against Constantius out of revenge for the murder of her husband and making promises to Eusebius, in exchange for playing a double game in her favor. Perhaps Constans is keeping her close for a similar reason? There's no brotherly love lost between our two emperors.'

'What does General Magnentius have to do with it?'

'Magnentius has shot up as the most powerful military man in the West. But why? *Why?*' Apodemius fingered a carved game piece on that checkered board near his chair.

'Who is he?'

'He is the son of a Breton freedman who served old Constantine's father, Chlorus, as a craftsman. His mother was a Frankish war refugee from the Rhenus resettlement camps who entertained Constantine's court as a soothsayer. Bit of a wild woman, they say. Now their son has made his name in the army as a rising man. He already commands both the former praetorian legions.'

'*Both* the Legio V Iovia and VI Herculia? Wait a minute. I believe I do recall his name. He was providing support forces for the fatal ambush on Constantine II, wasn't he?'

'And beyond that . . . all I have is rumors, rumors, and more rumors. We know that Constans once saved Magnentius from a mutiny of his own men. I need more on this Franco-Breton. I need to know where he stands. I have to know before Eusebius plays him like a "dog" piece on his *latrunculi* board!'

Apodemius knocked over the ivory playing piece with the flick of his twisted middle finger.

'Yes, *Magister*. And what is the General's relationship to Secretary Marcellinus?'

'Ah, Marcellinus is no game piece. He's an expert politician, perhaps the most dangerous man in the Empire after Eusebius. And for the last year or so, whenever I heard mentioned the names Marcellinus or Magnentius, I also heard of purple ribbons tied onto items of disgust or disdain. And then your report linked such a ribbon with Lieutenant-General Gaiso.'

'Why is this mission dangerous? It sounds like normal reconnaissance.'

'I'm placing another agent on a similar mission, but from another angle. You won't be alone but you won't work together. It's safer that way.'

'But why dangerous?'

'Because, my boy, you won't be there incognito. If my plan goes through smoothly, you will be immediately recognized as who and *what* you are by the man who knows you best. It will take all your talent to convince him that you're there as an innocent courier.'

The blood drained from my face. He was asking me to spy on my own former master, the Commander, while I, his bastard son, hoped only to be acknowledged for my merits—not hated for betrayal.

No wonder Apodemius had left me to stew alone. I was indeed the perfect man for this job. The Commander would welcome me back as a prodigal ex-slave unable to shrug off the deep loyalty I'd felt as the favored child in the house and later on the battlefield as his private aide and bodyguard. He would accept me under false pretenses. Whatever my official access to the top officers of the Herculiani as an *agens*, I would enjoy double the trust as Gregorius' personal freedman.

I had never been false to the Commander before. Mutilated and disfigured, Gregorius had trusted me above anyone else. He had tried to bind me to his side, even at the risk of breaking his word. Yet I'd openly abandoned him out of a greater hunger for freedom.

I looked at Apodemius with new respect. I'd wanted to protect the House of Manlius. Now I saw how clever the old man was. He had understood all along that the fate of the Manlius family hung, not around the fig-strewn courtyard of a rundown Roman townhouse, but around the Commander's political neck.

'You'll accept an attachment to the staff of General Magnentius?'

'Yes, *Magister*.'

'I thought so. You never struck me as the number-sifting type. Oh, yes, there's a new gadget we're giving all our men on dangerous jobs,' he said. He reached below his table into a wooden box and pulled out a varnished wooden handle about five inches long.

'Rather clever, this. It looks like nothing, but you see, if I pull here, a spoon swivels out—harmless. Or a comb, here. If only I had more hair to demonstrate! Oh, my fingers are stiff. But if I pull here,' he pried out a shining blade on a hinge which snapped into place. 'Or here,' and suddenly there was a deadly iron pick sticking out a right angles to the handle. 'You can hand over your weapons in any search and conceal this inside your tunic or boot.'

'What's it called?' I took the polished thing from him and pulled out a second twisted coil of iron and finally a file.

'I haven't the slightest idea. The armory just sent me a box of them,' he shrugged. 'Let's just call it a present for . . . Christ Mass?'

CHAPTER 7, THE BIRTHDAY PARTY

—AUGUSTODUNUM HAEDUORUM, GALLIA—

Apodemius trained us *agentes* to 'register and report' as soon as we reached a new posting. But I had no clue yet what I was really investigating. Vague unease triggered by purple ribbons?

If there was any disquiet, it was in my heart. How would the Commander receive me back on assignment?

He had fought against losing me because he thought I was his only issue. Now Kahina had given him a legal heir, the baby Leo. Perhaps because of Leo, the Commander could accept that I preferred taking my chances on liberty and an uncertain future to a half-life as some shopkeeper or foreman under his lifelong patronage. I would know from his expression within the first moments of our meeting again.

According to the latest report arriving at the Castra just before I left, the General Magnentius had shifted his base from Lugdunum up to the imperial city of Augustodunum. I stuck to the coastal state road as far as Arelate, then shot north through Lugdunum. Riding alone from Roma, I made it in eighteen days—not at 24-hour relay speed, but not dawdling either.

The Augustodunum I now trotted towards didn't look like a city simmering with political ferment. The city's walls were obscured on the southern side by lean-to's, vendors' stalls and a few huts. Most of the poor were sheltering inside from the harsh weather. Only one humble doorway framed a couple of bone-chilled prostitutes, their cheeks made rosy by the New Year's brisk winds.

They both waved to me. The buxom blonde even winked. I tossed her a *nummus* for trying and she caught it with a greedy fist.

'Come back for some luck, dark-and-handsome!' she shouted back, tucking my coin into her bosom.

After the new-built brashness of Treverorum's gray sandstone walls, Augustodunum struck me as a middle-aged woman with broader curves and a basketful of nostalgic memories. She was living off a fair chunk of glory from her Republican past. The Emperor Augustus had set up headquarters here to lord it over the conquered Gauls of Bribracte. Three centuries of wind and rain had smoothed down her rough edges. Today, surrounded by broad rolling pastures lying fallow for the winter and rippling streams stippled with ice floes, Augustodunum looked like a settled dowager. I passed a vast amphitheater standing empty, waiting for spring weather to fill its bleachers with laughter, cheers and tears.

But up close, Augustodunum wasn't such a shabby town, despite its weather-beaten facade. The elders had just added a modern gateway to Augustus' original one, no doubt paid for by ripe pickings from the trade route between Lugdunum and Bononia, the coastal Gallic boom town facing the Channel to Britannia. I'd heard everyone was speaking Germanic in Bononia these days. Even here in Augustodunum, when I asked directions where to register my arrival and deposit my mount, my ear caught a Latin enriched with barbarian slang that the Old Senator back in Roma wouldn't find in any of his authoritative tomes.

I had recognized no one *en route* and certainly had no informants or old contacts in Augustodunum. Crusted with dust and sweat, I rode through the city's arches thinking I was hardly likely to make any new friends in my current condition.

All these problems could be solved by one thing—a bath. I returned my mount to the city stables and registered myself with the *agentes* list, then rambled down the main street in search of the *thermae*.

A trio of stable boys laughed when I asked for a good bathhouse. 'There's one on every street.' They pointed me in three different directions at once, so I narrowed it down by saying I wanted a chance to see the town's true fat cats without their fur.

'Then you want the Baths of Tonantius,' one of the urchins said. 'But my father says they charge too much for towels,' he added, extending his own grubby palm for a tip.

I strode down a well-paved boulevard full of busy locals until I spotted Tonantius' sign. It was painted with two body-scrapers, a pair of sandals and bright blue letters that read, 'Salvum Lavisse, a bath is good for you.'

As soon as I entered the crowded vestibule, I realized one thing was certain; these baths were good for the proprietor's bottom line. Under the wintry light struggling through the domed glass ceiling, I threaded myself between gaggles of men in various stages of undress as I looked for an available clothes hook. Reaching some benches lining the walls, I was crushed between two men, one of them portly and bald and the other as tall and stooped as a shepherd's hook. Two dressing room boys vied for their tips to guard their belongings.

The heavier man lost his patience with the press of other bodies. 'This is ridiculous. On a normal day we wouldn't have to wait for the Tepid Room.' One of the boys reached out a hand, waiting for the man to remove his numerous neck chains. 'No, thank you! I'm keeping my gold on my chest where it's safe, you rascal! Watch what you're doing, lad, I'll be counting those items when I collect them later and I know your face only too well!'

'What do you expect on a day like today? You were invited, I assume,' his stooped companion asked.

'Of course, but you won't see me there. A previous engagement.'

It was obvious to me that the fat man hadn't been included in whatever the event was. The stooped man suppressed a knowing smile.

'It's not an invitation I'd dare refuse. All the big families will be there. I'm sorry I won't be seeing you. I'd hoped to share a few laughs with someone I trust.'

I followed them as they made slow progress towards the baths' various chambers. I had the impression that for some reason, Augustodunum's elite wanted to gossip more than bathe *en masse* today.

'What does trust have to do with it?' the fatter man shrugged. 'It's just a birthday party for a kid and not a very nice one from what my granddaughter tells me. Why should I bother?'

The tall man leaned down to whisper and I caught his expression, full of meaning, 'Because you and I both know it's more than a birthday party for Marcellinus' brat.'

There was more to be heard, but if I glued myself to these two, they'd turn suspicious. I needn't have worried. After all, what might they see in their eavesdropper but an olive-skinned Roman African youth with calloused hands and reeking of horse?

After a quick scrub, I did short laps for some twenty minutes in the cool swimming pool alongside half a dozen young men like myself.

Spotting some scarred and muscle-bound army veterans through the warm mist, I considered joining their loud and ribald conversation. While resting between laps, I'd overheard some juicy boasts about humping Pict redheads for the price of a drink or seducing white-haired 'princesses' begging for bread in the barbarian refugee camps in Upper Germania.

But there was nothing useful in their boisterous jokes. I might have looked relaxed, but I was very much on the job. As I toweled off, the veterans moved away to work off their excessive energies on some exercise balls. I wandered back to the vestibule to see if I could get into the Tepid Room for a light sweat.

I settled on a bench next to two elderly Gallo-Romans, their saggy chests covered in grey tufts, their flabby backs bent over to be oiled down and scraped clean by minions. One of them suffered from a goiter and the other from legs swollen with gout. Six months of guarding the Rhenus on simple army rations might have cured their complaints.

'Look at his villa. Count his slaves. The man's got everything he wants.' Goiter Man sniggered as he was massaged. 'Why upset the turnip cart?'

'Because Marcellinus hasn't got everything he wants. A man like this doesn't come along every day and he knows it.'

'He'll be there tonight . . . Have you met him?'

The gouty man winced as the boy scraped his swollen calf. 'Saw him once, riding into town for winter provisioning at the head of the Protectorates. That was years ago. He must be in his late forties by now.'

'Illyrian, I heard. Or Dacian?'

'You heard wrong. He was born up north, in Samarobriva, I think.'

Goiter Man slapped his thigh. 'That settles the question. He's a Gaul. Or a Gallo-Roman.'

'No. He's definitely not one of us. His father was a Breton—a slave who got himself freed and married a German girl from one of Constantine's refugee camps on the border.'

'A real barbarian then.'

'In all but name. He has spent his whole life in the army fighting his way up through the ranks.'

'And probably never sat behind a desk in his life. What does Marcellinus see in such a man when he's already got the Treasury?'

Gouty Man sighed, 'Oh, Lucius, you are well behind the times. Marcellinus has piled up political resentments as fast as he has piled up private riches. He's sick of the Constantines and their Eastern favorites. Constans is just the last straw. Last week I heard Marcellinus tell Thaumastus that General Magnentius is *The New Roman*.' He kicked away the bath slave. 'Stop that, you ass, can't you see you're hurting me?'

The two old men had soon had enough, but I hadn't. Wrapping my loins in fresh linen supplied by the boys, I made my way through the crowd into the steamy *caldarium*. I could hardly see the bright-colored mosaics that decorated the floor above the subterranean furnaces churning beneath our bare toes. The great flues along the hollow walls belched their hot gusts into the air over our heads. I thought of poor Apodemius, his *hypocaust* turning off at midnight, leaving his office walls humid with cold.

Everything in this room was built of fine white marble. Through the thick mist, I saw few empty seats and already that told me a lot. I was new to Augustodunum, but I wasn't new to society's ways. Most of these men looked well fed and sharp-eyed. Having ridden past miles of villas flanked by gardens and orchards earlier today, I knew these customers had baths at home. They weren't here for the doubtful pleasure of being anointed with cut-rate massage oils by light-fingered cloakroom boys.

These men were here for the very same reason I was— information—and the obscurity of the Hot Room masked the murmurs of Augustodunum's powerbrokers.

I picked my next quarries well. I watched the rows of faces to see who was doing as much watching as I was. Finally, I spotted two men who in their younger days might have served the imperial throne from a horse or under a banner. Their muscles were softened with time, but their spines were still straight as spears. Each wore a seal ring, but apart from that, their only adornments were the towels tossed across their laps. I sat to their right, leaving a good foot of discreet space between the customer closer to me and myself. His long jaw and high forehead gave him the look of a patrician and possibly a former officer. I thought of him as the Tribune.

'. . . in it for us? We can manage as we are,' he murmured.

'Why not make reality official?' the other said. This one was less aristocratic in stature than his friend, but he was more of a merchant type. He must have prospered in retirement from military service, to judge by the size of his belly. He dragged his thick fingers across his brow and flicked off the perspiration.

'Draw the poison to the surface and purge the boil. The gods know I don't care what people they do in their bedrooms, but when they devastate the economy, it's another thing. He has devalued our coin once already and the bastard might do it again. He installs Easterners as prefects where he should promote reliable Romans. Someone has to put the economy and administration back to rights.'

'Is that what the praetorians are saying?' the Tribune asked.

'And more,' the Merchant replied. 'I know, I know, their complaints are based on pride and disgust, not hard business facts, but they have a point. You can understand how they feel about the disrespect. We both served, but not under a festering, pus-filled boil like—'

'Better the boil we know than—' the Tribune warned.

'The point is not *why* the praetorians are fed up, but that they *are* at the end of their tether. Once the military leadership is unhappy, then we're not safe in our beds.' The Merchant jabbed the air like a man addressing his trade association. 'We have to keep the army happy or that border will snap wide open and we'll be entertaining Alemanni for supper. Do you think our enemies don't know how fragile the situation is?'

The Merchant lowered his voice quickly as some acquaintances passed and nodded to our bench. Men were eager to talk, but not to be overheard.

'I'll make up my mind when I see the man in person,' said the Tribune. 'Anyway, it's not my head on the block Marcellinus should bide his time. Let this wretched family continue to kill itself off and we'll get a solid Roman ruler back on top. That's what I say.'

The Tribune nodded to his friend and rose on bare feet to mount the marble steps for the *labrum* in the corner, where a slave doused his naked body with fresh cool water. The Merchant glanced at me and smiled, which I took as a courtesy. Making the most of this, it was my job to take a gamble:

'Citizen, I'm an imperial rider with a message from Roma for one Prefect Marcellinus, but the town seems in such a hubbub, I'm unable to find his villa among so many strangers. The directions I got at the relay station are worse than useless.'

'I'm not surprised,' the Merchant laughed. 'Marcellinus is a rising man and he's hard to pin down. He's moved house twice in the last four years.'

I leaned back against the dripping marble wall and wiped off my face with an air of casual resignation. I was a messenger in no hurry to get back to work. I fooled him.

'But you're in luck. The Prefect of the Treasury is giving a birthday party tonight. If your business can wait a few hours, you can follow my carriage to his villa. We have a brown roof festooned with dark red braid and bronze pommels shaped like bulls' heads. It's less than a mile. Wait for us to pass by at the main gate at sundown.'

'I'm very grateful, but my message isn't that urgent. It sounds as if I may be intruding on a private family celebration.'

'If you worry about that, then so should the entire elite of this diocese,' he laughed, tightening his towel. 'Half the men in this room are from out of town. They're cleaning up for the big event. There will be a veritable Triumph of Litters heading out the gates tonight.'

'An anniversary? Is this Marcellinus so very old?'

'No,' The Merchant lowered his voice as he rubbed his face with a towel. He continued added in a muffled tone, 'and neither is his son, the birthday boy. That's not the point. Stick around, rider, and you may have a much bigger message to take home.'

He tossed me a knowing wink and headed off for his own cold dousing.

⚱⚱⚱

I'd paid the bath boys extra to clean up my uniform and trim my hair. Wafting neroli oil in my wake, I had no qualms trailing hundreds of chattering guests towards the Villa Marcellinum. It stood on the slopes not far above the amphitheater. It also enjoyed a view of a massive temple to Janus featuring a Christian cross freshly engraved into its facade.

Nobody asked me to produce a written invitation but I was careful to nod to my neighbors in the crush on either side, even though neither of them was actually talking to me. I waved to a man ahead of me in the queue as we filed into the walled garden. I acknowledged his mystified and hesitant wave in return. I kept all this nodding, smiling and waving up so that by the time we reached the entrance to the house itself, I was practically an esteemed member of the town council.

I'd seen big society parties before. In fact, as a slave child among the Manlius elders in Roma, one of my duties had been to scamper and skip around the banquet table while Commander Gregorius entertained his military friends. I'd been expected to recite poetry, sing little songs and be teased and ordered about. As the evening wore on, Gregorius would gather me onto his couch and let me fall asleep while he kept on debating battle tactics and weapons with his fellow officers.

But the gathering tonight resembled something different— not so much a private party as a massive public display of local power and luxury. Set off by the glow of garden braziers and the rustle of silk flowers, it seemed there was more raucous music and loud greeting than you'd see on Circus Day in Roma.

People weren't so much settling in for a good time as counting heads and registering the names of those who hadn't yet passed through the garden gates under pine boughs tied with green ribbons. The arrivals never seemed to thin out and people who had got into the reception halls stood around sending darting glances of curiosity at each other. We all seemed to be waiting for something, even as we picked at passing trays of roasted meats, honeyed fruits and grains steamed with exotic seeds from the south.

Yes, waiting for something . . . but what?

I scanned the crowd for the one face, mutilated, and embittered, that I'd last seen in North Africa streaked with tears at my 'betrayal.' I searched for the Commander, but he was nowhere to be seen.

A former slave never forgets how to stay inconspicuous, and amidst all the nobles and officers in attendance here tonight, I slipped through the crowded atrium much like a minnow might move unnoticed in a school of distracted and exotic tropical fish. Everyone had made an effort to distinguish themselves in dress or makeup, with the result that before my eyes, the great and good of Gallia appeared as one lavish, glamorous, yet provincial mass of people straining their bejeweled necks to see who was yet arriving and glancing away from their partners to see whether they'd missed greeting a more significant companion.

One thing that struck me within the first half hour was the outlay of money. Everyone looked astonished at the over-generous bounty straining the catering tables and banqueting bars. Even by wealthy Gallo-Roman standards, we were being stuffed like pigs ready for the spit. There was double the usual number of musicians, too. The tweeting and bang of their flutes and drums made conversation a sort of competitive sport.

The second thing that struck me, and this was as much thanks to my childhood as a slave as any observation drills at the Castra Peregrina—I was sure that nobody was having a good time.

'Where is he? You'd think he'd have greeted us by now. I've paid my respects to his boy, but I'm getting a headache in this crush,' a woman in a grey wool cloak thick with red embroidery whined to her tipsy husband.

'Just stand over there, then, by the garden, for fresh air,' he muttered. 'It's too early to go home.'

The tension wound like a current through the guests. It was about to break any minute like a wave of impatience. Suddenly, the assembly in the main dining room parted into two wavering seas of heads and headdresses.

A man with a well-formed head and thick, compact shoulders over a taut torso descended the steps of a *tablinum* at the end of the atrium. He smiled and nodded to the first cluster of guest. This must be Marcellinus, our host, at last.

The lady on his arm would be his wife, I had no doubt. She had once been a pretty woman, I thought but no match for her husband's dominating presence. She looked almost buried under jewels too large for her tiny frame and hair too overdone for her bird-like features. She looked like a bookkeeper's daughter. I wondered if the luxuriant coiffeur might be a hairpiece.

He was shaking hands and taking time to exchange welcoming words with each couple or family. Surprised and half-drunk, some of them shoved the bread down their throats in time to pay their respects or dropped half-peeled fruits on his priceless Persian carpets in a hurry to get to the front of the crowd.

None of this obsequious or obnoxious hustling seemed to ruffle the Prefect. He had that knack of listening closely with rapt attention, so that each person received the impression that he ranked, after all, among the most essential guests.

The mood changed from anxiety to relief. Everyone relaxed and the wine flowed even faster. The evening's end was within sight, so why not make the most of his generosity now?

I drank nothing and ate little. I watched Marcellinus. His hair was close-cut, his complexion pale for a dark-haired Gaul and his body held taut and close to his torso—as though by disciplining his limbs he demonstrated his greater care with the Western Empire's accounts.

Still, no man controlled mints and coffers without benefitting himself over time. It was part of the job. I judged that the purpose of this party was to pave the way for his boy to meet the most important trading and civil service families of the province.

Yet this wasn't so. Marcellinus had only appeared half an hour after his son had gone off to bed. Now, having satisfied the social ambitions of one roly-poly merchant after another, our host paid special attention to his military guests.

I spotted the insignias of high-ranking officers from both the legions wintering over in the area but I didn't recognize any of them. With these men, Marcellinus lingered longer and smiled less. He nodded, murmuring agreements and giving short, sober replies to their questions. If he had an eye for treating imperial servants in uniform well, I was hardly going to remain invisible. I checked my *agens* insignia and straightened my sword belt as he approached.

'Do I know you, agent?' His smile seemed genuine as his hand braced my forearm with a firm grip but he knew he hadn't invited me to his party.

'I've just arrived, Secretary, to serve as state courier under the General Magnentius.'

'Attached to the Ioviani or Herculiani?' Both legions answered to General Magnentius. As they were the leading fighters of the entire Empire, this single soldier wielded more force than a simple headcount would indicate.

'I don't know. It's a technicality. Wherever the General thinks best.'

'Ask him now,' Marcellinus answered. He extended his arm in a wide circle. As the partygoers cleared a space in the center of the floor, he said, 'Welcome, please, my guest of honor. He graces this house and my son's special day tonight, bestowing on our humble hospitality all the glory that is the Empire's!'

I've seen matrons swoon over celebrity gladiators. I've heard senators who should have known better gush over a precocious rhetorician as if they'd been listening to Virgil himself. But the appearance of General Flavius Magnus Magnentius that night struck the crowd like a thunderbolt from Mount Olympus.

Slaves pulled aside the rich green drapes under an archway. In the hush, we heard heavy boot steps mounting stone steps from some inner chamber behind the dining room. Suddenly Magnentius appeared before us, framed by marble, shoulders braced back and head high, like a carving on a memorial frieze.

'He looks like a god,' murmured a tipsy young beauty next to me. The problem to my male eyes was that this god flexed his charismatic muscles only too well, one well-made calf turned out in a pose. He was indeed in his late forties, but still enjoying the prime of maturity and strength.

He had a full head of light brown hair cut in a bowl fringe over large, expressive eyes and a strong, high-bridged nose. His head sat on a bull's neck set between wide shoulders. He stood a head taller than most of these Gallo-Romans with their darker curls and rotund bellies.

He pursed a pair of generous lips set over his prominent chin with confident amusement at his gaping audience.

This was no Roman, no Easterner, no Gaul, and no Mediterranean of any ilk. It was as though his exotic personality sucked the incensed fug out of the overheated rooms into which we all squeezed. Here was a man whose blood coursed with the freezing winds of the channel dividing Gallia from Britannia and who stood as tall as the dark northern forests where savage bears and boars held sway.

My back straightened like a rod. I hadn't wasted my years serving the Commander Gregorius in North Africa. I knew how to react to the sight of the General's polished cuirass and fringe, his bare arms laced with scars and his pristine woolen socks tucked into immaculate parade boots.

Behind his left shoulder a familiar face now appeared— none other than Gaiso, that hearty boar hunter. He descended the steps behind Magnentius. I was glad to see him walk with ease, showing scarcely a trace of his autumn hunting accident. A second officer, so like Magnentius he could only be his brother, followed.

But then my eyes darted, despite myself, to a fourth man behind the general's other shoulder, someone who was an even more riveting sight to me—but for all the wrong reasons.

The last two years had been kind to my former master, even if the ambush up on the Rhenus so many years before had not. The livid scars that distorted the ravaged cheek under the emptied eye socket had finally lost their magenta fury. They were a dead white now. The full ferocity of his injuries was masked underneath a festive bandanna he twisted around one side of his head for the sake of the festivities. The embroidered head wrap gave his twisted smile a *louche* but worldly air that set off his brilliant armor.

I was happy to see that his outer swagger had recovered and perhaps some of his inner spirit as well. No doubt his appearance at the side of the supreme western commander reminded these comfy burghers that there were bold men who paid dearly for Gallia's security and prosperity. Commander Gregorius had once been a man who turned the ladies' heads. Now I saw he drew their fascinated stares to his scars before they could help themselves and lower their gaze in shock.

I was glad he had Kahina back in Roma. I was content that she'd forgotten our brief embraces and had learned to love the Commander Gregorius instead.

I didn't wait any longer to be recognized—it would have seemed unnatural, even derelict in duty, not to announce myself immediately to the men who would make use of my services. The other top men were gathering in force at one end of the room, eager to bask in the reflected charisma of the great general.

I greeted Magnentius and presented him with my identifying papers. With a bow of my head, I nodded to Gaiso and greeted Gregorius in turn, my heart pounding with fear that he still harbored all his rage and grief at my defection back in Africa. He might even sabotage the first few minutes of my appointment with some sour dismissal.

'Marcus *Gregorianus* Numidianus?' Magnentius read out loud, turning to the wounded veteran behind him.

My fears vanished as I heard Gregorius answer the General, 'Formerly our own *volo*, General, and dear to our family as the only child of Lady Laetitia's Numidian seamstress. Marcus earned his freedman status and much praise through his surveillance of the Donatist extremists during the Macarius affair.'

'Joined the *agentes*, I see,' Magnentius said. He examined my expression, as if searching for the telltale mark of Apodemius on my forehead. 'I already have enough aides on my staff, but you lads have many talents, I've learned, some of them less obvious than others. What's your specialty, boy?'

'High-speed communications, postal route control and relay delivery, road inspection, basic accounting and first-class secretarial certificate, Latin and Greek, General. I look forward to liaising with your legions' communications officers.'

We had drawn an audience of fascinated civilians. I'd omitted mentioning my training in poisons and antidotes, surreptitious memorization, silent assassination skills, night surveillance, invisible and coded communications, surprise arrest, and finally, detention and escort skills—and the General knew it full well.

And I almost blushed, because once again, I'd been caught showing off, trying to impress Gregorius with how far I'd come from serving canapés and sweeping out the foyer back in Roma.

Magnentius chuckled and glanced over at Marcellinus who suppressed his own amusement at my youthful boasting. 'Thank you, *Agens*. Report back to me before dawn.'

I bowed and retreated. For at least an hour, I mingled and made conversation with the ranks of junior officers wending around the lavishly decorated rooms. I sipped my wine with care and listened to the gossip, all of it growing more and more irritable and querulous.

After four hours of nonstop plucking and tooting, the hired musicians were taking longer and longer breaks between sessions. No guest dared leave until the Prefect of the Treasury signaled that his star general was finished with us all—but where had our host and guest of honor gone now?

Both men had finished their rounds of the different banqueting tables and had disappeared back into the study. The excitement was over and the atmosphere grew fidgety. Slaves aired out the suffocating rooms, letting in the winter's chill. Hundreds of women asked for their warm wraps and held their inebriated husbands up by the elbows. They were all depleted of conversation and hoping for release. It was past midnight and yet the wealthy Marcellinus was not to be denied his fabulous party. He'd paid the musicians to keep going. There was an audible sigh of frustration as they tuned up and resumed yet another round of familiar strains.

'Marcus, you've done well for yourself.' Here was Gregorius at last. I could not help but look at him with love and hope for forgiveness with every ounce of my soul.

'Thank you, Commander. You're looking much improved since I saw you last.' Up close, I saw how much not only his scars but also his pride had softened in a few brief years.

'My new lady Kahina is the elixir, Marcus. She has given us an heir—and what a child he is!'

'A great joy for the Manlius House. I paid my respects to your family while in Roma but—'

'Everything fine, then? Good, good.'

I didn't want to worry him just then with Verus' tattling on Clodius or Kahina's worry about his father, the Senator.

'It's like a second chance at life, Marcus. Not much could separate me from such happiness if I didn't think my duty held me here to counsel the General.'

'If it's duty to Magnentius that keeps you so hale, Commander, then I welcome serving him, too.'

'He's a soldier in a thousand, boy. More than twenty years in the field, undefeated in any skirmish, a fighter to the very marrow of his bones. Let's drink to him.'

Let's drink to us, I thought. We had survived our first encounter well. Considering the old days, it was a stiff and inhibited conversation, but he'd held back whatever anger or hurt he still harbored.

I poured wine into my ex-master's empty cup for him. With half of one hand lost in battle, he had trouble pouring his own drink. I knew the man better than myself, as the knack of anticipating his thirst or hunger before my own needs wasn't forgotten that soon. I could see now by the blaze of wall torches and bright oil lamps that he, too, was more than ready to get to bed. But decades of service had trained him to betray not an iota of fatigue. We watched the flagging crowd eyeing the door behind which our host and his military celebrity still lingered.

'Let's hope our Emperor Constans appreciates the General's talents. During my time in Treverorum, Commander, I heard not one single word of praise for General Magnentius, but only admiration of the Emperor's captive German archers.'

Gregorius paused over the lip of his ornate goblet and dropped his one good eye to study the intricate mosaics on the floor. The pregnant pause warned me that while I'd wangled myself into the ranks of the *agentes in rebus*, I'd still breached my lowly status in his eyes by alluding to Constans' vices.

At last he said, 'Right now Emperor Constans is hunting less than two hundred miles from here. Perhaps he'll come to stay in Augustodunum. Then he might realize how the strength of his reign rests on this General's shoulders. Long live the Emperor.'

'Long live the Emperor.' I drained my own cup and took this chance to study Gregorius' face—at least as much of his expression as could be seen through his ruined features. I read great faith in the dependability of this professional commander-in-chief. Apodemius' reports of unrest in the military might be exaggerated. Mere dissatisfaction at Constans' titular command hardly constituted a political crisis. My first report in the morning would allay these rumors of 'roiling' soldiers' troublemaking.

Within another five seconds, the Commander's expression had turned from concern to shock. For all my months of training and ambition, the next five minutes of this deadly night proved me a total failure as *agens*.

Marcellinus reappeared in the study doorway and lifted both hands to make a final speech. His guests greeted him with dutiful applause and readied their soggy smiles to bid him thanks and farewell. The musicians stopped cold and with studied determination, slung their instruments into leather carrier bags.

'Friends, I haven't gathered you here tonight to merely mark a family anniversary. By now you must have realized that there is not a single leading family of Gallia without a representative here—a cousin, a nephew or an in-law, someone who will be able to carry tonight's news to all corners of our province—maybe even farther—and rally the honor of the Western Empire behind a man who deserves our respect.'

Magnentius suddenly strode into the center of the room, draped in the only color forbidden to all but the imperial family. A purple cloak of silky velvet was anchored to his shoulders with golden braid. It swung down to pool around his heavy boots. A gold diadem studded with emeralds sat on his thick curls.

The crowd gasped in confusion and exhaustion. 'Why is he wearing purple?' a thick, deep voice shouted from the back.

'I will tell you why, Lucius. As a young man, Flavius Magnus Magnentius lived among the Gallic Laeti tribe, where he acquired a proper Latin education. Then he joined Constantine's forces in the final campaign against Licinius. He distinguished himself at both Adrianople and Chrysopolis. I fought under his command against the Alemanni on the Rhenus four years later and against the Goths on the Danube four years after that. So I was not surprised to hear that it was he who engineered support for the defenders along the banks of the Alsa River where Constantine II perished.'

'We demand to know why he's wearing purple.' The shouts grew from curious murmurs to an angry, drunken clamor.

'Because our treasury is being emptied out by a spendthrift pansy party boy who is destroying our defenses and lowering our state's morale. Romans up north are expected to march in the dust behind—no—even *serve* upon German favorites, prisoners-of-war who have lost all sense of their own honor or shame.'

'But at least he's a Constantine!' shouted one loyal loner.

'Constans had disgraced his robes. Let someone worthy take up the diadem. Here is a man who has already protected our welfare for past decades at risk to his own life and limb. He is prepared to strengthen our resources, not weaken them. He will restore our Empire to its fullest potential, not drag it deeper into the mud. Tonight the Ioviani and Herculiani legions lead where honor dictates. I humbly pledge before you to follow their example and serve their *comes*. Be proud to hail our new Emperor, Flavius Magnus Magnentius!'

An army cornet sounded in the dark night outside. All heads turned. As the horn faded, we heard a thunder of thousands of horses' hooves pound the soft earth around the villa's garden walls. A dozen tribunes from the Ioviani and

Herculiani wearing full battle dress marched into the house. Lining up in two columns under their red and blue standards, they saluted Magnentius with an orchestrated sounding of their swords upon their shields.

In the pregnant darkness of the night, the Ioviani and the Herculiani troops, some three thousand men, had surrounded the prefect's villa.

It had all been perfectly orchestrated. It was nothing less than a coup.

Magnentius stood braced on both sides now by devoted officers, all of them hailing their new sovereign. He beamed at the open mouths of the civilians gaping at his confident splendor. Marcellinus stepped aside to make way for the procession of hardened warriors led by Commander Gaiso and the General's brother, Decentius, parting the crowd for the General himself.

So these were the New Men of our world. They'd served the Constantinian throne faithfully for decades and gathered to their breasts all the power, acclaim, treasure and freedom the Empire offered. Such men had no private need to risk their necks and hard-won fortunes on a frivolous political gamble. Nothing could express better the army's final disgust at the reign of Constans than committing treason by moving to replace him.

I closed my eyes for a moment, horrified and fascinated at what we were witnessing but a voice inside me could not protest or condemn them. I'd seen that weakling myself bent over a granite rock, naked and vulgar as the rough stone that supported him, inviting the Empire's enemies to express their ridicule and contempt on his person in the most personal manner possible.

So, as so often in past centuries, the Roman Army had decided. They'd been driven by a sick, self-destructive family and corrupting court to a noble cause. They were staking everything to save the Western Empire and yet ... I saw only dismay and confusion cross Gregorius' face as he heard the familiar shoulder horns blare forth outside to answer the cornets.

What I saw was so obvious, it required no special training in observation skills. I could read it on my ex-master's expression. Marcellinus, Magnentius and Decentius had not warned Gregorius. They had not trusted *him*, a Manlius and the scion of one of Roman' oldest families, with their momentous plan. Half hypnotized, half-dazed, he moved forward to hail Magnentius.

I was already calculating the minutes and hours it would take my report to reach Apodemius. The purple ribbons symbolizing an imperial prince discarded on the dung heap of history had warned the old spymaster. My report would merely explain how and when.

Already, I feared that for the Commander, this news came too late.

CHAPTER 8, HUNTING CONSTANS

—THE VILLA MARCELLINUM, AUGUSTODUNUM—

The night was nearly spent by the time I found myself a place to sleep. I endured one hour of restless tossing on my rented pallet and then I abandoned the effort. I spent the next two hours or so hanging around the city gates. I sipped diluted wine in a tavern and breakfasted on a little curd cheese and nuts, always keeping my ears wide open to any news entering the city.

Deliverymen bringing in the season's scant pickings for the morning market grabbed a snack at tables around me. I now heard the common man's version of the party at Marcellinus' the previous evening, with all the extravagance and astonishment multiplied ten times over in the telling.

Whores returning from luxury villas in the hills beyond slept through it all on top of bushels of pitted apples and the last harvest loads of turnips.

I entrusted my sealed dispatch for Apodemius to the first rider leaving the main gate station. He was a young Romano-Briton. I hoped I could trust him but then, only a few years ago I'd been starting out myself, a North African taking messages from the hands of a more senior man. I authorized him to wear the white helmet feather reserved for urgent messages to ensure him first priority as he changed horses *en route*.

'My first white feather,' he said, fixing it into his headgear's leather strap. 'For the Senate?'

'Oh, that left last night by the *cisium* post,' I lied. 'This is a fuller report for the Castra Peregrina only.' The Senate could wait a few hours, I figured.

The feisty compact little islander checked the name penned on the parchment flap.

'The old man? Got it.' He winked as he flung himself into his waiting saddle.

The gossiping tongues in the tavern's dining room confirmed that all of Augustodunum knew Gallia now had a new 'barbarian' emperor. Within hours, minor landholders in the suburbs and towns farther out would learn it from their servants and field hands. Major landlords were already pocketing payoffs from Marcellinus with a satisfied smile. If the Ioviani and the Herculiani had been ordered to stand by, then suppliers and camp girls making the most of the winter quarters season might well have carried the rumors for miles already towards Constans' private aides on the hunting trail.

'Less than two hundreds miles away . . .' If Constans was so close, then Magnentius and his brother were racing with their supporters against time and imperial reprisal.

I got myself a horse and rode back past the amphitheater and Temple of Jupiter to join the rebel officers as commanded just before the winter sun made its lazy appearance. My horse knew the road. I returned to the Prefect's villa just as a rim of pink daylight showed over the eastern slopes where I now made out the legions moved into in their predictable rows behind a temporary palisade.

The burnt-out charcoal ends of Magnentius' festive garden stuck into the morning mist like stubby blackened thumbs. Hollow-eyed slaves plucked banquet debris from the bushes and moved Marcellinus' carved and upholstered couches and chairs back into place around the summer dining area outside the house. I stepped over a tiny girl on her knees in the atrium archway scrubbing wine strains and mud clots off the Prefect's precious floor mosaics.

The door to the study was open. I tightened up my bootlaces one by one and adjusted my ears to the voices within. Then I stood upright and at the ready I bowed my head, as if protocol, not guile preventing me from announcing myself. I saw the majordomo smile to himself as he passed me by. My *agens* insignia didn't fool him. One clever slave still recognized the eavesdropping tricks of another.

'. . . They'll all come on board.' It was Magnentius, carrying the others along with his physical enthusiasm.

But Decentius sounded worried to me. 'These are merely formalities, of course, but someone must confirm the allegiance of Claudius Silvanus. Without him, one entire flank remains open.'

'Silvanus is a special case, my brother, as you well know.' I could guess tell that Magnentius was used to dominating Decentius from childhood.

'Why? Why is Silvanus so special? Does he suffer Constans better than the rest of us?' Marcellinus' impatience broke in.

'Study your Franks as closely as you play politics among your Gauls, Marcellinus.' Magnentius sounded smug at his sponsor's expense. 'Silvanus is special because his father Bonitus was the first Frank to ever rise to the rank of *magister militum*. He fought right beside Constantine against Licinius. You think a soldier tosses that kind of credit with The Family out the window so lightly? '

'Silvanus will fall into place once Constans gone. Then we bargain for Constantius' answer with all the cards in our hands.' Gaiso sounded weary. He had obviously said this many times already during the night.

'No, Marcellinus is right,' Gregorius weighed in. 'We should wait for Silvanus. Give the go-ahead this morning to release your profile on a fresh pressing. Put your portrait in everyone's hand and your slogan on everyone's lips before Constantius countermands the order. Control the money flow and perhaps we can neutralize the little brother without a regicide on our conscience. Send Constans into exile.'

Magnentius sounded doubtful. 'I would prefer the imperial blessing before I release my new coins.'

'Is there a message in that pile for the Senate?' That was my ex-master again, peevish at Marcellinus' neglect of historical precedents, including requesting the approval of the Senators in Roma.

'Fuck those useless farts. They'll do what they're told sooner or later,' Marcellinus growled. 'With almost all the Western legions behind us and new coins in circulation, they'll have no choice but to grovel.'

It was dangerous for me to eavesdrop any longer. I removed my helmet, rapped on the doorframe, and took three smart steps into the study. The general sprawled at a marble writing table behind an impressive pile of documents. The others were spread at random on ornate couches, stools and chairs. Again I was struck by the General's heavy, expressive eyes and thrusting jaw. He ran a meaty hand through his hair, exposing for an instant a deep dent under his hairline left by someone's iron sword years before.

'The *agens*? Is it dawn already?'

He sighed and gestured for one of Marcellinus' attendants to open the heavy wall hangings. Feeble gray light gave the sleepless conspirators a spectral look. '*Agens* Numidianus? That's right.' He peered at me in the dim dawn light. 'You're sure you're Numidian? You're not Egyptian, passing yourself off as Numidian, are you?'

Gregorius' eyes widened. He'd introduced me himself to the General only few hours before.

'No, General. I'm Numidian.'

'That's right, that's right. Mother a seamstress. Good. Numidians are always good on a horse. Egyptians are so useless and sly. You never know where you are with Egyptians, right, gentlemen? Here. These documents of allegiance must go out immediately.'

'The municipal service left the gates within the last hour, General, but I'll clear these for military riders, marked urgent.'

Magnentius threw up his hands and grunted. 'Some things never change, do they? Now I'm Augustus, but I *still* can't use the *Cursus* express service without a clerk to license my riders! Here, here, take them, young Numidianus.'

Marcellinus blanched. 'General, you're overcome by the night's triumph. You haven't signed them.'

Magnentius chuckled as someone fetched pen and ink. It was the kind of moment I was trained for. I scanned each dispatch upside down through lowered eyelids and memorized another report for Apodemius. I tamped down my breath as I realized that via these letters Magnentius was calling in the Empire's military fighting power from his power base in Britannia to lesser forces stuck out in southwestern Hispania. By roping in these allies, he would secure for himself all of the territory under Constans' command. That meant nothing less than control of Roman Africa, Italia, Gallia, Hispania and Britannia.

Apodemius would have loved watching the proceedings now, if only to admire how well Prefect Marcellinus had prepared his coup.

These letters proposing an alliance across the Western Empire were written on the finest vellum. It was obvious, at last to me, that General Magnentius was not the author of these documents. Their formal salutations, proclamations and exhortations were recorded in the even, clear work of a professional scribe. The General signed his name and new titles with a bold and semi-lettered flourish. The signing took many minutes but eventually I held letters not only to military and civil authorities across Gallia, Britannia, Italia and Hispania, insisting that they needed to pressure Constantius into acceptance of Magnentius, but also to the most powerful bishops as far as Carthago.

By reaching deep into the strongholds of the new faith, this northern pagan might sway anti-Arian Christian support towards his new regime and away from the Arian Constantius in the East.

With studied indifference, I folded the expensive papers and readied the wax.

'Hah! I need a new ring!' Magnentius roared, rolling his general's signet ring in his palm. He was still digesting the enormity of what the night—and the soft-spoken financial chief—had dropped in his lap.

'I still say we're in danger until we have Silvanus,' said Decentius, that lesser physical echo of Magnentius. He had equally limpid but larger blue eyes and longer, more Germanic gold hair. There was a resigned curve of the same sensual lips, but the jaw was less prominent and the head set on a more gentlemanly neck and shoulders.

'You may be right, Decentius,' Magnentius said. 'so you ride this morning for the north. Put our case to Silvanus before Constantius' alert reaches him from the Persian front.'

There were a few protests, notably from Gaiso, until Magnentius slammed a wide, hard hand on the polished desk.

'My *brother* goes. The rest of you might threaten or bribe. But Decentius has always known that truth is the best coin.'

Marcellinus raised one eyebrow but uttered no objection. He seemed satisfied with his plotting for the moment. As he helped me pack the thick pile of letters into my satchel, I noticed he gave them a proprietary pat with a hand bearing two valuable rings, their colored gems embedded in the thick gold circles.

Magnentius wrapped up the business of their long night. 'Marcellinus, give the mints their instructions to prepare the fresh dies. But we wait, I repeat, we *wait* until Decentius signs up Silvanus. Constantius might still come around and if he does, then you'll see, my modest reticence will do me credit.'

I could see Marcellinus was balancing his role as conspirator with courtier. For the moment, the cautious courtier won out.

Magnentius turned to my ex-master. 'Gregorius, I spoke too rashly of those old women in their togas back in Roma. You're good to remind us that there are certain niceties that still matter in the mustier corners of this vast empire. There's no harm in observing the ritual of asking the Senate for their blessing.'

'I'm relieved to hear you say so, General.'

'Draft me an address to the Senate in your finest Latin. You know, the kind of thing your father would appreciate. Tell them I'll be appointing a new prefect for Roma in all peace and goodwill.' Gregorius nodded and then marched out the room without a glance in my direction. We had stood six feet and yet worlds apart from each other. He had looked strained and anxious.

Gaiso was the only man among them who seemed as fresh as a schoolboy spying on the ladies' baths but of all the officers, he'd abstained from the drinking the night before. I'd spotted him, aloof and sober, admiring the musicians from a comfortable brocade-stuffed perch.

'Gaiso?'

'Yes, General?'

'Why do you dawdle like a lady's maid?'

Gaiso gave his new emperor a wide grin of understanding and rubbed his hands.

'Hunting time?'

I'd seen that smile in the forest valley outside Treverorum. His famous bloodlust was up again.

Magnentius nodded and sank his out-sized head on the back of his chair. He closed his eyes at last. His deep baritone voice was more impressive when he whispered than when he proclaimed.

'The runt is yours.'

⚔⚔⚔

'You're riding with us, Numidianus!' Gaiso yelled to me as he dragged some junior officers and a *turma* of about thirty cavalry riders from their comfortable tents on the slopes of Augustodunum. I'd returned to the gatehouse to catch the next outgoing *Cursus* messengers. I'd registered all the dispatches and encoded a private update for Apodemius. The work had been rushed through in ten stolen minutes. The code I used could be broken by anybody who knew the low-security system but speed was more important now and it was the best I could do.

None of this race against a time-candle would matter if Constantius accepted Magnentius as Emperor of the West. But if Constantius opposed himself to the ambition of his commander-in-chief, everything hung in the balance. Our careworn Empire would shatter into a patchwork of uneasy alliances and betrayals.

Gaiso shouted at me again. 'Come on, Numidianus, we need a state escort if the arrest is to be done properly.' He laughed at his own preposterous gesture to legal procedure. 'Besides, I know you love a good hunt!'

We rode four abreast, heading north in the direction of Augustabona. We sought the hunting grounds last favored by Constans' entourage, which lay between the two towns on a straight north-south axis. However a sharp-eyed scout half an hour ahead of us galloped back with the news that farther up the road where there was much less traffic, the tracks weren't churned up at all.

It was obvious that Constans' party had headed south by a minor road instead. We raced back and turned onto the southbound highway. It took a wide curve of about eighty miles to reach Decetia. Perhaps we could surprise Constans there.

By the end of that same afternoon when, parched and dusty, we raced dusk to reach Decetia, a town councilor on the road told us that Constans had heard the news of General Magnentius' bid for the purple—they all had—within hours of the Marcellinus' announcement. Constans' court had ridden through Decetia at noon, scouring the river town for food and riding clothes.

So we'd lost the advantage of surprise. Now the hunter's canny stealth gave way to brute speed.

'He's going to try to hold us off in Avaricum until he gets backup troops,' Gaiso's scout suggested. The boy was a local with good common sense, but I could have drawn the same conclusion based on my reading of *The Gallic Wars*. The fortress town of Avaricum once held off a siege by the great Caesar for twenty-five days. They fell only to a massive assault, after which Julius massacred the region's 40,000 resistant Gauls.

We rode on and rested for only a few hours in a state *mansio* permitted to our party by the permanent licenses I carried. The next morning Avaricum stood in the distance, peaceful and prosperous-looking. After three centuries, its famous walls looked as impregnable as ever. But closer to hand, we passed empty granaries and barren fields. We encountered no welcome and no resistance. For the first time, I saw the destitution Constans' court of luxury and indolence imposed on innocent citizens.

We trotted into the city past beggars covered in lice. Our horsetails brushed aside children with swollen bellies. We found no imperial court waiting for us. But we did see that Marcellinus and his merchant contacts across central Gallia were right—the towns were running short of food and spring was still months away The welfare rolls were lengthening without relief as Constans, Constantia, and their costly entourages emptied the imperial coffers on personal luxuries and frivolous travels.

Despite their confusion and poverty, the Avaricum elders rallied at the sight of Gaiso leading us into the forum. They rang their church bells to call the townspeople away from their hearths and in from their labors to line the main thoroughfare and watch us make our way towards the state hostel. They cheered us when Gaiso handed the mayor pouches hefty with silver coins for repairs and social welfare. Not for nothing did they call Marcellinus the 'Count of Imperial Largesse.' Even our back-up horses were curried and watered while we listened to the city councilors. The old gray heads bore no love for Constans, but expressed fears that a dispute over the throne meant only disorder and more hungry mouths for them.

'What are we getting for our taxes if there's no relief, no grain and no oil from Roma to keep us going until spring?' one gnarled wise man complained.

'Under the General Magnentius, you'll receive all the assistance you need,' Gaiso promised. He swore an oath on his battered sword that Avaricum would not be shortchanged any longer.

And so we continued travelling and after witnessing a handful of such brief exchanges, I realized that Marcellinus had prepared Gaiso well. However drastically Constans had impoverished Gallia, the Prefect was confident finances could recover fast once the junior Constantine was out of the way.

Meanwhile, I was learning new roads and making new contacts at every stop, all of it useful for my *schola*. I marveled that, even as fast as we were travelling, news of the 'Usurper Barbarian' was always well ahead of us, invisibly flying forward and outward between villages, fields and relay stations via the network of human nature that even the imperial roads or Mercury's wings couldn't have equaled.

We'd been riding nonstop since dawn, snacking in our saddles and urging our horses up and down steep ravines and craggy cliffs as the terrain turned thick-wooded and rough. We rode at a steady pace but found no trace of Constans. We got no tipoffs from random travellers, either, including a group of pilgrims for Jerusalem following their noses stuck into the latest guidebook.

Nothing was fast enough for Gaiso. His energy never flagged. Our scouts were returning to us, more discouraged each time, with mere rumors, especially when we met them at a forked junction giving no hint of Constans' direction.

To the southwest lay Augustoritum and the freezing waves of the sea, and to the southeast sat Augustonetum, the volcano-ringed city between us and the teeming metropolis Lugdunum farther east.

'We'll catch him at Aginnum,' Gaiso shouted over his shoulder to all of us, which meant no rest for anyone in Augustoritum's comfortable baths. Instead we'd be charging due south into the night by torchlight.

If I ever doubted that Gaiso was a formidable hunter, that night proved it. He had a way of making the hunt the entire focus of his mind, body and spirit. He was like a man that the mythmakers conjured up in their rolling sagas full of gods, goddesses and their mortal favorites. Any prey filled his heart with courage and drive.

His enthusiasm was contagious to me, but not necessary all the others. Aginnum was almost in each but some in the squadron wanted to turn back. They grumbled that it was impossible for Constans to move that quickly and discreetly, for all the bribes between Londinium and Antiochia. The trail had gone cold. We'd underestimated the guile hidden under those blond curls and long eyelashes. How could any emperor so flamboyant have passed through this countryside unseen?

Only then, those gods that watched over the Gaisos of this world gave us a lucky break. We were riding hard when suddenly our horses were blocked at a junction on the paved road by a bold-voiced redheaded shrew of about thirty. She looked like a refugee with only her fading beauty to sell—or so we assumed. She stood, her frozen toes gripping the stones, her hands blue with cold. She clutched the rope of a heavy sack balanced behind her weather-reddened bare shoulders.

'Imperial business!' I cried, moving forward to clear her off.

'Piss off, German slut!' Gaiso was not above trampling her. His fine horse reared over the woman but she didn't flinch.

'I've got something for you, Officer, something worth a year's earnings in gold. Maybe more.'

Her Latin was guttural and ungrammatical. Her sneer needed no translation.

'We've got silver for an honest woman with information, but no time for worn out bags like you. What are you selling, besides a night of stink and toothless snoring?'

She took her pretty time untangling the sack's drawstrings and brushed off the stones so as not to dirty her already filthy patched skirt. She smiled, enjoying Gaiso's mounting temper at her delay. With knowing and self-satisfied precision, she extracted her bundle and spread it out on the road.

To his credit, Gaiso's mouth dropped open. He leaned forward in the saddle with a look of amazed satisfaction. The woman had spread out a multi-layered cloak. The underside was made of heavy white damask embroidered with trails of gold ivy. The outer layer was made of deep purple silk velvet, imported from beyond the eastern border of the Empire where such rare silks were woven somehow from the cocoons of precious worms.

'The fancy owners of this stole my client's farm clothes while we was sportin' in bed, didn't he?'

Gaiso leapt from his saddle, took the girl in his arms and kissed her with the passion he usually showed for larger, four-footed prey.

'Give her a whole pouch,' he cried. He leapt back on to his horse, clutching Constans' regal garment by one hand and pressed its stiff, high collar still riddled with strands of curly golden hair to his armored chest.

The trail was hot again, hotter than ever. Gaiso ordered that we take three hour's rest in Aginnum. Then we remounted, aiming to make it to Tolosa by dawn. I don't think our animals or we could have done more mileage without a full day of rest before tackling the wide slopes that range east to west along the foothills of the Mountains of Pyrene.

We finally hit the Via Aquitania and decided to overnight at Tolosa's main hostel. It was there, of all places, that we stumbled on some two dozen stragglers abandoned by Constans in an effort to lighten his pace.

A mixed bag of now-penniless, low-ranked imperial valets and toadies mashed in with German archer love-boys, they'd run out of pocket money and sold their clothes and finery for food and shelter. Now they were borrowing from local cardsharps to gamble their way out of a ramshackle tavern on the outskirts of the towns.

'Which way did Constans go?' Gaiso ordered his cavalrymen to stretch a couple of the court secretaries up between a stand of trees to encourage their tongues but they were too drunk and wrung out by their sudden flight to be of any use. Gaiso left them hanging to dry out.

He turned to the Germans. Using an auxiliary from the Ioviani as interpreter, he questioned them but got only jeers and rude taunts in response. Money was all they wanted. Gaiso ordered that two of them be whipped until they talked. He chose the two prettiest lads, but it turned out that not only did they not know Constans' route, they hardly knew enough Latin to understand the hunter's interrogation.

'Obviously capture didn't improve their linguistic skills,' Gaiso said, giving up after an hour.

'From what I witnessed in Treverorum,' I explained, 'they weren't encouraged to converse with anyone but his Excellency. And with him, conversation was hardly the point.'

Gaiso spat out the day's dust and wiped his grimy face clean of sweat with a chamois rag. 'Fetch me some clean drinking water,' he told an aide. While the youth scuttled off, he muttered to his lieutenants, 'I can't believe we've lost him. These dregs who masquerade as "men" are like stag spoor on a hunting trail.'

'Two days to get over that range and we'll have crossed into Hispanic Tarraconensis,' said one horseman.

Then one of our best scouts lost confidence in his own tracking. 'Do you think these pathetic leftovers are a decoy, Commander? Sent southwards to draw us away? Perhaps I've misread those hoof marks. They could belong to a cohort moving winter quarters or a party of officials with a *diplomata* to use the highway?'

His doubts went ignored when just then, one of Constans' courtiers scuttled up to us to the rear of our conference and whispered, 'For gold coins, I'll send you on your way and you won't regret it.'

Gaiso sneered at the intruder from his seat on a tree stump. 'Tell me what you know or lose your tongue, bastard.'

The man turned white, changed his mind and tried to run, but a lieutenant and scout grappled him to the ground.

'Pay me,' he shouted, but the lieutenant kicked him in the jaw. The scout gave him a sound stomp of a boot into his flabby stomach. It wasn't enough to cow the courtier. An angry glint flashed from his eyes.

'Money first.'

Gaiso pulled his short blade and held it to the man's mouth. The courtier flung his head from one side to the other, but Gaiso grabbed his jaw and would have gone to work on his tongue in the next second without hesitation, so the man blurted out, 'They're heading north by the Garona right there,' he said with a snort and a cock of his head towards the river nearby. 'In less than three days, they'll reach the port of Burgidala and head for the East and safety with big brother.'

'Impossible. All ships are dry-docked until the fifth of March, the Feast of Isis. He'd be in danger of shipwreck if he left port.'

'Even the winter winds soften for a price, Commander, for a price,' the courtier said with a sneer.

I weighed this and turned to Gaiso. 'It's just possible. Cicero sailed once in November from Actium to Brundisium. Ovid was dispatched into exile by boat to Tomi in December.'

Gaiso shook his head. 'Then we've lost him. The most important hunt of my career.' He kicked the informant in the temple with frustration. 'Still, if we set off now . . .'

I thought again. There was something 'off' about the greasy little man's confession. He'd given us the information in anger and fear but now he looked smug. 'Perhaps Constans did not take the river route . . .'

'What? What do you mean?'

'I overheard Emperor Constans boasting one night in Treverorum that an oracle predicted he would die in the safety of his mother Helena's bosom.'

'So?'

'So . . . it is possible that Constans has sought sanctuary in the exact opposite direction from the one this man indicates. Perhaps he's going to a place on the southeast coast known as Vicus Helena, named for a temple there dedicated to his *mother*. You see, the bosom of his mother?'

'But why head to a place the oracle said he would die in?'

'It's only my guess, but Constans is playing with irony, a sort of bluff, Commander. He was once a clever strategist. Consider that when Constans ambushed his brother Constantine II from the *fortified* town of Aquileia, he won. Perhaps Constans is putting his faith in a fortified town once again. The Vicus Helena is a fortification of some kind, even if fallen into decay. And at least we can be sure that Constans had heard of it.'

We were within a day's ride of the fortress on the coast. The next morning the walls of Vicus Helena stood silhouetted against the Great Middle Sea. Goats along the main road turned their bearded chins in the direction of the sounds of our hooves as we raced past them across a narrow plain between the mountains far to our right and the sea ahead.

We rushed down the final slope towards a coastline teased by fog. The peasants fell to their knees as we passed and the looks on their faces told me my guess was right. Their knowing fear filled Gaiso's nostrils with the guilty stench of his terrified quarry.

The Temple of Helena stood on a small hill. Our squadron encircled it. Gaiso ordered half a dozen of us to follow him into its cold marble foyer.

'Constans!' Gaiso shouted at the altar far ahead of us in the darkened reaches at the far end.

Years before Constans had forbidden pagan ritual. Yet the chilly stones of the somber, neglected inner chamber still stank of incense and a century of spilt blood. The stones echoed only a faint, 'Constans!'

Perhaps I'd been wrong after all. Perhaps this final day's ride was only a fateful detour allowing the deposed ruler his escape.

Gaiso would not forgive me for that.

There was a scuffling sound, like a rat crossing the hard flagstones. There in the dark reaches behind the sacrificial stone basin crouched Constans, his pampered curls matted with dust and great sweat circles staining his stolen tunic.

'Come out and fight!'

''I'll take exile,' Constans yelled back.

'I'm here to arrest you,' I started to announce but Gaiso drowned me out.

'*Fight* for your throne, you bugger!'

'There's a boat waiting for me down at the port,' Constans whined. 'Let me retire in Carthago.'

'FIGHT!' Gaiso couldn't disguise his disgust. 'Even the grossest pig puts up some resistance,' he said.

'I'm supposed to arrest him, Gaiso!'

'Well, go ahead,' he shrugged. 'I can't just slaughter a Constantine. It's against my training.' He stood undecided under the dead-eyed gaze of the statues of Zeus and Hera. He sheathed his sword and started back in the direction of the small sunny square outside.

'We'll starve him out,' I said.

'Wait!' Constans yelled. 'Drop your weapons and I'll come out.'

Gaiso signalled the men circled around us along the edges of the open space. Following his lead, we all unsheathed our blades and laid them in a pile at the door of the temple.

'Send your men back to the foot of the hill,' Constans screamed.

Gaiso signaled the men to retreat. We waited as they disappeared down the steep slope and just out of sight.

I brace myself to make the arrest as trained. But Constans panicked. Racing out of his craven position, even tripping in the borrowed trousers too big for his delicate stride, he made straight for Gaiso. Once in his youth, he'd been an admired fighter but now, he brandished only a ceremonial sword wrought in the softest gold. It was practically a toy, better meant for opening letters and gracing his banqueting wardrobe than piercing the leather cuirass of a senior veteran but Constans had won important battles in his early career. He was expert enough to make his thrust pay off if he could reach Gaiso in time.

From under his helmet, Gaiso didn't hear Constans' leather slippers skipping across the marble, but fifteen feet away, I wore only my Pannonian hat and I did.

I reached into my boot where Apodemius' small Christmas gift was safely fastened at the folded cuff. Opening out the knife in a single move, I intercepted the running Emperor just inches before he had plunged his weapon into Gaiso's back.

My short blade sunk deep at an angle and the force of his momentum finished my knife's work as it slid through Constans' spoiled belly, disemboweling him before our eyes. His intestines gushed out of him like huge white worms. His blood spurted onto the polished marble as he groaned into a sagging pile of flabby limbs and dusty hemp cloth.

A cavalryman ran back up the slope and tried to lift the dying sovereign into his arms, perhaps out of belated respect for the Constantine family. Within a minute, Constans' eyes had rolled backwards in their sockets. He breathed his last.

I extracted the small knife. I expected the blood smearing my palms to shine royal purple, but it was only a dull bluish red.

'Is that in your mandate, *Agens*,' Gaiso asked, 'to save my life, not once, but twice?

I smiled. 'You were right not to murder an emperor, Lieutenant Commander, even in self-defense. Politics can change with the month, the week, and even the hour. But an *agens* cannot be prosecuted for any crime. We answer only through our *schola* to the *Magister Officiorum*. It is the law.'

'Which makes you fellows so handy to have around,' Gaiso said, but added with a grim expression, 'and also so dangerous.'

CHAPTER 9, A GENERAL'S OATH

G regorius had counted on a future in exile for Emperor
Constans, not death. When he heard the news that
Gaiso had been the hunter, but that *Agens* Marcus Gregorianus
Numidianus had been Gaiso's catch dog, he turned his back on
me in silent dismay. Amidst the cheers and garlands heaped on
the Lieutenant Commander, Gregorius walked without a word
right past our returning party and out of Magnentius' council
chamber.

No one noticed but me.

In all the tumult of rebellion, I'd found no private
opportunity to warn Gregorius of his father's debility, Clodius'
venality or the estate's vulnerability. Now, it seemed, regicide
was too much for the Manlius House to discuss—much less
digest or celebrate. As I watched the Commander's lonely
retreat back up to the Herculiani tents lining the slopes, I feared
he could never acknowledge me as his son after this. At the very
least, estrangement between us made it all the harder for me to
protect him from the risks of this rebel action.

Yet danger seemed remote for now. Gallia held its breath,
then nothing happened, and soon daily life resumed.

As the Western Empire's new *Magister Officiorum*,
Marcellinus took charge of the imperial transition. The first
weeks of the Magnentius Era were like a bloodstained
honeymoon between the great barbarian soldier and the
dioceses surrounding his new headquarters in the palace at
Mediolanum.

I accompanied the rebel leadership from Augustodunum
attached to the official staff, but not counted as one of the
conspirators. *Agentes in rebus* were tolerated as a fact of life in

the Empire. We served courts, customs offices and road networks with an impartial face—equally useful, equally intrusive—no matter whose mail we delivered or which road we inspected. And we watched and listened. For the first time in my career with the *agentes*, I copied and coded reports to Apodemius every single night for the dawn dispatch bag to Roma.

Some days the reading was downright gruesome.

Over the first few weeks any provincial mayors or religious leaders who'd resisted Marcellinus' plan for a new era of 'peace, reform and prosperity' died in their sleep.

The smarter money, led by Marcellinus' business cronies primed from Londinium to Carthago, soon fell into place.

Pro-Magnentius mayors and councilors took their seats across the face of Gallia and the key prefectures of northern Italia. Christian bishops kneeled and powerful landowners donated. Each day, fresh delegations carrying tribute arrived at Mediolanum's outer gates and asked for an audience to hail the new sovereign.

Nightly, I coded their names and addresses for Apodemius to pin onto his map measuring Magnentius' success. As the lists lengthened, I pondered how long the financial chief had been paving Magnentius' road to the throne with bargains and bribes. I suspected that this usurpation had been in the works for at least six months, and I filed every piece of evidence to support that theory back to the Castra in Roma.

My daily duties and my evening's secret paperwork kept me busy, but I had to appear disinterested. I took precautions, but patience and modesty weren't my virtues. If I showed too much interest in positioning myself at the center of decision-making, I'd be uncovered as more than a postal director. If I pushed too hard or fast for information, I'd be transferred.

I kept my head down and made no effort to consort with Gregorius or Gaiso. I left all communications among the Ioviani and Herculiani staff to army couriers. I followed protocol to the letter.

The first time my expertise in communications brought me to the great man's attention was when I advised his improvised council, or *consistorium*, that Constantius II would probably have received news of the rebellion in no more than sixteen days from the night of the birthday party in Augustodunum.

The Emperor of the East was pinned down fighting the Persians for Nisibus, but the announcement that he had lost the West would have flown to him on the battlefield via Constantinopolis and the postal hub in Antiochia.

I registered the officers' shock at the efficiency of our *schola*. None of these senior men had served in the East. They had underestimated the advantage the Eastern state services enjoyed in both climate and wealth. Mail moved faster in the bright sun and clear skies, between Sirmium and Mesopotamia.

So they'd been warned, but they showed no panic just yet. Constantius was famous for putting the protection of the Empire before family. For fear of losing the East to the Persians' invasion during the height of a battle season, he had allowed his younger brother Constans to defeat and kill their elder brother Constantine II without lifting a finger in support of either sibling.

He might do the same again. After all, what had changed? The Persian challenge still kept Constantius pinned down. The rebels could hope this gave Magnentius time to consolidate his civil administration and put reforms in place. But who knew how long the Persian king would keep Constantius preoccupied? The Roman forces might prevail at last or the Persians might offer a negotiated peace.

And after that, Constantius was sure to turn his vengeful gaze westwards.

Each day, at the first glint of sunrise, I trotted up the marble steps of the imperial residence in Augustodunum with more letters for the General—from governors in Roman Africa, Hispania and soon, Britannia—guarantors of manpower if it came to civil war.

And to the undoubted quiet satisfaction of Apodemius back in Roma, I was not only standing behind 'the Usurper' at his new headquarters, I was discreetly reading over his formidably brawny shoulder. I noticed that whenever he was alone, Magnentius studied maps of the pivotal territory that hinged our western provinces to Constantius II's eastern territories. This territory included Pannonia and Upper and Lower Moesia on the Peninsula of Haemus, home of the Danubian legions under the weathered command of a renowned commander, Vetranio.

Vetranio was proving as coy as General Silvanus up with the Rhenus garrisons.

'No salutation yet from General Vetranio?' Magnentius barked at me one morning when we were alone.

'I certainly wouldn't expect one, Your Excellency, at least not in his own hand.'

The General rounded on me with a jovial smile in mock irritation. 'You're lucky I just downed a good breakfast, you sly African smart-ass. And why in Hades' name shouldn't the Danube legions support me?'

'They may well do so, *Imperator*. But the General Vetranio was *Magister Militum* under Constans. Now you're proposing to put Gaiso, a much younger officer, in the same position.'

'Yes, that's true. A bit of poke in the eye, I suppose.'

'Of course, there may be a simpler explanation. As a postal cadet, I rode that route and I never once carried a letter written by the good and noble Vetranio.'

'So what?'

'I only meant that the old general is well known for his simple heart, his humble birth in Moesia, his loyalty to the late Constantine, his devotion to all the great families of Roma,' I lowered my voice, 'and *his almost complete illiteracy*. They say that despite his advanced age, he still studies his alphabet by oil lamp after supper and even reads letters in the wrong order.'

Magnentius burst into a hearty laugh. 'And to think all week I've risen early just to see his letter pop out of your satchel! Well, Vetranio's legions are the linchpins to the East. Without his support, I can't march through the Gates of Trajan between Thracia and Macedonia to Constantinopolis.'

To Constantinopolis? The discovery of his ambition made me swallow hard.

'Did you ever want to, General?'

He cleared his throat. 'Of course not, course not. Nonetheless, our reform memo seems to have been lost somewhere on the road between here and Sirmium. Perhaps we'll have to deliver our message of unity in person to Vetranio sometime soon, right, *Agens*?'

Magnentius' confidence was breathtaking—and a little frightening. Power was dropping into his lap too swiftly and too easily. Was it because the gods found this upstart Franco-Breton so irresistible that they showered him with good fortune? Or was it because Marcellinus had bought the blustering general the entire West using hidden funds siphoned off from Constans' private treasury?

My money was on Marcellinus, not the Fates' favoritism for his hearty Frankish Mars. I no longer wondered how, from that dusty, underheated office back at the Castra Peregrina, Apodemius had sniffed the wind and smelled treason over the previous year.

For his part, Apodemius now kept his own head low, as he gauged the shift in political winds. To the new *Magister Officiorum* in Mediolanum, the old spymaster acknowledged the rebels' administration in a curt, correct message with neither embellishment nor obsequious groveling. He confirmed my appointment as the court postal officer, *Praepositus Cursus Publici*, without praise or comment and issued Magnentius' officials *diplomata* for the free use of the state roads.

Yes, Apodemius had seen this coming but surely not just by counting purple ribbons tied to latrines?

One day, as I supervised the sorting of official mail, the solution hit me. I smiled at the simplicity of it. Apodemius had informants at the imperial mints. Of course Marcellinus had told die makers in Treverorum, Arelate, and Lugdunum in advance to carve Magnentius' outsized profile for pressing, 'just in case.' The triumphant barbarian had insisted a whole new mint be opened in his hometown, Samarobriva, as well. Coin was one of the main tools of legitimacy in the Empire.

Nothing crossed the known world faster than its currency, unless it was news of an imperial death. Pocket change was the quickest form of proclamation known to the Empire. It was the surest way to pass your victory slogan and confident profile through everyone's palm or purse, from Hadrian's Wall down to Numidia Militaris.

Now coins brandishing Magnentius' jutting jaw, cow-eyes, large nose and thick fringe of hair were moving from soldier to streetwalker, from trader to farmer and from penitent to priest. Within weeks, we were all fingering shiny new gold *solidi* and bronze *centenionales* bearing rallying cries like 'Victory and Liberty,' and 'Happiness to Roma.'

Although, happiness down in Roma was far from a sure thing.

Constans' grieving sister, the *Augusta* Constantia, had disappeared in the direction of Roma. Some said the Lord Chamberlain Eusebius himself had escorted her into the metropolis' imperial complex but I didn't believe that.

Back in Treverorum, I had delivered mail into the hands of that vixen's maidservants. So I knew all her regular addresses. My best guess was that she had fled to the sheltering embrace of her aunt Eutropia, one of the old Constantine's younger half-sisters by his stepmother Theodora.

Eutropia resided at a country estate outside Roma on the Via Nomentana. She had married into the Nepotianii, a formidable clan of aristocrats that could stare down any impertinent eunuch or upstart barbarian soldier. They'd produced two consuls—including Eutropia's husband fourteen years ago, when I was still a little slave running around the Manlius House and catching all the Roman ladies' gossip.

In any event, Constantia's departure must have left hundreds of notaries and scribes, factotums and court hangers-on, lawyers and tribunes idle up in Treverorum where they awaited fresh orders from wherever real power had slunk off to.

For Magnentius, real power only came on the blade of a sword wielded by trusted family or army mates. He chose his imperial praetorians from among crack officers in both the Ioviani and Herculiani. Gaiso was to be the *Magister Equitum* and Gregorius the *Magister Militum*. Magnentius readied his brother Decentius to move northwards to consolidate control of Gallia and the Rhenus.

Beyond that, Magnentius kept his heavy-eyed council close to his breast.

We all knew what Marcellinus and he were *expecting*—that Constantius II would resign himself to Magnentius as co-ruler of the partitioned Empire. Perhaps only Apodemius and I knew what the Franco-Breton was secretly *hoping*—to advance farther into the East and conquer the entire civilized world.

☩☩☩

'Don't talk to me anymore about Claudius Silvanus!' Magnentius pounded a thick fist on his table. His roars could be heard bouncing off the marble pillars outside his council chamber. 'We've got all the other Frankish officers recruited from beyond the Rhenus on our side now—Malarich, Mallobaudes, Laniogaisus and yet this—' he almost sputtered.

His brother Decentius finished his sentence, 'This Silvanus sent us his "maybe" before I even reached his camp. He's still biding his time, measuring the options and testing the waters. But he's the biggest catch, worth a dozen Malarichs. Be patient.'

'Be patient? We Franks have suffered for two generations, some of our families even longer, waiting for this moment. It won't come again in our lifetime. Silvanus is a Frank, isn't he? What's that bastard's problem?'

'I didn't expect more. The man is careful,' Gaiso said.

'He's out for himself,' Decentius said.

'He's waiting for Constantius out in Persia to give a sign.' Magnentius said, calming down a bit. 'I'd do the same in his position, which is why he makes me so angry.'

Gregorius got in the final word on the reticent General Claudius Silvanus. He trained his one good eye on Decentius and Gaiso for support and then counseled, 'Once we win recognition from Constantius, we don't need Claudius Silvanus—or his legions. There's such a thing as being too careful—and paying a price for it later.'

I overheard this conversation because at the first pound of Magnentius' fist, I had entered with some tardy mail, held back for just such a moment of eavesdropping. I left it with one of the praetorians standing attendance over the Council. Then, as so often during a heated debate, I retreated in a roundabout route to lurk on a stool behind Magnentius' scribes, two little balding men inherited from the previous regime. They scratched at their wax tablets and snuffled their dripping noses into handkerchiefs all day. They were there to take down letters and record decisions. They never spoke. No one took any notice of them from hour to hour.

I got my best intelligence for Apodemius by keeping those two clerks company. Unfortunately, Apodemius wasn't the only man who appreciated my inroads.

Marcellinus himself began to watch me out of the corner of his eye. I noticed other signs of the new *Magister Officiorium*'s displeasure, too. The senior officers who felt kindly towards me just continued to call me 'the *agens*' but more than once I overheard Marcellinus use the nasty nickname '*curiosus*' within my earshot.

I could swallow insults easily enough, but then he introduced extra guard checks at each stage of the approach to the new ruler's inner chambers. He was trying to squeeze me, the neutral agent, farther from the inner circle of rebel confidants. Even the Emperor himself sensed something was happening. It was a freezing morning when he decided to speak up.

'Numidianus, why do you deliver the civil communications later and later each day? The sun's been up for ten minutes already and we're in "winter hours." I feel like I've lost half the morning.'

Magnentius was already installed behind his desk in the main imperial building overshadowed by the old Emperor Maximian's famous fifty-foot towers of twenty-four sides each. He might have become an emperor in title, but at heart he was still a soldier, shaved and uniformed for business at an hour when dilettantes like Clodius were just crawling back to bed down in Roma.

'Sorry, *Imperator*. There are certain new protocols installed. I now require special clearance at the gate of the inner courtyard, at the door of the palace and again before entering this council chamber.'

'By the gods, *why*? We all know who you are! Do you carry a concealed weapon on your person? Ha!' He gave a great belly laugh. I thought of the swivel knife inside the high cuff of my boot. I laughed right along.

I dared not point a finger at Marcellinus outright, though he was encircling and isolating Magnentius from independent voices more each week. The *Magister Officiorum* was buffering and cocooning his emperor deeper inside new layers of civil servants and cumbersome procedures with expertise. You would have thought a military man would have noticed he was falling under an invisible siege of bustling clerics, visiting bishops, economic experts and finicky administrators, but Magnentius was too enthralled with his shiny new coins and military maps to notice.

No, in answering Magnentius that morning, I could not blame Marcellinus for my tardiness. His power was growing, so I chose my words with care.

'I'm sure tightening up security is necessary, General. It's up to you, of course, to decide your style of government. But happily, Roma's long and rich history gives any new *Augustus* so many models on which to style his government.'

Magnentius lifted his bull-like head to look me square in the eyes. It was a provocative mouthful for a glorified mail boy. Intrigued, he said, 'Go on, Numidianus. Cough it up.'

I stood straighter and cleared my throat. 'They say, *Imperator*, that Trajan was the most beloved of all our emperors since Octavian Augustus himself.'

'So he was. Spit it out, boy.'

'Because Trajan was first and foremost a military man, like yourself, General. Tacitus writes that Trajan's imperial office was no more fortified than the flap of his tent. He was always receptive to the lowliest petitioner or soldier, or any civil servant who sought his favor or brought him news, without appointment or introduction or . . . obstruction.'

'I see. Well, lucky ol' Trajan, but I too know my Roman history. That was over two *centuries* ago. We live in the modern world. In a way, our vast empire is *shrinking*, son.'

'Shrinking?'

'Yes, *shrinking*, Numidianus! Marcellinus always explains it better than I can but you see, our sophisticated economic links bind our concerns tighter with those of distant regions. It's not just a question of defending fixed borders any longer. As the Empire expands, our administrative affairs become more intertwined and complicated, *Agens*. Procedure is important to keep our priorities straight.'

He spread his hands with bewildered distaste over the neat piles of reports Marcellinus had prepared overnight to occupy the Emperor's morning hours.

'With respect, General, the Roman Empire might be shrinking when it seems to be expanding, but all I know is, human nature never changes.'

'How true.' Magnentius smiled up at the ceiling frescoes, as if fascinated by pastel visions of the Three Great Matrons overseeing our destinies. 'Where did a Numidian freedman learn about Trajan?'

'The great Trajan built many of our best roads, aqueducts and towns in Africa. And as you'll recall, General, I grew up as a slave in the Manlius townhouse in the old capital. My job was to read to the Senator Manlius every morning.'

'I see. It seems you are doomed to spend your entire life a slave to letters, ha?' The hearty soldier enjoyed his little puns.

'Keep reading your history lessons, *Agens*. You come from the edges of the Empire, like myself, but look how far a humble, hard-working man can travel.'

He slapped his chest. 'We're stronger and more robust than those inbred old families. I bring Germanic valor and a Breton's wit. You bring Numidian speed, not to mention the stubborn endurance of a desert people, I'll bet. We're a shot of fresh blood into their inbred, oyster-sucking cliques.'

'Yes, General.'

'But all the same, perhaps we provincials can still learn a few things from the wise Romans of old.' His expression turned wistful. 'My late wife was always telling me that.'

'Yes, General.' I nodded and turned, nearly stumbling over my own boots into Marcellinus who had slipped into the chamber and now lurked right behind me. 'Outside, *Agens*,' he muttered.

Red-faced, I marched back double-time in the direction of my cubicle near the courtyard gates.

'*Agens* Numidianus!'

'Yes, *Magister!*' I turned and trotted back. Marcellinus waited for me at the palace entrance. He held out his palm to stop me at the foot of the steps, looking up at him like a penitent in a temple or a criminal in a public trial.

'From now on, you report to me alone before dawn with the mail sack. We'll decide together which dispatches need to trouble the Emperor. He's a busy man. We mustn't waste his time.'

'With respect, *Magister*, that's contrary to procedure. Each and every message addressed to him must reach his desk.'

'You question my judgment, *curiosus?*'

I stiffened. ''Course not, *Magister*. But our training is rigid for a reason. Mail goes to the name written on the front.'

'I'm the *Magister Officiorum* now. The heads of all the *scholae*, including that of the *agentes in rebus*, report to me.'

I bowed and nodded, playing for time. 'And in his wise reforms, the Great Diocletian ruled that each *agens* reports from post or province to his *schola* superior in Roma. Only the *schola* master himself answers to you. Our Lord Constantine upheld the system and so does Constantius in the East.'

'Cumbersome and unnecessary. It may be time for reform of that, too,' Marcellinus sneered.

I kept the mail satchel pressed tight under my arm. 'I regret if the current system frustrates intended reforms. Meanwhile I follow orders, no matter my personal inclination to do away with *unnecessary bureaucracy*.'

I raised one eyebrow and directed his gaze around the courtyard. The sun had cleared the eastern wall of the palace. Hundreds of secretaries, notaries and clerks hurried under their cloaks across the windy space. Marcellinus' mushrooming palace staff had arrived for the start of another workday.

'That's quite a mouthful for an African nobody. I'm astonished Gregorius breeds such arrogance in his slaves. The Manlius household in Roma must be quite a hotbed of democracy.'

'If you'll excuse me, *Magister*. The outgoing rider leaves any minute.'

My face burned with self-reproach. How stupid, stupid, stupid I was! Back in Numidia, my recruiter Leo had warned me—an over-educated slave heading off on a *volo's* mission—not to betray my cover story by showing off. Leo's own mentor, Apodemius, had taken me on. But he viewed my fancy education at Senator Manlius' knees as much an Achilles Heel as an asset to the *schola*. If I shot off my mouth in the wrong direction, my mission could be ruined.

And now for my cleverness, I'd done *exactly that*. I had made a firm enemy of arguably the most powerful man in the West, Marcellinus.

It was a frosty morning but I rinsed the nervous sweat off my face in an icy basin back in my private cubicle. I returned to my post and steadied myself to liaise with the next rider. Over the next hour, the *agentes'* routine pushed the *Magister Officiorum* out of my thoughts.

But Marcellinus hadn't forgotten me. Within that same day he tried to have me transferred from the Mediolanum court.

Magnentius overruled him. One week later, as I sorted the dawn dispatches, I discovered a scrap of a letter addressed to me, but bearing no visible message.

Later that same evening, when I was finally alone, I heated the scrap over my oil lantern. As I expected, the writing in acetum became visible. I read only a humorous poem: 'Which rules the World? The Coin or the Sword? The shining weapon catches the sunlight but the edge of the coin seems sharper than the blade.' There was no signature—only a cartoon of a field mouse.

And I could not yet answer the Mouse's question, despite public tensions that told their own story.

One day Magnentius mustered his Ioviani and Herculiani legion commanders, their tribunes and centurions from their winter quarters to an assembly in the outer courtyard of the palace.

'We're marching eastward, men! For Aquileia!'

A cheer went up from the troops. At least Aquileia was warmer this time of year.

A startled Marcellinus, his arms full of documents, pushed his way through the ranks of officer to protest.

'*Imperator*, we discussed this in the Council. We agreed to wait until spring. We have open-ended correspondence with the court up north and the Julians are still covered with snow. The mountain passes will be—'

'Undefended!' Magnentius lifted both arms. The officers took his cue and cheered.

'We've just got things started here,' Marcellinus said, running after Magnentius. The hefty barbarian was already marching back through an arch into the inner courtyard of his headquarters.

Magnentius rounded on his sponsor. 'Marcellinus, we're leaving Mediolanum.'

'No!'

'This town is too riddled with your secretaries and accountants, not to mention those argumentative bishops—especially those blasted Arians. I know they support

Constantius behind my back. Don't argue with me—I can *smell* their treachery.'

'I've tried to keep your schedule under control. I'll cut back your appointments and—'

'And isn't this where old Constantine married his daughter to Licinius and feasted with these townspeople for weeks on end? I don't like this city. I don't like sitting, stewing in imperial halls like this, waiting for Constantius to make the first move.'

'Wait—'

'We're leaving, Marcellinus and that's an order!'

So, that very afternoon, the Western Empire's two crack legions took to the paved state highway, heading southeast to tackle the snowbound passes for the smaller but better fortified town of Aquileia on the shores of the Upper Sea.

'He's thinking like a soldier again,' Gregorius confided to me as he rode past my horse.

We hadn't spoken for weeks, not even to exchange polite greetings. We hadn't discussed the Emperor Constans' gory end and I now realized, we never would if Gregorius had his way. It was a blot on the family's history to which he turned his blind eye.

'Indeed, Commander. This is a wise move. I know these routes like I know all the corridors and corners back home. From Aquileia, General Magnentius will control the Via Postunia, the Via Popilia, and all the routes into Italia from Illyricum and even farther to the east. With luck, he'll secure Emona as well.'

'*We'll* secure everything,' Gregorius said. He fixed his eye ahead of us, on the peaks towering ahead, white, cold and unpredictable. The Roman aristocrat in his nature was trying to reassure himself that his provincial half, through his noble Gallo-Roman mother, hadn't cast his dice too soon.

'You're committed to this man beyond doubt, Commander?'

'It's for the honor of the Empire, Marcus. I'm not alone. It's been many generations since these legions were manned by Pannonians. You realize half those men signed up on the promise they would never serve east of the Alps? And yet, listen to them sing as they march toward those mountains,' Gregorius said. Extending easily half a mile behind our mounts, our column had taken up a boisterous chant, marking by the tramping of nailed boots.

Feed the poor and tax the rich,
No more rulers' sister-bitch,
No more eunuchs, fat and sly,
No more archers, riding high!

We were slowed a bit by the melting snows, but in six days, the Ioviani and Herculiani legions, almost three thousand strong, descended towards our destination. There, stood the old walls of Aquileia, formidable and proud. We stretched our bleary eyes as far as the naval station and its dry-docked ships overlooking the white capped wintry waters.

It had been a good decision. Magnentius had advanced his position to one of the busiest junctions of the imperial road system. More importantly, he was now facing eastward— towards the crucial provinces that bound West to East. He was facing Constantius.

'He's a military genius,' Gregorius told me one evening shortly after. He had offered to help me with the set up, organizing the cubicles and dispatch flows for our service. I didn't overlook the importance of his kind gesture. We were sitting near the very city gate where the Commander had led the ambush to kill Constantine II for the dissolute defender Constans. It had been his last big battle as a whole man before the debacle on the Rhenus cost him an eye and half a hand.

Perhaps he needed the comfort of a child of Roma that night, even an ex-slave boy with olive skin and a Numidian accent. He was brooding over home and his tenuous ties back to the old capital.

The 'old women' in the Roman Senate were making trouble for Magnentius, despite Gregorius' constant overtures and lobbying contacts back in the city. The Senators were showing some mettle, for once, and withholding their support.

Happily for the Commander, Magnentius' priority wasn't the impotent old coots of Roma, but the security, freedom and economic recovery of vast new dominions that Constans had robbed and neglected. After many weeks of assassinating more regional politicians who were idiotic enough to voice loyalty to Constantius, Magnentius got serious about his governance of the 'reformed' West.

For one thing, he hadn't shown any interest in religion back in Mediolanum, but he made up for it now. Following the laws initiated by old Constantine in the East, Constans had prohibited pagan sacrifices and seized temple treasures late in his reign. In a two-handed signal of his own liberality, Magnentius now overturned the prohibition restricting the pagans, but at the same time, he printed the Christian *Chi Rho* on his coins.

As for his own beliefs, Magnentius played a canny game. Some said the General was baptized into the new religion, but I never saw him worship their Christ or read a catechist's lesson. One hundred per cent barbarian blood, he aspired to restore pagan strength, not Christian humility, to the Eagle Standard. He assumed he could do it through money and brute force, not prayer.

So Magnentius played the religious game but he neglected Roma. He was unable to imagine that he risked his stolen throne because of technicalities like a thumbs-down from an irrelevant group of old senators.

Gregorius was there to remind him. 'We aren't home and dry by a long shot,' he advised the General after supper one evening in March, 'Not until we've got you approved and a pair of consuls properly elected in Roma.'

Marcellinus had retired to his apartments for the evening, complaining of overwork. It was a rare moment when the two rebel brothers, Magnentius and Decentius, were left alone with their military officers. Magnentius had commissioned me to annotate a set of road maps—all facing eastwards—using whatever I remembered from my hard-riding days on that postal loop to Sirmium.

Tonight they were poring over my work. I lingered on, ostensibly to answer any questions. The senior men had forgotten me within a few minutes.

'There's another essential matter still pending, General.' You could rely on Gaiso to pinpoint the target and spear it through. He wasn't talking about ballot boxes.

'That Frankish bastard Claudius Silvanus will come around in the end,' Magnentius cut him off. 'He has to now. But Gregorius has drummed into me that I've got to deal with Roma without further delay. I'm re-appointing the impeccably pedigreed Gaius Maesius Fabius Titianus to resume his previous position as *Praefectus Urbi Romae*.'

'A very shrewd move, Emperor Magnentius. I approve. As you say, gentleman, I am a bastard, but I am an essential bastard.'

We all turned at the amused baritone that addressed us from the doorway.

Standing there, in full uniform under a mud-soaked cloak, rain-spattered helmet in the crook of his arm, was the delinquent general, Claudius Silvanus.

Like all these Franks, he was tall and broad-shouldered. A thick head of dark brown hair waved over his high forehead. He had green eyes that crinkled with humor. He'd made a dramatic entrance, like the protagonist in a Greek play where the lesser characters have warmed up the audience for his arrival—and he knew it.

Magnentius rose to his feet and lips pressed together, waited. Was Silvanus here only to deliver the feared ultimatum from Constantius? Was the Empire already at war with itself?

Silvanus strode into the center of the room and shivered. 'This is a cold palace for such a heated group of warriors.'

'What do you bring us, Claudius Silvanus?'

Silvanus chuckled and took in the anxious faces around the table. You could have heard a *fibula* drop in the apprehensive silent that swept through the rebels' breasts.

'My oath of loyalty, Magnentius.' Silvanus dropped to one knee and laid his sword at the General's boots.

They broke out into cheers. One by one, the officers rose, whether Franks or half-Franks, Gallo-Romans or purebred Roman, to embrace the latecomer. He needed a shave and a bath. I had no doubt he was growling with appetite as well. I summoned a page to take his cloak, prepare a room, and bring him a hot supper.

Silvanus accepted a goblet of wine. He leaned across the tablecloth. 'Good gods above, is that you, my dear old *contubernalis*, Atticus? I hope somebody covered this man's mirror.' He raised his drink in salute to Gregorius and added, 'I heard about it, old friend. You did well. To your health and good spirits.'

'We're all cheered by the sight of you, Claudius,' Decentius said.

'And no wonder. I look around this table and I see a dozen battered, over-ambitious and lonely old veterans.'

Magnentius chuckled. 'Lonely? I haven't heard any of the local brothels complaining for lack of business.' A couple of junior officers at the end of the table laughed along.

'As I expected,' Silvanus said, setting his drained goblet down. 'Our new Emperor strikes the nail smack on its head. *Brothels*. This is the report that I have heard, all the way up there, in every garrison facing the Rhenus. You're still little more than an army camp, Your Excellency. You are not yet a *court.*'

'Tell that to all those paper-pushers Marcellinus hired up in Mediolanum,' Magnentius grunted. 'Besides, I prefer camps to courts, don't you? It's all I can do to stop Marcellinus from changing my sheets to purple and making me wear a toga so little clerks can kiss my hem.'

'That's not what I meant. I've just sworn my allegiance to you, but—'

'It's all we needed. The addition of your cavalry forces makes the Western Army complete,' Magnentius answered. 'Let's have another pitcher of wine to celebrate tonight. Our purse is full of funds and we're ready to rally thousands more troops to our standard on a week's notice. We can only pray that our over-manicured Prefect Titianus will worm his way back into the hearts of his fellow Roman snobs and senators, but—what is it, Gaiso?'

'General Silvanus brings a fresh eye,' Gaiso answered, with a glance at the others around the table. 'You heard what he just said. We are not yet an imperial court. He sees that our rebellion is still missing the jeweled buckle that would fasten our legitimacy the West.'

Magnentius poured himself another goblet and gulped it down. 'Oh, gods, you're always too sly for me, Gaiso. I'm not one of those elks you have to sneak up on. Spit it out. What do you mean by jeweled buckle?'

Silvanus took in the room of determined, tired faces searching each other's expressions through the shadows.

'Gaiso understands me. Isn't it obvious? The Senate in Roma may be powerless, but they have long memories, right, Atticus? You're still a barbarian at heart, Magnentius—wait, wait—coming from me, that's in your favor. But one hundred years ago, the Praetorian Guard foisted a barbarian peasant soldier, the ignorant giant Maximinus, on the Empire. It was a disaster. You won't get confirmation from the Roman Senate unless you give them some way of saving face . . .'

Magnentius leaned forward and glared at Silvanus. 'I don't appreciate such a comparison with Maximinus from the last guest to our party. Are you suggesting I step aside for some puppet?'

'Nothing so drastic, General. I was just . . . thinking out loud, rhetorically, as an honest Roman might?' He shot a quick glance at Gregorius and with studied indifference, sunk his spoon into a plate of tender baby lamb roasted in honey and wine that had just landed on the table in front of him.

Gregorius lifted his tragic face. 'Then let me say it.'

The red glow of the coals winking through the heavy brazier caught the shiny white plane of flesh sewn down tight under his eye socket. I looked up from my maps, no longer pretending to stick to my business. I knew he was about to speak up for Roma, out of the memory of his family, tradition and no doubt, for sanity. For the sake of our frayed blood bond and my unclaimed son, I prayed whatever Gregorius said now would prevail.

He stood up and tucked his wounded hand into his cuirass. 'I've lain on Roman supper couches all my life, listening to after-dinner jokes and stories of the old capital. Marcus Numidianus, the *agens* over there, was a tiny boy romping around our dining room at the time. I'm sure he'll agree with me that at heart the Roman senators are a bunch of old ninnies.'

'Excepting your father, Commander,' I said.

They all chuckled in their cups. Greg nodded, 'A loyal joke, but *apart* from Senator Manlius, they are impotent aunties reduced to regulating district sewer permits and festival days. And like all little old ladies, their crabby hearts soften at sentimental stories. *Dynastic* stories.'

Gregorius leaned on Magnentius' table with his maimed palm.

'Touch the Senate's nostalgic soul, General. Solve all your problems on the pillow, not the battlefield. Spare the Empire disorder and bloodshed Send a delegation to the *Augusta* Constantia carrying a proposal of marriage. You have an unwed daughter to exchange, do you not?'

Magnentius' eyes had widened as he took in what his Silvanus and Gregorius were advising.

'Yes, Magnentius. Every court requires an *Imperatrix*.' Gregorius said. 'Marry the Constantine shrew.'

CHAPTER 10, CONSTANTIA'S MAN

—THE ROAD TO SIRMIUM—

Magnentius was a healthy widower of forty-seven. Many mornings I caught a glimpse of one comely face or another, some shadowed by a discreet *stola*, some brazenly unveiled, slipping out of the Palace at dawn. These lovely women crossed my path from the direction of the general's private quarters towards the luxury baths across the Forum, next to the Law Court.

No one commented. We all understood that the new Christian values of abstinence or chastity didn't top our imperial pagan's list of reforms. I was curious to see how the idea of a state marriage sat with him.

'Well, if I have to marry, I don't want Constantia. Let it be the little Helena,' Magnentius said the morning after Silvanus' arrival. He shoved his honey and pancakes aside with a stoic expression for his morning council. 'I think I saw her ten years ago in procession. She was just starting to push out the bodice of her tunic.'

Ever the soldier, he made suggestive circles in the air over his cuirass. 'Where's the imperial chickling now?'

'In Constantinopolis, General,' Gregorius said. 'Of course, she's hardly a child any longer. She's twenty-five but, by reliable accounts, still virgin.'

'On the shelf for a decade? What's the matter with her?'

'Nothing, General, so far as we know.'

'So why didn't you put her name forward instead of that Constantia's?'

'Helena is a devotee of the Nicene Creed, General. She's a fervent Christian and a favorite of the Empress Eusebia. The

Empress dotes on her sister-in-law and she is unlikely to part with her company during the Emperor's long absence from court.'

Magnentius gave Gregorius a steely look. 'That's a roundabout way of saying I'm not good enough for the saintly Helena. So I'm stuck with the older one.'

'Only a few years older, *Imperator*, and already a widow, thanks to the cruelty of her own brother. She's in Roma, not so far away as Constantinopolis. She's more likely than Helena to view marriage to you as a welcome escape from her brother's watchful eye.'

'If I might mention it, Commander, the *Augusta* is known to me personally.' Before I could stop the very showing off that Apodemius always warned me about, I couldn't help but offer Magnentius fair warning.

The *consistorium* turned as one to where I stood at attention with two praetorians near the door. I was waiting for the clerks to copy the outgoing imperial dispatches from their wax notes onto paper.

'Has she improved with age, *Agens*?'

'She is still lovely, General, but . . . perhaps in a more exotic vein than the virginal Lady Helena.'

'Well, that doesn't rule her out. Perhaps Hannibalianus taught her some bed tricks from the East, did he?' The General rubbed his hands with relish.

'Indeed, General. Summoned to her private suite in Treverorum to pick up some letter, I did observe that the *Augusta* decorates her chambers with whips, ropes and even jewel-encrusted gold bracelets that lock like shackles.'

The faces arrayed around the long conference table drained bedsheet white.

Magnentius broke the painful silence. 'Well, the Constantines are a family of extremes, aren't they?'

He braced his meaty shoulders with resolve and removed a rugged gold ring from one of his fingers. 'Someone take this to Roma and make the proposal. That's enough of marriage matters. Any news from the Rhenus . . .?'

But Constantia was no longer in Roma, the well-scrubbed Urban Prefect Titianus messaged back. I'd already sent my own coded update to Apodemius and by return mail I got more coded information back, 'An imperial letter for Constantius left Via Nomentana for a fortress near Nisibus end January. Bridal coach departed along eastern road on February 3.'

I should have given this information to Marcellinus, but instead passed it to Gregorius to use as he thought best. Silvanus might keep pushing for this deadly marriage, but I hoped that, in light of Constantia's departure for the East, Gregorius might improve on his original advice with a better negotiating ploy.

⚖⚖⚖

Despite my warning, the Constantia plan prevailed. Gregorius was to supervise the proposal that Gaiso would make. But first we had to find the woman. Gaiso happily shook the snow off his boots and rounded up a dozen cavalrymen. He carried Magnentius' chunky Germanic gold-and-garnet ring for the intended. I was seconded again as escort. If we were lucky, we'd catch Constantia on the road somewhere.

We rode sixty-five miles with few horse swaps, slowed only by the passage of a lengthy slave-train trudging to the markets in Mediolanum. We arrived at the state *mansio* in Emona, an old legionary camp turned boomtown, on the same night to eat and rest.

Gaiso and the others were soon washed and back downstairs feeding their faces at rows of communal tables. I could hear them trading jokes with a party of tax collectors heading north.

I found Gregorius still upstairs in the senior officers' quarters. Across the bedroom, I watched him struggle with his uniform alone, using his good hand to detach his sword belt and work his way out of his tunic.

Now that I was no longer his slave, he had proudly rejected my offer of help. So without asking, I ignored his protest,

141

fetched a basin of fresh hot water and scraped his back clean with a *strigil* for him in equally stubborn silence. He suffered my attention, gave me a curt nod when I finished, and wrestled back into his tunic.

He watched as I took my turn to scrape my hands and neck clean of the day's grime. 'You still wear the Senator's *bulla*?'

My hand shot up and enclosed the crude little lump of bronze-covered clay dangling from its cord. Was Gregorius still resentful enough of my freedom to demand it back?

'He told me to keep it always, Commander. It's brought me the good luck he promised, though I've been mocked for wearing a boy's token.' I waited for him to add his ridicule.

'The Senator was right. *Never lose it . . .*' He replaced his *pugio* in its belt scabbard. 'You saw my father at home? Was he well?'

'I've seen him in far better health, though the Lady Kahina is taking good care of him, I'm sure.'

'Clodius writes me that the Senator is "not himself." He asks me to transfer over legal control of the Manlius estates to his management.'

'I see.'

I made no further comment. It was no longer my place to interest myself, much less meddle, in the family's affairs, though no one cared more than I did about its future.

He hesitated. I could hear a note of appeal temper his proud diction.

'Do you think that's a wise idea, Marcus? Being on campaign all these years, I hardly know my nephew. And whenever I am at home, he's always 'out' and busy with friends. I don't pretend to keep up with the city's high society doings when I'm there, nor do I understand the ways of civilians now any more than when Laetty forced me to use fingerbowls.'

'I broke one of those fingerbowls by accident.'

'But you grew up with him. You must know him.'

I thought of the bruises I'd suffered from Clodius' vicious little boots but I wanted to seem as impartial as possible. 'I believe your son's interests and those of your nephew differ by a very long shot, Commander.'

'Well, yes, that's my worry. Leo has displaced Clodius as my heir. Am I wrong to put Leo's interests first? Am I being unfair to Clodius? Could I trust him until Leo came of age?'

'You are not wrong to hesitate, Commander. That's my opinion. I'd give my life to protect your blood from theft, fraud or someone's bad luck at the races.'

It was the most honest answer I dared put into words.

'Thank you, Marcus.'

'You had a right to ask me,' I swallowed hard.

'You owe the Manlius House less than you know, Marcus. Such unexpected loyalty—from a freedman . . .' His voice took a bitter twist.

'All the more valuable for being willingly offered, Commander.' If my Numidian blood churned at my natural father's continuing rejection, my Manlius honor stood watch.

He detected the anger underneath my pride.

'We've stopped over here before, Marcus. Do you remember?' He gazed out the window at the stable hands currying and watering our dozens of mounts and spares by torchlight. He was recalling a ride taken when he was still a whole man, leading his ambushers towards Aquileia to lure Constantine to his death. He'd followed orders on behalf of the young Emperor Constans who hung back in the safety of Naissus. Magnentius had been the only source of concrete support. How much did his love of Magnentius feed off a secret hatred for Constans using him as a 'catch dog'?

'I remember the peasant girls stared up at you, Commander, wherever we trotted past.'

'I was handsome in the old days, wasn't I?'

'Sure enough, Commander, the best-looking officer in the entire legion.'

'Marcus, if something happens to me, I mean, something worse than this,' he touched his empty eye socket, 'I would value your promise to look after Leo and his mother.'

'It would be only natural, Commander.'

'Indeed?'

He went down to the dining room, leaving me alone with his anxious, ravaged face imprinted on my eyes.

The next lap, taking us to Siscia, was twice the distance and the best we could hope for at the end of that ride was a sub-standard *mansio*. With any luck Gaiso would let us rest. There might be clean beds for our saddle-calloused bums, even if the chambermaids were worn-out 'ladies' on their second careers.

Riding at the head of the line with Gaiso and Gregorius, I hailed an outgoing *agens* as soon as we dismounted at the stopover. He was heading back towards Aquileia. We asked him if he'd seen Constantia on the road ahead of us.

'I passed her about a few hours ago in a gold-framed livery dragging four carriages and a dozen pageboys in her wake. They might be hoping to take the river route to the Danube and the East by sea,' he said.

'The Imperial party? You're looking for the Imperial party? She stayed here last night,' the stationmaster said with obvious pride in his services.

The commander handed his mount over to a stable boy. He looked tired as he flexed his good hand, sore from hours of clutching the reins. He protected his reduced sight against the winter drizzle and dust of the road with a fine woolen bandana. But he never complained.

'She must be desperate to contemplate a winter crossing, even a coastal one,' Gaiso said.

'She must be truly afraid of Magnentius' tightening control over Roma If she's fleeing to her imperial brother,' I added.

'Then we've lost her.' I could see Gaiso felt torn. His own horse tugged his head back towards Aquileia, as if anticipating a twitch on the reins signaling a return to the West. But Gaiso's gaze stayed eastward. I could see how badly he took the possibility that, at this very moment, Constantia was tossing in flatboats down a turbulent water network and beyond his grasp.

The stationmaster came back snacks. We drank deep and gobbled down the food. Whichever way we were headed now, Gaisco didn't like delays.

'It's too early in the year for a sea journey,' I said. 'And I know this woman a little. The Lord Chamberlain told me that Constantia fears Constantius more than she loves him. How can she trust her own husband's murderer?'

'I hope you're right, Numidianus.' Gaiso turned to my ex-master. 'So, where could she go, Gregorius?'

He took a deep breath, bit into a blackened meatball, and thought hard as he chewed.

Finally he swallowed and said, 'There is only one man kind and powerful enough in his own right to shelter Constantia between here and Constantinopolis.'

'Who's that?'

'General Vetranio.'

'Of course! Old Vetranio! She's gone to Vetranio!' Gaiso roared. He threw down his food and roared to the other riders with relief. 'She's hiding with Vetranio!'

'I'm not *sure* they were boys,' the stationmaster interrupted us. 'They all wore masks in gilt and colored paint and never left each other's side, eating and sleeping in a cluster away from the other travellers. They might have been maids in disguise.'

'What about a fat man, *Manceps*? Was he beardless? Perfumed?' Gaiso's nostrils were flaring again as if Constantia were a deer bounding just out of his reach.

'Oh, yes, *Magister*. The eunuch gave orders for us to water and brush down the horses, but said the *Augusta* and he would eat their meals on couches inside her carriage. We supplied fresh water for her wine, of course, but the Chamberlain said our food was too poor to feed her lapdog.'

'Quite right, too,' jeered a cavalrymen as he wolfed down the last of the cold meatballs.

Despite Gaiso's excitement, the next day's ride was more tedious. As we moved eastward, heavy traffic had helped to melt off the frost covering the Empire's most vital artery but the road was crossed by a junction or blocked by official traffic every few miles. Only two lanes of fitted stones carried the flow of all the world's bloodlines moving their riches and news east or west, north or south, to the four capitals of the Empire and its hundreds of busy markets beyond.

I rode a few miles ahead of our group, checking *diplomata* for forgeries and clearing any traffic off the *Cursus Publicus* if I could find the excuse. Despite my diligence, we saw no more sign of a gold-wrought carriage or masked entourage.

By dusk we neared a river hub. Through the clopping of our hooves, we heard the rushing torrents of the Odra tributary and the heavy currents of the colder Colapsis colliding into the broad Sava spreading out ahead of us. Clumps of ice bounced past us on white-capped rapids swelled with mountain runoff.

'We ride through the night,' Gaiso ordered. 'I'm getting tired of traffic jams.' And so we kept on, under heavy woolen cloaks pinned fast at three places. I felt we were rushing to catch the sun itself, and forgetting politics and private woes, I rejoiced in the rhythm of man and horse thundering freely as if one body.

At dawn we crested a hill and stopped to catch our breath. There, nestled next to the river under a heavy granite sky, stood the walls of the seven-hundred-year-old Sirmium, one of Diocletian's great capitals.

From this sleight elevation, I made out the elongated horseracing arena, the bishop's imposing palace, and the imperial buildings. I'd been here many times already, as a soldier and then *agens* turning around here at the border city that marked off the Eastern Empire.

I loved Sirmium's western vigor and laughter mixed with eastern comfort and warmth. It was the birthplace of nine emperors, including Constantius himself—and who knows how many more to come?

Some of the Gauls riding behind me hadn't ever seen until this bright morning what one writer nicknamed the 'glorious mother of cities.' But Sirmium the city was not our destination.

'Look, over there!' Gaiso pointed beyond the city walls, where stretching for half a mile, a grid of army tents stood, taut and filed as neat as a child's game.

'The army of Illyricum, including the Danubian legions, the IV Flavia Felix and the VII Claudia,' Gaiso said.

Gregorius scanned the horizon. 'With only one eye, I can see a camp of well over ten thousand men, perhaps even twenty? Vetranio must have called them all together for a winter conference.'

'Or to council Constantia?' Gaiso raised one eyebrow.

Both officers were right, of course. Embroidered bulls flapped on the pennants of half the encampment. On the other side of a broad boulevard wide enough for twenty horses, standards carved with the Capricorn and Pegasus swayed.

And through the very center of this temporary city of fighters, between thousands of men moving about their first chores of the day, we trotted towards a tall, wide carriage shining with oxblood varnish and fitted on all its corners and windows in gold.

The *Augusta* Constantia was here.

'We have Magnentius' letter ready?' Gaiso asked Gregorius.

'I have it here, Lieutenant Commander.' I patted my dispatch satchel.

'And I have the ring. Good. Let's go.'

On foot, our delegation approached the General's headquarters, a complex of half a dozen tents at the very center of the camp for himself and the legions' top officers.

But before we could hear ourselves announced, the grizzled old Vetranio himself emerged from under the furry leather flap shielding his tent from the cold. He threw himself at Gregorius, pulling the Commander to his barrel chest.

'A Manlius hero! Your father must be proud of his clan!' His eyes squeezed shut as he held Gregorius to his breast, but over the edge of the commander's shoulder, I saw that the shock of seeing my ex-master's vicious wounds sent a few tears of pity down the General's cheeks.

'Come in. Get warm,' he said, releasing Gregorius at last. 'So glad to see you. Send your riders along with Gaius here. They'll be well looked after. Now, I really want to hear the news of your rebel hero, Magnentius. Share my delicious breakfast.'

'Happily, we can combine two pleasures in one, Vetranio.' Gaiso said, stepping in between Gregorius and the robust older man. 'We need to see the *Augusta,* General,'

'Oh, you'll see her all right. She hasn't been here long. But let's use an *augusta* as our excuse to indulge our bellies first, right?'

We entered Vetranio's meeting tent and saw a long table set for breakfast surrounded by camp chairs. Vetranio's command staff rose to their feet as we exchanged greetings. The only person who stayed seated drew all eyes to the far end.

There she was, sunk deep in her own wide-armed gilt *cathedra.* Her journey had not been comfortable. She looked like an unmade bed of maroon velvets, bronze wools and teal silks. As before, both forearms glistened with female armor—stacks of embossed cuffs and bracelets of heavy gold studded with gems.

There was no man standing there among us that morning who could refuse his admiration for her resilience and speed on the road. If she was tired, some trick of cosmetics or medicine disguised it a little. If she was bruised by days of painful jouncing over hundreds of miles, her soft garments revealed nothing but a moist neck and shoulders.

There was no sign of the Lord Chamberlain Eusebius. Artful inquiries outside General Vetranio's tent told me that the eunuch had left the camp that morning on the main road for Naissus to the southeast.

I suspected another falling out between the two grasping personalities, if there had ever been a falling in, for that matter. Eusebius could no more linger in Magnentius' West than she could. They were foul weather friends at best. He was speeding ahead to Constantius' protection.

Instead of masked eunuchs, two young waiting women stood sentry behind Constantia. They were unused to hours of exposure to the unrelieved cold. Their teeth chattered and they clutched their fashionably thin cloaks close around their shoulders. Their faces betrayed the exhaustion and fear that their mistress refused to let show.

For a moment, seeing her huddled under Vetranio's protection, I forgot Constantia's unattractive tastes in private recreation. I felt sorry for the friendless woman widowed so violently by her closest kin and now surrounded by hardened soldiers. But for all my sympathy, I was relieved she didn't recognize me standing back a little behind Magnentius' high-ranked representatives.

Then she smiled at Gaiso and Gregorius. Those teeth were the same—as pointed as ever and even more unnaturally white.

Gaiso offered Vetranio a letter. He and Gregorius had cooked it up the night before, to pretend that they'd known all along where to run Constantia to ground.

Vetranio looked at the folded packet with hesitation. He dreaded the possibility of these envoys expecting him to read something out loud and reveal his illiteracy. But he was an old underdog, a survivor in a field of warriors. He knew all the tricks. The old soldier waved it back and said, 'Please. Do us all the honor.'

For a moment, Gaiso looked taken aback. Then he began to read out: 'A message from the Emperor of the West, General Flavius Magnus Magnentius. *Ave.* We greet General Vetranio and extend our warmest personal greetings with a gift for the *Augusta*—'

Vetranio nodded in appreciation and stretched his arm towards the unhappy woman glowering at us from under thick black lashes at the end of the tent.

'Our imperial guest takes precedence above any further salutations between soldiers, no matter how welcome,' Vetranio said with a chuckle. Gaiso bowed and handed the expensive vellum to one of Vetranio's military secretaries.

Gaiso strode down the line of officers and fell to one knee at Constantia's feet. He bowed his head again and removed his leather gloves. From a lambskin pouch wedged under his cuirass, he pulled out the vulgar ring, laid it on his right palm and held it out to her.

'Flavius Magnus Magnentius sends you his warmest salutation, *Augusta.*'

'I salute the bloody usurper and murderer right back,' she said, tossing her thick dark coils of hair with undisguised contempt.

'He also sends his respect and admiration. With this jewel, his most cherished possession, long in his family, he bids me to propose marriage to you. He offers to lay the Western Empire, from the wild lakes and moors of upper Britannia to the lush olive orchards of the Aurès Mountains, at your feet. He humbly begs you to accept his material protection as well as manly love and devotion. He implores you, the most beauteous fruit to ever ripen on the Great Family Tree of Constantine Chlorus, to become his wife and empress.'

I appreciated that the 'beauteous fruit' bit was Gaiso's own improvising but all his mountains and moors weren't going to help at all. Constantia curled her lip, repeating with astonishment under her breath, 'Long in *his* family?'

Gaiso tried a new tack. 'In return, Magnentius offers his own his own child, a precious daughter, the treasure of his heart, as a bride for Constantius, His Imperial Excellency of the East.'

'You are ridiculous,' Constantia spat out at Gaiso. 'My brother is already married to Flavia Aurelia Eusebia, the daughter of a former consul of Roma from a pure Greek family in Thessaloniki. You think he'd divorce Eusebia for the mongrel daughter of our brother's barbarian assassin?'

With a sudden kick of her pointed travelling boot, she sent the Lieutenant Commander Gaiso toppling right onto the pounded earth. Gaiso was left scrambling to recover Magnentius' ring in the pounded dirt underfoot. I was grateful Gaiso suffered this indignity and not Gregorius.

'You're *all* ridiculous!' The howl came from the mouth of a Fury rising up from her chair. 'You think a granddaughter of the Great Constantine who subdued the Franks in battle, now needs to *marry* one? I bring a present of my own—for Vetranio, the Empire's loyal servant and and I offer nothing to that superstitious tyrant, Magnentius.'

She turned to one of her girls, who lifted a large travelling sack off the ground and then, with a portentous clunk, dropped it back down.

'There are no more words needed between the good Vetranio and myself today,' Constantia said. 'I have to eat and rest. Tomorrow morning, I'll reward Vetranio for his loyalty to our family before his assembled legions.'

Fumbling with his sword pommel, Vetranio cleared his throat and stroked his stubbly jowls. His sidelong glance reminded me of a guilty man who's been caught plucking olives off his neighbor's trees, as he cried, 'Eat up, gentlemen, eat!'

The preserved figs, fish paste flavored with capers, fresh bread and chunks of roasted lamb with anchovy gravy was as good as promised, but I noticed that Constantia ate only food separately prepared and tasted by her women. Her studied chewing while we feasted didn't make for a jolly breakfast. I was relieved at last to leave the table.

I accompanied Gregorius and Gaiso into a tent lent to them for the stay and helped the Commander out of his riding gear. A small iron brazier heated the shelter but it was a mixed blessing. Its goatskin walls reeked of the eight busy men who usually occupied the space, giving off the familiar perfume of leather and sweat, washing oils, wet tunics and riding tackle.

'What's in her sack?' was Gaiso's first question to Gregorius.

'It was too solid for coins.'

Gaiso shrugged. 'We're the ones who brought bribes, just in case.'

Gregorius' twisted mouth attempted an ironic sneer. 'Just in case is *now*. She may be on the run, but she doesn't seem short of money and nor, it seems, does Vetranio if he enjoys her support. The troops love that old man and they'll march whichever way he pushes them—East or West.'

Gregorius had forgotten I was there. I finished storing his gear and commented, 'As you always said, Commander, an officer is loved by his men only because he loves and looks after *them*. Do these troops think Magnentius loves them?'

They looked at me. I picked up my dispatch satchel and left. Then I eavesdropped outside the back of the tent.

I heard Gaiso ask Gregorius. 'Do we dare? In broad daylight?'

'There are too many centurions and legates out there. The shares of this wouldn't be large enough to make any difference.'

'We have to try. We buy ourselves claques of supporters—but we're careful. We distribute only to faces we can trust, any man we know or any unit we've fought with. Leave it to me.'

The night closed in early. As the two senior men dossed down on cots, I went off to discover a corner for myself nearby. I drafted notes for Apodemius on my wax tablet by torchlight and kept an eye on their tent.

Sure enough, well past midnight, I spied four figures leaving the tent. One of them had a slight limp. Another wore a kerchief around his head. They were carrying heavy saddlebags. I heard the chink of Magnentius' coins as they snuck away down the empty lane of silent tents and disappeared in all directions through the rows of tents.

I didn't enjoy spying on my own travelling companions, but I still worked for the Empire. For me, during these confusing times, that meant Apodemius.

⚳⚳⚳

The first day of March dawned over mountains glowing lavender, orange and blue. I'd slept well. It was great to be lying once again on honest ground in a bedroll near a campfire, my head wrapped in a wool blanket and my eyes opening in the morning to the last star of the night sky. I felt again the simplicity of my years as bodyguard to the commander. The possibility of liberation from *volo* to *agens*, from slave to freedman, hadn't entered my mind in those innocent days.

The horns sounded an hour before dawn. There was freezing river water for my travel basin and warm honey cakes from a canteen tent. I shaved and washed, then headed off for the IV Flavia's messenger team to make myself known to them. Every Roman army camp in the Empire stood staked out along the same layout. I knew where they'd be. I was nearly at their tent when more horns summoned the legions from their breakfast routines.

Suddenly, I was caught up in a tide of hundreds upon hundreds of men trotting in the opposite direction towards the central parade ground in front of Vetranio's tents.

More trumpets blew and I answered the summons too, running alongside infantry and cavalry, medics and ironmongers, surveyors and engineers. It was impossible to get to the front of so many men massing loosely now, as trained, into their units, so I stood in the rear.

Vetranio shouted to the assembly, 'Here is your *Augusta*, paying respects to the men who march under the pennants of bull, Pegasus, Capricorn and lion!'

A cheer from the men on both sides blasted my eardrums.

'Loyal soldiers,' Constantia shouted, pulling back her cloak hood to reveal her fabulous jewels and elaborate hairdo, 'I bring you a message from my last and most beloved brother, your Emperor, Constantius II. Putting all consideration for family and private interests aside, although he mourns our brother Constans' death deeply, he shows where his duty to you lies. He will fight on at the frontier, defending Roman Mesopotamia from our enemies in Persia, until the end of this year.'

I could imagine Gaiso's smile at this news. Now Magnentius had longer to consolidate his hold on the Western Empire.

Or not—because Constantia continued, 'In his stead, my brother asks you, the Empire's most faithful fighters, to accept as your Emperor in his stead your own Vetranio, the Commander of all the Danubian and Illyrian forces. He sends this diadem to his loyal servant Vetranio to signify how sincerely he confers his authority and favor.'

The troops relayed this announcement back through the ranks with a hushed gabble of excitement. Out of her mysterious sack, Constantia now produced a finely wrought

153

circle of gold, studded with amber, garnets and emeralds. The heavy figure of Vetranio stooped over as she placed it on his thinning hair. For a moment, it looked like slipping off his balding pate but he straightened it and stood up to receive the acclaim of his legions.

He gave an awkward smile and looked right and then left as if sure that any moment, Constantius himself would gallop through the parade ground and snatch the diadem right off his head.

'Hail, Vetranio!' Constantia screamed. She reached into the sack again and within seconds had placed a flowing purple cloak across his shoulders.

'Hail, Vetranio!' shouted the cohorts who were standing far forward, well beyond my sight but just beneath her boots. They started up a rhythm of swords beating on shields.

'Hail Vetranio *AND* Magnentius!' came a sudden shout from a soldier deep inside the ranks far to my right and underneath the bull standards.

'HAIL Vetranio AND MAGNENTIUS!' More shouting rose into the gray dawn, matched with enthusiastic stamping. Vetranio's smile wavered and froze into a grimace. Constantia's shoulders heaved under her thick, soft cloaks with rising fury.

So everyone's bribes had worked only too well and the troops, their pockets full of gold from all directions, ended the assembly in a stalemate of enthusiasm.

Much embarrassed, the abashed General Vetranio rubbed his sagging chin and told Gaiso he was willing to co-rule with everybody for the peace and security of both East and West. After all, the late Emperor Diocletian had allowed for four heads of state under his Tetrarchy, so three should be no problem.

From the speed with which Constantia's caravan abandoned the tent camp for the comforts of the city of Sirmium, it seemed the illiterate old man had promised the Constantine family the very same thing.

Vetranio might have been a poor scholar, but he was a good enough field tactician. He waved goodbye to our retreating delegation with a disingenuous smile—one imperial diadem, two rival emperors and an *augusta* in his worn-out army kit.

CHAPTER 11, FETCHING AN EMPRESS

—THE PALACE AT AQUILEIA—

'There is no other conclusion. You both failed. Where's your Constantine Empress?' Marcellinus shouted across the council table at Gregorius and Gaiso.

I'd just entered the room to collect the late morning dispatches. I suspected things were going badly. The meeting had lasted too long. Even if there were no late morning dispatches, it was essential that I report the debate to Apodemius. Marcellinus was going to use this upset to gain the upper hand over Magnentius' military advisers. He had never liked the idea of a Constantine retinue, even a distaff one, invading his 'reformed' regime.

'Not entirely,' Magnentius said. 'From what I've heard this last hour, if they hadn't swayed the Illyrian troops with their long night of bribing, we'd be facing two—maybe even four— hostile legions fencing us off from the East, with its riches. Isn't rebuilding our economy your department, Marcellinus? You should be grateful to these men. We've had a close shave.'

'You still have no bride,' Marcellinus insisted. 'As you'll recall, Your Excellency, marriage to a Constantine was not my idea. Better to be rid of them than to wed them. We were halfway there. Now these bunglers have only showed our hand to be suppliant and weak.'

Magnentius didn't honor Marcellinus with an immediate answer. 'Where's my ring?'

'Here, General,' Gaiso returned the clunky boulder to its owner.

'There's no point in trying the little sister?'

'None.' Gregorius shook his head. 'That would be a religious misstep that would turn all the bishops of the West against you. You've printed anti-Arian Christian symbols on your coins. It's too late to woo an Arian.'

'Well, scrape the barrel, men! Surely there are more kittens in that golden litter? Constantius massacred his uncles and cousins, but he didn't slaughter all the little *girls* as well, did he?'

I spotted Gaiso suppressing a smile. Gregorius suddenly had to straighten his cross belt.

Marcellinus smelled victory. 'You should marry a Gallo-Roman noblewoman, *Imperator*. I have a list of candidates—'

'Yes, Marcellinus, I know your cronies are thick on the ground up north, but it's too late for that. I'm the Emperor now! I want peace with Constantius and I need a Constantine female for the Roman Senate's approval.'

'Then choose a Roman,' Gregorius said, looking up with a crooked smile. 'Choose a *Roman* Constantine.' He rose to his feet and beamed at Gaiso and Silvanus. 'I've just remembered someone.'

All eyes shot to Marcellinus, who scowled down the council table but nodded for Gregorius to continue.

'Thank you, *Magister Officiorum*. She's the daughter of Justus, Your Excellency, a praetorian prefect of Licinius. His mother was a Neratius and his father—my own father knew him well— was Vettius Justus, consul in—'

'That's still a plus?' Magnentius interrupted him with a barbarian's dismissive sniff.

'Consul is a double plus, *Imperator*.'

'Well, good. Titianus has fixed it up that Gaiso and I will be elected consuls later this year and Decentius next year, isn't that so, men?'

Gaiso gave the Emperor a brisk nod of satisfaction. '*Ave*.'

Gregorius plowed on. '*More important*, the candidate's mother is the daughter of Julius Constantius and his first wife Galla. Julius Constantius was the son of Constantius Chlorus and therefore a half-brother of Constantine I, making this young lady the great-granddaughter of the great Chlorus himself and some kind of cousin to the Emperor Constantius himself.'

Magnentius rolled his eyes to the ceiling. 'My God, do you Romans really carry these family trees around in your heads? It's a miracle your brains aren't as tangled as an hedge row, Gregorius.'

'It can be useful,' Gregorius said, resuming his seat with an air of triumph.

'Not for much longer,' Marcellinus thrust in. He turned to Magnentius. 'Happily, we live in modern times when courage and wits, not lineage, make the man. Forget this Roman brat.'

Gregorius took a patient breath. 'The lady was born in Picenum while her father served as governor there. Her name is Julia. No, I beg your pardon. Justina. Yes, of course, Justina Piceni.'

'More Roman than Constantine, I'll bet,' Marcellinus sneered.

Silvanus slammed his palm on the table, 'She sounds perfect.'

Gregorius nodded his thanks.

'I just hope she doesn't pray too much,' Gaiso muttered.

Magnentius rose and strode down the length of the table. He handed the bulky gold ring to Gregorius.

'Tell her father I'm kind with women,' he said. 'Propose the old-fashioned way, Atticus, the Roman way, whatever it is. And fetch her yourself. Gaiso would race her back at such speed, she might not arrive in one piece and Silvanus is too handsome.'

Only I noticed that Gregorius gulped through acceptance of this honor. Once he had been compared to Adonis himself. Now he looked more like Cyclops.

⚐⚐⚐

'You said, *Magister* Apodemius, that there would be another *agens* on this posting. Either I misunderstood you or my colleague is a champion of discretion and disguise.'

159

The old man chuckled with satisfaction. Swaddled in fine wools against the chill of a broken heating system, he sat huddled behind his desk. There was a small pot of water boiling eucalyptus leaves in the corner. It filled the room with a cleansing cloud. From time to time, the deaf masseuse came into the office and refreshed the steaming basin from which the master was taking deep inhalations under a towel.

'You didn't mishear me, Numidianus. I miscalculated, that's all. It seems that I sent the other agent on a wild goose chase in the wrong direction. That's going to be remedied soon. Now tell me more about the new emperor.'

'Magnentius is no Socrates, *Magister*, but he has a soldier's feel for the lay of the land and the strength of the wind. He knows you can't win battles without allies. He knew patience and timing with Claudius Silvanus was as important as force and bluster. And he has managed to keep the various voices in his council evenly balanced. You can tell he wasn't born to the purple because he actually listens to all his advisers and sometimes changes his mind, on their counsel. That irritates certain people who would have him act more imperial—or imperious.'

'Like Marcellinus.' Apodemius shoved aside his basin and wiped the steam off his face. He started playing with an ivory stylus.

'For one.'

'Your reports are excellent, Numidianus.'

'Thank you, *Magister*. But Marcellinus doesn't trust me and has started sending all his messages by a private rider. Nor does Gaiso, for that matter, although he claims to be in my debt for saving him from Constans' dagger in his back.'

'Watch Gaiso carefully, son. Watch out for Marcellinus. And Silvanus?'

'He keeps his own council, but when there's a disagreement, he acts like an adjudicator of a horserace, his eyes always trained on the finish line, not the riders.'

'Yes, yes, I can see it, now.'

Apodemius busied himself, fetching his attendant to remove the medical water. While I waited, I went over to the wide map of the Empire hanging behind his desk. I noticed golden pins at Edessa and Antiochia punched into the cork backing, marking Constantius' anti-Persian base camps. There were silver pins at the harbors, and dozens of ordinary pins for the legions' positions, as well as a tight cluster of bronze pins knotted on Aquileia.

'What are those scattered pins so far to the northeast?'

'Oh, some raiders harassing Shapur on his border. Possibly driven towards the Persians by drought of some kind. They're called the "Xions," or "Huns," or something like that. The report comes from a very inconsistent source.'

'Are they a variety of Hephthalites?'

'No, no, just some hungry nomads with funny-shaped skulls. I peg them around the Persian border for amusement. They're a headache to Shapur but not important to us. "Huns" are unlikely to darken our gates! Where's Gregorius right now?'

I'd heard the fourth hour after dusk ring out. 'Just finishing his dinner at the Vettius clan's mansion, I expect.'

'He won't have an easy evening of it with that Justus. Nothing's prouder than an ambitious man fallen on rocky times and trying to hide it. He'll negotiate hard. He has no spare daughters to waste.'

'I suppose he might say "no"?'

'No, Justus won't decline this honor,' Apodemius said. He scratched at his ruffled white hair. 'I sent a quiet word to a few senators this afternoon and I'm sure they ran into Justus at the baths before dinner, by coincidence, of course.'

He took off his slippers and began to rub his feet with camphor oil. 'Constantius won't stay in Persia forever. The gift of an only daughter to keep the Empire out of a civil war will bring that family much honor.'

'You think it might come to civil war, *Magister*? General Magnentius has put Constantius on all his coinage and conveyed every possible message sueing for peace.'

'Oh, Magnentius! Magnentius? Apodemius scoffed, 'He's the last man to decide, Marcus. Ask yourself, how much will Constantius swallow? How long will the army's outrage at Constans' insults to their honor and authority prevail over their deeper loyalty to imperial claims? Time is running out! What's happening on these borders, here, here and here? Goths everywhere, settled all along the Dniester River basin. These Thervingi, Greuthungi, Heruli, do you expect them to go home now that they're addicted to Roman luxuries seeping across the border into their poor markets?'

The old man was on his bare feet now. He was stabbing back and forth across his worn out map like a conjuror calling up barbarians. 'Yes, Marcus, they're on the move, sniffing along the northern Rhenus, here and here. They're testing the strength of our lines and challenging our garrisons. Do you know why?'

'Because they've heard that Magnentius has moved all the key legions of the West to support him down to the south.'

'Exactly.'

'Magnentius will need them if it comes to a fight, *Magister*.'

'Fine, fine, Marcus. And then, what will the Persians do if Constantius turns his face to reclaim the West by force?' He rubbed his hands up and down his wrinkled, sun-blotched cheeks as if to wake himself up. 'Most important, *what will Eusebius tell him to do?*'

⚔⚔⚔

For the second night in a row, I slept in the Castra's barracks, listening to a trio of trainees rattling dice in a neighboring cell. Apodemius' de-briefings inevitably came after dusk, so the corridors always stirred with trainers or agents shuffling, one by one, in and out of the barracks—some of them headed to the toilets, others to the hub of imperial intelligence— one never knew for sure. I got three hours of sleep. Gregorius had told me to wait for him at the city's northeast Porta Collina the next morning.

I was delayed by the Castra's pencil pushers. They'd been slack in renewing my identification papers.

'I was starting to worry, Marcus. You've never been late. I raised you better than that.'

'Yes, Commander. I'm very sorry. I had to collect new documents.'

'Yes, of course, Marcus. Sometimes I forget you answer to new masters.'

The Commander waited on horseback alongside an unfamiliar carriage, tightly curtained and embossed with the insignia of the bride-to-be's clan. An elegant old driver the parents had spared for their cherished girl soothed the horses with a handful of oats.

I gestured at the carriage as I fished out my *agens* identification for the final gate. 'Congratulations. I see you've been successful, Commander. Are you and the lady ready to go?'

I refrained from mentioning that one wheel's iron binding was warped, despite the well-intentioned efforts of a smithy's hammer. The carriage's suspension and brakes looked worn down as well. I hoped the vehicle would make it to Aquileia.

'No, but tardiness is a lady's privilege, not a freedman's.' Gregorius' expression was more troubled than my lateness warranted. I marched to the gatekeepers, excused myself from the warm embrace of Great Mother Roma's ancient walls as required by law, and remounted.

'Who are we waiting for, Commander?'

'The future Empress's pleasure, of course.'

'I don't understand.' I glanced at the curtained wagon.

'The Lady Justina *forgot* something.'

I was just digesting this information when a second, high-roofed carriage trundled toward us along the inner wall of Roma, the Agger Servii Tulii. I knew that transport well. It had once ferried Lady Laetitia to and from her afternoon salons. I saw that time, fashion, and no doubt the new Lady Kahina's taste, had wrought changes. I admired its fresh coat of silvery lacquer and dark blue brocade curtains swinging in the windows.

To my astonishment, the Lady Kahina now stepped out of the Manlius carriage and hurried over with her bundle to climb the steps of the other carriage. Even in her travelling clothes, her soft hips and graceful neckline under an elaborate concoction of curls and waves hinted at the pleasures I knew she could give and I was always trying to forget.

So the woman I secretly loved the most in the world was to join the Usurper's court I turned away, fearful that a mix of admiration and affection blared like a *cornicen*'s horn from my eyes.

We exited Roma at a crawl through the morning crush of merchants, pilgrims, farmers and slave trains using the Porta Collina for the Via Nomentana. I led the carriages with the Commander riding at the side of the Vettius wagon. A trip that would have taken me a day and a half riding hard, demanding the best relay horses and racing past official carriages and state cargo, was going to take us many days at this rate, provided the Vettius' discarded wagon held up. I suspected a nice new model was parked back at the family's mansion on the hill at home and that it had been ordered on credit in expectation of Justina's departure for glory.

For his part, Gregorius didn't seem as happy as he should have been. He had thrown in his lot with Magnentius who now commanded all the troops of the West and controlled Roma through Prefect Titianus. To secure the rebels' legitimacy, the Commander was delivering a Constantine bride to his new emperor. Such a marriage could bring the Empire nothing but peace and, if fruitful, nothing but honor to the Manlius marriage broker.

Privately, I thought of our tiny Leo with contentment. One way or another, this honor would be part of his inheritance.

Yet, the Commander seemed preoccupied and sullen the whole day.

At dusk, we pulled over at the state *mansio* in Oriculum, a minor stopover I'd sped past a dozen or more times. I took charge of handing the horses over to the stable hands while Gregorius inspected the ladies' bedchambers and then returned with a slave for their luggage.

'Where's Leo?' I asked Kahina.

'With Lavinia and the Senator in Roma. The farmhouse got too cold for them. Verus promised he'll keep an eye on things.'

'Verus is more than the sum of his parts,' I said and changed the subject. 'So! It looks like we're in for an *extended* tour of the countryside.'

Kahina lowered her eyes and suppressed a smile. 'Lady Justina has never travelled farther than her family's suburban villa before tonight. Come, ladies,' she called, 'We'll be comfortable here and dine well.'

Kahina knocked on the old carriage door. A tiny, white hand devoid of rings or bracelets reached out for assistance. Then a ruby satin slipper appeared on the uppermost step and a veiled head tipped low and cleared the door.

With a light jump, the future Empress landed on the paving stones and laughed. 'Oh, I forgot Claudia, *again*.' She jumped back up the stepladder and reached into the carriage.

Another veiled woman now emerged, carrying a doll in her arms. She handed the toy to Justina with a polite nod.

'Come, Claudia, suppertime!' Lady Justina cried to the doll. She clutched her bobbing treasure and with Magnentius' enormous gold rock of a ring bouncing on a delicate chain from her tiny neck, she dashed pell-mell for the *mansio*'s dining room.

'Well, both mistress and doll seem to share a good appetite. How old is our new *Imperatrix*?' I croaked.

'About twelve, I would say?' Lady Laetitia asked her veiled travelling companion.

'If that,' the other woman answered in a low note of dry humor. She lifted her veil and gave me a challenging stare.

'How do you do?' she asked.

'I'm . . . just fine, thank you,' I gagged out somehow.

The other woman was Roxana.

Chapter 12, A Tiber of Blood

—AQUILEIA, SPRING, 350 AD—

'Well, she won't be the first Roman female to grow up overnight,' Roxana muttered in my ear over dinner.

'Magnentius will be gentle. He's a decent man,' I said, 'although he is a *big* man.'

'How old is he? Forty-seven? Forty-eight?' Roxana shook her head at the slight child nearby. Justina looked nervous under the pathetic, pink circles of rouge daubed on cheeks and lips. Yet I could see she was trained to adult conversation and determined to make Gregorius her first courtier. She sat a few feet away babbling to the Commander over dishes of preserved oranges in honey. To her credit, she took his ghastly visage in her stride.

Roxana didn't seem moved by the painful prospect of this cheerful child in a middle-aged barbarian's lusty arms. Her cynical expression made one wonder what unpleasant path had led to her own recruitment as *agens*.

I gazed down the bench at Kahina, from whom all traces of girlish innocence had also disappeared. But unlike Roxana's aura of feline tension, Kahina exuded the relaxed glow of a confident young matron. I saw no hint of cynicism or unhappiness. She grinned with contentment across the table at the ravaged features of her husband. Guilt at our deception stabbed my conscience as sharp as the secret weapon hidden in my boot cuff.

The dining room was full of traders from the East, braving the late winter thaw to grab high prices for scarce goods in marketplaces around the imperial courts. They were a noisy bunch, smelling profits in the air as they compared price lists and delivery routes.

I admired Roxana's generous breasts wrapped tight under her demure blue woolen bodice. Staring at her lush charms was certainly safer than sneaking peeks at the married Kahina.

'You're looking very fine tonight, Roxana. Travel agrees with you.'

'I enjoy seeing new places,' she said, sucking on an overpriced fig.

'And bumping into old friends?' I smiled with a touch of familiarity that recalled our 'exercises' back in the Castra. I tried not to sound too hopeful, but failed. Under the protection of the wooden table, memories of our lusty bout together were already heating my thighs. The unexpected prospect of having Roxana as a colleague in Aquileia was certainly a juicier bonus than what I deserved for my services to Apodemius thus far.

'Old friends are a comfort, but new friends are a duty. I wouldn't expect much bumping in the night if I were you,' she said, wiping her rosy lips clean of juice.

'No, no, Of course not,' I struggled to recover my dignity. 'No. I assume you're here to help me keep an eye on our *Magister Officiorum*. I certainly need help. He's clamming up around me.'

'I wasn't thinking of Marcellinus. The wealthy Gallic conspirator is all yours.'

'Then, why *are* you here? Surely not to chaperone Lady Justina and her "Claudia" doll?'

'To watch *Silvanus*, of course.'

'Yes, of course, but I . . . I just didn't think you'd say it out loud,' I fumbled. My face reddened at my presumption that Roxana had any role in assisting me, much less sporting with me on off-hours.

She looked me straight in the eye as if I was the stupidest man of her entire acquaintance, and at that moment, perhaps I was.

⚔⚔⚔

Magnentius took one look at the child Justina and gave her an imperial welcome but announced himself in no rush for the wedding. The date was set for late May. Now that he'd won an uneasy accommodation with the Illyrian legions under Vetranio, there was less excuse for him to sit on the border facing the East and resist Marcellinus' insistence we all return to the larger palace complex in Mediolanum.

The move to Mediolanum also meant that the imperial wedding would be the biggest event of the capital's social season—a week of festive political horse-trading, consultation, backstabbing, bribery and bargaining. With a female Constantine in his bed and Constantius on many of his new coins, Magnentius was philosophical about being yoked to a little girl.

'Perhaps she'll ripen with the weather, like spring into summer,' he joked. 'Until then, I leave her to her dollies. Remember, I have a grown daughter of my own.'

Roxana spent her days tasting Justina's food or sewing with the other maids while the child herself played in a suite laid aside for 'the Empress.'

Whenever I caught sight of Roxana in the evenings, however, the woolen dress was gone. Layers of rose silk under a long sleeveless tunic of forest green velvet took its place. But there were changes that dress couldn't disguise. Each week that passed, dark hollows under her wide brown eyes deepened. With a pang of remorse for my lustier urges, I realized that Roxana was working double shifts for the old man back in the Castra Peregrina. No doubt she was also paid much less than I on some specious argument that she didn't have to ride express relays or carry a weapon.

I wanted her to know that she had my sympathy. 'You have my respect, dear colleague. It seems your devotion to duty leaves you no time for sleep,' I said one day as we passed each other in the outer courtyard.

'Sleep? I have no time to write my reports.'

'Is there so very much to say?'

She shrugged, as if any assignment was easy for her, but I could see she was exhausted and troubled.

'Would it help you, Roxana, if I took the Empress for a walk into the countryside? Long enough for you to rest this afternoon?'

'Oh, Marcus,' she sighed. 'I would love to sleep more than three hours at a time. The mother of a newborn gets more sleep than I do.'

'Then I give you five hours with a word to no one. I'll return the child for the evening meal, but sit with her until you fetch her, just as you like.'

'You won't find her quite the child she looks,' she said, lifting an eyebrow.

I fetched a palace driver and a two-wheeled cart for the expedition. Since her wedding day, Justina had had the run of the Palace. She knew me by now as one of the friendlier aides who lingered on the margins of her betrothed's *consistorium*, not quite in and not quite out of the inner circle.

After the midday meal, we rode into the hills beyond the city walls with her driver as chaperone. It was a brilliant day in early June. I shed my cloak and Pannonian cap after twenty minutes riding horseback next to her cart.

'You know, Marcus Numidianus, my father did not want to give me to His Excellency, General Magnentius.'

'I see. Did you have someone else in mind?' I wiggled my eyebrows at her in jest.

'Sadly, he couldn't really afford his own taste in sons-in-law.'

'I see.'

'Yes, but now I don't understand. That one-eyed officer handed over a lot of money for this engagement, but Magnentius ignores me day after day. Perhaps I wasn't worth all those bags of gold.' She still had the chubby cheeks of a child under those wistful hazel eyes. One day she might be a beauty. Already she was graceful and well-spoken.

'I'm sure you are worth far more, *Imperatrix*. Your husband rules the West now. He's a kind man, but a busy one.

Shall we walk up to that hill with the olive trees soaking up the sun? Or head over to that glade? I suspect there's a brook there where you can rest.'

She chose the glade. The driver unhitched the horse for a needed drink and followed us. She bathed her hand in water and giggled.

'It's as cold as snow!'

'That's exactly what it is, Alpine snow.'

'If I put my feet in the water, will you tell on me?'

'I tell on everyone. It's my job. If you hadn't noticed yet, I don't blame you. You're not supposed to see me doing it.' I gave her a broad smile.

'I've never met one of the *agentes in rebus* before. My father says everybody *hates* them. I asked my maid Roxana if that was true and she said that everybody *fears* them, although what would she know about it?'

I shrugged and watched the *Augusta* remove her slippers.

'Roxana says you get to look at everyone's mail and check their accounts, and—is that really interesting?'

'Not always.'

'Would you like to know my secrets?'

'I'd be very grateful, *Augusta*. It would save me opening and resealing your mail.'

'Ha! Well, I had a very strange dream last night, no, more like an oracle appearing in my sleep.' She sank two pale and perfect feet into the icy flow. 'Woooo! Marcus Numidianus, you have to bathe your feet, too. I'll bet you can't stand it!'

I did as she commanded. It felt like a test of trust. Unfortunately, my feet turned blue as fast as hers, but to my surprise, she seemed determined to outlast me.

'A goddess made of silver appeared. She said I would be the mother of a great imperial dynasty lasting many generations.'

'Hardly strange, *Augusta*. I'm losing the feeling in my feet.'

'But it was very strange, *Agens* Know-it-all. Because when I asked how many children I would bear the General, she turned her back and faded away.'

'My blood is turning to ice water,' I said, laughing as I jerked my feet out of the water and put on my socks and boots. 'You win.' I waved to her driver to hitch up the horse. 'You must be made of iron, Lady Justina.'

'Well, I hope after I die that all my statues are cast in gold!' she answered. Only then did she pull out her feet and rub them dry on her priceless brocade over-robe.

I watched her hoist herself back into the imperial cart like a bounding deer. I noticed she wasn't carrying her doll any more.

⚜⚜⚜

That evening it wasn't Roxana who relieved me of my babysitting, but a cornet summoning the imperial council from its various dining rooms scattered around the city and palace. Entering the anteroom of the Council Chamber, I stood at attention as a white-faced Decentius passed. Then to my astonishment, Gregorius asked me as he raced past, 'Is the Prefect in there?'

'*Praefectus Urbi* Titianus? Surely he's down in Roma, Commander.'

'The gods help him if he is. Julius Nepotianus declared himself emperor the night before last and stormed Roma at the head of an armed band of gladiators, felons and slaves. Titianus couldn't hold them off. We heard he was trying to flee back here.'

Titianus was indeed already with us, barely alive. I followed Gregorius behind a cluster of other officers arriving to listen to the Emperor's debriefing of the City Prefect.

'So you just abandoned your Praetorian Prefect of Italia to the mob, Titianus?' Magnentius stood in front of his desk staring down at what remained of Titianus. At first I didn't recognize the aristocrat in that kneeling mess of mud-covered uniform, blood-crusted hands and bandaged face.

'Five of us escaped the municipal complex, but most were slaughtered in their offices, *Imperator*.'

172

'Where were the *aediles*?'

'The Senate quickly recognized Nepotianus, only to save their own throats, but still, the *aediles* did nothing to help us.' Titianus wailed, 'People were cut down as they ran... The Tiberis is running with blood, corpses fill the doorways, children...'

He panted and someone gave him water to drink.

'Some of the plebs who'd been for Nepotianus, well, they changed their minds when they saw those beasts raping and killing with *smiles* on their faces. They were like ravenous shades out of Hades. We fought hard and managed to drive most of them out of the city. But it wasn't safe for us. So Anicetus, the prefectural aides and I headed for the river by the Via Aurelia. The citizens secured the last of the gates behind us.'

'You stuck together?'

'Yes, of course. We made for the docks. Some people got us that far, but even they were picked off one by one from the back by these... *animals*. We stole a boat and held a *pugio* to the boatman's throat to work us upstream, when these... this... *horde* grabbed a faster boat and chased us down. They... they got hold of Anicetus by one of his arms and then... There wasn't much I could do to save...' Titianus broke down in sobs.

'Any warning of this, *agens*? What good are all these reports you deliver if we aren't warned of revolt?'

'There was no notice, *Imperator*.' I said, but thought at the same time, *why had Apodemius detected no sniff of this?*

Gregorius said, 'Because there *was no plot*, General, there was no *movement*. Julius Nepotianus is nothing more than his mother's feeble-minded dupe.'

'Eutropia. Is that old crow still *alive*?' General Magnentius' huge eyes bulged in surprise. 'Oh, someone help that pathetic excuse for a man.' Titianus staggered out of the Council, propped up by two praetorians.

'I heard she survives on nothing but pride and anchovies,' Gregorius said.

'It has to be her, Your Excellency.' Silvanus said. 'She's no soldier. This is not a well-planned coup but a desperate fling at power. Anyone else would know that an uprising on the backs of men who live in cages and dungeons can't hold the hearts of decent Roman citizens.'

Gregorius stepped in. 'He's right. Rely on the Senate, Magnentius. As soon as the streets are clear of this scum, the politicians won't support his bid for long.'

'On the contrary, Gregorius.' Marcellinus countered. 'The Senate is another bunch of old women you can't trust. They can use Eutropia's bid for Nepotianus to negate your claim to succession by Justina, *Imperator*.'

'Nepotianus is nothing more than the runt of the litter. The Constantines should have left him on a hillside at birth,' Magnentius growled.

Marcellinus stepped forward, 'Let me deal with him. I've been out of armor too long.'

'I'll go back, *Imperator*.' Gregorius said.

'No, Gregorius. You're too close to those senators for my comfort. I want you and Gaiso to concentrate on pulling in all available forces,' Magnentius barked. He stood up and shouted at Gaiso, 'Pull down *all* moveable troops out of Britannia and along the Gallic frontier—'

Silvanus protested, 'Magnentius, you've moved the roving legions south, but you can't empty the defensive garrisons and leave the northern border open.'

'I will.' Magnentius pounded his enormous fist on the desk. 'I want every Frankish, Celtic and Saxon soldier standing in formation behind me—ready to move on Roma if necessary. Vetranio's game is bad enough but at least he's a *man* leading four legions. Do they think I'll just stand aside for an inbred weakling hiding in his mama's sedan chair?'

'Ride with Marcellinus as escort,' Gregorius whispered to me outside the council chamber.

'But my posting is here, Commander.'

'Do what I say, Marcus and let your *schola* blame me if there are any questions. Find any excuse but make sure you go.

You saw the way Magnentius refused my offer to relieve the city. He thinks my ties to the Senate would stay my hand from doing what may be necessary. I fear our *Magister Officiorum* has more than Nepotianus in his sights.'

𐌓𐌓𐌓

Magnentius got hold of his temper and held back Marcellinus for a full two weeks. He clung to the possibility that the Senate would revoke their support for Nepotianus or that Constantius would signal disapproval of his cousin's claim.

Meanwhile, troops were moving southward, abandoning garrisons and border patrols to the absolute minimum number of squadrons.

Then one morning Gaiso placed in Magnentius' hand a freshly-minted coin. It had Nepotianus' profile on one side and Constantius' profile on the other with the words, '*URBS ROMA.*' When he saw that, Magnentius tossed all hope out the window—along with the coin.

That same day Marcellinus galloped with four cohorts out of Mediolanum onto the Via Aurelia. I kept my promise to the Commander and rode out with him. We barreled past other travelers, sending them spilling off the road and into the dust. Our riders' spare horses thundered behind us, swapped for panting, sweating mounts twice a day.

Marcellinus may have become a wealthy treasury secretary, but he had kept in good physical condition over the years. The ordinary rigor of military service returned to him quickly enough and as if to prove he had lost none of his physical power, he gave no quarter to the cavalrymen under his command.

He was also a driven man, desperate for this operation to make up for long years of counting expenses for Constans and mollifying Gallo-Roman businessmen with bribes and favors.

I rode one hour's distance ahead of their procession, clearing off anyone using the road illegally and checking for obstructions. It was like my old days ranked among the *equites*, galloping along the soft verge of the paved road to save my horse's hooves from wear. When I wasn't regulating the road, I had a lot of time to think.

For one thing, I suspected cold politics, not any affection for Roma, fuelled the *Magister Officiorum*'s fury to save the city. Marcellinus hadn't yet lost the crumbling abandoned capital from the Usurper's control—at least not until this battle was decided—but he was furious that Magnentius had slipped out of his control.

Since those heady days in Augustodunum of planning the coup, matters had slipped gradually away from Marcellinus' autonomy. Every day he had to defend his policies to real warriors—powerful and confident field veterans like Silvanus, Gaiso and Gregorius and the others—who filled out the *consistorium*.

It got worse for Marcellinus with each passing week. More legions marching down from the north meant the inclusion of yet more outspoken military leaders into the strategic circle. They offered their expertise and often dissension. Some even questioned why Marcellinus had any claim to the final word.

And yet Marcellinus had been the engineer of the whole rebellion. He had financed it, planned it, politicked for it for months and years behind Constans' back. Marcellinus didn't welcome these new senior soldiers for one reason—the former treasury chief didn't like working with men he couldn't buy.

I think he believed that the coming battle for Roma could swing his bid to regain the upper hand—even make him one of the next consuls.

There were other developments I considered as I galloped ahead of his cohorts. I had noticed that in choosing the fighters to ride against Nepotianus, Marcellinus had favored units remarkable for their barbarian blood. So it was coming to that, I thought, as I kept ahead of them, hearing their faint trumpet signals marking their progress behind me throughout the long day. It was coming down to that uncomfortable fact. The original conspirators did not trust true Romans to attack a

Constantine—even a puny one. They thought their advantage lay with men who'd never seen Roma before in their lives. Marcellinus intended to show us all what a Gallo-Roman could do without any help from Gregorius or his aristocratic kind.

But how could Marcellinus retake Roma alley by alley from scum who knew every ally, fountain and sewer hole?

By the time I reached the naval port of Pisae, I saw that Roma had caught wind of our approach. A river of refugees blocked my race southwards to the old capital and by the time I'd cleared the road, the rest of Marcellinus' forces had caught up with me.

As we cantered down the Via Flaminia towards the familiar domes and roofs, I saw that Nepotianus' ragtag rebel camp had swelled up with every creature of Roma's underbelly. Released from the jails and scoured up from the sewers, these filthy, brawling drunkards swarmed the slopes east of the Tiberis in front of the Aurelian Walls.

Even from a distance, they looked like a human inflammation or infestation, not an army.

I wasn't ranked as part of the fighting force and I felt grateful for it. I left Marcellinus on the excuse of reporting to my *schola* at the Castra Peregrina for further orders and headed around the city walls.

But first, I knew without asking what the Commander had wanted me to do. Marcellinus had personally guarantee the safety of the Manlius household, but now that I had seen the rough and hardened foreign troops who were about to wage a crackdown, I knew that nothing and no one could be guaranteed security in the chaos to come.

My identification papers unlocked the guarded gates of the Porta Aurelia. I registered and then rode into a silent Roma— eerier than anything I remembered. Where had half a million souls hidden themselves? All I saw were shuttered windows and refuse-strewn streets. Wagons and carts rolled driverless in the streets. Gates swung back and forth on their hinges. A socialite's gilded litter sat in the middle of a main junction where its bearers had dropped it on a dash for their lives. The food and repair stalls stood empty. The barbershops and bathhouses were locked up.

The great cradle of the Empire had become a playground for rats scurrying to the music of fountains gushing in the sun.

I skirted the Caelian district with the Castra looming high above me, and instead urged my horse up the steep Esquiline streets towards the Manlius townhouse.

'Verus! Open up!' I pounded on the gate under the fig tree. 'It's me, Marcus Numidianus!'

A slave girl I didn't recognize peered at me through an opening high in the wall. Her face dropped away without a word.

'Open up! Verus! OPEN THE GATE!'

I waited many long minutes before I heard footsteps and the bolts lifted with difficulty, one by one.

'Marcus Numidianus! What in Hades are you doing here?"

Clodius was drunk. I pushed past him and ran through the *fauces* and into the atrium. In the summer's heat, the gardens beyond had gone to seed. Wildflowers and weeds smothered the stone bench where Lady Laetitia had once gathered elegant friends for snacks and gossip.

'Where's the family?' I shouted back at him.

'I'm head of the family as long as Gregorius is away.'

'The Emperor's *Magister Officiorum* is riding through the city gate with troops to remove Nepotianus,' I said. 'I'm here to warn you. But tell me quickly—how did the Senator vote?'

Clodius rolled his bloodshot eyes. 'The Senator's too feeble to vote. You should know that. I sent his vote for him *in absentia*. The Manlii support Nepotianus' claim, of course. He's a Constantine, after all.'

'Are you mad?' Where's everyone else?'

'Cook's getting lunch. My slave is preparing my—'

I shook him by the shoulders. 'Where's the Senator? Where's Leo?'

'Stop that. You're rattling my brains. The brat's in the nursery, I suppose, with that nurse. The Senator's in his study, probably having a nap—or dead. How should I know?'

'Get them out of the city, Clodius, NOW.'

He screwed his bloodshot eyes up at my forehead. 'You're wearing Gregorius' Pannonian hat. Did you *steal* it?'

'Clodius, if the Senator's vote for Nepotianus is public, you're all in danger. Lock up the whole house. Take the baby, all the servants and the old man out of the city right away. Verus, where are you? Get them all to the apartment in Ostia by side roads. Wait for news. If it gets bad, and Magnentius takes revenge, you sail with them to the southern estates.'

Clodius' eyes widened and he leaned away from me. 'And leave my friends? Abandon my sponsors?'

'Verus!' I shouted again in all directions at the doors facing the atrium. 'Verus, where are you? Verus, it's me, Marcus Numidianus!'

At last the old servant came limping out of the kitchens, his arms wide in greeting. 'Thank the gods you're here, Marcus. The city's going to Hades in a pisspot.'

'I know. Verus, there isn't time to talk. There are four cohorts poised to attack Nepotianus' supporters this minute. They won't give up until they regain control of the city. One of their targets is the Senate. Fighting will have reached the Forum within the hour. Collect Lavinia and the baby. I'll go get the Senator. You're going to take them to Ostia. Try the Porta Ostiensis first.'

'Yes, Marcus.' Verus ran off towards the nursery.

'I'm telling you, Clodius, if the Senator's vote is held against him, no one can save any of you.'

'Tell him yourself.'

I ran up the short flight of steps to the old man's study door.

'Senator Manlius! You must prepare to leave for Ostia. Verus and Clodius will take you there now.'

'Who's that?' he asked, turning a vague white gaze in my direction. 'I can't possibly leave my books.'

'You *must leave now*, Senator. Verus will come for you in a few minutes. What do you need? I'll tell the maids.'

'I never leave my books unguarded,' he said in the steady voice that had once moved Roma's rulers to vote yay or nay. 'Someone is trying to take them.'

'You *must leave*, Senator.'

'I will not leave.'

I couldn't persuade him, and the clock was running on me now. Trusting him to Verus' speedy care, I left the Senator standing there, in the middle of his piles of books, one hand on his reading couch for steadiness. He gazed up at his wooden ceiling, carved with gods and nymphs, looking dazed but unmovable. Verus would have to carry him out.

I'd been absent without permission too long. I descended the north-facing slope of District V down into the Subura slums, my horse wending its way between looted furniture and refuse piled into stinking barricades. Clusters of ragged plebeians stood cheering a gang of gladiators breaking into a weapons warehouse. The *vigiles* who should have been guarding against fire were nowhere to be seen.

I heard screams coming towards me. The street battle between Nepotianus' ruffians and Marcellinus' cavalrymen was moving closer.

I now saw the fighting straight ahead and rode smack into Marcellinus' men slashing their way through a mob of Nepotianus' fighters on the Campus Agrippa. They were driving those who weren't cut down dead straightaway to stagger backwards as they were herded into the horseracing arena.

Someone grabbed my leather toe loop, and then got hold of my trouser leg. I looked left, down into the face of a man giving me a vile leer. His clean-shaven head reached almost to my shoulder. His hand was pulling my *spatha* up and out of its scabbard by its hilt. I drew my *pugio* and made to stab his upper arm, but he dodged me. I turned the horse towards him, shifting my sword out of his reach, but he grabbed my reins, dodged my thrusts and now yanked hard on my sword belt to dislodge me from the saddle.

'Get off me, bastard!' I shouted. With an upward thrust, my *pugio* caught him under his bristled jaw and cut his chin open to the jawbone. With a powerful blow to my wrist, he knocked the short blade from my hand, sending clanging into a gutter across the street. If he tried to retrieve it, my *spatha* would enjoy the rippling muscles of his naked back as a target.

But even he wasn't that stupid. He left the *pugio* where it fell and kept hold of my belt, hanging off my horse as I twisted the animal one way and another. I couldn't shake the creep.

Finally, he reared up at me, roaring something unintelligible. With beefy arms, he pinned me in a deadly embrace and dragged hard on my whole torso, using my horse's barrel as resistance with his massive knees to get me to the ground. I kicked hard, my arms pinned underneath his massive weight. I fumbled at my boot cuff to get at my hidden swivel dagger. I could feel the wooden handle, but my horse was bucking too hard to me to work the blade open. I kneed the man with all my might. He grunted in pain, bending over and loosening his grip of me.

My arm free again, I pulled my *spatha* out of its scabbard, took hold with both hands, and swung it wide at his thick neck.

My blade cleaved deep. His head and shoulders were thrown back as he slammed against a wall, spattering brains and blood all over graffiti reading, 'Ball players! Vote Lucius for *aedile.*'

If this was what Marcellinus' men were up against, they'd need all their experience of fighting the hardiest Germans to win the day. These men were more brutish than trained soldiers. Unlike enlisted men, they were criminals with nothing to lose.

But Marcellinus had everything to win. I kept my grip on the saddle and plunged ahead, using my horse to scatter their gangs and using my sword to remove some of them permanently.

As the hours dragged on, I had reason to hope that the tide in the citywide battle had turned against Nepotianus' foul mob. I saw these sub-humans, rags flying, scuttling this way or that, one by one, down narrow alleys no horseman could negotiate.

I followed the thunder of hooves and cries ahead. Reaching the open piazza around Flavian's Arena, I saw the flanks of

Marcellinus' cohorts hounding the last of Nepotianus' gangsters through its arches for roping together—or worse.

I melted into the cohorts. Marcellinus himself now reared up from behind and galloped past us, raging at the top of his lungs with the ease of his victory. He carried a lance topped with a man's severed head, shouting over and over. He dashed his horse around the perimeter of the amphitheater brandishing this gruesome trophy into the faces of the filthy, bleeding horde forced to their knees in the blood-soaked sand.

The dead eyes of the bleeding head looked vaguely familiar, although I had never seen this man before. Then I realized, that I had seen many of his relatives up close. It was what was left of Nepotianus.

'Who will hunt down the mother?' Marcellinus crowed, dispatching a *turma* to hunt out Eutropia's head for a lance of its own. It was a challenge Gaiso would have loved, but he was safely out of this hellish mayhem. 'And the senators! Get me the heads of the Senate!' Marcellinus cried.

Another unit dashed out of the arena. I tried not to panic. By now Verus must have smuggled the family onto the southwestern road, possibly even to the gates and beyond.

But I couldn't be sure. It would take time for these strangers from Gallia to locate the Senator's townhouse, unless they had special informants. Judging by the speed of their departure for Eutropia's whereabouts, I feared they did. I'd banked too much on their ignorance of Roma's elite neighborhoods. Marcellinus had planned better than I thought. He had never shown loyalty, much less respect for the decrepit Roman Senate that had delayed and thwarted his new government. If he ever intended to revenge himself on those remnants of Roma's lost greatness, if he relished handing them over to the mercy of a mob with nothing but hatred for patrician authority and tradition, it was going to happen tonight.

There was no choice but to slip away again, to defend the Manlius House until I fell under some sword, if necessary. I shouldn't have left Clodius in titular charge, no matter how much I relied on the trustworthy Verus.

Marcellinus' legionaries had split into two groups. One group was storming the Caelian Hill and the second searching the Esquiline. The summer skies shone full blue, but as I rode fast, back up the slope toward Trajan's Baths, I saw the first signs of blood running through the gutters right under my horse's hooves.

Screams came from other houses as doors were battered down, gates cracked open and street walls scaled to invade the lush gardens of the privileged.

I hurried on now, closing my eyes to scenes so cruel and savage, only my loyalty to the Manlii carried me past atrocities I would otherwise have fought to stop. I finally reached our old street and clattered up the road, leaping off my saddle. Under the sprawling fig branches, the oak gate barring the Manlius House from the street stood wide open.

I sighed, thinking that the family had fled in too much of a hurry. That idiot Clodius had left the valuables accumulated over centuries—statues, rugs, ancestral funeral masks, golden tableware and priceless murals for any brigand to loot and vandalize. I dropped off my horse, shut the gate and bolted myself in.

I walked through the vestibule, then the atrium, stifling hot now under the glass roof and stinking of weeds rotting in the moss-covered fountain basin. What servants still reported to Verus had fled as well.

It wasn't too late to secure the house up tight again, especially the priceless library books. I dashed up the short steps to the old study and then fell back against the doorframe in horror.

The Senator lay across the floor, his sightless gaze meeting mine. He looked now for all the world like a bag of bones covered in white linen and wool stained livid with drying blood. His two scrawny feet in their goatskin shoes had kicked over the bin of scrolls he always kept by the side of his favorite chair, ready for the vanished slave boy Marcus to return and read out loud.

I sobbed and ran to the old man's corpse. Wrapping him in a tight embrace, I cried out to any gods who were listening, '*Unjust murder! Injustice!*' My breast pounded with shock. My brain was blank and dizzy. No heat of the battlefield at Gregorius' side had ever drained my mind of thoughts and strength so fast. The empty house didn't answer my screams of rage, yet I howled all the same.

This was the only person in the world who had truly loved me. I pressed my breast to his as if we could swap his lifeless heart for my broken one. I heard someone wailing with grief and realized it was myself. And all the time I held the frail and lifeless body to my heaving chest, my horror reverberated. How could Gregorius ever forgive his father's murderer? Who would avenge it?

CHAPTER 13, THE COIN OF UNITY

'Marcellinus' massacre in Roma made you look barbarian, not imperial,' Gregorius said. 'The Roman fathers—those that survived—will never accept you now, whatever Decentius does, *Imperator*.'

'Who cares?' Marcellinus retorted across the council table. 'You already rule Roma and all the West, *Imperator*.' He scoffed at my ex-master. 'Move with the times, Commander Gregorius, move with the times.'

'My father's ashes are hardly cold in the Manlius mausoleum.' The Commander's distrust of the Gallo-Roman *Magister Officiorum* grew by the minute.

Marcellinus' gaze turned stony. 'I've sworn on my ancestors, though they are not as illustrious as *yours*, that I gave specific orders to spare the old fool from retribution. Don't raise the issue with me yet again.'

I listened to them wrangle in front of General Magnentius and his *consistorium* as I had for the last five months. Always more thoughtful than his older brother, Decentius had tried, but failed to make peace between the council members.

Decentius had never felt comfortable surrounded by these senior veterans with years of service for other emperors under their sword belts. I thought I had detected downright relief when no one challenged his elevation to Caesar. Decentius even had his own *solidus* now, too, embossed with *RENOBATIO URBIS ROMA, MAGNENTIUS DECENTIUS*, but from what I observed, the coins embarrassed him more than anything else.

With Titianus shamed in the eyes of the Roman street, Magnentius now had to dispatch his own brother on bended knee to the old capital to appease its wounded pride. Decentius didn't care for pomp but at least he took his new responsibilities for the security of Gallia and the Rhenus border to heart.

Gregorius himself had returned to Roma to oversee the last rites for Senator Manlius and to commission his death mask. He'd left Kahina with us under Magnentius' powerful protection. Clodius declined his uncle's summons to the funeral by pleading illness. He remained behind to enjoy the sundrenched terraces of Ostia. Perhaps it was just as well that the Commander's nephew and heir stayed with Verus in the port town, well out of Marcellinus' sight. If Marcellinus had distrusted me from the first, the Manlius camp consisting of Gregorius and myself now hated Marcellinus with equal sincerity.

The time for avenging the Senator's death wasn't ripe, but the enmity was there. Marcellinus knew it only too well.

So the Usurper and his court argued out the summer, distracted only by a move back to Aquileia. Magnentius disliked the stifling bureaucracy of Mediolanum more than ever. In Aquileia, he was free to spend his leisure time the way a rough-and-tumble soldier sees fit under less judgmental eyes.

By fall, Constantius' bouts over Nisibus with the Persians had reached an uneasy truce. He now turned his vengeful attention towards the West. Aquileia was rife with rumors on the streets, whispers in the wine shops, and gossip in the baths. People shivered at the scent of conflict in the wind.

'Unity, men, unity is our first priority. Does this coin lie?' Magnentius tossed one of his *solidi* on the table. It twirled and circled, and then fell flat with Constantius facing up. Magnentius pressed his thick index finger down on the Emperor's profile. 'He and I can split the Empire or we can share it. I'm determined to try once more for peace.' His heavy eyelids lowered as he added, 'But in the future, tell the mints to take the bastard's face off my coins.'

'War's inevitable,' Gaiso said.

The hunter's hunger for a real fight was palpable. He trained his forces harder than anyone else. The cavalry units under his demanding eye knew how to wheel and charge, retreat and regroup, circle and reverse in the saddle with the seamless grace of palace dancers. Training fresh *tirones* how to mount horses at a run carrying full arms or how to charge down steep bushy slopes without breaking the mount's legs now bored him and his deputies. They'd done their job all summer. They stood impatient to test their skills.

'I hope you're wrong, Gaiso,' Silvanus said.

General Silvanus always played it safe. I wasn't surprised to hear the caution in the handsome Frank's voice. He was in charge of pulling the legions, one by one, farther south towards Magnentius' expanding front line. Silvanus knew better than the other commanders what vast territories lay stripped of defense as these troops vacated the northern borders of the Empire.

As so often these days, Silvanus this morning played the arbiter enjoying the decisive word. 'You still have Vetranio halfway on your side, Magnentius. Unfortunately, he suffers from his humble origins and poor education, making him susceptible to a peculiar malady.'

'Sick? Vetranio's sick?' the Emperor asked.

'Our roughhewn Moesian suffers from a case of *Constantinophilia.*'

'What in Hades is that?'

'A rash that spreads from head to toe whenever he comes near the color purple.'

Everyone but Marcellinus chuckled. Silvanus continued, 'Employ the legions massed behind us as an antidote without delay. Team up with Vetranio and together put it to Constantius that a civil war would be fatal to his campaign against Shapur. Even propose marriage again to Constantia—if you must—and send the virgin bride home to her father.'

'Silvanus is right. Justina is still a child. I can't wait years for heirs to the Great Constantine. My so-called "marriage" to her could be annulled. She could be sent back to Roma . . .'

Silvanus held the floor. 'Vetranio is asking Constantius for more money while pledging his loyalty to us. God knows we have enough money to reverse that, what with Marcellinus selling every imperial post from here to Lutetia...We should send another delegation to Vetranio...'

I left the room on time with the morning's dispatches for the relay rider. It wouldn't do to linger and feed Marcellinus' suspicions. Not all of us were so discreet. Roxana blocked my exit from the council room Her ears stretched a full yard in front of her.

I'd helped her out once or twice since my afternoon with Justina, trying to squeeze her some free time between her duties as chaperone and her exercises as military mistress. Sooner or later, I confess, I hoped for some personal reward. Silvanus was handsome for a man in his forties, with that sleek dark hair and those friendly green eyes, but time had proved him cold and calculating.

I could be tender and kind. Now I reached for her shoulders wreathed in expensive Eastern silk, but she brushed my hands away with impatience.

'Did Silvanus propose another peace delegation? Quick, tell me. I must get back before I'm missed.'

'Yes.' I didn't like taking orders from women. 'Don't act as if a delegation was your idea.'

'To put over with all my persuasive skill.'

'Not *your* idea, surely?'

'Oh, shut up, just play your role and let me do my job!'

'Roxana,' but she was already flying down the marbled hall, back to playroom duties. 'Roxana?'

My face burned at her insult. Everyone knew I was an *agens* with authority over all the court's post, ready to record and report any factional split or crime to the Castra Peregrina's master. The suspicious eyes of Marcellinus hampered my movements. Meanwhile Roxana stayed invisible and free to carry out Apodemius' tactics to keep the Empire intact.

I flushed even deeper when the stark truth hit me like bolt of Zeus. *Apodemius had set me up*. If we *agentes* were told to put the Empire over all our private ties and political sentiments, the old chief put the Empire ahead of the interests of his individual agents with ruthless utility.

I was just a *decoy* so Roxana could do the important work. I was there to distract Marcellinus and feed council room debate back to Roma while she was feeding policies and strategies across the pillow to save the Empire from itself. Apodemius planted an idea through Roxana into the Council and then read my reports to see how the argument presented by Silvanus had played out.

That night things got worse. Resting in my cell-like quarters as chief of the postal riders, I received a letter bearing only a wax seal embossed with a small mouse. Even playing the decoy wasn't enough, it seemed.

It read, 'To Sirmium as escort. Report *daily*.'

Escort again. Clearly the old man in the Castra Peregrina had more confidence in his feline brunette than in his Numidian informant.

⚔⚔⚔

Magnentius gave Vetranio ample warning of his dissatisfaction with their 'pact' in a string of letters, all of them drafted in the distinctively elegant handwriting of Marcellinus' personal secretary. The ground was laid but the path littered with traps. The Usurper's negotiating delegation set off for Sirmium in the second week of December. It included not one single key member of the Council. Magnentius sent ten tribunes and a half dozen *protectores domestici* from Gaiso's military staff, protected by units of the Ioviani with none other than the disgraced Prefect Titianus riding at the head.

I was the state escort in charge of the route. We were all disposable.

Marcellinus smiled at the scene as we mounted our horses in the outer courtyard of the palace before the gray dawn. How utterly vulnerable we must have looked, riding into the enemy's maw! Any failure on our part would signal success for those who wanted civil war.

Vetranio was hardly likely to be moved by our puny mission. I was riding out for a lost cause. Only Magnentius himself, in personal conference with the wily old Moesian, could have brought about a solid alliance against Constantius.

I felt a sudden shiver, despite my thick woolen tunic and socks, sturdy riding trousers, armor and short riding cloak. It was as if Justina's silver dream oracle had warned of danger looming over me. I shot one last look at the fortress walls as we trotted eastwards in the direction of Illyricum. What I saw over my shoulder sent another kind of shiver through me.

Framed by a high window in the imperial quarters, Lady Kahina stood alone watching my departure.

Her face was red with weeping.

ЖЖЖ

The rocky Haemean slopes, emptied of troops or peasants by frozen winter, were all that now stood between Sirmium and our party. The glaze of ice on the paving stones was treacherous to our horses' hooves. Teeth chattering and shoulders shivering under blankets, we walked the horses over the last mile towards the city with care.

The Illyrian legions had moved into more solid winter quarters. The old general Vetranio, his stubbly jowls still wagging like a bloodhound's, welcomed us into the entrance hall of a large suburban villa commandeered for the senior staff. Although he was Constantius' anointed buddy, he sported neither borrowed diadem nor purple-trimmed cloak, just a battered cuirass over his uniform tunic, patched trousers and worn boots.

'Eat, gentlemen! Our grub is better than anything you get from any tavern on the *Cursus Publicus*.' We quickly made ourselves at home. Vetranio had risen to the top because he knew soldiers' ways and the men loved him for it. Food and warmth came before political talk.

Vetranio's jovial humility fooled me no longer. I watched him. He eyed Titianus over the edge of his wine goblet as our party devoured a hearty dinner of olives and fruits, roasted capons marinated in *garum*, blood sausages and wheat bread, all washed down with an oaky wine.

The other officers in our delegation could never have judged by the generosity of Vetranio's board that he feared Magnentius' displeasure at his last-minute double-dealing. I alone had read in secret the word-lashings doled out by Marcellinus, letter by letter. And I could trust that literate or not, someone had read those letters out to Vetranio.

Tonight I saw in the wary warrior's eyes a mix of curiosity and peasant canniness. Vetranio might still be studying his alphabet but he needed no lessons in politics. He knew he commanded the critical military hinge that buffered a legitimate Emperor from a popular and powerful upstart.

'We Romans like to pay for our meals,' Titianus said, smiling as he called forward four adjutants, each laden with two sacks of Magnentius' *solidi*. 'This is a just a small expression of our gratitude for your continuing alliance.'

'For that kind of money, I should have served you gold-papered dormice stuffed with dates,' Vetranio said. 'But I'm happy to see that Magnentius has returned the West's finances to health in only one short year.'

'The *Magister Officiorum* has regularized taxation. He has straightened out the budget irregularities that crippled the Empire during his days as Treasury Secretary taking instructions from Constans.'

'And grown fat in the process, I bet!' one of Vetranio's staff volunteered.

Titianus didn't smile along. 'Marcellinus serves the Emperor Magnentius, for whom the army will always come first. Have no fear of that, Vetranio.'

'Oh, I believe it, I sure do. It was the army's misery that drove him to treason and murder,' the old fox chuckled.

'Justice, not treason. An arrest gone wrong, not murder. All the legions west of this room salute Magnentius. The defenders of the Roman people have spoken.' Titianus spoke with impressive authority for a coward who so recently had fled for his life to a stolen boat on the Tiberis. Perhaps that event crossed Vetranio's mind as well.

'I hear that there aren't many real Romans left, thanks to you and Marcellinus.'

Titianus tried to chuckle it off.

'You might laugh, Prefect. Oh, not that Nepotianus or his mother were friends of mine. But I didn't like what I heard. They should have been arrested or exiled. Let's call it peasant sentiment. I was born not far from here on a rough pallet laid with a borrowed blanket under a leaking roof.' Vetranio's thick fingers picked the very last morsels of meat off a bone with concentrated precision. 'In my childhood home, a meal like this would have been stretched to feed the entire village. So forgive me, Titianus, if I trust a system that promotes a yokel like me right to the top.'

Titianus nodded, 'Magnentius had also promoted his men on the basis of merit.'

Vetranio spit a bit of gristle out, thinking perhaps of Caesar Decentius but he didn't quibble. Instead, he pressed his point. 'Oddly enough, I respect the family who gives a simple man like me a fair chance, provided I follow orders and fight with courage.'

'Magnentius only wants peace within our Empire. We all need peace to use our forces to defend the borders. Barbarian incursions grow more frequent with each year and even when we win, the enemy holds more imperial ground than the year before. Magnentius wants you to join us in getting a formal settlement face-to-face from Constantius. The marriage proposal to Constantia is back on the table.'

Vetranio let out a snort and polished off more wine. He stared at the hot coals in the brazier.

Titianus grew testy with the rough Moesian. 'Surely you've had time to consider this, Vetranio. You've *read* the messages from Mediolanum?'

'Messages? Scoldings, you mean! The arrogance!'

'You must know by now what your answer is? Will you ride with us to Constantius, or not?' Titianus used too much condescension. His allusion to Vetranio's educational shortcomings was a fatal insult.

Vetranio rubbed his stubbly jowls with a calloused hand. We waited. He looked around our delegation with a mix of resignation and disdain. Then he belched in our faces.

It was clear my report to Apodemius on this confrontation was going to disappoint anyone praying for peace. Vetranio's lavish meal had just been showing off. He might as well have served a bowl of salt to rub into our saddle sores. His refusal to make good on his partnership with Magnentius was going to be the bitter dessert.

I was wrong.

'Yes, there is only one solution to this. Constantius will meet us next week in Naissus to discuss terms.'

Titianus visibly started in his camp chair. Tribunes, legates and centurions from our two camps exchanged smiles and shook hands down the length of three long tables. The banquet was adjourned. Vetranio said goodnight like a Roman patriarch blessing his grandchildren as they scampered off to bed.

I lingered in the emptying dining room to inquire where to deposit my night's report with the dispatches leaving at dawn. An officer wearing the Pegasus insignia offered to escort me in one hour's time when I had collected whatever self-serving puffery Titianus was drafting himself to send to Marcellinus and added my own unvarnished version.

As usual, my report to Apodemius took time. I had to write two messages, as I'd been trained. Tonight's cover letter detailed our arrival time, the money transferred to our host and his proposal we all proceed to meet the Emperor in Naissus.

Then around the margins of the page, I added a coded message in invisible ink that was sure to outshine any intelligence that vixen Roxana could come up with for weeks to come. It felt good to know I had useful information for once, but as I wrote it, my heart sank knowing that Gregorius had gambled the future of the Manlii and my son with dice now loaded against all of us.

The evening had been long and the wine strong. Before the meeting had adjourned, I'd excused myself to take a piss and a gulp of fresh air. Instead I caught a whiff of sweet and cloying perfume. In the villa corridor I spotted an unmistakable silhouette that drew me back into the shadows with a gasp. I prayed to the gods he hadn't detected me, but I couldn't be sure.

Now I could add something to the margins of my report that would give Apodemius a shock of his own. 'Eusebius eavesdropping from adjoining room.'

CHAPTER 14, HOPE ABDICATES

—DACIA MEDITERREANA—

We set off a few days later for Naissus. I could deduce that Vetranio's assurance we were to meet Constantius was based on information delivered by the eunuch.

I'd never ridden so deep into the East in my life. We crossed three hundred mountainous miles of frost and snow. It took six days, via Singidunum, Viminacium and Horreum Margi, just to reach Constantine's birthplace. The great Emperor had once nicknamed Naissus, 'my Roma'—before he built himself an even better one.

Naissus was all right, but to my eyes, no Roma.

The last surviving imperial son had moved on and now waited for us at his winter quarters in Sardica.

We set off on another three days of bone-chilling travel. It all came back to me now from my army days serving Gregorius—the stench of twenty thousand men and their horses, the thunder of tens of thousands of hooves thudding on dirt next to wheels on the paving stones, always ending with the pounding of palisade stakes around a fresh camp at dusk. Only discipline and habit saved us from chaos as we bedded down in a rectangular metropolis of tents.

Surely Constantius' forces, weakened and whittled down by the relentless Shapur for years on end, could never match Vetranio's muscle? I imagined all the legions of Britannia, Gallia and Hispania, massing ever closer and closer to Magnentius, matched with this horizon of hardened fighters, all the Danubian cavalry legions plus infantry units from the central northern frontier. Logic told me the sheer weight of the allied armies of the West and Illyricum had Constantius cornered.

I was sure Magnentius had a deal.

Yet my nerves tightened on a winch of apprehension with each day's leaning in my saddle against the chilly winds. I got no chance to tell Titianus my fears that the eavesdropping Eusebius had had ample time to set a trap.

Our Magnentius delegation had been split up on purpose, a move I credited to the perfumed eunuch, riding under silken covers in a cushioned litter somewhere back with the baggage-train of bullion and supplies. Our Ioviani Gauls and Franks rode pinched behind some ten thousand men fast-marching or riding ahead, followed by another ten thousand on horseback and the trains behind.

Singled out to ride at Vetranio's side, Titianus was in no position to counsel the rest of us, even during our nightly stopovers. Vetranio kept his chief guest busy with flattery and toasts at his private table.

Even from a distance, our noble Roman spokesman didn't look any more confident than I felt, but not because he knew Eusebius' labyrinthine ways hidden from our view. He was no doubt busy rehearsing the terms of a treaty which would acknowledge the superior standing of the legitimate heir in the East over the reformer of the West in exchange for a peaceful division of rule.

If that failed, Titianus was to allude to the interests of the united Empire over the high price of a civil war.

As a sweetener, the Urban Prefect carried in his army kit a small portrait of the Magnentius daughter. Unfortunately, the virgin was no trump card, even as part of a dubious exchange for the widowed Constantia. I'd caught a quick glimpse of the tiny image and noticed a pair of cow-like eyes and pointed nose curving down over her father's massive jaw.

After so many days of riding, obscure and silent, in a flowing river of disciplined men, I felt nothing but relief as we finally crested the mountains that ringed Sardica's valleys.

I gulped at the vista below. For miles and miles, Constantius' forces—in lines as regular as a Roman boy's grid in the sand at Ostia—stretched in wait for the Moesian's forces. Under a gray sky heavy with snow, I could just make out

Constantius' pennants marking the center parade ground and military headquarters. A wooden podium stood twenty feet high and fifty feet wide in front of the imperial tents.

Hundreds of horses slowed ahead of my own to negotiate the rocky, narrow descent. I had to rein in hard to keep in position. I exchanged worried glances with any of the Gallic tribunes I could spot near me in the procession.

Sidling down, hoof by hoof, stone by stone, I spotted Vetranio's standard and picked his heavyset figure out from the advance riders speeding up their pace after they reached the safety of the flatland. I would have known Titianus anywhere for his upright bearing and white horse specially chosen in Aquileia departure to dazzle, but I was surprised that Vetranio himself now wore the long purple cloak and diadem Constantia had tossed his way in Sirmium.

On the descent, my horse lost his footing and stumbled. I slipped farther behind our party and was struggling to keep my place on the road. A brutish Thracian with thighs as thick as tree trunks was edging my own mount off course.

Then he barked over his saddle to me, 'We've got instructions. When Constantius finishes speaking, hail him with a full throat. Pass it on.' He returned his eyes to the treacherous final stretch.

'How do we know when he's finished? I can hardly see the podium from back here, much less hear anything.'

'Don't be a clod. When Vetranio kneels, of course.'

'Why would Vetranio kneel? He's here to sign a—'

'Just pass it on.'

We melted into the sea of tents. I passed Constantius' cavalry in various stages of war exercises. These were men who lived for constant battle, ferocious and unforgiving, ungallant and duplicitous, against the Persians. Even during their winter rest, they were honing their battle skills, preparing to face Shapur's formidable cavalry all over again in the spring.

I was astonished by my first sight of a mounted unit clad *entirely* in metal armor, with only slits for eyeholes and rotating scales of metal plated over their arms and legs. Each rider on exercise carried lance, sword, mace, bows and battle-axe, all dangling from belts and scabbards and sheaths. More extraordinary, each horse wore armor over its head and body that hung down to its knees, making the whole of man and mount one glittering engine of death.

I could not stop staring. I had to see more. I was about to slip forward for a better look when a roar from the troops engulfed me. I'd only heard such a sound, like a bellowing, hungry beast, in Roma itself and only at the arrival of a celebrity gladiator or the death throes of a royal prisoner-of-war in the center of Trajan's Arena.

I strained high in my saddle over the clamor and bang of spears and swords on shields just in time to catch Vetranio and Titianus dismount. Our two envoys followed a heavy-footed man with a proud, heavy-featured head on wide and rigid shoulders underneath the imperial banners and into the ceremonial imperial tent.

I had just enjoyed my first glimpse of the true Emperor.

☩☩☩

Across the plains, horns summoned the armies into loose formation. Overnight I'd managed to rejoin the other Magnentius delegates. We now carved out a space for our party in the ranks among the cavalry officers of the IV Flavia but before too long, the Flavians had jostled forward, obliterating all sense of order in the eager crush.

Above the imperial tent poles, a fierce northern wind sent the open mouths of the Emperor's gold dragon banners, the cylindrical *dracones,* snapping at the breeze. Fixed to the ends of the stage, two placards painted with Chi-Rho insignias twisted and banged against the handrails of steps wreathed in purple silk on both sides.

Nothing seems quieter than thirty thousand or more soldiers standing in rigid silence, broken only by horse's neigh, the intermittent order for attention, a cough here and the wind there whistling through thousands of upright lances.

I imagined that for Constantius, nothing was lonelier than facing us but then I saw the sharpened point of a pike and remembered his cousin Nepotianus' head bleeding from Marcellinus' weapon.

Such men as Constantius couldn't afford human frailties like loneliness.

We heard the bells of Sardica's Christian churches ringing. They chimed on and on, for ten, fifteen, then twenty minutes. Soon it seemed they would be chiming all day. The clanging pounded on my tired temples.

'Why don't they stop?' I asked a centurion next to me.

'It's a feast day. Sardicans will spend today on their knees.'

'For Constantius?'

'The birth of Christ.'

I must have looked too tired or too foreign to take in his meaning, because he repeated more slowly, 'Today is Christ Mass.' He made the Sign of the Cross against his breastplate as if to underscore his message.

Finally the bells swung down to a standstill, leaving echoes for a full minute in our ears. Constantius' praetorians emerged from the imperial tent at last. Now, without straining, I scrutinized the Emperor himself—his long face framed by a short bowl haircut. With his large, heavy-lidded eyes fixed and expressionless, he reminded me of a stronger version of Constans, but with all the prettiness hammered out of him and replaced with builders' concrete.

He led Vetranio and Titianus up the steps to the center of the stage.

The officers at the front of the crowd sent up the salute. Whatever Vetranio's shortcomings in a library, he was obviously a hero in the field. Cheers rolled backward from their ranks and engulfed me like sea waves and then onwards to the foothills behind us. I noticed in the clamor that Titianus stood well back from the two senior men. Constantius put his arm around Vetranio's shoulder and began his oration.

His voice hardly carried to where I stood. Like everyone else, my eyes read the pantomime of embraces and gestures that matched sentences floating back and forth according to the whims of the chilling breeze.

' ... for reasons I shall make clear ... As you know, for the good of the Empire ... I delayed any course of action ... in the West.'

He went on, but I was heaving a sigh of relief already. So, the treaty was set and global peace secured. Tomorrow we'd head back to Magnentius with the East-West accord in our dispatch bags.

'But last night,' Constantius shouted, 'the shade of my father, the great Constantine, appeared to me ... the corpse of my murdered brother Constans in his arms ... voice called me to avenge ... He forbade me to despair of the republic. He assured me of the success and immortal glory that would crown the justice of my arms ...'

Someone cued a cheer at the front and again, roars and hails of support swallowed up and deafened me, then rolled onwards to the rear and finally subsided. I even saw tears rolling down soldiers' cheeks as Constantius' oratory moved their hearts.

But I had stopped cheering. Something wasn't right. My face flushed at the mention of Constans, though no one there knew his killer stood right there in their midst. Irrational fear deafened me to Constantius' next words, but I felt more than personal alarm. To my horror, the political theatre staged for the troops was veering off our script.

Vetranio removed his purple cloak, dropped to one knee and handed the Emperor the diadem from off his hoary old head.

There was an explosion of noise around me and I lost my footing for a moment as a crush of men cried, 'Death to False Emperors! Death to Constans' killer!' There was a great sound of scraping metal as swords were drawn and the rhythm of blade on shield started up again.

I joined my croaking voice with theirs, 'Death to False Emperors!' Anything else would have triggered a stampede of hobbled boots on my torso for simple disobedience.

Vetranio finished his charade, unbuckling his thick sword belt and laying his weapon in its battered scabbard at the Emperor's boots. Stiff as a living statue, the Emperor laid his palm on Vetranio's cowering head with one hand. With the other, Constantius saluted his army, now trebled in size thanks to the capitulation of our erstwhile 'ally.'

We were trapped. I tried to calculate the distance to my horse. Should we wait for Titianus to rejoin us in defeat, or muster the group without him for a dash back over the mountain road towards Naissus?

Even riding in twenty-four relays at twice the speed of our fast-march here, using my *agens* permits and pulling every string of privilege, we couldn't reach safety in the West for at least four days, maybe five.

I needn't have bothered. My horse and travelling sack were gone, confiscated. As I searched for them with frantic speed, I was spotted and pointed out to two Dacians under a tribune's watchful eye. Within the hour of Constantius' public condemnation of Magnentius, they had gagged and dragged me straight out of the vast camp for the imperial palace in Sardica.

⚜⚜⚜

'It was so very kind of you to come to us, Marcus Gregorianus Numidianus. The Emperor would have had us wasting months chasing you through the wilds of Gallia or the slums of the Subura. Speak up. Where are you?'

Paulus 'The Chain' Catena had entered our subterranean Hades. He was moving among us prisoners in the dark. I'd heard his voice as the guards let him pass through the corridor of cells until he arrived at our door. It opened and then clanged closed behind them. In the blackness it took me only seconds to identify a voice I hadn't heard in so many months.

When I realized who it was, I shrank back against the slimy rock. My slave's training to virtually melt into the walls unseen was letting me down now when it mattered most.

So far, I'd seen out two days and nights in this pit of death, measured not by a single changing ray of light but by the arrival of coarse bread tossed through a grate on the floor.

I'd had time to think. When had Vetranio decided to betray Magnentius? From the moment we'd left his Sirmium tent, or earlier? Had Constantia returned to threaten or flatter the old fool? Or had he intended from the very first, even before we arrived, to convert our overtures into Constantinian gratitude?

Catena held out a flaming torch at the height of his sword hilt to guide his steps between the shit and groaning bodies. The blinding flame lit up my fellow unfortunates, one by one, as the Hispaniard's heavy boots trudged past their terrified eyes.

Until now, the pitch black of the jail had been a sort of blessing, sparing us the sight of each other and offering a pathetic privacy to our suffering. On all sides, men retched and shat where they crouched their fleshless bones. After only three days, I was coming to recognize fellow inmates by their particular smells but at least I didn't have to see what torture and starvation had done to them and was going to do to me. I'd retired into what most men did with such a living death and tried to sleep away the hours or recite poetry to myself, remembering safer, happier days back home in Roma.

About ten feet from my hiding spot, Catena thrust his torch closer to the face of a prisoner who started shrieking, 'No, NO, not HIM!' Catena's flame swept back and forth only inches from the victim's face. Instead of teeth, all that remained in the poor man's mouth were gums crusted thick with blood. His chest was covered with smeared gore as well.

Catena moved on.

There were five or six other men in the darkness not far from the corner I'd fought hard for because the dirt floor where the rocky walls met was slightly softer and higher, a little nest of debris and dust. From all corners of the low-ceilinged chamber, vomit and piss ran in streams to the center of the cell. Those with limbs too broken or diseased were left there in the foul pools. But all of us suffered from the freezing draft that stabbed like sharpened rods right through the rocky wall.

I'd been detained before—as a runaway slave in Vegesela, North Africa—but at least that jail had had a single window that allowed prisoners to look at the ankles and shoes of passersby in the marketplace outside. This was not so much being jailed as buried alive. Of course, we had no need of light if we were, for all intents and purposes, already dead.

As Catena's torch inched nearer, I covered my face with my hands, but that was enough to give me away. My limbs were far too clean and unbruised to belong to a long-term resident of Hades.

Catena crouched low and wrapped his fist around my collar, half-strangling me with the twists of my tunic.

'Hello, Numidianus. You're the man we hope to present to Constantius. You're the assassin who robbed him of a brother and a co-emperor.'

'That's a rumor. Gaiso led that expedition. Ask Gaiso how Constans died.'

'I don't have to. Did you forget I was up in Treverorum when Gaiso rode south from Augustodunum for the Pryenes? You were riding right along behind. And next thing we knew, the Emperor was no more, thanks to *you*, I heard.'

My *agens* papers had been torn away, along with my satchel, *spatha* and *pugio*, belts, armor, and cloak. My treasured Pannonian hat, the formal gift of Gregorius on the day of my manumission from slavery, was stolen or lost back in the massive tent camp with my bedroll and cooking kit. I felt a wave of naked despair. Was there any point in arguing?

'Try talking while you still can,' Catena said.

'Where's Titianus?'

'Your delegation marched westward the same day as Vetranio's abdication.'

'Where is my *agens* insignia? My *Cursus* papers? They prove I'm neutral.'

'Neutral nothing. You're the ex-slave of Commander Gregorius, his freedman, nothing more than discarded family property. You still do their dirty work for them, Emperor-Killer.'

'You want Gaiso and you'll never find him here. I'm protected by imperial law.'

'So you are, like all the other citizens here.' He laughed as he waved his torch behind him to display the dying sprawled around the cell. If they didn't have rights, they'd already be dead.'

'A soldier follows commands. An *agens* goes where he's posted.'

'So he'd better choose the winning side. We'll get a confession out of you soon enough.' Catena got up from his crouch and looked down at me. 'If you say you don't know my reputation, you'll hurt my feelings.'

Catena's guard yanked me up and together they dragged me out of the dank pit into a corridor carved whole out of solid stone. Then we entered a tunnel lined with granite blocks lit only by wall torches. I heard screams echoing off the wet damp stone. Dizzying flames blinded me and I stumbled as my boots dragged through cold puddles too dark to identify as blood or rainwater.

The guard unlocked a door and we entered a small chamber, lit by two torches set in the walls. I stared at a set of three huge wooden tubs. Each lid had a hole large enough for a man's head. I saw a large hive of insects sitting on the lid of one. The buzzing and shifting waves of shiny black backs and tiny wings was like a lump of molten lava.

Then the whole hive moved. Its mouth opened to emit a low moan. The hive was the head of a man, still barely alive, being consumed alive by flies. Judging by the stench leaking out of his wooden coffin, I guessed that Catena's victim was swimming in his own rising shit. Thick white maggots coursed out through a crack at the top of the tub and moved down the side in a determined path for the floor.

'I see the unmistakable look of admiration crossing your face, Numidianus. I learned my trade on the Persian border,' Catena. He favored me with a smile from that oddly small mouth of his. 'The Sassanids are more artful than any other people in obtaining information.'

'The law forbids torturing anyone but slaves or foreigners. I'm a freedman. You're the criminal, Catena.'

'You'll confess.'

'It appears your other customer hasn't talked yet.' I fought back my rising terror, which blocked out any intelligent search for escape.

'Oh, I never asked this man anything. He didn't do anything wrong. He doesn't know anything. He doesn't even know my name. He's just a slave. I bought him to keep in practice for bigger prizes like you.'

He suddenly slapped me hard across the mouth. 'Take off your boots. You wouldn't want to get them dirty.'

He glanced at his guard as if to promise him my footwear as a tip for services rendered.

This was my only chance but there were two of them, fully armed. Each bootlace was reinforced with thin gold wire. Garroting one might hold back the other. Catena expected a lace in my hand, not a knife, and there was no time to swivel out my concealed weapon in front of two men. The guard had turned away. He was rolling one of the empty tubs forward. Four bolts held down the lid. He released the first one, but the second was rusted down by damp.

I unthreaded my right lace and laid it on the ground, then held the other and stood up, an end in each hand and then made to faint towards Catena, falling on his breast. He pushed me away and then gurgled with the realization that his thick neck was caught in the loop of my garrote. I pulled it tight around his neck just short of strangling him. While he gurgled for help and his frantic fingers tried to work their way underneath the wire, I kneed him hard right up between his legs. He tumbled and I grabbed the other lace, wrapping it over and over around his wrists so tight, a vein burst and spurt blood all over his uniform.

The guard had turned around and pulled his sword. I finally had got Apodemius' knife in my hand, blade out, but it was no use against the *spatha*'s deadly reach. So I held its razor-sharp blade against Catena's muscle-bulging neck and faced off with the guard.

'An *agens* carries other proofs of his training besides insignias,' I said to them. 'Drop the sword or Catena dies now.' The torturer's blood was flowing fast from under the wiry bootlace. I didn't want to kill one of the Emperor's most senior officers—another unlooked-for crime on my record—and I was in luck. The guard didn't want to end up in a tub himself. He halted, unsure what to do. Catena's words were too garbled to understand.

'Drop those down the hole,' I told him. 'No, the one with the flies.'

He dropped his *pugio* and *spatha* down the neck hole of the slave's barrel of shit. An angry swarm of flies flew up and clouded the air around us.

The instant I felt I had a second of advantage, I dropped the gagging Catena on the honey-slimed stones at the guard's feet. I stripped Catena's weapons for myself, and with one in each hand, made a dash for it.

I slipped and banged down a nightmare maze of low corridors and short steps leading to yet more tunnels and turns. Panting, I slid out of the granite passages into tunnels with rough rocky walls. I stayed out of sight as best I could and listened over my panicked breathing for any sounds of their chase. I heard dripping water, screams, but no boots running after me. I hesitated more than once, fearful any minute of hitting a dead end carved into impassable rock.

Then I heard another, terrifying sound. It was the barking of dogs and the rattle of chains. Catch dogs or bay dogs, whichever, I knew what they could do. Which was safer—to seek out the light and be arrested, or get trapped down here in the pitch-blackness by ravenous dogs?

How many animals could I kill with a *pugio* in one hand and a *spatha* in the other? How many men held their leashes?

Catena's guard had sent up a cry for help but for the moment, I figured, he'd brought in other guards to help save Catena's life. If they weren't hurrying after me, they must have assumed that I'd trapped myself. It was a chilling realization. And just then I hit a wall, hard. I ran my hands in front of me. I was facing an impenetrable wall of wet and solid stone.

The only course was to backtrack and risk getting closer to them, but it was my only hope to discover some exit to freedom. There must be other ways out. Dogs would be the end of me and they'd be on me soon. I felt my way back until a narrow passage opened up on my right. I took it—I had no choice—and followed the dim haze of flickering oil lamps on a slight incline of the gravel-strewn tunnel.

The passage widened slightly, but as far as I could guess, this might lead to the women's cells, more torture chambers or a funeral pit for the dead torture victims. The stench was growing overpowering, tempered only by the indifferent chill of mossy rock. At this point, all I had to go on was my nose and fingers to lead me forward. My ears kept the sounds of screams behind me. I wouldn't be able to run faster, even if I knew the way, in flopping boots with no laces.

But the dark made me nearly canine, as I depended on my nostrils for survival. Suddenly the scent made me nearly faint. I had reached a pit filled with the corpses of torture victims, some still recognizable as human and others mere hills of unspeakable rot. And trapped there, I heard eager panting, claws tapping on stones.

Suddenly there in the dark, two dogs rounded the dark turning in the tunnel. They bared their gums at me with hungry grins and satisfied barks.

I had no choice. I backed away from them slowly and reached into the foulness at my heels. I selected the freshest piece of flesh to offer them and reeling with disgust, I tossed it at their paws. I was lucky. It was just the sort of menu they had been raised on. As their heads dipped down to fight over the generous morsel of limb, I dodged and ran past them, frantic for another exit.

I must have scrambled back for a minute or two when my fingers fell into an open space—some turning that offered a new direction. Now my desperate nose picked up a very different smell scent. It was both civilized and nauseating, the smell of sweet bath oil mingled with nervous sweat—belonging to neither man nor woman.

I tracked it like one of Gaiso's dogs, raising my chin and drinking in the fetid air for any whiff.

The smell faded and I was lost again. I stopped for breath, a fool in a maze of frozen tunnels dripping with winter's thaw from above. I blinked, but there was still no helpful light. I threw my head back and rested against the nubbly rock. Then I worked forward again, inhaling more deliberately now, regular and deep.

I caught another whiff.

Someone had been down here recently and I was working my way back to the entrance they'd used. I spent more minutes, slipping along, bent over, desperate not to lose their track. Then I hit it—a wooden door, unlatched from my side, but hooked closed on the other, giving on to a room just visible through the crack between door and frame.

I heard nothing on the other side.

I laid down Catena's weapons for an instant and slipped the thinnest blade I had on my swivel knife into the space and worked the latch up and off the hook fixed on the other side. Taking up the weapons again, I heaved my shoulder at the heavy door. It hit the resistance of a thick wall hanging. I wrenched the tapestry aside and nearly fell onto the flagstones of a large room. I squinted for a moment, blinded and scrabbling forward, swinging Catena's *spatha* against all comers in the open air.

'I'm sorry, Numidianus, but you don't have an appointment.'

Eusebius stood in the center of the room, holding a handkerchief to his nose, his egg-yolk eyes bulging out at me.

'Will you help me?' I held the sword directly at his soft chest. 'Or send me back to Catena's *carnificina* for monsters down there?'

The chamberlain walked around me and re-bolted the door to the underground passage. He replaced the heavy tapestry.

'Catena is an unpleasant freak of nature, isn't he? Coming from me, that's saying something. Nonetheless, he does his job, his way.'

'He has no right, no right.

'Follow me.'

Only then did I discover it was night. We padded and shuffled side by side through the shadows of a side passage in the Sardica imperial compound. For his size and heft, the soft-bellied man moved like silk. He pushed me into a small office, more a porter's cubicle than a room, and slammed the door against intruders.

'You would go back to the usurpers' camp?'

'I have no choice in the matter. It's my posting. I serve the Empire. That's where the government of the West is now.'

'They're doomed now that we have Vetranio. The Roman world will never bow to a barbarian slave's grandson.'

'If that is the dark message I must deliver, so be it, especially as Titianus will try to paint the painful truth purple.'

'You value the truth?'

'It will be hard to tell it.'

'But you have friends on that side, don't you? Treasonous loyalties, I hear.'

'I said, I serve the Empire.'

'You'd do better to say you serve *me*.' Eusebius was powerful but vanity gave him away, like the inch of fine rose linen peeking out below the hem of his brown brocade robe.

'Do you know what Apodemius says about you?' I choked on the fumes from an incense burner somewhere just outside the door.

'I'd give a lot to know,' Eusebius said, turning his wide girth in a half circle and pulling aside his heavy skirts to rest his wide hips on a stool.

I wasn't fooled by his lazy manner. I kept my weapons readied. 'He says Constantius II has *some* influence over you.'

Eusebius gave a high-pitched giggle. 'He flatters me.'

'Why would you want me to serve *you*?'

'Perhaps I should say *help* me. You freedmen are so touchy about who and what you serve.'

I took a deep breath as my wits came into focus through the subsiding fear and panic of the chase. 'Help me and you help yourself, Your Excellency.'

'Why? How?' He ran a fat finger across his thick upper lip.

'Surely the great Chamberlain sees the obvious. Paulus Catena wants my confession to murdering Constans to feed the Emperor's terror of assassins that you so carefully keep at a constant simmer. With me as the prize, Catena proves he's on the watch at all times, the more valuable man. He displaces you as the favored confidant.'

'Then why don't I just turn you myself and win the game?'

'Catena won't let such a trophy slip into your lap unchallenged. The Emperor won't believe you captured me yourself, not while Catena bears the deep cut of my strangulation and more than one guard as witness.'

'Oh. That's tedious.' He waved the handkerchief as if he'd lost a toss in a Knucklebones game. 'All right,' he said at last. 'Men in my debt are more useful than men in graves but I warn you—I always collect my debts. I can think of uses for you, but first, I will have to hide you for some time. Catena will have every exit post from Sardica on alert . . .'

Chapter 15, Constantia's Boy

—March 15, 351 AD, The Castra Peregrina—

'Catena survived, just, but you must've cut him deep. I hear his voice is ruined forever.'

The old man lay on his sagging couch, his long tunic lifted up to his gnarled knees. His deaf attendant was rubbing some resinous liniment into the joints that, from where I sat, looked swollen into balls of painful bone. 'From now on, his revenge will be as personal as it is political.'

'Yes, *Magister*. Catena had already set up checkpoints and spies on every official road, cart track and goat path out of Sardica. Eusebius kept me hidden for two months working as a slops boy in a brothel—the last place Catena would search.'

'A brothel? Why is that?' Apodemius never missed a chance to add something to his dossiers.

'Because the beast uses the girls at that very house every week. He wouldn't look for me under his very nose, but I saw their bruises. I heard their screams.'

'Was the price very high?'

'He can afford what he wants.'

Apodemius rolled his eyes and I flinched.

'No, Numidianus, I'm asking you for the Chamberlain's price for letting you go.'

'For letting me go?'

'Yes, Marcus Gregorius Numidianus. What deal did you make with Eusebius that he would let you escape?'

Apodemius gestured his thanks to the masseur and rose with a grunt from the couch. He wriggled his distended toes back into the cowhide slippers worn so thin they were like a second skin. The servant packed up his ointments, bowed, and closed the door behind him.

I had hoped Apodemius wasn't going to ask me that question. I stood there, washed, shaved and fed, but still haggard and bruised by weeks of struggling back to the West without money, friends or road permits. I had hoped to be excused from the inevitable debriefing long before it came to this.

Now I realized that 'this' was the point of Apodemius' midnight summons.

'Then let me tell you.' Apodemius pulled on his outer robe and walked to the window. He paused, as if listening for something outside. 'Eusebius threatened you.'

'Not exactly.'

'Then he kept you prisoner in that Sardica brothel for his own purposes.'

'He never touched me—!'

'Oh, don't be ridiculous! I meant to serve his ambition, not his appetite for, well, whatever interests that oddity. Why did he let you go?'

'Well, *Magister*, I warned Eusebius that Catena wanted my corpse and confession to gain favor with Emperor Constantius over himself. So he sent me back.' I shoved to the back of my mind my secret vow to that wily mound of perfumed lard back in Sardica.

Apodemius turned away from the window. 'If only life were as sweet as a eunuch's perfume, Numidianus. I suggest another explanation. I believe Eusebius sent you back here to spy on me for him.'

'I beg your pardon?'

'To spy *on me*.'

Nobody got a lie past the old man, so I said nothing.

'Oh, don't waste my time! I'm expecting enough bad news tonight as it is. You agreed, I suppose. Didn't you?'

'Yes, *Magister*.' My shoulders flagged. 'I vowed to report on your service.'

He rubbed his gnarled hands together. 'You're cleverer than I thought, African. Now the game gets interesting.'

'You really believe I would betray the *agentes* to Eusebius?'

'Of course not! I'm going to do it for you.'

He returned to his desk and got out a tablet to take notes. 'Now I will decide what corrupted information to send east. You give me all the details on how—code words, signals, whatever you two agreed—so I can carry on while you're put to better uses.' He waved his knobby knuckles at me. 'Sit down, for gods' sake.'

I half-collapsed with relief onto the stool opposite his desk while he jotted down my arrangements with Eusebius. While he scribbled lines in the wax, I mumbled, 'I hope these better uses for me are more than serving as a contemptible decoy.'

Apodemius laid down his stylus and uttered a knowing 'Ah.'

'Roxana's reports were twice the thickness of my own. She's bedding Silvanus, whispering your policies into his ear, as if she were the Oracle to the great Julius Caesar himself and . . . she treats me with utter contempt.'

'It's your own fault, Numidianus, for putting yourself in the limelight with Marcellinus. Once he had decided you were an obstruction, I could only make use of your, shall we call it, "youthful glow"? That girl's got a difficult job. Without you, she hasn't a true friend in that court. Don't resent her. Was that a bell?' He cocked his ear towards the window again.

'No, *Magister*.'

'Well, it's the Ides of March. Maybe it makes me a little jumpy.'

I doubted that, but only said, 'So then, what's my mission now?'

'With Vetranio's betrayal, Constantius has now equaled Magnentius' troop strength. Did you spot the *cataphracti* modifications Constantius has copied from kidnapped Persian forces?'

'Yes, *Magister*. An astonishing sight. Even the horses are draped in mail to the knees. No arrow could find an inch of flesh to pierce.'

'I've had secret sketches sent to me. Are these accurate?' He fumbled through mountains of fresh reports with his painfully clawed fingers and unrolled an ink drawing in front of me.

I leaned over by the light of an oil lamp.

'Yes, that's close, but the armor is more like woven chain and covers even the riders' toes and hands, so flexibly that he can bend his fingers. The armor also hangs lower on the horse, down to here. The riders carry maces, swords and axes as well, loaded back here or over here, the carrier fixtures hitched to one of the four saddle horns. The champrons obscure the horse's whole face, not just his cheeks.'

'Formidable.'

'And terrifying for other horses not used to it. The only disadvantage is when this man is knocked to the ground. I saw it in an exercise in Sardica when we first arrived. A lighter rider can hop back into the saddle, but not a man encased up to his armpits.' I thought back to the drills I'd watched as we settled into camp that frigid morning. 'On the other hand, it's quite hard to knock the rider off because he's carrying the *contus*.'

Apodemius raised a questioning eyebrow.

'It's longer than the normal lance, *Magister*, as long as a barge pole. It requires both hands to wield. So this rider has no shield. He relies only on the grip of his knees to keep his seat and direct his horse.'

'That must require much training.'

'Yes, but it's almost impossible to get within reach of him with any regular weapon.'

Apodemius sighed. 'I see. Constantius has stolen every trick of the Sarmatians and Sassanids to modernize his side. He might actually have a choice—to resume the campaign against Shapur or take on Magnentius.'

I remembered Kahina, weeping as she gazed down on me from the high window. I had not seen her now for over three months. Perhaps she had sensed the coming danger, even then.

'With all respect, *Magister*, Constantius can't leave the East undefended. As long as there's a Persian challenge there, Magnentius has got time to consolidate his reforms. I know he's trusting that Caesar Decentius will get on top of barbarian raids in the northeast. Justina will come of age within a year or two and maybe there will be a Constantine bun in the oven in time.'

Apodemius fingered a roll of expensive *vitulinum* in his stack of reports but said nothing.

'Peace might still take root, *Magister*. The Empire might heal under two emperors or even more, just as the Great Diocletian ordained—' I was pleading now, but at Apodemius' dour expression, I cut myself off.

'I fear it is increasingly unlikely.'

'Apodemius, why do you do anything to support a usurper in the West when Constantius has the claim of legitimate succession on his side?'

'I was wondering when you would ask me that, Numidianus. And I'll tell you. Succession hasn't always been everything. You know your history. For one thing, Roman tradition holds that the approval of the imperial army is almost as good as a divine right, if honestly earned. And second, because the centuries bring change and we must change with them. The barbarian commanders have become the undeniable backbone and muscle of the Western forces, whether Roma likes it or not.'

'There are times I watch these northerners and feel their fresh energy, the way their irreverence for the old ways gives them a freedom but also an unpredictability that alarms Romans like Gregorius or even that shit Titianus,' I said.

'There is no snuffing out the candle marking the passing of time, Numidianus. Personally, I'm not so sure about this Christian cult. It may spread or just die out. But the new citizens of barbarian stock are woven deep now, as deep as the threads in my tunic, into our society's cloth. Only ... this Franco-Breton, this Magnentius, may have moved too fast and too soon. His sponsor Marcellinus misgauged the moment—but not by much.'

He turned away from the window and examined my thoughtful expression. 'You realize your ex-master Gregorius is probably doomed now, don't you?'

'No. No. Surely there is hope for peace?'

'Hopes hangs by a thread, and only as long as the tension holds between Constantius and Shapur, first, and second, no one else in the West defects in the meantime.'

'Who might defect?'

Apodemius hobbled forward with fresh eagerness. 'Now that, Marcus, that is for you to tell me. I've read your reports, very carefully, as well as those of Roxana and other *agentes* in the field.' He pointed to the wide map above us on the wall. Now I saw all the pins of the northwestern and southwestern forces had shifted far to the southeast of Gallia, leaving swathes of unpunctured space on the upper Rhenus, and the coast of Britannia with no pins at all.

'I've narrowed the risk down to one of the leading commanders—Gaiso, Silvanus, or your dear ex-master. Gaiso is Constans' true killer. Oh, I know you wielded the blade, but he was the hunt master. He's impetuous and passionate but not likely to suddenly swing the other way. He knows he has no chance of securing friends in the East.'

'Silvanus?'

'For her part, Roxana reports that Silvanus is cautious, but loyal. That leaves one man who might tip the balance, one man so angered by the murder of his father and so true to the values and loyalties that built this Empire, including loyalty to the imperial line, he might change his mind. A defection would tip the balance, and Constantius might launch a wave of painful and crippling reprisals destroying the military leadership of the West.'

'Gregorius. You're asking me to catch out Gregorius in treason?'

'It may never cross his mind. I'm asking you to protect the Empire. I recall your earlier request for an assignment close enough to Roma to protect the Manlius House from corruption and theft. I persuaded you then that you could better protect that clan by sticking close to Gregorius.'

'But now you're asking me to betray my own—?'

'I'm asking you to monitor him night and day. At the first sign of communication with Constantius, at *any* hint that he's thinking of leading troops to the other side and tipping the scales of power, you know *what you have to do*. For the sake of thousands upon thousands of innocent people, this stalemate must force a negotiated resolution, or—' his long white fingers brushed the game board on a side table. All the black pieces toppled over.

'You can't ask me to—!'

Apodemius never raised his voice. Worse, when you roused his anger, he hissed like steam from an ironforger's oven. He'd been agitated and distracted all evening. Now he lost his temper as I'd never seen before. 'You signed up with this service to *obey* orders, to *protect* the mails and roads, to *ferret* out the truth, to *escort* the high and the low, even traitors into exile, and *to execute on command*, if necessary—all in the interests of keeping this Empire whole. That's why imperial law protects you from prosecution—'

'I know, *Magister*, but—'

'Did you think that particular clause in your contract was just decoration?'

'I swear, I'd kill myself first before laying a hand on the Commander.'

'You still talk like the slave you once were. I tell you, you'll do what a *Manlius* would do—they raised you, didn't they? May I remind you that if it came down to the survival of the Roman Empire, Atticus Manlius Gregorius wouldn't hesitate to run you through?'

⚜⚜⚜

Later that evening, I finished off a bottle of very rough red and a reheated chickpea stew in the back cubicle Verus called home. Cheap, salmon-colored emulsion flaked off his plaster walls. Worn out reed mats stained with fish sauce and lamp oil covered his humble floor.

Otherwise, his tiny space was immaculate. It was bad enough to cross the slums of Subura with sewage and shit dropping on your head from the cheap apartments of the wretched *insulae* leaning over the street. The best Roman families made sure that, once inside their gates, life was fragrant. The Manlius townhouse had running water piped straight into the atrium fountain, thanks to thirty-five miles of ancient aqueduct running from the mountains north of the city. Lady Laetitia had always made sure her household made use of it. The servants' quarters were kept clean and healthy. Every week she inspected our basins, chamber pots and pallet mattresses for vermin or lice.

I couldn't speak for the slaves working here now, but I could see Verus had helped his new mistress, Lady Kahina, maintain the old standards as best they could. Coming from Numidia, where the air was dry and disease was rare, she no doubt had been shocked at Roma's fetid valley slums and turd-strewn walks.

'It was no use. I couldn't budge him. We could hear those bastards coming up the street, savages they was, neighbors screaming for help and all. I tried to carry him off, I did, I promise, Marcus, but he wouldn't have it. Said he was going to stay and fight'em off. I told him to lock hisself into his study at the back and don't let nobody in, but I swear, Marcus, I tried to get the Senator out the back with the others.'

'I know, Verus.'

We sat for a long minute in sorrow. Verus didn't think I noticed him wiping his eyes with his threadbare sleeve. I went for more of the cheap wine reserved for the servants. When I returned, his voice had returned to normal.

'After the ceremony at the mausoleum, that there Clodius skipped off, "to see to the farms," he told the Commander.'

'So Clodius is getting a little dirt under his nails at last?'

Verus sniffed. 'He's measuring out vineyards to sell off, if you ask me, just as soon as he can lay hands on those deeds.'

'How's the little boy doing? I wish he were here, so I could see him.'

'Oh, a miracle child, that's what he is! Lavinia says he can already count up to twenty!'

'No kidding. He's not even two years old.'

'He'll be reading before you know it.'

'Are the Senator's books still there or did the creep sell them off?'

'I locked up the library, with the master's permission, before Clodius got back from Ostia.'

'Very wise. More?' I filled his pottery cup to the brim. 'You keep all the keys safe?'

'All but one the Lady L wore on her finger, sort of a little ring-key, folded over, in the style society ladies thought was fashionable in the old days.'

'But surely Gregorius knows where the deeds are kept?'

'Maybe, maybe not. He's not saying. The Senator was in charge of the estates' income. Lady Laetitia ran the household. The master was always fighting on the frontier. He probably thought he'd catch up on all the family account books when he retired and put on some fancy politician's robes. Nobody saw this disaster coming until it was too late, that's for sure.'

'That's what the Greats always warn us.'

'Yeah, well, with all respect for your learning, my boy, you don't have to listen to a bunch of airy-fairy Greek poems being shouted on the street corner to know that the Fates can strike you down, just like that—if you don't keep a lookout.' He tapped the skin under his right eye. 'Ol' Verus, here, he's on the watch. The master and his new lady can count on me, their own personal Cerberus, guarding their gates.'

Not long after that, we two called it a night. It was too late to trudge back to the Castra, so I bunked down in my mother's old room, displacing a sullen slave boy who slept rough on the floor. Perhaps by returning to my childhood room, I hoped to shrug off the awful responsibilities set on my grown shoulders by Apodemius in his office on the Caelian Hill.

I knew what I would do and wisely, Apodemius had not actually forbidden it. I'd warn Gregorius of my assignment and urge him to lie low if things broke in the wrong direction. With that resolution for flimsy comfort, I managed to doze off.

It must have been around the sixth hour of the night, when the moon is highest, that bells rang out across the vast city, echoing from hill to hill and reverberating off the side of the great arena.

I went out into the corridor. Verus' door stood open and I heard his footsteps padding across the marble leading to the entrance vestibule. I followed him out to the gate and we slid the bolt.

'What's the racket?' Verus yelled down the street to a servant peeking outside his own gate. From one gate to the next, slaves and porters stuck their heads into the night, rubbing the sleep from their eyes and listening to the pealing bells.

'Ludo's run down to the temple to see,' cried a woman, still adjusting her *stola* over her mussed-up hair. 'Is that you, young Marcus? How's the freedman's life treating you, love? Come here. Well, I must say, you're a sight, you African bastard, you! I'll remember to watch my honey cakes now that I know you're back prowling the alley outside my kitchen!'

Verus and I stood there without any cloaks, feeling the spring night's breeze tossing our hair. We waited. The bells finally stopped. The vast city fell back to rest.

'Well, that was a big nothin',' Verus shrugged. 'For a minute I was scared silly that it was another fire breaking out.' He was just about to bolt the gate behind us when we heard feet pounding up the street. Little Ludo had brought back news.

'There's a new Caesar,' he said, panting. 'A rider just came in from the East and woke up the Senate.'

'A new Caesar? Who?' I was about to grab him by his tunic front, but checked myself.

'Constantius has crowned his cousin Gallus. He's made him the new Caesar of the East!'

Verus shrugged. 'Fancy that! Gallus who? I thought he killed all his relatives in their beds when the old man died.'

I shut my eyes and forced down my anxious breathing. 'No, Verus. The army got orders from Constantius to massacre everyone who could threaten him or his two brothers, including two uncles and six cousins, which left his two brothers—'

'Constantine II and Constans—' At least little Ludo knew that much.

'And three boys too young to stage a challenge, youngsters like you, Ludo. You know what happened to Nepotianus. Gallus was eleven, so now he must be . . . about twenty-five.'

'Were the little boys brothers? Who's the other one?'

'Half-brothers. The younger one was Julian. They were locked up for years with a bunch of eunuchs standing guard. No one knew they were still alive.'

'But that doesn't make sense!' Ludo's face suddenly wrinkled up.

'And why not?' Verus looked ready to reprimand the boy.

'How can he marry his aunt? Euuuw! She must be an old bag!'

'What're you saying, Ludo?'

'Well, that's the rest of the news from Antiochia. "The Caesar Gallus has been joined in matrimony to the *Augusta* Constantia, widow of the great Hannibalianus and sister of the *Dominus* Constantius II".'

So Apodemius had got warning of this somehow. He'd been preoccupied by rumors hinting at this. *I'm expecting enough bad news tonight as it is.* He was waiting all evening, listening for bells at his window for confirmation of this grotesque turn of events—an embittered young widow swooping a boy just out of house arrest into her royal bed.

I didn't even try to go back to bed myself. I'd lost my gear in Sardica, so packing up a new kit with supplies scavenged secondhand at the Castra over the past week didn't take long.

I squinted into the rising sun as I tightened the harness on a fresh horse plucked from the relay pack at the Porta Collina. I double-checked my new identity papers and slipped them into my satchel next to thick packets of documents addressed to all points east.

'Good ride, Numidianus,' the stable boy said. 'Sestus said to tell you, he's sure grateful for the lie-in this morning.' He gave a last brush to the horse's flanks. 'There's something in there for the Emperor Magnentius himself.'

Emperor Magnentius, yes, but for how long?

I galloped through Roma's garden suburbs at reckless speed. Apodemius' warning had become reality in a matter of hours. Constantius had tied up the problem of his ambitious, angry sister and the threat of the ferocious Shapur in one nasty package. What was the use of has-beens like old Vetranio, now that Constantia had a fresh Constantine of her own to whip about and Constantius had an energetic new Caesar to guard the East—all in one and the same cousin?

Magnentius' opportunity for consolidation had just slammed shut in his face. The last Constantine Emperor had freed his hands for revenge.

CHAPTER 16, AN INTRUDER'S NOTE

—AQUILEIA, LATE JULY, 351 AD—

On my return to my *agens* duties at the fortress in Aquileia, even the ordinary task of managing the imperial post ate up all my waking hours. Each night as I flung myself down on my narrow bed, I tossed a prayer of thanks to Apodemius for relieving me of my duplicitous commitment to Eusebius' purposes. Every other member of the court worked night and day the same way. Through the warming months of March, April, and May we all bustled about our tasks with a preoccupying air that masked unspoken tension.

Time and again, when I tried to snatch a moment alone with Gregorius, he brushed me off in his haste. He had no inclination during these politically uneasy days to be seen associating with any *curiosus* like me. He didn't even inquire where I'd been during my months of absence. The Sardica episode was officially recorded, filed and forgotten. The tribunes who had survived it better than I gave me a wide berth. My escape was suspicious, not to say embarrassing, to those who had abandoned me, but no one had the authority to interfere with my *schola*.

As the summer heat mounted, the women of the palace retreated deeper into their cool and sequestered world of seamstresses, lady's maids and bath attendants. As a rule, I glimpsed very little of Kahina, Roxana or the slender young Empress. I suspect the Emperor himself saw his virgin bride not at all. Once I thought I saw Kahina lingering in a crowded marble corridor that I traversed every morning, but someone called her away before I could greet her.

Eighteen months into his reign, Magnentius had indeed sunk roots into the troubled soil of the West. True to his reputation as a barbarian bull, he scorned the gilt chairs and flapping dragon banners of his Eastern superior, but he indulged his love of horseraces, social baths, loose women and military sport with the gusto of a rugged northerner not exactly born to the purple.

As *Magister Officiorum*, Marcellinus had his greedy hands as full as he wished, liaising with the ranks of civil servants left back in Mediolanum. For the time being, it looked like his butchery of Nepotianus and the Roman senators had slaked his provincial resentments.

He now managed every corner of the West that measured success by coin. Dodging Gregorius' festering anger, he fortified himself by selling off any insignia or positions at hand. Then he invented more honors and ranks and sold those off, too. Clearly, Marcellinus was banking that even the disruption of a looming civil war wouldn't unearth his secret horde of gold back in Augustodunum where his wife safely managed their booming estates.

To make sure everyone knew he disliked getting so rich and powerful, Marcellinus complained nonstop. He condemned uppity Christian bishops controlling ever-bigger estates, dishonest tax commissioners, and hard-bargaining middlemen driving up the price of food and wine handouts for the vast welfare hordes down in the city of Roma.

This summer of anxious peace didn't suit the agitated Lieutenant Commander Gaiso, either. He stayed friendly with me even as Gregorius kept his distance. The brusque horseman took on the job of upgrading and inspecting the arms factories. When he wasn't on the move—this week to see Ticinum's new shields, next week Carnuntum's stronger bows—he was touring with the Commander of the Stables, inspecting the supply and health of the horses. He had to make sure that the equine taxes were buying the best horseflesh possible and not disappearing into the officer's pockets.

I said nothing to the vigorous hunter, but Gaiso's labors left me wondering what difference a sleeker arrowhead or a faster mount could make against Constantius' Persian-style armor encasing the Eastern cavalry from top to toe.

Gregorius liaised with the praetorian prefects running the crush of legions stationed in a wide crescent to the northwest of Roma and up into central Gallia. Restless soldiers, displaced from their usual job of pushing back barbarian border raids, clamored for food, sex and distraction.

As for Magnentius, over recent months, he'd raised more money to throw thousands of fresh German mercenaries—none of them Christians—into the ranks. He was sure that money and barbarian blood would bind their hearts to his standard.

'None of them has ever even seen Roma and never will,' he scoffed. 'But they've seen *me*. Now *I am Roma*.'

Meanwhile, these droves of longhaired warriors strained the resources of town after town. Field workers and slaves suffered in silence but educated Gallo-Romans and Italian city fathers were unnerved by the demands of these vast encampments. Their growing sea of tents lapped like a tide, gaining yards of ground closer and closer to the protective town walls each night. The various city elders sent a constant stream of delegations to Magnentius to beg relief. Aquileia's imperial reception rooms crowded up like provincial meeting halls.

Of course, the Aquileians didn't complain. What wealth still remained in the Western Empire swiftly made their money purses bulge. Quick-thinking food vendors set up lean-tos against the outer walls of the imperial courtyard to sell cool drinks against the midday summer heat. Even the prostitutes were making enough off imperial military traffic to leave off work by mid-morning for a solitary siesta.

In his attempt to avoid constant interruption, Magnentius shifted his morning exercises to a pre-dawn stint of weights and running. He held his dawn council in the privacy and cleansing steam of the imperial baths. I reported daily, twice with the dispatches from Mediolanum and beyond before his main meal and twice again in the afternoon and end of the day.

'It can't hold, Magnentius. Decentius needs help, now.' Gaiso was saying in the baths one hot day. Wearing nothing but a towel, he'd just read a report from the Caesar up on the Rhenus. 'Constantius is funneling gold to these tribes behind our backs in secret. It's a betrayal of his own Empire, but effective. Decentius can't get the upper hand. He needs more forces to push back each time the Alemanni gain ground. They can't break through walls but they besiege the towns with weapons as good as ours.'

'Time to return the legions to their border fortresses?' Marcellinus had finished with his rub down. He tipped his slave well and sat up on his couch. 'This morning's report does it for me. If Constantius spends June in Sardica, I'll wager that's it for the summer. We don't need any blessing if he leaves us alone.'

'Send me back as the head of the northern legions to help Decentius mop it up, *Imperator*,' Gaiso said. For him, hunting any prey—feckless emperor, ferocious boar, or Alemannic chieftain—was better than sitting out the summer on the southern coast like a holiday maker.

'No. It's too soon to lower our defenses,' Gregorius said. 'We have no Constantine heir, the Senate still has empty seats, and Nepotianus' skull may be picked clean but thanks to you, Marcellinus, it still rattles on the gatepost over Roman heads. We must negotiate again.'

Provoked by heat and steam, Gregorius' savage white scars and empty eye socket looked all the more shocking without the pomp of a uniform to dignify them. He pulled a bath sheet tighter around his shoulders as if only he felt a sudden draft chilling the room.

Marcellinus stood up and commanded our attention with both hands on his solid waist. 'Gregorius, exactly what is this peace worth if it bankrupts every merchant and landlord between here and Lugdunum? We end up ruling an empire overrun with Alemanni. They can't read so much as a bar tab, much less a tax bill. As we sit here, the East only gets richer and stronger.'

'Some people in the West are getting rich, too,' Silvanus said, eyeing Marcellinus. He dashed cool water from a bucket over his head and groin. 'So, we send Decentius temporary reinforcements, but no general retreat?'

As usual, General Silvanus was the moderate voice, the man who kept the peace among the councilors. Roxana's reports of Silvanus as the inner circle's calm and steady core matched my own observations. He was always ready to flatter Marcellinus' vanity or soothe Gregorius' seething grief over the Senator. He commanded great loyalty from the thousands of troops he'd added to the rebel side. For his part, Gaiso made it clear that he respected the Frankish general's fighting skills.

I also noticed one other important thing. General Claudius Silvanus only chose battles he was sure to win.

But now, it seemed, none of them might have a choice. As usual, I'd read and memorized the mail in advance for sending the most salient intelligence to Apodemius. And one early June morning, I learned before any of these men running the western world that something momentous had occurred overnight.

Now out of curiosity, I'd lingered almost too long at the bathing conference for a chance to warn Gregorius. With reluctance, I made to leave. I'd reached the passage leading out of the large echoing central pool room when Magnentius looked up from the morning's dispatches and called, 'Wait, *Agens*. Wait over there.'

I sought a bench as far from the furnace flues as possible and watched.

'Constantius has made his move. At last.' He looked up from the report and nodded at each of the rebels, one by one. 'He had moved west and camped halfway between Sardica and the Alps.'

'We blocked the passes. He can't get through,' Gaiso said.

'He's aiming for Atrans. I know it.' Magnentius slapped his naked beefy thigh.

I knew Atrans, a vital and fortified postal hub on the Cursus network between Emona and Celeia. It nestled next to the Sava River coursing down a narrow green Alpine valley marking the border between Italia and Noricum.

'Gaiso is right. Atrans is secured. There's nothing Constantius can do.' Gregorius seemed satisfied with that. I hoped Gaiso was right. I was relieved to think my ex-master was out of danger.

'No, we can do better,' Magnentius said. 'We're not a bunch of helpless girls weaving baskets around a fire. We wait for Constantius at Atrans and wipe him out in an ambush—'

'No!' Gregorius shot to his feet. 'There's no *need* for war.'

'Sit down, Atticus,' Magnentius ordered. 'We're going to finish this, once and for all. We've got every Gaul, Celtic Iberian, Frank and Saxon warrior behind us. We've got the fiercest legions of the Empire, all drawn up and standing ready, right out there! We've got thousands of barbarian auxiliaries and mercenaries chomping at the bit. They came down here because I promised that every prisoner they take will become their personal property, from the generals and commanders to the last javelin thrower, and that all captured baggage and property will be their plunder. They want to see that promise come true.' It was not the heat of the baths that sent the red blood coursing through his cheeks.

'You're not describing civil war. You're describing the end of the world,' murmured Marcellinus. 'For once, I agree with Atticus Manlius Gregorius. To lose such a fight, which we could only take to the bitter end, would be the end of all of us, of everything.'

Magnentius exploded with pent-up energy. 'But we're sure to *win*, Marcellinus! I know what makes men fight. I know how to lead such soldiers—not from the rear like Constantine's cowardly runts, but from the front, like a *true* emperor.'

'So you're resolved?' Gaiso closed his eyes with relief and then leaned forward to shake Magnentius' meaty hand.

'We meet Constantius at Atrans.'

Stark naked, the Emperor of the West strode out of the baths for his offices. His advisers followed one by one, with divided hearts.

₽₽₽

'I will speak to you, Commander, whether you like it or not.'

I had blocked Gregorius from crossing the outer courtyard on his way from a briefing for lower-ranked officers.

'I have no time,' he said. He brushed past me.

'You have no choice, Commander.'

'How dare you!' He kept on striding across the broad pavement towards the offices he shared with Gaiso.

I drew my sword. It was the first time in our long decades together that he looked at me exactly as one man looks at a complete stranger. I was undeterred. 'You will listen.'

He stopped, aghast at the sight of my blade catching the summer sunrays.

'I will listen, Marcus, because then I can prosecute you as a freedman for threatening the very master to whom he still owes allegiance under law. Do your job, whatever it is, and leave me alone.'

'True, I answer to others now, as well as to the memory of your house. And I tell you out of love for that house, Commander, as well as loyalty to the Empire, that if Magnentius fights, the chances are that he will lose. The Manlius family risks ruin. I have seen with my own eyes that Constantius leads a formidable force, not just in numbers—'

'We have more troops by far—'

'Not in armaments. You're *not* balanced in armaments, Commander. The cavalry under Constantius rides like impenetrable statues cast from molten metal hammered out by Zeus himself.'

His eye twitched. He hesitated for an instant before asking, 'You've seen this?'

'In Sardica. Cataphracts they call *clibanarii*. Constantius stole the designs off the Persians, probably by torturing them for information. I saw Constantius' mounted legionaries exercising in these encasements of armor. They were riding and fighting, as flexible and invulnerable as gods.'

'What are you suggesting I do with this information? Warn Magnentius? Or defect out of cowardice?'

'If you only could, Commander, for the sake of Lady Kahina and the child. But if you try to defect, I have orders from the highest authority of my *schola* to stop you—for good. Any defection would shatter the last illusion of a stalemate that's holding the peace by a thread. It would tip the West right into the Emperor Constantius' lap. And too many people support Emperor Magnentius now for the reprisals not to be horrendous. A negotiation from strength is the only hope for peace.'

His face, already twisted by hardened cords of scar, grimaced with irony. 'You seem to have learned an awful lot—'

'At the Senator's knee, Commander.' I bowed my head.

His ruined face crumpled. Despite himself, grief washed across his ruined features. He turned away, stiff with indignation and remorse. If he blamed me for not preventing the Senator's death, I had to ignore it now.

'The only way out, Commander, is a truce that saves the Western Army. Negotiations must go forward.'

'I agree.' He turned back to me, composed again. 'We can only hope that a solid defense at Atrans will set Constantius back on his heels. I'll fight to keep this peace, Marcus. I'm no Gaiso or Silvanus. You know better than any man alive, I have no more eyes or hands to spare.'

I sheathed my sword and knelt on one knee in front of him. 'Commander, I can now add that when ordered to kill you if you defected, I swore I would kill myself first.'

He laid a hand on the back of my neck and fingered the familiar neck cord of my *bulla*. For a moment, I felt he was leaning on me for support. He withdrew his hand and in a kinder tone, asked, 'You loved my father very much, didn't you Marcus?'

'I could not have loved my own grandfather more, Commander.'

I saw the few fingers of his maimed hand clench into a sudden fist, turning the shiny scars white with tension. Then, with a sudden turn of his back, he paced off into the late summer dusk.

☥☥☥

Later that night, footsteps pattered past my sleeping cubicle towards the gate lodge where we kept the dispatch bags under lock and key. I crept out of bed, armed with my small swivel knife hidden up my tunic sleeve. I looked harmless enough, but if someone was trying to tamper with the imperial post, I had to be prepared for a struggle. I took a deep breath, ready to make an arrest that would stick, no matter how ferocious the resistance.

Nobody disturbed our communication lines without paying a painful price.

Through the lodge window, I saw a dark, hooded figure rustling from one spot to another in the shadows. He didn't seem to be stealing anything, because in a minute, he'd slipped back out through the small wooden door, as unencumbered as before. He replaced the latch with the perfect silence of a trained burglar.

I slunk along, following him back through outer courtyard, and then the inner courtyard, sticking close to the walls as we both slipped past dozing sentries and into the imperial palace. It wasn't hard to shadow him in my bare feet as he slipped through the corridors with a surety that told me he was no stranger to these halls himself.

We moved like this for nearly ten minutes, stopping and then continuing on in absolute silence. This was no amateur. He stayed nearly invisible in the gloom, making no sound. Twice I nearly lost him, but a slight movement in the moonlight shining through a window or the shift of a grey shade along a corridor told me he was making his way deeper and closer to the private recesses of the imperial chambers.

If this were an assassin, I'd have to make my move in seconds before he had the time to kill. It was too late to raise the palace praetorians. After months of boredom and summer heat, they had dropped their guard. The intruder was seconds away from gaining access to one of the sleeping commanders.

I dashed forward and cornering him, I lunged and got him to the ground. I pressed my short blade to his neck and ripped off his hood.

Roxana smiled up at me in the dark. 'They should have given you better marks back at the Castra.'

I dropped her and stood up. 'I suppose you've got some explanation. The mailbags are my job.'

She shrugged. 'I can't help it if your hours and mine don't match.'

'What were you stealing?' She made no resistance as I searched her. In fact, she made it seem like an embrace. Suddenly I felt her drawing me close to her with a different kind of urgency.

'Don't play with me, Roxana. Your job is Silvanus.'

'Who says it's fun?' Her voice was a mere whisper.

'It won't last much longer. He'll be leading his forces to Atrans along with the others, I guess.'

'We're not supposed to corrupt our information by comparing notes. Maybe we shouldn't talk at all.'

She pressed her mouth to mine. Her velvety tongue slipped between my lips and began to stroke in and out, a little deeper with each thrust. She opened her cloak. Underneath, she wore little more than a bronze undertunic made of the same imported Cathay silk that the *Augusta* Constantia often wore. I already knew Silvanus bought her jewels, but I saw the general hadn't spared any cost on nightwear, either, for Justina's 'nurse.' This evening, however, all her ornate necklaces and bracelets were removed—for stealth.

I pulled myself away an inch or two. It was hard. 'Roxana, you don't need any more "practice".'

Her eyes shone, desperate and bright. There was a point beyond which any man no longer resisted a woman—the wrong or the right type. I didn't want to reach it.

'Silvanus won't know.' She reached for my waist and ran her hand farther down with such expertise, I wondered if it was a job or not.

Instead, I weakened and let her stroke me into a sweat of desire.

'I can't take you like this, within a few feet of the general's quarters,' I panted.

'You must now, or I *will* tell,' she said, lifting the thin silk above her thighs and rubbing my fingers back and forth between her moist private lips. From then on, I remember only closing my eyes and lifting her slightly so I could sink into pleasure that lasted even longer than I would have predicted.

After many minutes, when we'd finally finished, she steadied herself against the marble wall, smoothed her hair and pulled the hood back over her face. She slipped away towards Justina's wing, still as light and soundless as a passing dream.

The corridor was stone quiet. No one had witnessed the scene. Roxana had seen to it that I wanted nothing now but to collapse my drained body into sleep. I smiled with a vindication of the resentment I'd nurtured since our night together in the Castra Peregrina's dormitory. She *had* enjoyed my touch then, and wanted more.

I slipped back to the lodge to check the latch. I was wrung out, but I wavered. They didn't call us *curiosi* for nothing and I convinced myself that my curiosity was innocent, not professional. It didn't take long for me to check the outgoing mail against the registration book. I found a new letter carrying an unfamiliar address—a Greek tavern, of all things.

Maybe Roxana had some little brother hidden away or even a nest egg of a business starting up. I knew how to open letters without damage—we all did—but I needed wax to reseal it.

I carried her letter back to my room and felt it from side to side. There was an inner envelope. I took an impression of her seal with wet plaster, and then loosened the wax with a candle

233

flame. With patience and care, I worked the inner envelope free. There was no proper address. I opened the letter itself and saw only one line of code.

I worked for two hours or more at breaking her code, but it was only after the first pink glint of a summer dawn that I realized with horror, I'd known the key all along.

I thought back to the notes I'd left with Apodemius and checked my small notebook from Roma. Then I tackled her letter with ease.

It read, 'Ambush in Atrans.' I glanced again at the inner envelope. A few faint penstrokes of code deciphered made the letter, 'E.'

So, she was reporting to Eusebius under Apodemius' supervision, just as I was. I shook my head at the old man's counter-intelligence web. But if so, why was she writing the eunuch the truth? Against all my training, I burned it. We'd talk about it first chance.

Troubled, I lay down on my bed. I put a linen cloth over my eyes to block the first morning sun but something was wrong. I felt my neck, then my shirt and then turned my uniform and private pouch inside out.

My *bulla* was gone.

CHAPTER 17, JUSTINA'S NOTE

—AQUILEIA, AUGUST 351 AD—

The summer heat grew unbearable to those who hadn't endured an African childhood, so now the court started work well before dawn. I was comfortable enough. The heat reminded me of returning to my homeland in 347 under Gregorius' command. The Numidian noon there sent our European federates panting for the shade of their tents. Even the pack mules rested in the meager shade of the olive trees.

The next few weeks found Magnentius back in his element again. He shoved horseracing touts and whores aside for military tacticians and physical trainers. He rode off with Gaiso to inspect the legions stationed within reach of Aquileia. General Silvanus and Commander Gregorius liaised with the Caesar Decentius along the Rhenus to interrogate *legati* and their tribunes in command of the legions farther out.

My workload doubled as the council's marching orders flew west, north and south by twenty-four hour courier relays. We beefed up the regular postal staff with secondments from army riders, coordinated with military checkpoints to register all communications and tightened up *evectio* inspections to keep the state roads as clear as possible.

Magnentius ordered a unit of cavalry and engineers to move forward off immediately for the fortress at Atrans. They would extend its defensive walls into an impassable roadblock spanning the entire pass. Next to leave were units of archers and specialists in the repeat-action ballistae, both equipped with sulphur-tipped weapons that water only made burn all the hotter.

Gregorius selected army scouts and signal experts from among Illyrians who knew the Sava River region well. They rode off next, to secrete themselves beyond Atrans in a string of signal stations along the hilltops towards Celeia. They would relay alerts of the enemy's approach to our central command.

As long as Aquileia was the hub of western imperial communications, I stayed in place. But Aquileia was beginning to empty out of officers I trusted. Gregorius remained in charge of the wider military forces, but he was shuttling between the legions not yet engaged, pulling them into the plan.

Meanwhile, Marcellinus' grand staffs in Mediolanum and Aquileia stuck to their own routines and devices but they still played their part preparing for the confrontation with Constantius. Bustling with mint officials, clerks, notaries, secretaries and tax collectors, his bureaucratic offices funneled forward all the money Magnentius had raised to pay for his mushrooming troop numbers. The *Magister Officiorum* was hardly subtle in lining the war chest. Private property tax on some large estates shot up to fifty per cent. Other prominent landowners were compelled to purchase imperial property 'by invitation.'

Finally, the day came when I stood at attention in full armor with the rest of the usurper's forces to witness General Silvanus and Gaiso parade out of the imperial courtyard behind Magnentius and his cortège of praetorians heading for Atrans. As the scorching sun rose over the hills outside Aquileia and glistened on the sea beyond, thousands upon thousands of fighters waited in formation. When the imperial standards appeared, we heard a cheer for each go up and echo over the distant throb of the waves pounding on the shore to the south of us.

Staying in Aquileia suited me fine as long as I wasn't sure of Roxana's game. If she was waiting for secret instructions from the East, I was going to know it first. Even routine signals from 'the Mouse' in Roma addressed to her now got scrutinized first by me. Judging by his questions, Apodemius was playing it straight and for all I knew, so was she.

Though I watched her like the Greeks' mythical giant Argos—that one in Hesiod's poem with a hundred eyes who kept watch over the seductive nymph Io—I couldn't catch her doing anything else suspicious. But then, I was a mere mortal, with only two eyes and twenty-four hours in a day. When I wasn't racing to keep up with my postal duties, I was searching the imperial grounds for my lost *bulla*. I hated myself for being so distracted by the disappearance of a lousy hunk of bronze-covered pottery, but childish superstition dies hard in times of uncertainty.

As for Roxana, with Silvanus gone into the field and festive imperial dinners suspended, she never left the women's quarters now. For weeks, I despaired that our curious night of stealthy lovemaking and the mystery of her letter to 'E' had hit a dead end.

Oddly enough, it was the Empress who triggered my next encounter with Roxana. The gentle young woman had ventured out of her suite of rooms one day in search of me.

'*Agens* Numidianus?'

I turned to see Justina standing in one of the main reception halls. She looked like a fragile doll on display in a vast empty stall. Two things caught my attention—her long curls were bound up with ribbons and stuck with jeweled pins. It was a hairstyle I associated with grown women like Kahina. The vulgar betrothal ring Magnentius had given her hung from a gold chain around her slender neck.

She held out a small letter.

'I've written *ad imperatori*, to my Emperor Husband, but it's a very, very private message. I would be so grateful if you delivered it to him in person.'

'So solemn, *Augusta*? I am sure he'll be happy to hear from you.'

I lied, of course, but with the kindness the gentle child-woman inspired in everyone. I doubted Magnentius would make time to read anything from his 'wife,' given his joyful departure at the head of a barbarian imperial force for the real work of winning more Empire.

Nevertheless, I held my tongue and took the pathetic packet, sealed with her imperial insignia and tied in a bow with a thin purple cord. She watched as I slipped it under my cuirass with care. I nodded and turned to get on with my day's many tasks.

'*Agens*, do you recall I told you of a dream that I would someday found a dynasty?'

'I do, *Augusta*. I also recall I froze my feet off listening to you.'

'The oracle appeared to me again last night. She repeated that I would found a dynasty.'

'This time did she predict how many sons you would have?'

Justina's face turned even paler than usual. 'Yes, she said I'd bear one son and three daughters.'

'You don't look happy about it, *Augusta*.'

'No, because, Marcus,' and my heart softened as I heard her forget all her grown-up protocol, 'the oracle said Magnentius was not to be their father.'

'Oh, *Augusta*! Forget about dreams that upset or confuse you! In Roma sophisticated people stopped paying attention to those predictions long ago. Oracles are always changing their meanings to suit events. I hope this letter isn't full of such worries about a little dream. Right now, the Emperor has victory on his mind, not siring little caesars.'

She let out an affronted gasp at that ill-considered phrase of mine, and bit her tongue. 'Well, thank you, anyway.'

'Shall I accompany you to the Ladies' Wing?'

'Yes, I suppose it's not correct for me to be wandering around like this, with my husband off at battle. I await his return with new eagerness and anticipation.' She blushed, drew up her slight frame in its robes too heavy for the season and thrust out her small, high bosom with a self-conscious smile.

So that was what the letter announced. I didn't need advanced observation training back at the Castra to guess that Justina had grown up at last. She was now a proper, fertile woman inviting her husband into her bed. Magnentius was a decent man, himself a father of a grown daughter. He didn't ravish little girls. Still, things might be different now. I hid my discomfort at the sudden image of the rough-hewn Franco-

Breton celebrating his imminent victory at Atrans by deflowering the delicate Justina.

I was just about to deposit the Empress at the entrance to her wing with a salute when female shrieks echoed down the marble corridor. Justina turned and dashed towards her private wing. I saw no guards or ladies-in-waiting in sight, so I shouted for backup and with *pugio* ready, I followed her at top speed.

We found Roxana and Kahina on the floor of Justina's reception room, dragging and sliding around on priceless Eastern rugs in a vicious struggle. They pulled each other's hair and screamed with equal force. Justina froze in the doorway, appalled at the sight of the two most trusted women in her life tearing at each other like wrathful Furies.

I pulled the sash tying Roxana's waist to yank her up and off Kahina. At least I got the two of them parted. Kahina panted, red-faced and disheveled, her bare legs exposed on the marble stones. She lay on her back and glared up at Roxana like a lioness at bay.

Both women were dressed lightly, as if just back from the baths. Their hair coils hung loose over their brows and ribbons straggled around their necks, but whether that was from the heat of bathing or the result of battlefield engagement, I couldn't tell.

'Don't trust her, Marcus,' Kahina yelled.

'So you *do* know him.'

'Of course I know him, you bitch. But he's just a freedman from my husband's household in Roma, nothing more.'

'So why fly into a rage over such a little trifle?'

Kahina seethed in defeated silence. Poor Justina mustered enough maturity to ask, 'I command you both to explain.'

Roxana didn't answer. She cast a disdainful glance at her young Highness that would have got her dismissed on the spot—were Justina anything like Constantia.

Kahina turned her face to the floor and broke into tears. I stared at her. This was not the weeping of embarrassment or even pain, though the honey-colored skin of her upper arms was scored with deep scratches from Roxana's nails. Her very soul sounded wracked. Her sobs turned to wails that turned my stomach.

Justina tried to assert her authority. 'Lady Kahina, please, go to your rooms and rest. Roxana, explain yourself or—'

'She's just a jumped-up African nanny,' Roxana spit out. 'She dared to accuse me of flirting with that horror she married.'

'One hero isn't enough for you, you sewer slut. I come from a decent family. I worked for a respected African citizen. I married into a leading Roman family. But who are you, really? What slum did you climb out of?' Kahina spat back. 'As soon as General Silvanus leaves for the front, you're chasing my husband. You're a Messalina, rubbing almond oil and rose lotion over your thighs like some cut-rate Cleopatra—'

'That's enough!' Justina held her own. 'Lady Kahina, get up off the floor. Roxana, Commander Gregorius is an honored *conciliarum* who enjoys my husband's trust. You're a servant here. You will apologize for insulting the painful wounds he suffered in the service of our Empire.'

'Yes, *Augusta*.' Fighting to control her temper, Roxana fixed her gaze on the mosaic at her feet, 'Indeed, I pity Atticus Gregorius' wounds . . . and I pity his wife even more.'

The two older women stood fast, the one still engulfed in sobs, the other adjusting her torn ivory tunic back over her lithe limbs with as much dignity as she could muster. I saw blood smears all over the expensive Egyptian cotton. Whether it was Kahina's or Roxana's, who knew?

'We need your other ladies, Empress. Where are they?' I asked.

Justina shrugged. 'I wouldn't know. Resting, bathing, amusing themselves in the market or down at the shore. They find my court boring, so I let them go when and where they choose. Only the Lady Kahina stays with me. We read or sew together when Roxana's busy.'

Roxana shot me a warning look. To inquire where she went or what kept her busy might shed too much light on her true assignment for Apodemius.

'May I go now, *Augusta*? I recall you had business for me.' Justina's letter sat stiff at my waist and other duties called. It seemed safe to leave them now as a hen pack of curious chattering women rushed into the suite like birds poking their beaks into a pile of seeds.

I shot Roxana one last look of warning and started off for the gate lodge. I was halfway back through the echoing reception halls when I heard my name called.

Her arms still bleeding, Kahina rushed up to me across the broad marble expanse.

'Get those scratches seen too before they fester, Lady,' I said.

'Look me in the eyes, Marcus . . . Or are you afraid they'll say too much?' Her soft Numidian accent, so like my mother's, tugged at my heart.

I looked her straight in the face but kept at arm's length. She deserved a fair warning from me. 'You know I've always admired your eyes and now I admire your courage. That servant Roxana might know more about dirty fighting than you can imagine. You were right to defend Gregorius' honor, but not to abandon your Manlius dignity or risk life and limb in the process.'

'But I won, Marcus.' She smiled with a bitter irony that confused me.

'How so? I'm afraid, Lady, that I found you bleeding and on your back.'

'I won, because I got this off her neck,' She stretched out her fist and unfurled her fingers to reveal my *bulla* and its broken cord hidden in her palm.

I closed my eyes for a moment. Now I suspected what might have set the two women at each other's throats and it wasn't an insult to the Commander's injuries.

'Do you recall that night I discovered you rooting around for it in Leo's study? It was then I knew how much it meant to you. Later, in Rome, Verus told me you always wore it, even when other young men would have tossed such a childish thing away. Verus said it was the Senator's gift and that you would never part with it.'

'Verus told the truth.'

'Then how—?' She blushed. 'When I saw it on that woman's neck and I thought—I just forgot myself. I can't pretend to like or even to understand her. I know she's only a servant—of no importance whatsoever—but there's something about her that I don't trust.'

'Her duties might be heavier than you think. Did she *really* make a pass at the Commander?'

'Of course. With her, seduction is no more than breathing. I doubt he noticed anything. That's the advantage of having lost an eye.' She gave me a rueful smile. 'But she gave me enough of an excuse to fight her for this. Did she . . . steal it from you?' Kahina glanced away at the tall marble pillars surrounding us like a stern forest.

'Lady Kahina, it's a childish thing to lose your peace and position over. Thank you. Let's forget all this.'

'It was the Senator's gift, after all. You must never lose it again.' She searched my expression for reassurance.

'Don't worry, I won't.'

'You won't tell my husband?'

'It's the least of our secrets. Thank you. I've got to go now.'

'Marcus?'

'Yes, Lady Kahina?'

She reached for my arm to slow my leave-taking. 'He's the loveliest little boy in the world.'

I tied the *bulla* cord back around my neck. 'Yes. Worth sacrificing everything for.'

'Then you do feel our sacrifice, still?' She tightened her grasp of my arm.

'Not when I see Leo and yourself both thriving. Keep the boy safe, Kahina and give Roma a wide berth. Constantius may have it in him to send Vetranio off with a pension plan to Bithynia, but he won't be so kind to Magnentius or any of his officers if things go wrong.'

'But surely he wouldn't slaughter the old Roman families?'

'Constantius would not. But his lieutenant, Paulus Catena, "The Chain," would make certain you begged him for the mercy of death.'

⚜⚜⚜

Late that day I had a chance to remember Kahina's warning about Roxana. There was more than jealousy in her mistrust. I tracked my training mate down with stealth, lying in wait more than an hour among the columns lining the corridor to the palace toilets reserved for the ladies. I'd been too gullible, I realized, and too easily distracted by the feeling of her warm breasts moving up and down my chest.

I surprised her at last, moving in on her as she passed down a shadowy corridor well in the fading light.

'What did he offer you?' I twisted her arm hard behind her and held it fast to her back.

She knew the same training tricks I did, so it was hard work keeping her pinned down. She tried to kick back and knock my legs out from under me but I jumped and she missed. Her teeth were bared to take whatever chunk of flesh she could from wherever she could. It was like wrestling with an oiled stoat— soft and serpentine to hold but all sinew, spring and teeth underneath.

'Let me go or you'll never be able to piss straight again.'

'What's he paying you? You know I can snap that slender neck of yours so you'll have to beg to be put down like a crippled horse.'

'A hero like Silvanus gets it free—and often.'

'I meant that beardless slug, Eusebius, of course. What could he offer *you*? You like your *viri* well-endowed, as *countless* men no doubt could confirm.'

'You bastard. I'm better at everything than you, but I have to work days *and* nights—'

'Then you're working *three* shifts, not two, with the extra work behind Apodemius' back, aren't you? What does the eunuch offer you? More bracelets and earrings? What does he want? What do you want?'

She stopped fighting, but I braced myself for another wrestling bout all the same. Any minute now, I would dislocate her shoulder for the truth and she knew it.

'A good post in the East.'

Disbelieving, I waited for more.

'What of it? We're all one Empire, aren't we?' Her eyes blazed an angry defiance back at me through the dark.

'The eunuch is just using you against Apodemius.'

She gave a bitter laugh. 'And vice-versa. The old "Mouse" works me no better than a streetwalker. When I'm dried up, he'll give me some cleaning job at the Castra at quarter pay and a pittance of a pension. Let me *go*!'

'Eusebius won't deliver even that.'

She smiled even as she struggled. 'Who's waiting around for a pension? The East is rich pickings for an unattached girl.'

Suddenly, underneath the scent of her imported perfume and almond bath oil, Roxana reeked of raw jealousy—jealousy of Kahina and me. She'd flaunted the stolen *bulla* and now I could see it all—how Roxana's envious suspicions of a secret past between Kahina and myself had frightened Kahina.

'So you're alone. Don't take it out on the service.'

'The West is cold, confused, and sinking. Old Roma is a forgotten junkyard. I smell failure, Marcus—on you—on all of them. You stink of decay, all of you. Well, nobody's got *me* tied down, especially not *you*.'

She broke my hold with a sudden wrench and ran for it. I would've followed her—I knew there was more to her actions—but I had to sign off on the records before the praetorians locked down for the day. I was headed back for her when a horn less than a mile outside the town sounded an alert.

I ran out of the palace and down to the Aquileia city gates. One of our relay riders appeared on the crest of a hill about a quarter of a mile away on the eastern road. We delayed our sentries from bolting fast the gates. I sent a boy to fetch Marcellinus from his paperwork.

A few minutes later the rider thundered into the courtyard. He wore the white feather of victory in his helmet.

'Constantius' advance forces completely repelled, *Magister Officiorum!*' He dismounted and handed me the report. I passed it over in turn.

Marcellinus read it on the spot. 'Prepare your next team of couriers for immediate departure. I'll prepare summons to Gregorius and all the rear legions.'

'Yes, *Magister*. We have half a dozen fresh men just coming on shift.'

'Put *every single one* on duty to ride out tonight. It seems the Emperor Constantius fell into our trap. He's sending a delegation to negotiate.'

'I don't understand, *Magister*. If it's peace, why pull the rear legions forward?'

He waved the dispatch with displeasure. 'Magnentius' orders. We move the imperial council to the front, myself included, with the entire Western Army at our heels.'

'To strengthen his bargaining?'

'I pray to the gods that's all but I suspect that's not the reason. I'm afraid he's got his head swollen with a lust for yet more power.' The expression on Marcellinus' crafty features darkened. Despite his contempt for me, he muttered within my earshot, 'I curse the day I crowned that stupid barbarian.'

So it seemed I would be hand-delivering the Empress Justina's love letter after all.

⚔⚔⚔

'My gods, look at that. Who in Hades is she?' A rider named Caduceus stared, the packet of reports clutched in his hand frozen in the air.

We all looked out from the postal cubicle. Under my supervision, the couriers had been sorting up and registering the overload of orders and dispatches to be sent out, when a woman of around sixty had appeared at the outer palace gates beyond.

She wore her hair in wild reddish curls festooned with braids of twisted gold cord and fastened down with a golden headpiece studded with jewels. But for all her glittering display, she swaggered with impatience at the sentries' delay in clearing her with no more grace or dignity than a common potions peddler. Then to our astonishment, this garish creature obtained entrance and even a praetorian escort for her passed to the inner gate and courtyard leading to the palace.

It was none other than the Emperor Magnentius' mother, a formidable flame-haired barbarian clanking under her load of Frankish belts and bracelets—a German woman's armor indeed. She had arrived from parts north to make a rare visit to the salon of her straight-backed little daughter-in-law.

I'd heard of this crone. As an eye-catching young refugee, she had read fortunes to the officers around Constantine I, until his strategic conversion to Christianity prevailed over such amusements. The woman looked half witch even now. I scolded the courier clerks back to work, while I imagined Magnentius *Mater* being welcomed now into the *Augusta*'s suite with condescending hospitality, but not a Roman aristocrat's warmest embraces.

I was wrong about the welcome. However odd-matched, these two in-laws soon discovered a mutual love of soothsayers and omens.

As the staff finalized unprecedented logistical problems on the very eve of our complicated departure, the palace became a meeting point for a series of peculiar visitors. Each commander who brought in his dozens of centurions to report to Decentius for duty and detailed briefings found themselves stumbling over a bazaar-like hustle-bustle of praetorians escorting weird civilians in silk slippers crisscrossing the same crowded halls.

Each day, one wide-eyed old bat in rags or dubious harridan in gaudy silks after another threaded through the ranks of reporting officers en route to Justina's quarters.

If we men were summoning all the physical forces of the West into one powerful message for Constantius, it seemed that Justina and her steely-eyed in-law were calling in all their spiritual chits for the oncoming confrontation at Atrans. I much preferred the charming child Justina to this impressionable teenage *Augusta* made giddy with crazy predictions and incantations—but it wasn't my concern.

Soon after that, Marcellinus' fears proved well founded. We heard that the elated victor had abandoned the security of Fortress Atrans to push deeper into the East without waiting for his backup forces.

His impetuous advance forced the Caesar Decentius to hustle over fifty thousand men forward in a race to catch up with his brother. Lumbered down by baggage trains, *ballista*-carts, weapons, bullion and cook wagons, not to mention the fixed pace of the infantry filing at fast-march pace ahead of the cavalry units, we set off, expected to join the imperial camp in a mere six to seven days.

That assumed that Magnentius managed to stay put until we arrived.

I argued to Marcellinus and Gregorius that as an *agens* my job was to speed ahead of their stately progress to communicate the strength of our forces and any requirements in advance. Gregorius agreed, all too readily. He hoped I would carry his private advice to Magnentius to pull back to Atrans and reconvene the council.

To my surprise, Marcellinus shook his head, 'No.' 'You're free to solicit such a command from your *schola* superiors, Numidianus, but I would consider it a favor to myself, as well as Decentius, Gregorius and our fellow commanders, if you'd remain with our company.'

'Surely, *Magister*, there are some messages or intelligence that would be good to deliver ahead, to ease the merging of such vast forces?'

Marcellinus shook his head again and even laid a bejeweled hand on Gregorius' shoulder to cut off any dispute. 'Trust is not only delicate, but also unpredictable, *Agens*. You know a year ago, I resented your independence and even more, the insubordinance with which you, a mere freedman, flaunted it. Now, I'm not too proud to admit, I might come to value that very quality more and more—or at least to be ready to exploit it. I find I'm very very reluctant to lose you.'

I chaffed at his tightening control disguised as respect over my movements.

'But all the news from the East is good, *Magister*. Look behind us.' The line of spears, standards and banners reached to the horizon of hills we'd already crossed and behind which the late summer sun was now sinking. Like an explosive ball of flame, it sent orange light onto a shimmering river of armor winding left and right. 'My request to speed ahead is based only the need for logisitical warning, not strategic worry. Rarely has one emperor commanded such a modern, robust force—'

'Much less two.' Marcellinus looked uncomfortable in his military livery. He made me uncomfortable as well. Seeing him in full armor again, all I could think of was his savage, defiant ride around the Trajan Arena brandishing Nepotianus' dripping head with its blind, staring eyes.

I pressed Marcellinus to divulge his misgivings. 'Surely, *Magister*, there's too much to lose to risk all-out civil—?'

'Certainly!' He cut me off, adding, 'Indeed, why would the most powerful empire in the world commit suicide?' The he stared off at the horizon, unable to answer his own question.

Gregorius bit back some comment of his own and kicked his horse forward. I was about to fall back in line with more junior officers when the *Magister Officiorum* broke his restive pause.

'If I were not so modern myself, gentlemen, I might consult an oracle or better yet, slice up some poor goat to spill its fortune-telling entrails into a basin. But I'm a *modern* man, so all I'll say is that my own guts churn with uneasiness. So, no, *agens*, you'll stay with us and even after we arrive, I'll be watching you. You never know. You might make a useful weather vane, like that bronze Triton in Athens on top of the Tower of the Winds, pointing his trident in the opposite direction—should fortune stop blowing my way.'

When the moon was high overhead, I set off with stealth to Roxana's room. Silvanus was gone and Justina and her ladies long retired to their beds. I knocked again and again, softly. After considerable exasperation with lurking in the shadows of the women's wing, I forced her door open, using the thin wedge of my swivel knife to lift the latch.

Perhaps I had guessed already. Perhaps I just had to see it for myself.

Her room was empty. Roxana had fled Aquileia, taking all her clothes and jewels, not to mention her secrets, with her. Had Eusebius been merely receiving reports from the woman or worse? Was he scheming against Apodemius through her? What? What? She'd decided to run the moment she confessed. So there must be more to hide from me. Exactly whom had she betrayed and was it too late to save them?

Chapter 18, An Oath is Broken

Thus I was stuck in place for the duration, keeping my horse at the infantry's fast-march pace in the company of legion commanders. These were hard men, scarred by border duty and a life on the move. Franks, Celts, Hispaniards, even the odd refugee from farther north, they were all committed to the imperial barbarian's new regime.

It wasn't hard to understand their affection for Magnentius. Some of the black-eyed Hispaniards' ancestors had fallen to Pompey's slaughter almost four hundred years ago. Even as they rode, some of these Frankish officers might still have toothless grandfathers walking the earth, telling tales of forest warfare against Constantine around some refugee camp's ovens.

As usual, I listened like the slave child I'd once been, keeping my gaze forward but my ears cocked. These strangers had endured the long impatience of suspended mobilization. After months of reconnoitering and exercising while sullen Italian peasants looked on, they were keen to get their men marching to a purpose. All day they barked and disciplined their lines double-time, not only to catch up with Magnentius within the week, but also to quicken the troops' appetite for war.

The men took it with gusto, too. Marching meant more 'boot bonus' for each infantryman on top of regular pay, a fresh choice of women and more plentiful food rations. They'd eaten southern Gallia and northern Italia down to the last breadcrumb and shellfish.

We passed one last night of comfort camped around the walls of Atrans and along the valley floor before setting off again for the more uncertain territory beyond Emona.

We knew we were nearly in sight of the main Western camp because a full day before reach of Siscia's city gates nestling on the left bank of the Colapsis River, our eyes spotted a miasma of brown cloud hovering above the Sava River. Our ears soon picked up the unmistakable rumble of army—a true ocean roaring like breaking waves with the sounds of horses, oxen, hammers, horns, wagon wheels, metal-working, shouts and pounding feet. The fading skylight filtered through the smoke sent up from hundreds of cooks' and smithys' ovens.

And suddenly I was a child again at the Senator's knee, reading to him from *The Iliad*, . . . *as the countless flocks of wild birds, the geese, the cranes, the long-necked swans, gathering by Cayster's streams in the Asian fields wheel, glorying in the power of their wings, and settle again with loud cries while the earth resounds, so clan after clan poured from the ships and huts on Scamander's plain. And the ground hummed loud to the tread of men and horses, as they gathered, in the flowery river-meadows, innumerable as the leaves and the blossoms in their season . . . Like the countless swarms of flies that buzz round the cowherd's yard in spring, when the pails are full of milk, as numerous were the long-haired Greeks drawn up on the plain, ready to fight the men of Troy and utterly destroy them.*

A boisterous greeting broke into this reverie that accompanied my progress towards the parade ground where the Emperor waited. Magnentius' re-constituted council was going to hold their first field conference at dusk in the imperial meeting tent flagged at all four corners with the banners of the Ioviani and Herculiani hanging limp in the summer heat.

'Victory! *Victory*, Marcellinus! Hello, Gregorius! We chased their asses straight out of the valley. They ran like rabbits.'

Magnentius' face had lit up at the sight of his bean-counting sponsor as soon as our crowd of officers ducked under his tent flap.

'Congratulations, Magnentius.' I noticed that Marcellinus could not bring himself to smile.

'You're tired, sure, man, but you've got them here without trouble?'

'Just under two hundred miles with no incident, but a brawl over some blonde back in Emona. Hello, Gaiso. Silvanus.' The generals greeted each other as I presented my satchel of post to a tribune assisting Magnentius. The leaders resumed their lively arguments over how to get a nation of soldiers across the Sava—by building a bridge or commandeering boats?

I still had to find my own tent and work out the order of merging the messaging and posts with the army communications officers. More than 80,000 men now measured out an orderly space all around the hard-packed parade ground that bathed in the fast setting blaze of September's dry dusk.

'Halt, you! Yes, you!'

I turned, startled at the sound of his imperious summons.

'Did you deliver this, *Agens* Numidianus?'

The Emperor himself had thrust his head out the flap of the council tent and was recalling me across the parade ground. I trotted straight back into the tent behind him and stood at attention. I assumed he had already stumbled on his consort's letter, but as soon as I got up close, I realized Justina's tender announcement could hardly be responsible for the bull-faced rage in those huge eyes.

He waved an unfamiliar letter in spidery script in my face. 'Did you *speak* to my mother?'

'Your *mother*?'

'Yes, you African clod! Contrary to Eastern rumor, I have a natural mother and she wrote me this! Did you speak to her before you left?'

'No, *Imperator*.'

'What is it, Magnentius?' The hot-blooded Gaiso knew best the dangers of a temper.

'The old woman warns me not to proceed farther into Pannonia.'

Marcellinus sniggered. Magnentius rounded on him, his thick fist half raised to flatten his *magister officiorum*. 'Her prophesies have never been wrong. She warns us of Fates unfavorable to an engagement in Sirmium.'

Gregorius cleared his throat and a number of tribunes standing along the perimeter of the tent's wall looked uncomfortable. A long silence settled on the assembly in the tent.

'That's it, then,' Magnentius said. 'We've marched too far and we must appease the Fates. We are within a day's reach of Constantius. Gaiso, get me soothsayers and experts on ritual. Comb the villages.' His large eyes darted from man to man, all of them looking aghast.

The meeting disbanded with mutters and troubled glances.

Gaiso rode out of the central camp at the head of half a *turma* of fifteen cavalrymen plus their officer. I slept that night with seven other tent mates of my rank. I wondered if, among those thousands upon thousands of men bedding down in tents of their own all around me, there were any bands of Christian converts sneering at their Emperor's barbarian follies.

If such ridicule carried into the night, it was cut short at dawn the next day. Reveille sounded on horn after horn across the wide fields of our tents. The legions massed in an enormous circle around Magnentius' wooden platform to hail their Emperor.

A salute roared up from the men at the sight of Magnentius mounting the wooden steps but the troops' acclamation plummeted into a sea of confused buzz as we saw a girl of about fifteen in a long white tunic escorted up the wooden steps to the Emperor's side. A wizened old woman, so bent over with age her nose pointed down at the planks, pulled herself up the steps as well, followed by a small scruffy boy as her only escort.

I was positioned too far away to hear, but I wasn't too distant to note that Gregorius and Marcellinus—odd allies at the best of times—were nowhere to be seen.

Gaiso stood and enjoyed a borrowed moment of glory to acknowledge a spontaneous cheer from some upstart legion off to the east of the sprawling camp. Silvanus stood rigid to the far side of the platform, flanked on both sides by Frankish officers unknown to me.

Magnentius spoke at length, his voice reaching me only as a vulgar Latin shout riding the wind, something to the effect that the Fates needed propitiating to ensure that the army's courage and skill would reach its rightful destiny.

Then—without more warning than that—the Emperor took a ceremonial dagger off a pillow presented by the old woman, took hold of the maiden's long hair, jerked back the poor girl's head and slit her throat mid-scream.

A roar—half-horror, half-blood-lust—rose up from the legions. The girl's twitching white shoulders were held over a crude washing basin carried by the boy. Amidst a torrent of nightmarish incantations accompanied by rough gesticulations from the sorceress, the praetorians held out cups to collect the hot spurting blood for the troops to drink with a dilution of wine from vats waiting below.

I was desperate to find Gregorius or even Marcellinus, when horns blasted through this awful procedure. Even the Emperor Magnentius started at the unexpected signal.

Now I pushed forward, despite the resistance of hundreds of hefty pairs of armored shoulders, just in time to see Marcellinus riding into the parade ground. Behind him followed some forty to fifty cavalrymen, their banners carrying the unmistakable *Chi-Rho* logo of Constantius' forces.

I took a huge breath when I saw that. It was too·late to save the poor girl slumped limp and as white as her dress in the arms of a soldier. But perhaps this ancient blood magic had worked to save the peace after all. Why else would Marcellinus be escorting delegates from the Eastern Army into our camp?

I kept fighting to get a better position to overhear what happened next. 'Flavius Philippus comes to us from Constantius, to kneel and bargain,' Magnentius was shouting at the troops by the time I had worked my way within earshot of the platform.

This Philippus—a tall, noble-looking Roman—raised his arms in greeting and broke into Magnentius' oratory. He was determined to deliver his message in his own way.

'... does not become you, Roman citizens all, to make war on fellow Romans. Your Emperor is none other than the son of Constantine with whom you've enjoyed many victories, for whom you've erected many trophies and memorials over the barbarians who threaten our borders and our way of life.'

Philippus scowled at his host. 'Flavius Magnus Magnentius should remember the Constantines' kindness to him and to his parents. And how ironic that it was Constans himself who saved Magnentius from danger in a previous mutiny, and recognizing his long service to the Empire, exalted him to the highest dignities ...'

At this reminder of that murky episode from which the Constantines had supposedly rescued him, Magnentius' jaw shot up. He glowered in undisguised defiance at the enemy envoy's plea. I observed how this Philippus knew how to get his message across, even to the thousands of men too far to hear his actual words. He spoke slowly and waited between phrases, relying on reports spreading backwards like ripples across a vast pond of armor.

At one point, he spread his arms as if to embrace Magnentius who only shoved him away in rebuke.

Philippus persisted. 'Leave Italia, Magnentius. Retreat with honor. You shall rule the nations west of the Alps. This is the Emperor Constantius' offer. Our esteemed ruler desires only to husband the lives of all who stand here before him today. He makes this offer of peaceful joint governance to avoid a fearful struggle pitting the armies of Gallia, Hispanisa, Africa, Britannia against Illyricum and the East. Your Emperor Constantius desires only peace.'

The army was shifting at the visitor's imploring gestures. A few units started up a clamor of swords banging in rhythm on their shields to show their agreement. Magnentius had to decide whether to swallow Constantius' offer or fight back, but the troops made it clear they would welcome a peaceful partition of rule.

Magnentius' face flushed with indignation. He could see in Philippus all the grace, eloquence and breeding he lacked. He knew his command over the men rested on an appeal to their resentments and provincial passions, not their loyalties to the Constantine succession.

With an abrupt thrust of his right arm, he pushed the emissary aside and cut him off with, 'Men, have you no memory of the abuse, disdain and dishonor your service received under a Constantine *drunk,* a *spendthrift,* a *tyrant,* an enfeebled excuse for a man, a so-called leader who ranked even his prisoners-of-war above yourselves. He laughed at our desire to restore Roman honor, virtue, and order ...'

As Magnentius chided and cajoled, the refined Philippus was soon eclipsed by the sheer size and bullying energy of his host. Even when I realized with alarm that Philippus was no longer visible on the platform, Magnentius still hadn't stopped his rallying and railing.

I finally reached the back of the parade ground at the rear of the imperial tents. There I discovered Marcellinus in hurried conference with Silvanus, even as Magnentius' voice still bellowed and echoed across the valley plain.

I joined a set of tribunes awaiting their orders from the council.

'That was not pagan ritual. It was nothing more than barbarian savagery,' Marcellinus was saying.

'He's accusing Philippus of coming here only to spy on our numbers,' Gregorius interrupted, appearing from the scene of the debate. 'Silvanus has got Philippus in detention in his private tent now, on Magnentius' orders.'

'It's a stupid move, completely out of bounds to treat an envoy that way!' Marcellinus protested.'

'I believe Philippus came with a genuine offer. We should take it.' Gregorius' instinct was to preserve the Empire's unity, even in these final precious hours.

Gaiso shook his head. 'It might be a trap. Constantius could overtake our rear on the road as we retreat. He could pick us off, one *ala* at a time.'

'No, I believe Philippus is sincere—and yet, like you Gaiso, I don't trust the offer,' Marcellinus said. 'There is something wrong, something we don't know. I can't put my finger on it but we need Silvanus. I want to know how he reads Philippus.'

Behind us there was a deafening roar, 'To the Sava! To the Sava!'

All color drained from Gregorius' good cheek. Magnentius had won the day over Philippus. The Commander glanced at me and the others followed with a pregnant silence.

They were staring at me because that I was the only neutral officer, the only *agens* in sight. It was now my responsibility to stand by, near the tent where Philippus had been detained, and to collect any message he wanted to dispatch to Constantius on the other side.

I was discussing this with Gaiso when someone caught my eye.

Hanging to one side with other less senior officers, was that so-called Roman 'noble,' the aristocrat Urban Prefect Titianus who had left Anicetus to the butchery of Nepotianus' convicts and then abandoned me in Sardica for the pleasure of Paulus Catena's personal perversity.

It took me a few moments to recognize this helmeted man listening intently and silently to the ongoing debate around us. But he had already recognized me.

'I know you, *Agens* Numidianus.'

'Prefect Titianus.' I had nothing good to say to him.

'I'm glad to see you here.'

'I'm certainly lucky to be here, no thanks to you.'

'There is no time for recriminations or petty scores. I may need you. Magnentius has just decided to send me with a delegation to Constantius to urge his retreat eastwards to the Persian front. I know you are a trustworthy escort.'

'Magnentius wants Constantius to retreat?' I was appalled. 'The acclamation of so many soldiers can intoxicate even a great

man like the Emperor,' I said. 'He should reconsider. The entire
Empire might be too much, even for the reforming Magnentius.
Forgive me for declining your invitation but I serve my *schola*
first. Your delegation has no need of me.'

'But you know the court of Constantius well.'

'As I said, my posting is here.'

I nodded in salute and announced myself at the tent where
Silvanus still detained Philippus under Magnentius' orders. I
expected to find Philippus there under protest and the even-
handed Silvanus dominating him with his usual cool command.

Instead I stumbled on an unexpected scene.

Far from acting his warden, the Claudius Silvanus was
seated on a camp stool and leaning nose to nose in conversation
with the rejected envoy. I took up a discreet position and
watched from the anonymity of a cluster of guards. The two
officers continued their hurried and eager conference. Perhaps
Silvanus saw a chance to broker a peace for us all. Philippus'
expression was of concentration and agreement, not fear. The
two officers didn't notice me but kept on in rapid-fire
conversation for almost ten minutes. Finally, the two men
nodded, stood up and slapped each other on the shoulder with
an exchange of satisfied glances.

I slipped away to find Commander Gregorius at once. I felt
the rush of suspicion at Silvanus' calm expression now meeting
the memory of Roxana's sly smile. Was this her last, darkest
secret? Was this her conspiracy with Eusebius made reality?
Had she infected Silvanus with doubt as strong as a poison
concocted by Eusebius and honeyed with her pillow whispers?
Or could Silvanus be trusted to win over Philippus to some kind
of accommodation with his barbarian emperor?

'Commander, I strongly suspect General Silvanus of
making a deal with the court of Constantius. But what nature of
their accord, I can't say. He's in the imperial tent now, saying
goodbye to Philippus.'

'Silvanus is a sound man, as sound as they come. You're
talking treason.'

'No, Commander, listen to me. He was the last to join up to your cause—'

'I won't listen to slander.'

'Please, Commander. There is a doubt. Cast your mind back over the last year. Wasn't Silvanus always the man with the last word in any debate? Wasn't he the reasonable voice who weighed all sides first. Wasn't he the least passionate, the least headstrong, and the least *committed*?'

Gregorius rounded on me. 'Shut up, Marcus! How can *you* judge a man like Silvanus, commander of tens of thousands, who are cheering him out there right now? Do you think he's a man to stake his honor and give word to us and then simply turn tail?'

'I saw his face just now.'

'Leave him to it. He'll do his utmost to bring Phillipus around. I'm sure of him. Yes, the gods help us, perhaps the two of them can negotiate us out of this situation.'

'There's more, Commader. Silvanus is bedmates with Roxana—'

'A stupid housemaid—'

'A *spy* for the East.'

He paused, and his scarred mouth curled with disbelief. 'A woman? A woman! It's unheard of. And even if your fantasy were true, Marcus, does that make her any worse than yourself, an *agens*? I've seen the way you look at her, Marcus. You only wish she were your kind. You could have had a respectable life as my freedman in some trade or business, owing only homage to the Manlii instead of playing messenger boy to—oh, I don't know.'

The bitter roots of my defection from his family's patronage sank far deeper than I suspected but I had to keep trying before it was too late.

'You're wrong, Commander.' I chased after his brisk steps in the direction of the tumult raging beyond. 'Roxana is nothing to me. She's nothing like me. She's a *double* agent, working for Eusebius, the most powerful eunuch at Constantius' side. I know that person. He made me an offer to betray our *schola*, too. Whatever you do to beg Magnentius for a peaceful deal, Eusebius is working to annihilate any peace, so he can spread his web wider from Antiochia to Burgundium like a mammoth spider.'

Now Gregorius paused. I had called everything into question—his commitment, judgment, and even his survival. I faced him eye to eye and thought I detected for a flickering instant some wavering in his mind. For he knew that I was not only an ex-Numidian house slave, as jumped-up on the day of my manumission as freedmen come, but also his own unacknowledged flesh and blood. He could not help but listen to that, once he'd had a chance to digest my warning.

But who could think straight in this mayhem? The shouts and pounding on shields hadn't stopped rolling around us, wave by wave. In vain, the *tubicens* blew signals for retreat. Some over-excited units were already testing the cold waters of the Sava, boat or bridge crossing be damned.

'We'll talk about this tomorrow morning,' he said as if there was nothing more to say, but I noticed that he marched off alone still deep in thought towards his own tent. A dozen other officers huddled in conference turned to watch his retreating back, glanced at me and then returned to their anxious debate.

ΨΨΨ

I dreamt that night I was riding in a wagon. Its ironbound wheels thundered on the paving stones beneath my cushioned head and shook my shoulders as it trundled along.

I opened my eyes. The rumbling around me was no dream. Men shouted outside the leather walls of our tent. A couple of my mates, barely dressed, had gone outside already to see what was happening. I tossed my short cloak over my shoulders and joined the crowd gathering outside. Along the entire lane of tents, dozens of soldiers emerged half-naked from their slumbers.

'What is it? Did we miss a signal?'

'What's up?'

'We on the move?'

'Sounds like an attack.'

'It's on the far side, near the river. We're waiting for a report.'

I ran towards the center of the encampment. I had no intention of waiting for some half-baked rumor to reach me via thousands of sleepy men, some of them far from sober. Before I could even reach the command staff's central tents, I saw a forest of standards and banners ribboning off towards the East.

I mounted the driver's bench of a supply wagon and peered over thousands of men across the plain. The sun was just rising over the river. At first all I saw was the gray light shattered into a pinkish haze by a broad dust cloud lifting off our camp and hovering in the distant sky.

That cloud meant that a column of men and horses was already marching away from our camp. Thousands upon thousands of them, in tight formation and at a controlled and regular march, had set off without a horn signal or warning shout to disturb the dawn. If my estimate was right, they'd already been sneaking off for at least half an hour. The line extended so far, I couldn't see their standard bearers, but the standing body positioned at attention and waiting for their turn to file out was beyond numbering.

'What's going on?' I jumped off the wagon and stopped a pair of men trotting back to their tent-mates to report.

'It's General Silvanus. The bastard is defecting with all his legions to the other side!'

Why had Silvanus waited until our armies were poised for engagement, until men were sharpening their weapons and adjusting saddles? Perhaps because of honor or perhaps because of simple doubt, Silvanus had hesitated until he heard out the arguments of the envoy Philippus. I didn't know Silvanus as well as Roxana did but I could imagine him weighing the odds, comparing the numbers, and finally balancing the envoy's persuasive words against the dangling white corpse of a girl murdered out of superstition.

The last man in turned out to be the first man out the rebellion's door. Now it was too late to argue him back.

Thirty thousand men were on the move and there was nothing Magnentius could do to stop General Silvanus leading them away. The balance of power held by the blind Fates, so delicately poised between the forces under Constantius and those under Magnentius, had just tipped towards the imperial son.

For one afternoon, Magnentius had held peace in his burly hands. The opportunity to share an Empire whole and strong with a rightful heir had been within his reach. He had spent a year waiting, angling for recognition, and grasping for just this offer.

But Constantius had made Magnentius wait too long. The weathered barbarian had come this far and now pinned his pride on a conquest. In his blustering greed, the so-called reformer had just tossed peace away, and with it all the people I loved.

CHAPTER 19, AMBUSHING THE FATES

'Constantius' army stands waiting for you here,' Gaiso reported, 'in Cibalis.' He placed a finger on a large military map of Pannonia spread out before the Council.

'We shouldn't follow him,' Gregorius said. 'It's exactly where his father defeated old Licinius. His morale will be too high—'

'I don't need your history lessons!' Magnentius raged.

I stood by, coordinating with senior army communications officers as we registered routine orders going out to legions and civilian support bases beyond. As the General signed off on one order after another, even that brutish bull could count heads and horses. What had been a field of evenly divided forces had slid dangerously in favor of his rival. The loss of Claudius Silvanus was like an invisible wound draining him of all reason.

'Concentrate on strategy then, *Domine*,' Gaiso said, giving Gregorius a cautioning glance. 'Constantius wants to draw us out onto flatter land for an assault that would favor his heavy cavalry. I say we stick with negotiating. Prefect Titianus is making his counter offer any time now. We should wait for an answer.'

Still angered that, Catena or no Catena, I'd thought better than to accompany Titianus again, Gregorius glared across the room at me. For we all knew that Titianus, mistaken in thinking that Magnentius still held the upper hand, was using his most arrogant patrician tones to suggest that Constantius to abandon his claims to any empire and hand it all over to Magnentius.

'With Silvanus next to him, Constantius will laugh in our face now,' Marcellinus said. 'No more negotiations. We fight it out before anybody else turns coat.'

The *Magister Officiorum* saw no future for himself in a co-rulership with Constantius and he never had. If he'd argued for negotiation before this, it was because he thought he would prevail. Magnentius' formidable blessing would have made him, Marcellinus, effective ruler of the Western Empire.

Fortunes had reversed. So had his prospects.

'So, our only hope with weaker numbers is a strategic use of this terrain here, to draw Constantius into another ambush,' Gaiso said. He ran his hand across the detailed landscape sketched out by the Illyrians under his command.

Magnentius stared at the map but he wasn't listening.

'We burn Siscia to the ground.'

'Surely—!' Gregorius started.

'BURN it!'

Heaving under his armor with impatience, the Franco-Breton's appetite for fresh Eastern ground was unsated and might have inexplicably grown in the wake of Silvanus' flight. He laid a thick forefinger on the map at a circled dot lying three days' march from us.

'We destroy Siscia. Then we move up the Drava, take every village on the way, and besiege Mursa!'

Within that same day, the walls of Siscia were breached and archers rained arrows down on the town. Within fifteen minutes of the first assault, it had gone up in flames. In the setting sun, lines of refugees—like living streams of weeping and stunned humanity that paralleled the quiet Drava nearby—flowed southeastwards towards sanctuary in Servitum. They straggled around the southern border of our vast encampment on foot or on mules dragging carts and wagons piled with their pathetic belongings.

Over the hours, we watched them being abused and harried by the carriages of one wealthy Siscian family or another shoving their way down of the center of the paved road.

'Frankish bastards!' some Siscian boys yelled as they passed our legionaries. Too young to shave, the bravest of them gathered stones to fling at a herd of army pack mules. The animals panicked, kicking and braying in the dust and straining at their staked ropes. I saw a couple of our Dalmatian stable masters trying to settle the youths down with shouts and gestures until one of them took a missile right in the eye. An archer raised his bow and shot the lead rioter in the right shoulder. The boy howled and his gang backed off with their wounded leader in sullen defeat.

Moving deeper into this, hostile territory was madness. Was Magnentius driving ahead into Lower Pannonia out of desperation, ambition or blind defiance of those barbarian fates he feared? Did he fancy himself a Pompey or Caesar of old, laying waste to primitive kingdoms and petty despots? This was the Roman Empire, more modern and richer than any civilization before it, not a wasteland.

Yet no one could dissuade him. To the braying of a thousand mules and shouts of a hundred centurions, the Western Army drove on the very next morning. An endless column of mounted soldiers followed the infantry tramping between the rushing Drava on one side and on the other, a flow of angry refugees who cursed and begged us for bread or coins in the same breath.

I rode alongside the army logistics officers, our mail tunics polished and rolled up in wicker baskets behind our saddles for safekeeping. For the first time in this campaign, I was unfamiliar with the road, the towns, or the foddering. This region, so far east on the *Cursus Publicus*, had never been part of my route as a junior rider.

When we reached the outskirts of Hadrian's colony, Aelia Mursa, we met Titianus' delegation returning from Constantius' lines. They returned in as much shame of failure as that ass could bring himself to admit. I was called forward to collect the dispatches recording Constantius' rebuff for posting to the bureaucrats in the West. In Treverorum, Mediolanum, and

Roma, clerks and secretaries could cluck over the news from the safety of their desks.

My secret reports to Apodemius would spare no detail. But it seemed that I might have little more to report. I was summoned to the General's tent amid frantic relays of officers and aides.

'*Agens* Marcus, this will be your last commission,' Magnentius said. 'You're already beyond the purview of your assignment to my court. You have no part in the fighting to come. Thank you for the satisfactory implementation of your duties. You may return to Mediolanum or Roma, as you see fit.'

'Yes, *Imperator*. Thank you.'

I'd been expecting dismissal for some time. The battlefield was not place for *agentes*. I marveled only that Magnentius had thought of so trivial an item of command protocol in the middle of preparations to destroy the ironbound gates of Mursa.

His specialists were even now leaning over his conference table conferring on the means of melting down more of the fortifying bands around the ladders to speed up scaling of the walls once Mursa's garrison extinguished the first flames. Rumors flew around the camp that Constantius had abandoned Cibalis and was even now marching to rescue Mursa.

But the Emperor took the time to rise to his feet and walk me to the tent entrance. I figured he must not have forgotten my small hints to think for himself instead of always following Marcellinus' bidding.

I tried to understand that his humble beginnings might feed an overweening hunger for revenge on the old enslavements and discarded notions of civilized nobility. His rough, embattled soul hadn't been lucky enough to grow up at the knees of the old Senator Manlius listening to tales of Greek democracy or Republican values upheld by a Cato or Brutus. Magnentius knew no other education than the poverty of refugee villages filled with superstitious old women for sages and then the melting pot of provincial army camps for a family.

Gregorius followed me out of the meeting tent.

'You heard your orders. Marcus. This isn't your battle. Go back to Roma and your new masters.'

He turned the blind side of his face to me and tapped the ground with the tip of one boot as if marking off the seconds left between us. This curt dismissal was his final comment on the long difficult breach that my manumissions had cleaved between us. If I wasn't to be his devoted bodyguard in the coming struggle—the same young slave who'd carried his bleeding body to safety across the bloodied waters of the Rhône—then I was of no use to him.

I could bring no further honor to the House of Manlius.

'I'm sure you'll need me,' I protested, 'It will be dangerous, even if Magnentius can't expect you to fight on the frontlines with only one good hand and eye.'

'I'll command from wherever I can be heard,' he said. 'I can strap myself to the saddle and fix my shield to my bad hand. I've done it before.'

'That was fine for parading and inspecting troops. Magnentius won't expect actual combat from you, will he?'

'Once the fighting starts, Magnentius won't have much to say about it.' His scarred lips twisted into an ironic grimace.

'Then I can still be of service, if not to you as body-guard, then to you as fellow soldier.'

'But you *aren't* a soldier now, you're a—' Even he bit off the insult *curiosus*, so as not to sully our last meeting.

But it was more than that.

If Magnentius carried the day, his personal victory would be to owe nothing more to me from now on.

If he was on the losing side, he couldn't bear the thought of my witnessing his ignominy under the hooves of the coming *clibanarii*. However much he tried, Gregorius couldn't suffer me to see the final failure of his misjudgment in backing Magnentius. By siding with a barbarian usurper against the febrile but legitimate Constans, he'd risked his father, his clan and even the future of his beloved Leo.

My very person, standing there with my *agens* insignia emblazoned on my tunic, was a reproach to his maverick decision, no matter how honorable.

If he wouldn't let me share the odds, I saw my hope of proving my loyalty to him was dashed on the packed ground under our boots. It hardly mattered now with the army machine rumbling past us, but my heart finally gave up.

Gregorius would never see me as his son—even in spirit— no matter how I was sired. He could only see in me the little bastard child he'd doddled on his knees and tolerated when grown. He'd been relieved when he was able to lift up in full view of everyone a nine-day-old Manlius boy in the ancient gesture of official recognition and legitimacy. He would never lift me to public view, even in spirit.

Once back in Numidia, at the moment of my demanding from him my promised freedom, I'd seen him weep over losing me. There were no tears today. He had his Leo now, a scion to carry on the name, burn incense to his memory, and carry on the line.

For a moment in Mursa, during the disciplined scurrying and fearful preparation for battle all around, I was tempted to take my revenge and tell him the truth. Then the memory of the Senator's kindness to me silenced my tongue. To tell the Commander that Leo was *my* child, his *grandchild*, at this moment would have either killed his courage or ended in my exile from his life forever.

'May the Fates be kind to you in your endeavor, Commander' I said. 'I'll wait for you in Roma.'

'You see,' he suddenly joked. 'There will be no need to execute me as a traitor to any cause. I'm traitor enough to my own.' With that enigmatic farewell, he walked back towards the council tent at the center of the parade ground.

I touched my sword in a salute to his back but he didn't turn around.

⚜⚜⚜

I had nothing much to pack. By the time dawn had fully blossomed across the plains, any man in his right mind would have seized the honorable flight I'd just been offered and have departed hours ago.

Instead, I lingered, unable to tear myself away from the astonishing sight spread across the broad horizon all the way to the orb of the rising sun itself.

The deep blue Drava flowed along the left of Magnentius' forces. The slanting sun suddenly hit the shine of a sea of armed men and their horses. But as terrifying as if the sun had come to join the enemy, spread out facing us with the river sliding along their right flank, stood thousands of Constantius' men encased in blinding bright Noricum steel. As one body, they stood still as statues, dark below the waist, illuminated above. As the dawn caught the reflection of helmets and plated shoulders, the enemy looked more and more like one huge fat, satisfied, scaly reptile sunning itself on a rock.

Their stealth and power in moving forward into our range overnight stole my breath. We'd heard no trumpets through the night. We hadn't seen them massing. Now the line of their formidable *clibanarii* extended up to the Drava, and for more than a quarter of mile on the other side of his infantry formation, in a second wing reaching much farther south than Magnentius' opposing ranks of horsemen. In their fantastic masked getups, the heavy cavalry looked faceless, fleshless and almost inhuman—at the very least Persian—but more like something from the Underworld.

Patient and deadly, the Eastern army held its position as the great gold sun rose directly behind them like the gods' own standard. What might these two armies have done as one if Magnentius had only accepted Gallia from one hand and peace from the other! Yes, Apodemius had been right to struggle for a balance that might sink roots, but it was too late now for regrets.

I spotted Magnentius' standard moving along his front lines, even before the winds brought his booming voice in my direction.

Then leaning forward on my horse, I heard a roar go up from the opposing forces. Constantius was galloping too, back and forth along his front lines, with one hand raised in salute at their bristling forest of lances and javelins. His horse was magnificently decked out in the knee-length mail issued to all his cavalry, but emblazoned on both sides of his imperial saddle in solid gold was his father's emblem, the Christian letters, 'Chi-Rho.'

I watched as the centurions rode back and forth between the vast lines of standing forces under the sharp orders of their decurions. The silent, anxious breath of over one hundred thousand men in full armor waiting to cross swords lay across the entire plain. Only the orderly commands of the officers or the whinny of a nervous horse broke the deathly hush.

The morning turned hot for autumn. I was thirsty, but that was no excuse to linger like this. Yet I couldn't tear myself away from the sight of the Empire poised and divided against itself. Glancing down the *Cursus*, I saw that my passage was still clogged with refugees.

I dismounted and led my horse to the outskirts of the emptied camp, seeking a medic's tent. I knew from the old days, that even though the doctor's surgery always lies on the outskirts of battle, bad news of any kind gets to his team first. I found them rolling their bandages and soaking instruments in acetum with a wordless professionalism. Their tents would fill with men's screams of pain soon enough.

'It's been a couple of hours,' I said to one of the Greek orderlies. 'What's happening? Are they negotiating?'

As long as there was no signal to attack, I held out hope.

'The fodder team tells us that Constantius met with the Mursa bishop, Valens. The old priest saw a cross hanging in the sky at dawn so he says the Christian god blesses their side. Constantius is off in some church of Arian martyrs saying prayers.'

'I heard he's having all of his soldiers baptized before they risk their lives,' said a supply slave, running in with boiled water.

'But he's not baptized himself! He'll leave it to his deathbed like his father did,' I said.

'All I know is that he's dismissing the soldiers who don't want to be baptized from the fighting,' the slave shrugged.

'He will leave the fighting to his generals,' the Greek said, rolling his knives and pincers in the sterilizing bath.

'Yes, well, the imperial family has form when it comes to letting others do their fighting for them,' I told him. 'Constans did the same thing. Did Magnentius see this Christian cross in the sky?'

'Did you? Did I?' the Greek slave scoffed. 'Nearly 40,000 men on our side missed the miracle sign? Funny we should hear of it, though, right?'

The supply slave shook his head. 'They're just trying to spook us.'

The morning wore on and the heat rose shimmering into the heavy air. On the other side, Constantius' heavy cavalry must be stifling, even cooking in those body ovens. Yet, from a distance, I could see none of the heavy lances poised for attack waver or falter. After years on the scorched Persian deserts, the Pannonian September might be just a clement spring day to these veterans.

I waited and watched, unable to tear myself away to safety. Perhaps the baptizing of thousands of men would take up the whole day. Or perhaps it was just a ploy to avoid engaging his metallic warriors during the hottest hours of the day. There was no standing down, not through the sun's highest point in the sky, nor even as the birds began to return from midday naps to peck and twitter in the afternoon shade of a few trees overlooking the plain.

I could not believe it they would actually fight. I prayed that these long hours of unnatural silence promised peace, compromise, safety and sanity for us all. It was coming, I felt sure at last, as I felt the sun sinking on my back now. That last warmth of late afternoon turning the sky rust-red with resignation. The day's danger would soon be survived. Dusk was less than an hour away.

I left the medics and went back to pack up again, unhitch my horse, and ride away. A horn sounded across the plains and echoed off one hundred thousand shields. The Eastern horns answered the signal. The medics ran outside and together we watched the horizon. Half a mile to the right of our tents, we heard thunder and spotted Constantius' limitless left wing on the move. His massive wing of thousands of *clibanarii*, were gathering speed, advancing at a measured gallop in a disciplined oblique line stretching southwestwards away from the river.

They seemed to be leaving the plains altogether. It looked as if any minute they would gallop for another quarter of a mile until they trampled right over the queue of straggling refugees on the *Cursus* far beyond.

But there came another set of signals and like a snake recoiling on itself, they pulled them up short. The noise multiplied as Magnentius' signalers blew their alerts.

Already the time for trumpets and cornets was almost over. From now on the legions had to act on standing orders issued through the cacophony of shouts and commands that barely reached my ears. Constantius' monstrous wing doubled its speed and suddenly almost folded right in on itself. Like a carrion bird swooping its deadly wing around its prey, the thundering charge wheeled around in a colossal arc. Their deadly lances shot down from the sky as they angled them forward, pointing sharply at the right flanks of the Western infantry's front lines.

Magnentius troops swiveled to their right, southwards, to face the onslaught. They closed their shields hard and fast to resist the coming impact. It was obvious Magnentius' formation had been foolhardy. Horns blew to reposition the northern-most cavalry, to bring from the river-bound rear, but they would be too late. Constantius was using his extra cavalry to shatter Magnentius' right wing.

And then Constantius' killers smashed into them. A cloud of summer dust rose up into the sky. We listened to the clamor and horns for many minutes. I should have gone, I said to myself, listening to the rising cacophony, but now I can't go, I can't.

The first wounded trickled in on stretchers, but for the most part, the battlefield had turned into a level of mayhem too ferocious for the stretcher slaves to penetrate. Discipline had kept the Western line tight for an anguishing half hour but suddenly, the Eastern forces, indifferent to the hail of missiles and arrows from the rear archers, recollected themselves for a second assault. With breathtaking choreography, they wheeled and reformed, and rushed forward to take on Gaiso's cavalry legions.

I could stand by watching no longer.

'Finally getting out of here?' the head Greek doctor asked as he wrapped a ragged thigh with a wide tourniquet. 'I don't blame you.'

'You'll see me again,' I called to him. 'Let's hope it's not feet first.'

For I had decided, not with my mind but with my heart, that I would not abandon my father to this—whether he recognized me or not, whether my orders were to stay or go, and whether I had failed in my mission or merely finished it. Half of me was a Numidian provincial ready to leave these Romans to their incestuous struggle over a diadem and purple cloak. But half of me was Manlius, with the noble blood of the lost Republic hardened by my grandmother's imperial Gallo-Roman valor.

The future of the Empire was also my future, *our* future, to lose.

Back on my horse, I charged hard eastward to clear the savage battle spreading as Constantius' troops pressed Magnentius' back northward towards the riverbanks. I was searching through the thickened air for the Ioviani or Herculiani banners. I wanted to find Gregorius somehow in the day's fading, dust-clogged light. With one hour to go before nightfall, the Frankish and Saxons legions were taking huge losses, literally fleeing into my path and falling mashed under the hooves of my horse, as heavily armored Syrian archers pierced their unprotected flesh with ease. The Hispaniards and Celts were holding, just.

I was within five hundred yards of the Drava now, close enough to see the dark forms of Saxon mercenaries sinking into the shallows of the water, failing in a last ditch attempt to wade across to safety. One by one, they suddenly disappeared, trapped without warning by a sharp drop into the swifter currents and dragged down to a cold and final relief by their heavy gear.

The Franks' infantry were rallying and suddenly gaining on the Easterners, sword for sword. Within a few feet of drowning, they were finally peeling themselves away from the riverbanks's deadly embrace, yard by yard.

Now, at last, I spotted Gaiso, still in his saddle and shouting to pull the Frankish ranks tighter. One of Constantius' faceless riders, an enormous *clibanarius* was tearing towards the hunter. That was my cue. Drawing my sword, I galloped into the fray, between skirmishes, until I had reached him. I rounded on the steeled horseman who had just started slashing at Gaiso's flank.

The Easterner kicked his horse away to elude me and I raced after him, but leaning forward in my saddle, I saw nothing I could aim my sword—not a single inch of exposed human flesh. This rider was a veritable Achilles, but without a single vulnerable heel. And there were thousands upon thousands of them all battling all around me.

I finally got into position at the left rear of his horse and without any chance to think, I poised my *spatha* point straight into the root of the horsetail swishing at my knees and rammed it home the one place a horse needed to leave unarmored.

The horse whinnied in agony and reared up in pain. My blade had found its target. As Constantius' cavalryman clung to the agonized steed, Gaiso had not missed his chance behind me. I had wheeled around in a dash to safety. Gaiso saw his moment from the other side and ran his own *spatha* clean across the animal's unarmored belly before he fell back to earth. Together we had downed man and horse.

A second enemy horseman was close to attacking me. Like a mad peasant, I'd gone into battle without a shield. My helmet was merely the leather riding helmet of an *agens* and my legs were bare of any metal protection. He swerved away from Gaiso's blood-drenched weapon and pulled his glittering axe, lifting it to slash at my reins and detach my forearms from my hand. Any second now, he would have my limb dropping into the churned up mud below my foot.

Gaiso's sword blocked the man's mailed elbow, denting only the metal, but opening the enemy's breast to a stab of my sword just above his neck plate. My thrust met flesh, he bled, and sank slowly off his horse.

'Get a shield, messenger boy!' Gaiso shouted—or at least I think that's what he said—through the deafening noise. He signaled for me to follow him. I raced after his horse, kicking my own terrified postal mount to keep up with his war-hearty stallion.

This was what Gaiso lived for. He grinned back at me, his reddened cheeks blanketed filthy with dust and sweat. It was the hunt all over again, another sunny autumn morning, innocently chasing a boar. But this time our lives were at stake and all around us, men were falling like hunted animals. Some of them rolled in their armor cages. Warhorses were trained to avoid men underfoot but the flailing metal objects pouring with blood confused them. The noise was deafening.

There was an hour somewhere when my despair started to lift. It seemed that what the West had lacked in armor, we could make up for with a quicksilver brute strength and creative courage these Easterners lacked. They relied too much on their steel carcasses. Shorn of a helmet or armored horse, the Western men didn't break and fun like Persians when their line was shattered. A German's ferocity or the Celt's quick wits were carrying more moments than then lost.

The tide shifted in Magnentius' favor, then against him, and then who knew? I battled on, breathing hard, thirsty, terrified. I realized there here were no more lines, no more assaults and no more horns blowing to call us to retreat and safety. Bewildered in the slaughter, officers were now just fighters. There were no longer two armies, just Roman men fighting Roman men in a slaughter without strategy or boundaries.

I'd lost Gaiso in the chaos. I went on and on, slashing and kicking. I fought off three, four, five, six, and now I had lost count past the first dozen, always relying on my eye to find the soft flesh somewhere on the heavy-footed enemy. I killed some and discouraged others and only hoped that these were enemies of the Commander. I no longer heard anything distinct, but just went on like this, each bout with an Eastern soldier lasting an eternity or an instant. I lost track of time, heard nothing but my own terrified, exhilarated breath and the panting of my courageous horse. The lowering sun touched the tips of trees in on the distant slope behind our position but if the day was ending, the battle raged on.

Surely it was over for the day. Yet no horns sounded retreat. The valley of Mursa was a mass of killing. I saw no one I knew in the fray. I'd lost Gaiso hours ago. I now galloped towards the south, hunting for any officer or standard I could recognize. An Eastern hellhound gave chase and caught up with me, plunging his long *contus* at my side, but missing again and again as my sturdy little horse dodged and turned at my command. Perhaps he thought he was simply avoiding a traffic jam or lumbering obstacle on the Cursus Publicus but he was holding steady underneath me. The fighter was well beyond my reach. I had to escape him or die.

I was again pinning my very life on Gaiso's tricks, making the other man's animal twist and turn, aiming for its eyes or unarmored knees, leaning low in my saddle to dodge the deadly lance that kept me at bay. Finally, I made a break for it and spurred my horse to charge as fast as he could go towards the Drava, to a high point where the water had eaten away part of the bloodsoaked bank. The featureless horseman took my bait and stormed after me, his lance tapping with frustration on my horse's flank, missing again and again. We were heading straight for the black waters rushing below, then I wheeled my agile mount clear of the drop and watched as my pursuer's momentum carried his heavy weight clean over the shard of crumbling earth and down on into the sucking mud up to his knees.

I caught sight of no one to tell me what was happening. No one knew. It was sunset now and still I had found no sign of Gregorius or his legionaries. I took down more than half a dozen heavy-clad men in bouts lasting what seemed forever on the strength of mad indifference to death and deft agility. I realized I was going to fight forever until I died and joined the thick landscape of corpses and groaning wounded blanketing the field. At least I wasn't going to die inside a metal coffin like these enemy riders.

Now yet another one Constantius' relentless devils made for me. I gripped my knees tight to my exhausted horse like an obstinate Numidian warrior out of my mother's legends. She had always said that I was as stubborn as a mule. Now it was paying off as I postponed my death through sheer bloody-mindedness. Rising up in my saddle, I got one deep stab right into his horse's whinnying mouth when it bucked with fear, but as it reared away in pain, it yanked my sword right out of my sweaty hand.

Then horse and enemy descended down on top of my smaller horse. We all crashed together into the mess of blood and white gore spreading underfoot. A second Eastern horseman reined in but his horse refused to trample me. I rolled to safety from the hooves and with only my *pugio* in hand, slashed at the horse's shins. I got at the small swivel knife hidden in my boot cuff and had two hands working now, back and forth, to catch his horse's kicking fetlocks. Deadly hooves pounded all around me, as the Easterner struggled with his horse to finish me off. The horse disobeyed again and again, flashing target spots I missed over and over. I waited for the blow from the fallen rider to come up behind me and dodged sideways only just in time. I was ready to take on them both if I had to. My postal horse had galloped away, no doubt to search in panic for the familiar pavement of the *Cursus*.

Then suddenly the Eastern horse and rider were gone, and the second enemy gone as well, all of them pulled back by horn signals I'd only missed. It was completely dark. Brutal duels and clashes rang out only yards within my reach but nearly invisible.

There was so little moonlight, my Eastern horsemen had given up. They could no longer make me out as alive or dead among the limbs, no longer even see me among the heads and torsos flung onto the ground at every turn.

The two armies were still fighting, but fighting blind as ghosts in the near-pitch black.

Wary and panting in the blackness, I struggled for my balance, both blades held out ready ahead of me. I waited for my next foe. I had no thought in my head but killing.

I started to walk, keeping the river at my back and ignoring the pleas for help that rang out in the night on either side. A *clibanarius* lumbered towards me on foot, his lance point racing towards my heart as I stood dumb and paralyzed, too tired to escape its aim. Then he fell over, dead right at my feet, his helmet crashing onto the shield of another fallen man.

He had collapsed from some invisible wound or simple heat and exhaustion. I stared down at him, my dagger waiting, almost willing him to rise up again and fight as hard for life as I was fighting. But he didn't move. Riderless horses galloped past me, slapping my dazed face with the foot loops and saddle ropes now emptied of man and weapons.

I felt dizzy but no pain. I suspected I had been struck somehow on the head or wounded. I wonder if a kind of shock was moving me along on my way to the Underworld. I had seen men in Dr Ari's medical tent unable to understand what had happened to them, and perhaps I was one of them now.

I heard wails of pain and horror and more desperate animal grunts all around me. I crouched and moved forward, hoping no one would launch a fresh duel that I no longer had the will to repel. Splashes and shouts of victims fighting their way out of the river behind me gave me the direction of the Drava. Clouds obscured the moon. The tents must be half a mile to my right and the medic's tents farthest away, along to the south. If I crawled along in this blackness, would I survive and return to life? Thousands upon thousands of dead men's parts strewn across my answered 'no.'

I slipped and fell. I rose again and slipped again. In the distance I saw torches moving. They might belong to either side, whichever had won, if any had won at all.

I stayed well clear of those moving flames. I crawled slowly, feeling other men's helmets, boots, shoulders, bellies and ears under my groping fingers. I crawled aiming for the medics' tents.

I was crawling through an abattoir. My hand fell on another man's fingers, still warm, clutching empty air. I stopped, disbelieving. I groped and peered at the hand wearing two rings. I gathered my strength and tried to pull the man up by the arm, hoping to drag him to rescue if he still breathed, but the arm came away with a sucking sound from the muck in which it had sunk. It was still bleeding. I explored around in the dark and it was as if the fingers I searched gripped at my heart. An army runner passed me carrying a flaming torch and by the frightening illumination I stared down at the rings. These were the very jewels I'd seen patting dispatches in my satchel bag and the same rings I'd witnessed on fingers signing off letter after letter.

I was trying to save the butchered limb of Marcellinus.

Carefully, ignoring the chaos all around me, I removed the rings for safekeeping to give his wife back in Augustodunum, as witness to his bravery to the last. With groping hand, I searched around me for the man himself.

I turned up nothing a grieving widow would welcome.

I crawled on, around dead horses and over men groaning for water. Other men were still on their feet, plunging here and darting there as they scavenged corpses for weapons, Eastern or Western, to fight on in the blackness. Some chased horses to regain their advantage. Some were skulking, trying to make a run for it. I gathered up a fresh sword and shield for myself, hardly knowing whether it marked me for one side or other, it was so covered in mud. All around me now, men kept on fighting in a morass of confusion.

Moving faster now on foot, I skirted a small unit of cursing Franks fending off a pair of mounted *clibanarii* with determination. They didn't need me. I hunted for an available horse, but every animal I found bore horrible wounds as it stood stockstill trembling in shock or laid itself into its muddy grave with gums bared in pain.

I must have circled in panic. I found myself at the river again. It glinted like a liquid sword itself now in the dim light, but where there had been no crossing to safety, now thousands of bodies stretched out as if the riverbank had molted into a new and ghostly metal shore. It made for an eerie pontoon of dead men stretching halfway across the water but no farther.

I saw more dead than anyone would ever be able to count. I huddled by the river, resting and shaking next to my shield. Some men found new fights to fling themselves at in the blackness. I was done with heroics. I'd seen enough and yet now saw no one. Although I wanted to lie low in the gloom, there was only one thing left. I knew that any of these stubborn heroes might be Gregorius himself, so I shifted my steps until I stumbled on two or even three men at a time, entangled in each other's arms or weaponless and gouging at each other's faces with muddied, bleeding fingers.

One man, part of a mob so covered in dirt and blood, I could no longer determine which side he was on, and tried stabbing at my back. He just missed my right shoulder but when I saw that he had just felled an Hispaniard and was going for a final, fatal blow at the man's bare head, I rounded on the Easterner and aimed for his neck with a swing of my sword. The blow was incomplete but he dropped his weapons and sank onto the ground trying to hold his head on, to close the deep gash. I kicked the Easterner aside and grabbed the Hispanic survivor by his good arm. There was a sickening sound of sucking mud as I left him up and dragged him forward, towards the medics' tents. He was gasping and sobbing as he looked down at the remainder of his other arm, now so chopped and hacked, it was probably too damaged to save.

There was a row of orderly lanterns and torches in sight ahead of us. The Hispaniard found his footing, mumbled some thick-throated thanks and staggered on his own for help.

But another, unluckier man wasn't making it alone. I nearly stepped on him. He was dragging himself towards the circle of light marking the medical station. He was grunting hard but gaining only inches. His strength was no match for the sucking action of blood mixed with slime and gore.

One hand still clenched his shield and the other his sword. They were making it impossible for him to gain purchase pulling himself forward. He had reached the very edge of the battlefield. Why didn't he go of his weapons to make better speed towards help?

Then my heart split in two. The soldier could not let it go because his crippled hand was bound tight to the shield's protective planks where another man's darts would have been mounted. Another runner raced past us holding a torch that pierced the darkness. For a second, the man and I were illuminated as if under a flash of lightning that disappeared a second later but it was time enough. I'd recognized the Commander dragging himself through the mud.

I tried to lift Gregorius up out of the mess, but saw he had a deep gash below his cuirass leaving his innards, white and glistening, exposed to the rising night winds. His one good eye rolled back in its socket as he felt my arms encircle him. His right hand dropped his sword as he flailed blindly for my help.

'It's me, Marcus. Hang on. Hang on. We've done this before. We'll do it again.'

CHAPTER 20, A WOUNDED DREAM

—BEFORE DAWN, SEPTEMBER 29, 351 AD, MURSA—

I wasn't sure the Commander had heard me or even knew it was me holding him clear of the filth. I watched his drained face closely as I inched him forward, fearful of pulling his wounds open wider. He couldn't speak and seemed to be passing back and forth between this world and the next. I might lose him any second.

The sliver of moon now hung low over the plains but the flickering forest of torches that lit up the medical tents only mocked our slow progress. At this rate, we'd never reach help. The whole rescue area had tripled in size with ordinary tents seconded for the wounded into a freshly sprouted city of the half-dead. Bodies were being discarded in piles as fast as the luckier of the wounded were carried in. After only a few dozen yards, I looked up to realized we'd found ourselves on the wrong side of an Alpine mound of corpses, rising higher by the minute as medical slave-runners tossed *legatus* on top of cavalryman on top of ballistics specialist without regard for rank.

We were being cut off from help by a palisade of the newly dead.

I collapsed with the Commander on the ground and fought for breath. I could hear the medical staff on the other side of the barrier shouting for able men to make way or help bring forward the cases that had any hope of surviving. I waved for their attention and shouted at stretcher-bearers trotting past us but no one paid us any heed in the dark.

They would abandon the hopeless cases where they lay, kicking away the desperate fingers that reached for their ankles and ignoring the savage curses of men left to bleed as they passed.

I'd heard it all before outside Aquiliea and along the Rhodanus but this was no mere battle. We were helpless in the midst of the end of the world. This time even an alert and healthy man could hardly make out the medics' instructions over the screams and groans of thousands of wounded stumbling and staggering forward through the dark or just left behind, thirsty, dismembered and friendless, in the muck.

The entire breadth of Pannonia had turned to blood and shit. The Roman Army had let loose one bloodcurdling howl to the gods.

By feeling through the gore with my feet, I moved us two yards or so to a patch of raised ground not clutched at by dead fingers or churned up by the death throes of a horse.

I held the commander in my arms.

'Wait for the dawn, Commander. Someone will find us. Rest for a minute.' I had no water to rouse him from his faint but he still breathed. His wound might get worse or it might hold—I couldn't see in the dark but surely light would eventually rise, even on what would be a hellish day?

The last distant clangs of steel hitting steel fell silent at last. The air was filled with the shouts of frantic men with no officers left to command them. We waited and waited. Suddenly half a dozen tribunes rode past, their horses' hooves dodging men underfoot. They were hunting for lost standards and fallen officers.

I screamed for assistance. They didn't hear me.

No one was coming to us. Lying in a sea of lost souls, I realized there was almost no one left to come.

The Commander stirred. There was a little daylight now. A cold blue whisper of dawn revealed his scarred gray face. He opened his eye and recognized me.

'Just wait, Commander. Someone will come. Someone will come.'

He tried to lift his good hand, but I took it in mine to save him the effort. 'Yes, it's Marcus. Hold on. It's almost over. Someone will come.'

But if I'd tried to shout for help again, I would only have joined the chorus of thousands upon thousands who wailed around us. I saw the first bright crescent of orange rising above the eastern flatland where Constantius had stretched out his lethal wing of *clibanarii*. There was no shining river of faultless riders over there now, but just more of the carnage. I scanned in all directions for a healthy man, a man on two good legs, within hailing for help. But there was no one within earshot of my call, even if I'd had the strength.

Suddenly the Commander's bad hand scrabbled at my tunic collar. Like a wraith rising from Hades, he pulled on my *bulla* with all the weight of his armored body. If he meant to lever himself up by the neck cord, it was futile.

The cord snapped and his hand fell back with the Senator's gift flipping into the gutted earth. His tight fight pounded on the ground as if to bury my *bulla* or with his last ounce of force, to smash it to pieces. Was this his last gesture? To tear away my last link to the Manlius clan? To deny me even that? Did his life cling to this world by the pathetic cord of so much bitterness?

'No, don't take that from me now!' I stopped his pounding fist.

He tried to answer. I laid my head low to his lips twisted by the old injury and listened. His words didn't come and his eye rolled back on its socket again. I sobbed, 'I'm here. It's me, Marcus. Someone will come. Someone must come.'

His chest heaved with effort. His lips worked until they found the breath.

'*Filius meus.*' My son.

'Yes,' I answered, bursting into helpless sobs, '*Pater meus, semper servio tibi.*' My father, I serve you always.

Then the mangled hand fell back into the mud. I untangled the cord from his remaining fingers and tied it back around my neck. His breath was growing fainter. His eye stared up at me.

His pulse was gone.

I held him until the morning unveiled its full horror across the plains of Mursa and I could stand the carpet of stench, bones and brains around me no more. There was no more need to worry about his wound. Straining under the weight of the Commander's armor, I stumbled with his lifeless body around the vast palisade of corpses and found help at last.

I added his body to a camp of thousands of dead. I had to walk up and down a maze of lifeless bodies, threading my way between the macabre corridors of the unclaimed and sightless dead, hoping to find an exit and a cup of water.

A head and pair of shoulders sticking halfway up a mound of slain stopped me short. Here lay the peerless Gaiso between two signalers from the Herculiani corps. His eyes stared up at the skies. His right hand clutched at the shaft of a Syrian's arrow piercing his cuirass over the heart. His death had been swift.

I felt emptied of emotion or grief. I stumbled on, my ears ringing with the screams of casualties in the medical tents and frantic commands all around me. Impatient army slaves jostled and bossed me out of their way. Only when I found the body of a legion commander I recalled in conference with Silvanus did I stop my ghoulish tour long enough to notice that deep gashes scored my own thighs and calves.

'Get those looked to, man, or the infection will take you next,' said a little Dacian slave. But the medical tents were so swamped with critical cases, I shook my head.

The sun had cleared the horizon. I laid down in despair and slept among the dead and wounded, no different from a thousand other men, or two? or three? who did the same, waiting for one world to breathe its last and another to take its place . . .

₽₽₽

'You're wanted in the command tent.' A tribune kicked me awake. He had found me bandaged and passed out with exhaustion on a tarpaulin stretched out on the grass.

Of course it would be the Prefect Fabius Titianus who had
survived. He lost no time as the sun rose in the sky to try to
impose order in the command tent. I found him flanked by
legion commanders from all over the battlefield reporting on
losses as they came to light.

Working my way through dozens of weary fighters, I
reported for duty.

'I heard you dismissed back to Roma, *Agens*,' the prefect
said. 'What are you doing here?'

'Fighting, Prefect.'

'That's not your job. Does your *schola* know where you
are?'

'I'm not sure, Prefect.'

'What's your rank, Numidianus?'

'*Circitor, upper class,* promoted a year ago.'

'Clean yourself up, if possible and stand by. We may have
use of you.'

'Where is the Emperor Magnentius, Prefect?'

'Unaccounted for.'

I waited some hours for Titianus to finish his awful task of
tallying the losses with the assistance of army secretaries.
Titianus was no champion as a fighter or diplomat, but I
credited him with the stamina of a god as the numbers mounted
up, passing ten thousand, then fifteen. By noon, the estimate
had reached twenty thousand.

The secretaries halted once, so that Titianus could leave the
tent. We heard him retching outside. One of the tribunes went
off in a futile search for a bucket of fresh water.

There was no food or drink. I saw no friend. I sat alone, like
hundreds around me. I thought of Kahina and wondered where
the court of Magnentius had fled. Magnentius . . . where had the
Usurper himself gone? And the Caesar Decentius?

The Prefect returned to the tent, brushing past us, just as a
decurion from one of the Frankish legions arrived on foot,
carrying a bundle of leather in his arms.

'For the command staff, urgent,' he said, pushing past those
of us ordered to stay out of the way.

Titianus watched as the gruff German auxiliary unpacked his burden. He unrolled Magnentius' huge purple and gold battle cloak on the ground. 'He was last seen by some of our men fighting late into the night,' he reported in the rough Latin of the Rhenus refugee camps. 'We found his horse grazing across the Drava to the west. We took it to the stable tents.'

'Any sign yet of the Caesar Decentius?'

'None so far.'

'We can't wait any longer. Get that *Agens* Numidianus for me.'

'Yes, Prefect. I'm right here.'

'You remember Sardica? You remember what Constantius looks like?'

'Of course, Prefect.'

'The hours are passing. I have no choice. As an *agens*, your *schola* is distinct from the army. That makes you neutral, although at this moment, you hardly look credible.'

'No, Prefect.'

'The men who fought for Magnentius are at the mercy of the victor. We face execution. But Roman law protects the *agentes* from recrimination. You are to cross the battlefield, locate Constantius, and deliver this to his hand and none other.'

He handed me a piece of vellum bound by a leather cord scavenged from someone's saddlebag.

I stared at the document in my hand.

'It's the written surrender,' Titianus said, 'as if one were needed.'

'Casualties at 22,000,' a tribune interrupted, 'but we're counting the fallen enemy standards as well, estimating losses upwards of 33,000 for them.'

'Is this possible?' Titianus burst out, pounding his fist on an upturned weapons crate. 'Is this *possible*? Where is everyone?'

I stood there, stunned. Titianus had just ordered me to return to the court of Constantius, whatever hellhole that court occupied now across the fields of slaughter. I stood commanded to march straight back and face both Paulus Catena and Eusebius, not to mention risking Emperor Constantius' paranoid and vengeful fury over the death of his brother—at my hand.

I stood frozen, unable to speak.

'What's the matter with you? You have your orders. Go now.'

'Prefect, I'm not even ranked *biarchus* class. I'm hardly senior enough for this honor.'

'I know it's an honor well above you, but from what I recall, you're a freedman from the House of Manlius. Gregorius thought something of you. Even Constantius, that Illyrian *bastard*, might have heard the esteemed name of Manlius. We Romans understand these things, right? Barbarians on one side, Arian priests on the other—but *we are still Roma*, I swear to the gods, and that Constantius has yet to even set foot in the Founding City!'

I may well be arrested. If there is an answer—?'

'You will take two signalers. Will you do it for the rest of us—for the thousands who've fallen today in defense of the Empire?'

He did not realize that he had just laid down my death sentence. With teeth clenched and heart frozen, I marched away to locate a fresh horse. This was the last thing I was destined to do. If Titianus had needed a way of twisting the blade of my loyalty deeper into my guts to bend me to his will, he could not have found a better means. *Titianus had just done something that as an ex-slave I could not resist.*

In the end, he'd *asked*, not ordered me.

Yes, I would deliver the surrender—as a Roman freedman proud of his last act.

It took us some twenty minutes of careful riding to reach the imperial tents pitched not far from the church where Constantius had waited out the massacre of the previous day in prayer with Bishop Valens. The imperial banners flew over a slight rise in the terrain marking out a string of tents forested by standards being returned by slaves and infantry medics.

They parted to make way for our trio. The signalers surrendered the muddied banners and standards of the Ioviani and Herculiani legions and remnants of other legions. I reported us to a group of officers gathered around a camp desk, shaking their own blood-smeared faces at casualty lists.

Leaving my escorts outside the main tent, I found Emperor Constantius with what was left of his advisers. He did not stand to receive me, but some members of his *comitatus* nodded with respect. Eusebius was nowhere to be seen. There was only one hateful face that leered at me with recognition as I advanced my way through the exhausted officers.

I identified myself and extended the roll of *vellum*, 'For the Emperor.' An officer on Constantius' left took it and with ceremony passed it to the Emperor himself.

Stony-faced, Constantius unrolled it and scanned the lines.

Now he stood up from his sturdy *cathedra*. I was astonished anew at his height. His rigid expression seemed calculated to give the impression of a statue already carved to his own greatness. Up close all his features were recognizably Constantine but thicker and masculine, unlike his younger brother's. His expression was unemotional and virile, unlike that of the viperish sister.

'We have lost more men today than the Tyrant,' he said in a low voice. 'Yet we have carried the day.' He seemed to be addressing me with an unblinking glare.

'Yes, *Imperator*.' I gulped and felt Catena's black eyes pierce my back with anticipation.

'We did everything to prevent him,' the Emperor murmured. 'We offered him forgiveness, freedom, and all of Gallia. Yet he pressed on.'

I nodded my affirmation and waited at attention.

'The Roman Empire has just committed suicide,' he said to the hushed officers. 'Look around you out there.' His voice rose, not in panic, but despair. 'What do you see? The Empire has just fallen on its own sword! What was that Plutarch called it? What did—?' his voice broke with sudden grief. 'What did he write about Pyrrhus?'

There was a dismayed silence in the wide space around him, as if only this man *saw* and *understood* the catastrophe of two short days. Would no officer answer the anguished sovereign? These lesser men hung back and simply stared.

I was a doomed soul, but not an ignorant one.

I braced my shoulders and touched my sword again to show my respect. 'With respect, *Imperator*, *"Pyrrhus replied to one that gave him joy of his victory that one more such victory would utterly undo him".*'

'That's it, *Agens*! What did Plutarch write after that?'

'He wrote, *"For he'd lost a great part of the forces he brought with him, and almost all his particular friends and principal commanders; there were no others there to make recruits, and he found the confederates in Italia backward".*'

'Go on. This is a message from our betters that we need to hear.'

' . . . *"On the other hand, as from a fountain continually flowing out of the city, the Roman camp was quickly and plentifully filled up with fresh men, not at all abating in courage for the loss they sustained, but even from their very anger gaining new force and resolution to go on with the war.*'

'Would that it were so. How do you know the wisdom of our forefathers by heart, Messenger?'

'I had an excellent teacher, *Imperator*, the Roman Senator Manlius to whom I read those pages many times. I am grieved to add that during the revolt of Nepotianus, the rebel *Magister Officiorum* Marcellinus murdered this venerable statesman.'

'We see. What strange events.' Constantius took a deep breath. 'Like Pyrrhus, we have no hope of fresh troops, no fountain of men rising up from this carnage to fill up our ranks . . . ' He stood stock-still. No one dared interrupt. 'There is no one left.'

Constantius glanced at the *comes* standing mute next to him. 'To whom do we award the *torc*, the *armillae*, the *phalerae*, and the *Hasta Pura*? What use are medals, honors and awards to dead men?'

Finally, Constantius looked again at me. 'This is the message we want you to carry back—that all division and enmity between our armies is forgiven. We order a complete truce. What's more, we order the immediate coordination of all our medical resources and staff to tend to the wounded of both sides. We are again one Roman Empire. Is our message clear?'

'Certainly, *Imperator*.' I fell to one knee and kissed the hem of his cloak to indicate gratitude.

'We ask only one thing of the gods on this sad day and that is revenge on the family of Magnentius and those who were individually responsible for my brother Constans' murder.'

The officers murmured their approval of the Emperor's magnanimity. Only one harsh voice broke the sad harmony.

'Then your day is complete, *Imperator*, for none other than Constans' murderer kneels before you right there.'

Paulus Catena had made his move.

Constantius could not disguise his surprise. 'This messenger is our brother's assassin?'

'Yes, *Imperator*.'

The hateful Hispaniard stepped forward, his mismatched features made only worse by the dust and blood smeared across his sweaty cheeks. 'I detained this Marcus Gregorianus Numidianus once before to make a formal arrest for your pleasure, but he escaped the Sardica jail before I could extract his confession.'

I kept my eyes to the ground and felt the Fates rushing in on me from all sides, invisibly encircling me and whispering my doom in my ears. They were saying that for the sake of honor, I was destined to pay this death. As soon as Prefect Titianus had ordered me here, I had foreseen it.

'Is this true? You bear the insignia of an *agens*.' It was the voice of the Emperor reaching me through the Fates' whistling, hissing warnings.

I needed to face this final hour standing up, looking the Emperor straight in the eyes as I sealed my doom. I rose off my knee and removed my helmet so that he would always remember the face of one who valued truth.

'I am a freedman, *Imperator*, and the illegitimate son of Commander Atticus Manlius Gregorius. I rode in the arrest party with Commander Gaiso. As *agens* attached to his detail, I knew the roads and the stations. I carried the documents for the Emperor Constans' arrest.'

'But all of that exonerates you from responsibility. Whether we like it or not, that's what an *agens* is for, among other things.'

Catena couldn't wait. 'He's playing games with you, *Imperator*. He's no road warrant inspector. He's the man who wielded the death blow that left your brother disemboweled and bleeding to death in the temple dedicated to your mother.'

Catena pointed his finger at me. 'That is the hand that struck down Constans as he surrendered his arms with honor.'

Constantius' eyes shifted left, right, left, right without moving his head a jot, as if Catena had pulled a lever inside the Emperor's uneasy mind.

'How do you know this, Catena? We've prayed to avenge our brother's death for over a year. We've delayed satisfaction while we fought back the Persians, even while our deepest family loyalty begged us to turn to the West to take our revenge.' Constantius turned his angry jaw on its stiff, thick neck and faced Catena with a stony gaze.

Catena's uneven little eyes blinked under his sovereign's scrutiny. 'He's the assassin. I swear it. It was the talk of Treverorum.'

'Then he must die, without honor, unlike the thousands upon thousands who lie around us this morning. Hand me my sword. It is my duty to our family name to execute this man myself.'

To my horror, an aide wasted no time in presenting to Constantius a jeweled scabbard hanging off a filigreed leather sword belt.

'Do you wish to confess or pray, messenger?'

It was the first time in my young life I could have wished to be a Christian, if only to gain another minute or two of precious breath. However, all the honor of my sacrifice as a man who protected his commanding officer to the death would be tainted by such a deception.

I shook my head, 'No.'

Constantius hesitated. He was a suspicious man by reputation. Perhaps he didn't trust Catena. Perhaps he found his prayer to settle this score was answered too easily. Perhaps he even thought twice about cutting off a young head so filled with Plutarch.

He laid the razor-sharp blade on the nape of my neck. My skin shivered at the tickle of cold steel. The morning light caught the jewels on the hilt. I saw the tent wall flicker a dazzling green. I realized that these dancing emerald glints of sunlight were the last things I would ever see. And my last act had been to proclaim my Manlius blood to the world. But would history add this footnote to the credit or debit accounts of the dying Manlius clan?

'Are you absolutely sure, Catena? There has been enough wasteful slaughter today.'

'He's the one, *Imperator*. If you don't believe me, ask Eusebius.' It was a deft move by Catena to call on his hated rival for corroboration.

I felt Constantius lift the sword off my neck and into the air to strike the blow.

'But he's *not* guilty, Constantius,' said a man at the rear of the tent. 'My subordinate officer, the notary Paulus Catena, is sadly misinformed.'

The assembly turned at the interruption. I thought I recognized my defender's voice but dared not glance up, for fear my mix of terror and determination to meet the Fates with courage might betray my guilt. The Emperor's blade hung frozen in the air.

'Catena, my dear fellow, we are all wracked with grief this morning. But even *in extremis*, we can't condemn a man, particularly an *agens* protected by the rule of law, just on hearsay and gossip.'

'How dare you—?'

'Wait, Catena, before you say something you'll regret. You forget I was briefly part of Magnentius' court, *Imperator*. I bear no love for the men who led us to this disaster. Nor will they—if any of their enemy council survives—live to praise the name of

Claudius Silvanus. But I do know them and I know their history in this affair. I know that Gaiso, famed for his hunting wiles and peerless in his warrior skills, is the assassin you seek. He boasted of it to me himself. This *agens* was a mere escort, a North African nobody. He is unworthy of a Constantine's retribution. Bring Gaiso forward from your prisoners and there you will find true justice.'

Constantius laid aside his heavy gleaming sword. 'Stand up, messenger.'

I stumbled to my feet to see General Silvanus moving forward from the door of the tent.

'Commander Gaiso lies dead, General Silvanus,' I said.

A strange smiled glanced across Silvanus' taut lips. 'I'm glad Gaiso's end came on the field then, and not in one of the cells under Catena's command. Are you sure?'

'This morning I saw his body pierced by a Syrian arrow laid out among the fallen.'

'What do you say to this, Catena?' The Emperor was an impatient as well as suspicious man. Eusebius had said so long ago. Now I saw for myself the way his large eyes flickered with nervous misgiving back and forth between the handsome, sleek Silvanus and the misshapen Catena.

Catena knew he was beaten, for now. His smile faded as he exploded with a curse, acknowledged the council members with a curt nod, and marched out of the tent.

I was excused from the tent myself ten minutes later. I now carried logistical details on emergency medical supplies and body identification-and-disposal procedures to be delivered back to Titianus.

'Marcus!' It was Silvanus striding from behind to catch up with me.

'Yes, General?' He had saved my life in that tent, but in my eyes, he was still a traitor to Gregorius. I wondered what he wanted. Was my reprieve just another trap? Silvanus had already proved himself to be fickle and deadly when others were counting on him.

'Did I hear you right in there? You are the *son* of Gregorius—his own blood, not adopted?'

'Yes, General. My father died last night with the others. His last words were to acknowledge me as his son.'

Silvanus closed his eyes for a moment as he took this in. Had he kept his troops with Magnentius, Gregorius might be alive today.

'I'm very sorry to hear that.'

'Thank you, General. I thank you for repeating Gaiso's boast. You saved my life.'

'But you are Constans' killer, aren't you?'

I stayed silent, standing at attention, new fear rising up from my boots and filling my chest.

He kept his voice low. 'You see, Gaiso never claimed credit. Quite the contrary, he was nothing more than an honest hunter at heart. He would never claim a trophy that wasn't his. You know that. He praised *you* for saving his life—not once but twice.'

'Gaiso was no politician, General. We all liked that about him.' I stayed on my guard.

'Yes, I too respected Gaiso for all his hotheaded urges. I knew he was dead when I spoke just then. I saw him take that Syrian arrow and fall from his horse last night. But that's not why I saved your neck.'

'You just said—?'

'That Gaiso was an honest man, yes. But that's hardly enough for me to put myself on Catena's enemies list.'

'Then, why?'

'I did it for that maid Roxana. I owe the girl that much. She has no family, no husband, no sister or brother. She told me one night that you were her only true friend in the entire world.'

I had to look away to hide my surprise. 'I wish I'd known. We never said good-bye.'

'She's the loneliest person I've ever met, both brave and foolhardy. I can't pretend to understand a woman like that. Despite all her talents, that girl is fated to walk a troubled path.'

'I wish her well, General.'

'Perhaps someday you'll meet her again and make things better for her because of my gesture today?'

'Yes, General.' It was easy to say. I doubted I would ever meet Roxana again. But Silvanus was satisfied. He nodded and marched back to the imperial tents.

I didn't dare ask such a senior officer why he chose to betray Gaiso and Gregorius as well as Magnentius and Marcellinus. These were difficult times. Perhaps Silvanus realized deep down that the Empire still needed the banner of legitimate succession to survive its coming trials. Magnentius had meant no less well, but the barbarian was brash, immoderate and premature in his timing. He was the wrong man rising at the wrong hour.

But maybe that wasn't the reason Silvanus defected at the head of thousands that fateful morning. I think deep down I already guessed who had tipped him in favor of Constantius. Whomever she reported to now, Roxana had applied her deadly Castra lessons well.

CHAPTER 21, ON THE IMPERIAL BLADE

—SOUTHEASTERN GALLIA—

To my surprise, I got promoted from *eques* to *biarchus* rank—for completing a mission 'requiring both discretionary judgment in difficult circumstances and loyalty to the neutral duties prescribed by our training.' The commendation came from none other than Constantius' senior staff now installed in Mediolanum. Apodemius must have raised his eyebrows with irony when he signed off on that memo.

I didn't deserve it, but who was going to argue with more pay?

I was certainly luckier than the fifty-four thousand fighters guys stacked on the cremation piles that September morning in Pannonia. Someday a new Plutarch or Virgil would write about them, but for now only men like myself survived to tell our grandchildren about the day the Roman Army committed suicide.

It was the biggest casualty total that anybody could think of and not something the Empire dared risk again. More than ever, Constantius was riddled with suspicion and anxiety—Eusebius was right about that—but the Emperor's distrust seemed justified when it came to the survivors of Mursa.

He did keep his promise not to punish the legions loyal to Magnentius' cause—even the Franks, Hispaniards and Celtic survivors who hated his family's guts—but that was the extent of his clemency. His Eastern forces had been shredded. He needed Magnentius' 'barbarian' Romans as battlefront fodder. He sent them marching off to an early death on the Persian border. We heard rumors of bands of legionaries burying their insignia, armor and standards in farmlands and forests in a rush to avoid Persian duty. They became outlaws instead. I heard some even crossed the border and hid among the Goths.

Either way, surviving Mursa carried its own punishment.

Civilian supporters weren't going to escape the Emperor's wrath, either. All across Gallia and Italia, recriminations and reprisals were turning ugly. Even as Constantius' elite forces entered the palace in Mediolanum to re-establish his court, they discovered that a boatload of Romans loyal to Magnentius had reached the eastern coast and set sail for sanctuary in Greece.

When they heard Magnentius and Decentius were on the run, the business cronies and friends of Marcellinus and his vast network of Gallo-Roman merchants and moneylenders took to back roads leading north. Constantius urged them to return and promised an amnesty but few believed in such mercy from a Constantine.

The political refugees fled so fast, we heard, they left the gates to their suburban gardens still swinging off the latch. They'd been sighted in dozens of different mule, carriage and wagon caravans making tortured progress along obscure farm tracks considered safe from *Cursus* inspectors. Constantius loyalists seized their property before the refugees had crossed the horizon.

But the refugees weren't safe no matter how far or fast they travelled. Paulus Catena posted undercover informants at taverns and market squares all across upper Gallia. Reading the accounts coming in, I pitied the lost reformers, searching for some wasteland where they could subsist on whatever coins lay hidden on them.

These people weren't the type to stay in isolated pockets of obscurity forever. It was only a matter of time before they banded back together with a false sense of safety and made themselves a juicy target for Constantius' implacable revenge.

Was Kahina among these refugees? Or had she hunkered down with Leo and Clodius in Ostia? Could she have fled to safer boltholes down in Numidia where she hide with family and childhood friends? There was nothing I could do right now, but I hoped the *Augusta* Justina, under house arrest in Mediolanum, could tell me.

With a little guilt, I thought of the jeweled rings I'd salvaged from the battlefield for Marcellinus' wife. They might be more than enough to buy her safe passage to Spain or North Africa but how could I return them? Was she still alive?

If anyone was keen to interrogate the ringleaders who still lived, it was that vicious Catena. Not to be denied his entertainments, I'd seen him gallop out of Mediolanum at the head of a cohort making straight for the channel. Magnentius still had sympathizers up in Britannia who remembered his British father enslaved by Constantine. Catena was planning a blockade to prevent the Gallo-Romans from finding shelter in the villages north of Londinium.

And the defeated Emperor Magnentius? He had first fled Mursa with what forces he could muster from the plains of slaughter. They had reached Italia from where he sent desperate messages by army runner offering a new settlement with Constantius.

Then as Constantius finally set up in Mediolanum, we heard Magnentius had reached Gallia. But when he rallied the survivors there and appeared before them, they'd raised their arms in salute—and hailed the name of Constantius instead.

Then we got a report that Magnentius was making a run for it with only his mother and brother for company. The trio had slipped past agents watching for them in Augusta Taurinorum. They'd headed up into the thick woods covering the Alpine passes still best known to the descendants of the Taurini tribe.

There was only one road through Taurinorum. Magnentius was leading his brother and mother to a two-bit walled village called Cularo founded by the Allobroges tribe to the west. They were falling straight into a trap.

Constantius requested a *ducenarius* from among the most senior *agentes* capable of tracking Magnentius down. There'd be no confusion this time about the authority to finish off an emperor—even a usurping barbarian one. But as someone who knew the man and his ways, I was called up as part of the arrest squadron.

I'd never ridden this road before. After we trailed out of Taurinorum and started climbing, it hardly deserved the name of road. Engineers had carved a trail out of nothing but forest, rock and fog.

Our leader, a man named Caelius, was no Gaiso—rash, passionate or fast. He was like a well-trained senior bay dog, always keeping his nose forward in the saddle, watching the ground, and riding carefully off the rocky track to spare his horse's hooves and keep our progress silent.

'That's it over there.' One of our scouts returned from a sortie and directed our gaze across a valley at a small walled town.

On Cularo sat next to a bridge spanning the navigable torrents of freezing snowmelt that tumbled across these Alpine ranges down into the Rhondanus River. If Magnentius had anyone keeping watch, we would be spotted filing across that bridge.

'We'll cross at night,' Caelius said.

'We have a contact—a stable hand—waiting to fodder the horses,' the scout said.

Caelius twisted around in his saddle. 'Numidianus, where would Magnentius hide? Where will we find him?'

'He's not the rat-in-the-hole type,' I answered. 'He's a large, burly man, brusque in temperament and a man of the people who prefers to stand tall. He can wear anything, eat anything and even sleep with anything. He'll feel right at home with the lowliest farmer, but he's not one to skulk under a bed. I bet he has already recruited all of Cularo to his cause.'

'I see. We don't want to take the whole town, just one man. Let's try not to rouse them.'

We spent the night hidden in the trees on the far side of the bridge, with only our heavy cloaks to protect us from the dripping trees. As far as we knew, no one but our stable boy knew we were there. An hour before daylight, Caelius signaled us to move forward.

We left the horses tethered with the boy and started toward the town. We were lucky. We were invisible under the sinking moon blanketed by heavy cloud, but the darkness made it harder for us to feel our route down the steep slope without tumbling into the deadly ravine rushing far below us. The ground underfoot was uneven and loose. One man nearly slipped off the cliff when he put his weight on an outreach of unsupported ground. He only caught himself by a branch long enough for us to pull him to safety.

The sliver of moon had hardly shifted down in the sky but it seemed a lifetime before we reached the bridge. It was no wonder of Roman engineering made of stone arches and even paving. It was made of rope and wood and just wide enough for a team of oxen to drag a wagon over.

Crouching low and moving slowly, Caelius crossed it in half a minute, only stopping to test a suspicious plank or two. I was astonished to see how this veteran could move like a slippery eel, low and noiseless, by favoring the soft wooden slats and avoiding the noise of his boot studs on the iron reinforcements.

I was the third man across but halfway over the treacherous white water, a dog barked. I dropped onto my stomach and caught my breath. The light of a curious torch might bounce off my armor and betray me. I pulled my cloak right over my head and waited, knowing at any minute an arrow might pierce my shoulder blades, but there was nothing.

I took a deep breath and looked up. Caelius signaled it was safe to come forward. Crouched over, I dashed to the end of the bridge, praying my boots wouldn't clank, and dropped onto my haunches to wait for the other men.

There would be a sleeping gateman or two but if Magnentius had bribed well enough, there would also be armed men guarding the town gates. We couldn't take a chance. We scuttled around the southern wall, loosening stones underfoot and cutting ourselves on thorn bushes planted all around. We finally found a hillock rising against the western length of wall where the shade of early dawn would obscure us.

One by one, we scaled the wall and landed in an alley of small mudstone houses shuttered for the night. We slipped along the lanes, avoiding the center of town, the market square or the front gates near the bridge.

We were searching for a stable where Magnentius have hidden his horses. He might have as many as six with him and maybe pack mules as well.

The drizzle that had kept up all night strengthened to a steady rain. Suddenly the gray skies cracked open with lightning and thunder. Under our heavy cloaks, we hoped to remain inconspicuous but our marching boots and drawn weapons were sure to give us away to any town dweller.

We worked our way through Cularo, alley by alley, and then street by street. One house, larger than the others, stood back from a low wall that gave us cover. We crouched and waited while our scout slipped away in the shadows to search for hidden horses. In a minute or two, he was back.

'They must be in one of the houses back there.' He pointed down an alley at our backs.

'Certain?'

The scout nodded. 'I found five horses and a mule. Saddles equipped with weapons' hooks and expensive leather mounts for heavy horse packs. The harnesses have military spoon bits for tight control. Fighting horseflesh, not draft animals.'

'Spread out,' Caelius signaled. We were stretching our line in a belt around the neighborhood when a startled cry broke the morning stillness.

'Aiiiigh!' One of our men in the rear dropped to his knees. He fell, head forward onto the street. A rustic wooden axe handle stuck up from his back. Blood spurted out around the wedged blade sunk deep through his armor. It was an ordinary woodcutter's blade, but no ordinary woodsman had slung it.

Gurgling with shock and pain, he stared into a pool of rainwater streaked with his own blood. There was nothing we could do for him without breaking cover. With faces flattened against the alley walls, our eyes looked upwards through the rain, searching for the killer's unshuttered window.

'Over there!' one man whispered. He pointed at a two-story house above the spot where we clustered. A shutter closed over one of the windows. From a second window an army dart shot from an expert hand. It pierced the gullet of the man standing right next to me. He grabbed my arm and almost dragged me down with him, then lost his grip and fell hard on the wet stone.

We scuttled for better cover, leaving my companion gasping for his breath as he pulled at the dart.

Caelius signaled half a dozen men to lay in wait at the front door. The rest us circled to a ground floor window on the rear side. We smashed open the shutters, then half a dozen of us clambered through, holding our shields out to cover us. We'd made enough noise to raise the whole quarter now.

The ground floor room was cluttered with stools, worktables and tools so we stayed close to the window and waited for Caelius' next signal.

Weapons poised, we crouched for might have been half an hour but there was no sound from the floor above. Now I could make out the dusty corners and a rickety staircase to the upper floor.

Who had attacked us? Cularo sympathizers paid off to distract and delay us? Was Magnentius even now making his escape while we snuck around an empty house?

'Come down!' Caelius shouted at last. I guessed he didn't want to risk any more lives just to storm an attic.

There was no answer.

As patient as we were, how could someone upstairs not feel the tension of a dozen men lying in wait below?

There was an enormous boom of thunder that shook the house. The rain pounded harder than ever now against the windows and I even felt it spatter my startled face. Perhaps the roof upstairs was open somewhere to the sky and the ceiling leaked. I wiped my cheek clean. My fingers looked dark red through the morning gloom. The man crouched next to me was spattered too. He wiped his own face with impatience and I saw it was streaked red as well.

'Caelius!' We showed him a crack between the ceiling planks overhead dripping blood on our shoulders and shields.

Then we heard a few footsteps on the floor above, the scrape of a stool, and a hollow thud, ending with a guttural animal noise.

Caelius signaled a scout to follow him, and they disappeared. The rest of us positioned ourselves to climb the steps after them.

'*Agens* Numidianus!' Caelius shouted to me downstairs, breaking the hush. I crushed past the others wedged with their weapons and shields along the narrow steps. I entered the room to find Caelius and his scout standing with their swords and shields lowered.

They were staring up at a man swinging by his neck from a noose hooked to the ceiling by a fat iron nail. His legs were still twitching and even as we took it in, his body voided into his expensive riding trousers and his clear eyes bulged from their sockets.

I recognized the profile once fingered by millions of Roman subjects, from the lookout towers along Hadrian's Wall to the markets of Carthago, on coins passed from palm to palm. No one could mistake the barbarian's curly hair, long-lashed blue eyes, strong nose and prominent chin. His boots just missed the stool he'd kicked aside in his death throes moments before our discovery.

A pile of gaudy silks and furs piled high on a low peasant bed was soiled by a mash of dripping blood and rosy gullet. I approached the second body, holding my nose against the fresh stench of death.

The corpse was Magnentius' mother. Her throat had been sliced clean across. The windpipe that had once cautioned her sons with prophesies and omens lay silent and gaping in the wet morning air.

'That's him, right?' Caelius barked at me, pointing at the hanging body. All around me, acute tension relaxed into a pregnant silence. I knew what some of the men were thinking, that Caelius and such a large patrol should have been able to take a single man and his mother without losing two crack riders.

In the end, though, this was why I—of all our number—had been necessary for the mission.

'No, Caelius,' I corrected him. 'It's my sad duty to tell you that this is his gentle brother, Decentius.'

♗♗♗

There would be no more lavish payouts from Magnentius or Decentius to the peasants of Cularo. So within an hour of dragging the Usurper's dead relatives into the rain-soaked marketplace, beggars, vendors, cobblers and butchers had crowded around us, flogging fresh information.

They told us that Magnentius had fled into the woods higher up the mountain ravine. Decentius had attacked our men to win his brother more time but it was a futile gesture.

The rain let up at last. We pushed our way up along a track through dense foliage. Morning sunlight glistened off leaves bashing into our faces and branches slapping our trousers.

It took us less than an hour to track the Usurper to a shepherd's cottage standing in a forest clearing.

We positioned ourselves in a circle around the hut. The lead scout dismounted. Five men followed him at a crawl towards the hut. They tested the door but it was bolted from inside.

Again, we waited. We heard the crash of shattering pottery inside. Ten more men raced forward with a fallen tree in their arms to use as a ram. They were just preparing to force the door when it opened with a bang and before it could bounce back closed, a military boot stopped it.

Magnentius stepped out onto the thick grass and looked up at the bright sun. He bolted the door neatly behind him. He had lost weight and his features were haggard, but I recognized the bold stance. He stood there now with the same vigorous defiance he'd shown donning a diadem and purple cloak at a party in Augustodunum.

'Name and rank?' he bellowed at Caelius.

'You can see our insignia plain as your face. My name is none of your business. We've come to arrest you and take you to Constantius,' our leader said.

Magnentius rolled his head to the side as if his brains needed exercise to answer. He squinted his eyes to focus on Caelius' uniform. I realized he had been drinking.

'*Agentes*. You'll have to take me.'

'That wouldn't be hard.' Caelius gestured towards the flanks of riders in three rows behind him.

'You need only one man to run me through. It would be cheaper and faster.'

'The Emperor has promised you a swift, clean death but he wants your confession.'

Magnentius snorted. 'I don't need any Constantine to determine my death. People like me know how to die for Romans. We've been doing it long enough.'

Caelius ordered his men to drop the battering ram and move on Magnentius. I kept my eyes fixed on the familiar figure braced on thick legs like a cornered bull. He waved an arm at Caelius and said, 'No, stop. Wait.'

Caelius stayed their advance with an upright palm. 'You surrender?'

'I want *that man* to come forward. No, not you, that one.'

Magnentius was pointing straight at me.

'Come here.'

I dismounted and walked through the swishing grass until I was only a foot away from him, just as I had that night I first presented my papers to him in a circle of dinner guests.

'You're that *agens*, Numidianus.'

I stood silenced, overpowered by the force of his rage so close and unable to proceed with the arrest.

'Well? What do you think of me now, boy? What's your advice, messenger? What would Trajan do, huh? Wasn't I first and foremost a soldier?' He shouted to the morning sky. 'Wasn't my tent flap open to every soldier? Where are all the men who followed me, who loved me, now?'

I found my voice at last. 'Where you led them, General, dead on the fields of Mursa.'

'I can read your expression. You wish I were lying there with them, don't you?'

'We've come to arrest you, General.'

'I'm not kneeling to Constantius! Will you run me through, boy, here and now? I haven't the strength, though damned if they'll say I didn't have the courage.'

'No, *Imperator*. We have orders to escort you alive to Mediolanum.'

'*Imperator*,' he mimicked. 'I said RUN ME THROUGH NOW!' he bellowed at me. 'Suddenly you're afraid?'

'Leave him alone. Why him?' shouted Caelius.

'Because this is the boy who finished off that buggered wimp Constans, that's why!' Magnentius lurched forward and made a grab for my scabbard. 'You're the imperial killer, aren't you?' He screwed up his eyes for a better look at my features under my helmet. 'Yes, it is you, the quick-witted escort who covered Gaiso's back.'

I glanced away, too full of pity to witness Magnentius' bloodshot eyes filling with tears. He peered over my shoulder at the men circled all around the clearing and yelled, 'Gaiso? Are you hiding back there, hunting with these bastards? Is that how they found me?'

'Gaiso is dead, *Imperator*.'

'You see?' Magnentius waved at the expressionless faces staring down from their saddles. 'You heard this *agens* call me "*Imperator*"? I'm no criminal! Yet you deny me the same treatment as Constans, you African bastard, with your famous "imperial blade," just because I wasn't born into the right family, while that little runt you put out of his misery ran around with purple ribbons in his hair. I'm ordering you to run me through NOW!'

He had stood so proud and fine that night in Augustodunum, appearing all of a sudden in his imperial raiment to the startled admiration of his new subjects. I laid a hand on his shoulder to help him surrender.

'Damn you, African! I don't want your pity. I want your sword!' He shook me off and grabbed my scabbard with his left hand. He slid out my *spatha* with his right. Holding the point against his belly, he made a sudden dash at the hut. Slamming into the door and pressing with his last gasp, he impaled himself on my blade.

CHAPTER 22, RETURNING AN EMPRESS

—ON THE LAST LEG OF THE VIA FLAMINIA—

For a young woman transformed overnight into a deposed empress and virgin widow, Justina seemed amazingly composed as I escorted her home to Roma. Some might say she was lucky even to be alive, much less dressed in fresh robes and with her hair done up in a crown of braids and curls under her travel veil.

Perhaps Justina was born under a luckier constellation than the rest of Magnentius' court. All witnesses called up before the Emperor had argued in favor of mitigating any punishment because of the young woman's maternal Constantinian pedigree and her father's devoted service as a governor for the Empire.

But remembering the child I'd escorted to Aquileia, I knew it was her personal innocence and steadfast courage that had won her reprieve.

After weeks of hearing everyone out, the Emperor Constantius gave Justina permission to return to her parents. Perhaps he felt sorry for his cousin, if such a stony soul could feel compassion. Perhaps he just didn't want more Constantinian blood on his hands. More likely, he was simply drained of vengeful fury by the sight of Magnentius' heavy corpse lying across the back of a horse as our hunting party rode back into the imperial courtyard in Mediolanum.

Escorting Justina back to Roma was the last task of my posting to the court of Magnentius the Usurper. We were making good time on the road. I hadn't spoken to her for hours. Only one more day's ride separated us from her father's townhouse. As the *agens* of her small escort unit, consisting of a few men scavenged from the surviving tribunes and *legati* of a northern legion, I carried the road permits and negotiated our lodgings station by station. The other officers, their army careers damaged but their lives spared, didn't personally know the young woman in their care nor did they take much notice of her now that Magnentius was dead and discredited. To them, Roma was just a stopover before another field assignment.

But I did know her and I watched over her with anxiety.

Justina had asked for the company of two maids I didn't recognize and they hid behind the curtains of her carriage, bumping over the *Cursus* paving stones. I kept my horse on the soft margin of the road. Our little party made few stops along the route, choosing the most comfortable *mansiones* through the Apennines where I reckoned she wouldn't be recognized or harassed.

We ate well enough and I assume she slept well, too. If any more precocious visions disturbed her rest, she kept them to herself, for which I was grateful. Women with second sight unnerved me. I was a man trained to analyze every last detail that lay in front of my eyes—not on my pillow.

I was having trouble sleeping. Night after night I woke up in a cold sweat, back on the fields of Mursa with screams filling my ears.

That's not to say Justina made the whole journey in silence. From time to time, her lively conversation as I rode alongside her carriage window helped the horrors of the last few weeks recede a little. I had to remind myself she hadn't lived through the carnage at Mursa or seen Magnentius plunge himself onto a blade.

Nor had that large-living husband ever really included her in his boisterous, barbarian life. She remained as poised as ever, mentally untouched by her husband's colossal failure. She was already considering her future with the pragmatism of the Roman society matron she was sure to become any day soon.

How could it be that I was not even a decade older than she, yet I felt weighed down in broad daylight by entrails and blood? I felt phantom hands clutching up at me from the filth. I saw men's faces splitting open with terrifying butchery over and over again?

I shivered with the horror of it all. I'd seen too much of the world to ever share her lighthearted joy in a sunny November morning. I fought back memories of the shrieks of men being maimed and dismembered across the plain that deadly night.

Now I rode at Justina's side, listening to her chat, reminding myself that even though Atticus Manlius Gregorius was gone and all the West stood like an orphaned child hungering for Constantius' healing attention, my companion was right to look forward.

Was any survivor as haunted as I felt those brilliant mornings on the road? I knew what was best but my resolve was weak. I must not make the mistake of Orpheus turning around at Eurydice's call from Hades. I could not afford to look over my shoulder. These ghosts would beckon me time and again, urging me to turn my gaze back at their lost dreams and lives.

I had to resist their plaintive call. I had to face what was to come. Only the future was important now, only the prospect of a single Empire made frail by brutal civil war but at least unified under one man.

And yet, I still saw them there, bleeding, pleading . . .

'Where are we meeting my father?'

'Someone from your household will wait at the Porta Flaminia to escort you through the city, my lady.'

'I hope Pater comes himself. I'll be glad to see Roma again, even though it's rundown and the streets are so badly designed.'

'Didn't you like Aquileia?'

'How could anything be as grand as Roma?'

'They say Constantinopolis is a fine city with astonishing plumbing, broad avenues and beautiful new buildings.'

Justina shrugged. 'Plumbing's important. So are baths, and sports grounds and *stadia* and all that, but lovely, smelly, old, crowded Roma is the heart and soul of the globe.'

I smiled and said nothing. If I missed the fresh fish and fruits, cheese and flatbreads of Numidia's market towns basking in the dry clean air of my early childhood, I couldn't explain those yearnings to a hothouse flower like Justina. I understood her affection. I'd grown to manhood in Roma. But a part of me burned with the pride of the provincial who loved both.

'Is anyone waiting for you, Marcus?'

'Not particularly.' I would hasten to the Manlius townhouse to ask Verus for news of Kahina and Leo before reporting to Apodemius, but that wasn't any of Justina's business.

'Where will you go this evening?'

'I suppose I'll go to my headquarters and bunk down in the *schola* barracks.'

'Perhaps my father could offer you some supper and a mattress softer than some nasty army cot.' She offered me a wide smile under those clear, watching eyes of hers.

'I doubt your father will have time to even notice me in his joy and relief at your return.'

'I'm not flirting with you, *Agens*. I was only being hospitable.'

'I didn't think you were, Lady Justina.'

'My father may already have some highborn new suitor in mind. He's very politically well-connected, you know, my father.'

'I hope your next husband has eyes only for you.'

'I don't care what they're saying now. Magnentius was not a tyrant or a bad man. He was a good man, but without much education. I hope my next husband at least has better taste in rings,' she added. I glanced down through her carriage window in time to see her small hand remove the chain with its large vulgar gold circle that Magnentius had placed around her neck. She tucked it into her belt pouch of quilted rose linen.

'He did what the gods told him,' I said.

'It was what he didn't do that made him kind, Marcus.'

'*Augusta*?'

'He never touched me, not once, except the night of our wedding when he held my hand to place that ring on my finger. It fell right off.' She looked up at me through the carriage window.

'You mean he never even caressed you? Or kissed you?'

'I mean he never touched me in any way. No one can say now that I wouldn't be a worthy bride for their eldest born son.' She paused and leaned out a little into the sun. 'Do you think he knew, somehow? Do you think he knew that I was never destined to be the mother of his children?'

'Perhaps the oracle was right after all.'

'Then do you think the rest of her prediction will come true? That I'll have a son and build the future of the Empire with a new dynasty?' She smiled up at me through the salmon silk that protected her pale skin from the slanting rays. 'Do you think I have the gift of the seers? I certainly don't want to end up like my mother-in-law.'

'Whatever your dreams, I'm absolutely sure you won't end up like that crazy bat.' The bloodied body of Magnentius' gaudy barbarian mother rose up in my imagination.

'But she was *right*, wasn't she? She told him not to press eastwards, but he did.'

We fell silent to the soft padding of my horse's hooves and the rattle of her iron bounds wheels on the paving.

'Whatever happened to that Claudia doll of yours?' I asked.

'I dedicated it to the Goddess of Fertility on the day of my marriage, of course. That's the custom of all new brides.' She shook her head at me in wonder. 'Really, Marcus Numidianus, sometimes I wonder what kind of Roman family owned you!'

⚖⚖⚖

There was no one waiting to meet her.

We dallied for over two hours at the bustling gate. We ate lentils and honeyed bread. I tipped the tavern boys to check all the roads leading to where we sat and told them to keep an eye out for a man answering the description of her father or the Vettius carriage.

One by one, they all returned after an hour or two. One boy felt so sorry at Justina's anxious face, he offered the tip back.

'Shall I take you home myself?' I offered at last.

'Let's wait until the sun goes down. I don't want anyone to see me travel like this without a proper family escort. It would set tongues wagging.' She pulled herself up straighter and for a minute, I wondered if she still saw herself as an empress.

We lingered at the tavern. I ordered yet more snacks to keep our claim to the discreet table in the corner. She didn't touch them. Suddenly her face lit up with relief.

'Cerealis!'

A striking young man pushed his way through the hubbub and embraced the girl even as she leapt into his arms.

'Why have I been waiting here so long, Cousin?'

He lowered his eyes and shook his head, as if tossing her question away. 'Your mother insisted we only leave the house after dusk, when we wouldn't be seen.'

I sensed worse things than unpunctuality were on the tip of his tongue.

'What nonsense! Why should we hang our heads in shame? Half of Roma supported Magnentius, and all of them bowed to him.'

'The city is fickle, Justina. You've escaped with your beauty and virtue intact, but the Emperor's forgiveness carries a price.'

She collapsed back on the bench and lifted her veil to reveal eyes sprouting with tears. 'What happened?'

'Your Father's dead.'

Her hand shot to her lips to stifle a cry.

'You see, Uncle Justus, the proud old fool had a *dream*, in which he saw himself drawing a robe of imperial purple right out of his side. You know your father. He looked down his nose on your husband, but dreamed of your imperial children, of you giving birth to a new—'

'Surely they don't execute people for dreams?' Her features clouded over.

'No, not for a dream itself, but for a dream that reaches the ears of Constantius' aides. Remember, your father only married into the imperial family. Who was a mere governor to sire a line of gods?'

'What happened to him? Did he kill himself?'

Cerealis shook his head, no, and pulled us closer so that no one would overhear him. 'A week ago he was murdered, knifed in the street as he walked through the crowds to the public baths with his friends. There was nothing they could do to save him. The assassin got away.'

'Who would—?'

'It doesn't matter *who*, Justina but the streets aren't safe for us. And be careful to whom you entrust your dreams.'

She glanced at me in alarm as her cousin gathered her under the shelter of his cloak.

'I'll take her home now, *Agens*. Thank you.'

The sad young man tried to tip me for my task, but I laid his palm aside and merely bowed. I was glad to finally hand Justina over to someone who would protect the girl rather than exploit her.

She looked back at me just one more time. I gave her a broad smile of reassurance. Her dreams were safe with me.

CHAPTER 23, THE *BULLA*'S SECRET

—THE MANLIUS TOWNHOUSE, ROMA—

The house stood, derelict and overgrown, like a dowager who still puts on her rouge but forgets to pin up her hair. Lady Laetitia would never have left all these dead fig leaves clogging access to the gate. I knocked and no one answered. I knocked again and then I pounded and finally shouted for someone to answer the gate.

The bolt slid back at last. A scrawny young slave peeked out at me with two great fearful eyes. He sighed with relief when he saw it was only the freedman Marcus Numidianus. I was astonished to see he wielded a plumbing tube of rusting metal in his other hand.

'Is your mistress in?' I asked.

'Wait out there. Verus will be back from the market.' He started to close the gate on my face.

'Wait.' I stuck my boot in crack. 'Is Clodius here?'

'No.'

'Who lives here now?'

'Only Verus and the rest of us servants.'

'Where is your mistress?'

'Can't say.'

I pushed the kid aside and fended off his silly attempt to knock me out with his ridiculous pipe. I lifted him off his feet by his stained tunic.

'Can't say or won't say?'

'No one knows! Let me go!'

'Tell someone in the kitchen that Marcus Gregorianus Numidianus is here. I'll wait for Verus near the fountain.'

Late afternoon had always cast a melancholy air over the garden, especially after Lady Laetitia died. There was no place among its ageing trees and neglected flowers where a pair of dead ancestral eyes wasn't gazing down at you. I sat on her stone bench, listening to the chilly fountain water slap onto a bed of dead foliage that should have been cleaned out weeks ago.

Staring at me now I spotted a familiar set of features set in fresh white wax. In all the chaos of this terrible time, Gregorius had managed to order a likeness of the Senator to join the Manlius faces lining all the corridors and walls of the atrium and garden portico.

And now? I put my head in my hands for a moment, realizing that there would be no likeness of Gregorius joining his ancestors. Leo might never know what the Commander looked like. I wondered if it was too late to commission a painting of him, as he'd once looked.

Verus found me there, sitting in silence as the light of everything I valued faded around me. I probably looked like a dead statue myself.

'Marcus? Is that you?'

'Where's Kahina, Verus? Where's the boy?'

'I wouldn't have known you. You're just bones, son.'

'What's happened, Verus? Where is everyone?'

He glanced around him as if he didn't trust all these dead aristocrats not to give him away. 'Come out for a walk with me, Marcus. My old pair of legs needs a good stretch.'

'I thought you'd just come from the market.'

I followed him back out into the street. Together we strolled towards the green park with its the little temple that marked the end of our neighborhood. A few sad drunken youths lounged around the perimeter but no one else took notice of us.

'We don't know where she is, Marcus. Clodius sent out messages to all the families that supported Magnentius, but half of them had fled and the other half was trying to pay their way out of trouble. Didn't want nothing to do with us.'

'How do you know she's even alive?'

'Because she sent this back for the boy.' He took out his leather purse and unwrapped a scrap of knotted kitchen towel. I saw Kahina's ring, a blue jewel set in gold, from Gregorius.

'She sent it back by a soldier who said he escaped Aquileia during the evacuation of the palace. She paid him a pretty price to stay honest, I'm sure.'

'What was the soldier's name? Where is he now? Where was she going? Did she tell him?'

'No one knows. It's too dangerous out there, Marcus, to keep asking questions. You know that. Men keep knocking on our gate to ask the other servants whether we've heard where the lady matron of Commander Gregorius has got to. They even beat up the cook's boy who didn't want to let you in. "Why don't she come home, now that the tyrant usurper's dead and gone?" they ask. They say they got loose ends to tie up. Loose ends, my foot.'

'I don't like the sound of any of this. Have you shown her ring to the child?'

Verus just sniffed and rolled his eyes.

'Oh, what am I saying?' I looked up at the sky, surprised by my own stupidity. Whatever one gave to the baby Leo would end up in Clodius' wallet or some pawnshop.

'Any word from Clodius? Surely it's safe enough for that reptile to come back and get to work. Nobody suspects him of counseling Magnentius to revolt.'

'He's busy in the gambling dens in Ostia, but I keep the nurse Lavinia on a tight leash, I do. I insist on weekly messages about the boy, and I makes sure her pocket money stays separate from what Clodius demands.'

'Who's running the estates, then?'

Verus slapped his wrinkled forehead. 'Who's been running them since the master and his lady moves out to that newfangled palace in Aquileia? What the hell's in Aquileia? I ask you.'

'You, Verus?'

Verus tapped his hollow, bony chest with a gnarled finger. 'I get one of my friends to help me with the accounts and I know who to trust when it comes to the payments and such. We've got steady tenants down south but with Clodius in place, the Ostia properties aren't bringing in as much as they should under a real dock man. From what I can get out of them up in Gallia, the herd numbers are way down because of the war. It's a holding operation, that's for sure.'

'I'll help you now, Verus.'

'There's enough income out there, son, but in this confusion, it's just not being collected. And I can't just gallivant around the countryside from the bee farm to the vineyards like a rent collector. Somebody's got to watch over this place. Vandals know the family's dishonored. They've got their eyes on our silver, I know it.'

'I'll try to help until it's safe for Kahina to come back.'

'When do you think that'll be, Marcus?'

'I can't say, Verus. But I've got to see her back and running this house with your help, the ways things should be, for Gregorius' sake.'

'What if she ain't even alive?'

I would not answer that.

We returned back to the Manlius kitchen. Verus roused the cook to make us supper. We ate in silence, each remembering happier days.

'What did the master say as he died?' Verus pushed his empty plate aside and leaned forward, his watery eyes staring at me. He had joined the household when the elder Manlius was still a thriving voice in the Senate, a nobleman of old Roman blood who'd just wed his controversial second wife—a Gallo-Roman woman of wealth and provincial lineage. He had held the baby Gregorius in his arms. Verus had spent his entire life looking after the Manlius household. No wonder he burned with a hunger to live Gregorius' life right to the very end.

I took a deep breath and stared at my hands. Just like in the old days, we sat by the light of a single oil lamp at a wooden table in the servants' quarters together, with two cups of cheap diluted wine in our hands. The early evening shouts and racket of kitchen servants scraping plates and tossing out scraps came in from the alleyway through the back window bare of curtains.

I paused, wondering what to say. Verus was so simple and true. No doubt he pictured the Commander's death like a scene carved on some marble coffin lined with a relief of perfectly formed men and graceful women, their figures surrounded by a Latin couplet chiseled into the stone.

'He died nobly but didn't say much.'

'He was struck down that fast, huh?'

'No, Verus. You're no simpering girl, so I'll tell you the truth. He fought for every last painful breath in agony. We'd been out there half a day and all through the night. I've never seen so many men die. It was a miracle our paths even crossed.'

'Stop shaking, boy. Have another drink.'

'I found him nearly finished off, crawling for help through the muck with his sword and the shield still fastened to his hand.'

'Oh, the gods have pity on our souls.'

'I hope I never see such a battlefield again, Verus. It felt like we were sinking to the bottom of a dark roaring ocean that tossed us back and forth . . . without any let up. I can't remember most of it. I remember going with my sword at . . . I killed a lot of . . . Some of them were completely sealed up in armor and they rolled around in the blood like . . . My ears just filled up with the death of all.'

'Calm down, boy, calm down.'

'And at night they still visit me in my dreams, Verus, and I wake up, and their hands are still clutching at me even once I'm wide awake. They won't let me go, Verus, they won't let me go.'

And then to my shame, I burst into tears. The old man took me into his embrace. We rocked back and forth together. He stroked my hair with his bent fingers and muttered, 'It's all right, son, you're home now.' He hadn't ruffled my hair since I was a little slave caught stealing sweets in the kitchen.

I nodded and straightened up, pulled myself together and finished the drink in front of me. I mopped up my face with a cook's rag.

'Then the Commander didn't say nothing?'

I had guarded my secret so long. 'I stayed with him until it was over,' I wavered. 'I'm only thankful I found him before it was too late.'

'He knew it was you? Out of all them thousands of men out there, he knew you'd found him?'

'Yes, he knew. For a minute there, he tried to hang on to my *bulla* cord. He pulled it right off.'

'Lucky thing it didn't get trampled under some horse, ain't it?'

I shrugged. Suddenly, after nearly twenty years, the Senator's *bulla* didn't seem so important as it had. It belonged to another time and place. In its stead, the Commander himself had named me his son, with his own voice and acceptance in his heart. I knew the blood of Mursa had washed away his bitterness. I had what I wanted, even if society would never recognize me as his son.

I pulled the clumsy amulet out of my tunic. 'I should give it up, Verus. People think I'm an idiot for wearing a boy's talisman.'

"A great lump of pottery and bronze like that, it wasn't ever much to look at. I mean, it's the Senator's present and all that, but he's gone and Gregorius gone with him.' He shook his hoary head. 'Well, it's up to you. The old man wanted you to have it. You never took it off once, not even when the other boys teased you.'

He paused and rubbed his white bristles with a calloused hand. 'Although I remember once he told me to take it down in a box to the smith's to have it mended. So you took it off then.'

'I don't recall breaking it. In fact, I'm certain I never did.'

'Well, it needed repairing. I paid the bill myself when I picked it up. You were a bit of a roughhouse.'

'If anybody was a bully, it was Clodius. The bruises I—'

'Well, you were both young. If you did break it, you didn't pay much attention. You didn't pay much attention to anything in those days, except all the stories you read upstairs in them books.'

'I never broke it, Verus.'

We cleared away our plates and spoons. He poured himself a fresh drink and swallowed half of it down. The word 'sip' wasn't in his vocabulary, although he had a sharp tongue for bad table manners when he saw it in his betters.

'More for you, son?'

'No, thanks.'

'You're brooding again.'

'Verus, why did the Senator send it to be repaired? You'd think Lady Laetitia would have taken care of a slave's amulet, if anyone.'

'Oh, she wasn't well by then. She was sick a long time, but boys aren't the kind to notice what's going on in women's quarters, not until she was too feeble to come out to dinner.'

'Are you sure, Verus? Why care about a slave boy's—?'

I pulled the cord over my neck and laid the *bulla* down on the rough wooden surface. It was the same old lump of bronze-covered pottery, embossed with an 'M.'

Wearing it around my neck, day in and day out, I hadn't really looked at it closely, if ever, for years and years. It was cheaply fashioned, with the metal covering formed into a hinge over the cord and, thanks to more than a decade of what Verus called 'roughhousing,' scattered with dents where the pottery showed through. It was nothing special to anyone but me and hardly ever worth repairing.

'What exactly was fixed, do you remember?'

Verus shrugged. 'It was in a box with a note, all tied up with string. And that's how I returned it to the Senator.'

I turned it over and over. I was so used to the dents and scratches, the small compressions of metal wide or thicker here than there, I couldn't figure it out.

'Was it always made of pottery inside?' I asked.

'Can't say. Yeah, I guess so.'

I saw the Commander in my mind now, flinging the cord up and down trying to smash the *bulla* on the ground.

'Verus, have you got a hammer? Or a rock? Just a rock will do.'

'You can't be serious. All right, you're a big boy now, you don't need it. But if you don't want it, save it for the baby. It'll be something of the Senator besides a load of dusty books to remember him by.'

'That's just the point, Verus. The Senator did something to this useless lump that cost him good money. I want to find out what that was. I think the Commander wasn't trying to take it off me the way I thought. He was trying to smash it open. Get me a hammer.'

Verus came back with a bag of tools and pulled out a hammer. We went out into the garden where the flagstones were good granite and I laid the bulla down with hesitation. It was my last tangible tie to the old life, to the old man whose stubbornness I'd inherited, and to the courageous warrior whose strength I now hoped would grow in my son.

'You're sure you want to do this?'

I held back, the hammer poised in the air. 'No, Verus, I'm not sure.'

Then I remembered something buried deep in my childhood memory. I was a little boy again. The Commander was entertaining his friends in the dining room. The couches were full of reclining officers. I was scampering around, encouraged by their jests and songs to entertain them as usual. I heard the Commander turn his handsome features to me. I felt him put his hand around my thin neck.

'Not too heavy, is it?'

'No, thank you.'

'It protects you. You must protect it.'

I smashed the hammer down with all my might. Verus jumped aside as bits of pottery scattered over our boots but it wasn't a clean hit. I had drunk too much. I pounded again and again, the third time with a more measured swing, hitting the *bulla* dead center at last.

I'd shattered nothing but clay and metal. A pile of shards and bent bronze lay where my treasured gift had been only a moment ago.

I sat back on my haunches and wiped away the clay dust clouding my eyes with my sleeve.

'Well, that's that.' It was too late to feel regret. So much else had been lost, my *bulla* was the least of it.

'That is that.' Verus tapped me on my shoulder. 'Let's go in and have another drink, son.'

'I've had enough.'

'Well, don't sit there staring at it all night.' Verus leaned over and picked at the flattened bits. 'I'll have the gateboy clean this up.' He pushed at the debris with a crooked index finger Perhaps he felt even more nostalgic for the past than I did.

A tiny round dull iron with a small set of teeth on a square hinge appeared through the grit.

'Well, I'll be damned,' Verus said. 'Will you look at this?' He picked up the iron circle and peered at it under the lantern light. 'It's Lady Laetitia's missing ring-key to the deed box.'

CHAPTER 24, AN OATH OF HIS OWN

—THE CASTRA PEREGRINA, ROMA—

The mists of winter coiled off the Tiberis and through the narrow streets of the city. At dawn, I descended to the Via Appia, slipped under the embankment of the Aqua Claudia aqueduct and mounted the Caelian Hill for the Castra Peregrina. Laetitia's ring-key dangled on my old cord now, along with Kahina's ring for Leo and the two rings I'd salvaged for Marcellinus' widow. It took me some time to get used to these new treasures hidden under my tunic. They were lighter than my old *bulla*, but I felt as decorated as a German chieftain.

Everything felt new for me this morning. We were all walking into an uncertain age under a single emperor, the unchallenged reign of Constantius II. His ruthless power had swept all the other imperial brothers, in-laws, usurpers and tyrants right off the board.

A sleepless night had blown away so much confusion in my mind. It was clear to me now what secrets the Manlius household had sheltered during those long years and what hidden plans had been laid to protect the family's future.

If there was no legitimate son, Marcus the slave was always there, known and watched but never named or acknowledged as such. My claims to property or social standing were deposited and buried in the *bulla* for safekeeping—even from me—in the hope that a rightful heir would come along. I was a lively, curious, quick child. Who knew what trouble I could make as an adult if I learned the truth for no good reason?

It wasn't just emperors that might have to strike down upstart claimants.

Gregorius and Lady Laetitia had endured their childlessness with grace, but they had suffered nonetheless. Bringing her nephew Clodius into the family was Laetitia's desperate attempt to import the kind of highborn blood society could cluck over with approval. She forgave my poor helpless slave mother her brief liaison with my father and she certainly indulged me. I think Gregorius made it easier for her, though, because he never once betrayed Laetitia again, not with my lonely, abandoned mother or any other woman, even during Laetitia's long years of illness.

How sad Laetitia must have been with the passing years as Clodius sabotaged his formal adoption by becoming... no Manlius. The longer the delay in his legal status, the more his character rotted like forgotten cheese.

But it was the Senator, not the Commander, who'd embedded the key into my *bulla*. It was the Senator who loved me best. Though bound to sealed lips by clan loyalty, he shared his library to bestow all the gifts he valued on me.

Then Laetitia had died. To Gregorius and the Senator's great joy and relief, the new wife Kahina gave birth to Leo. That longed-for baby—*my own son*—assumed my place as the beloved heir.

It wasn't only empires that watched usurpers seize the diadem but how I could not keep silent in his interests?

No doubt the Commander imagined me forever standing by, a grown freedman, serving as physical bodyguard over his household and a moral check on Clodius. Instead, I'd broken clean away and rejected him to carve out a life of my own.

Yet at the end, the Commander had looked up at me that hellish dawn in Mursa. He had realized that Leo was defenseless and beyond his protection. It was time for secrets to end and other plans to be laid. He sensed that within minutes, he would fall silent forever. If anyone was left to protect Leo, Kahina and the estates, it was only Marcus, that stubborn freedman, that upstart Numidian bastard, who could be trusted, after all.

These thoughts jumbled around my mind, as crowded as the market stalls jamming my progress up the last stretch to the

Castra's wall. I shook them off as I cleared myself at the compound gates and went straight to that familiar office full of files, maps and camphor oil where the old man was supposed to debrief me.

'He's asleep,' his deaf masseur gesticulated to me, using a sign language all the *agentes* learned to understand. 'Been up all night reading reports,' he spelled out, 'from Britannia.'

'I thought he was expecting me.'

'Look for yourself.' He cocked his head towards the inner door standing ajar.

I crept in and saw Apodemius' head on his desk, his lamps burned out and the morning light catching the sheen of his scalp through his thinning white hair. Above his sleeping form hung that battered map of the known world, so different from Eusebius' showpiece in its ornate frame. This map practically breathed in and out with pins, punctures, pencil marks and paper scraps. This was the world he monitored from Hadrian's windswept barrier down to the sands licking the crumbling African fortress I knew so well in Lambaesa.

Sure enough, most of his legion pins had moved to the Pannonian fields around Mursa, but there were far fewer now. A pottery bowl sitting on his desk spilled over with the pins he must have removed, one by one, as reports of casualties reached him here.

'*Magister*? It's me, Marcus Gregorianus Numidianus reporting, *Magister*,' I whispered. I touched his sleeve, stood back and stood at attention.

'Numidianus? You're back?' He lifted his head and shook it free of sleep. I waited as he signalled his aide to come back with a bowl of clean warm water. He doused his whole head, toweled off and smiled a sort of rueful welcome. He fed his mice some stale breadcrumbs off a plate.

'You look dreadful.'

'I got caught in the fighting.'

'That's not your job! We don't train you for that!'

'Was I was supposed to stand on a hill with the camp followers and their babies and just watch?'

'We lost, Numidianus. Eusebius won.'

'With respect, *Magister*, everyone lost out there.'

'There won't be an Empire left if this happens again.'

'What is my next posting, *Magister*?'

He squinted out the window and winced. He hated working during the daylight hours. 'I don't suppose you'd like to track Paulus Catena up in Britannia?'

If my face drained white, Apodemius chose to ignore it.

'He's on a rampage up there. It started as a purge of anyone linked to the Magnentius leadership or even sympathetic to reform.'

'But now?'

'It's a witch-hunt of torture and death spreading across the whole imperial territory with attacks on all pagan monuments and practices that Magnentius allowed.'

'Where is Marcellinus' widow? I have things to return to her.'

Apodemius shook his head. 'The whole of Marcellinus' family fled to Magnentius sympathizers in Britannia. They were among the first into Catena's clutches. If there are any heirs, they'd be suicidal to admit to it now.'

I thought of that bird-like wife weighed down with jewels and a heavy wig at the party in Augustodunum. She had no more need of rings now.

'Your intelligence seems more than fresh, *Magister*.'

'I have a two good agents across the channel, but I need more. The Vicarius of Britannia, Flavius Martinus, stood up to Catena, but that crazed wolfhound of Constantius managed to frame him. Now,' Apodemius pushed a folded packet of reports towards me, 'I read that Flavius Martinus has committed suicide.'

'There's no way I'd stay undercover around Catena,' I said. 'He has me marked out because I killed—'

Apodemius waved his hand to cut me off. 'I don't want to know. It's better if I don't.'

I fought back rising panic. Had Kahina fled northward right into Catena's clutches?

'Well, I didn't think you would jump at the idea. The other option is a little trickier. Perhaps I was too good at impersonating an ambitious Numidian with my two-faced memos over your signature.'

I'd forgotten Apodemius' game with Eusebius—his little fiction that I was a double agent.

'The eunuch took your bait?'

'Better than that.' Apodemius shook himself. He shuffled, stiff and sleepy, across the room to a simple tin box and unlocked its latch with a key hanging in a cluster off his belt. 'It's the sort of thing I don't like to leave lying around on my desk,' he said. 'This is Eusebius' letter requesting you be assigned to the Caesar Gallus' new court in Antiochia.'

I scanned the precise and elegant script and wondered if it was Eusebius' own hand or that of some doe-eyed Egyptian secretary.

'How is it I merit such a dramatic reassignment?'

'I'm afraid the *Augusta* may have something to do with it.' He raised his eyebrows in warning. 'Which is why I'm thinking of keeping you here in the West watching Constantius' court for a while.'

'May I take some leave first, *Magister*, to adjust matters here in Roma?'

Apodemius never liked vacations. As far as I knew, he never took one himself. He waited for a good explanation.

'Commander Gregorius fell at Mursa, *Magister*. I did put that in my first report.'

'Yes, of course. A shame.' He slammed his hand on the desk with surprising force. 'He was just the sort of man Magnentius should have listened to.'

'I never told you, but on the night Magnentius announced himself as emperor, I saw surprise all over Gregorius' face. If he knew Magnentius was ambitious, he didn't expect him to go that far that night. We had just finished toasting Constans. And he spent all his time in the Council arguing for negotiation and peace with Constantius.'

'His death was a waste.'

'He died nobly, whatever his allegiances, and not before we had time to settle our differences. If I hadn't gone into battle, I would not won earned my father's blessing.'

Apodemius said nothing. A twitch of a smile crossed his lips as he put Eusebius' letter back under lock and key. He had known my own recruiter in Numidia, the brave retired *agens*, Leo the merchant. Perhaps Leo had even told him I was the bastard son of the Manlius house?

Of course he had. Apodemius had known all along.

'I only need three months, *Magister*. But I need them.'

He leaned over and examined my face. 'You look gaunt. Are you eating enough? I can give you two.'

'I'm very grateful.'

'Oh, just call it an early present for Christ Mass.'

I cleared away my paperwork with Apodemius' aides as quickly as I could. In the yard outside the barracks, some men were warming up for exercises. I waved to a couple I remembered from training days. I could hear language lessons going on as I passed the class doorways one by one. Persian, Germanic, then some awful barbarian garble I couldn't even identify. I was tempted to say hello to an instructor or two, but my stomach growled in protest. I was ready for a good hot breakfast of sausages and flatbread from the street stalls and a long walk through the forum to clear my head.

But I stopped and turned, tugged back at the gate by an invisible voice. Was that a shout from the wrestling sandpit or a lonely howl from the invisible demons that disturbed my sleep?

I found myself standing in front of the Castra's temple to Jupiter Redux. I had no offering in my satchel. I wasn't even a praying kind of man but my heart felt suddenly full.

I crossed the silent stone threshold and peered into the interior. The temple was swept clean but the altar stood empty and neglected. There was no one inside, no penitent and no priest to read the hundreds of plaques and inscriptions covering every inch of marble.

I walked up to the altar and gazed around me.

Never before had I felt so grateful to have survived, to have walked away on both legs, to have simply returned—*redux*. Thousands of other men must have experienced this flooding relief. Thousands of them had sacrificed here before this altar to give thanks to Jupiter.

At last I understood why this temple stood in front of the Castra, the ancient barracks built for all of Roma's non-Latin fighters, its *peregrini*. Some were grateful to have returned to Roma, while others must have prayed they would someday go back covered in glory to their distant families.

My thoughts were full of such men—the Celts, Hispaniards, Illyrians, Franks, Syrians, Numidians—and of all those soldiers of the East and West whose scattered bones whitened with each passing day on the bloodstained plains of Mursa.

Standing before Jupiter's altar for returning men, I suddenly felt more Roman than Romulus or Remus themselves. For we were all part of the Empire's blood—my Gallic grandmother and my Numidian slave mother, my aristocratic grandfather and my proud and stubborn father.

I knew no particular prayers for the dead, so I swore an oath to their memory instead. I pledged that I would return to this shrine with Kahina, that I would wash our family name of the Usurper's taint, and that I would give Leo and his mother a secure and happy life from all the fruits of the restored Manlius estates.

The key to the deeds slept on my breast. I would find the missing deed box. All I needed was time and a little luck to give both the dead and the living the legacy they deserved.

After a long while, I emerged squinting into a brighter sun. I headed for the Subura district—nasty, slummy, lively and cheap. I needed new shirts, new socks, some city sandals and a haircut. If I wanted to feel alive again, it would be in the Subura, among men and women who grabbed the gift of every single minute with a passion and greed as if it were their last.

As I dove downhill and into the busy throng, I felt someone grab my tunic tail.

'Eh, Soldier? I heard your sword bang into something. Are you an honorable man?'

I looked down at a man crouched for safety against a graffiti-covered wall.

'I hope so, my friend.'

He was a disabled veteran, his uniform in tatters, still bearing the insignia of the Legio I Martia. He stared up at me through white eyes blinded by fire or oil. The shiny bloodless scars disfigured the upper half of his face.

'You served on the Rhenus?'

'Castrum Rauracense, guarding a bridge over the river. Took it full in the face from some fucking Alemanni with a bucket of pitch.'

'Bad luck, but I've just left 50,000 dead in Mursa, Pannonia. Take some joy from the day. Here's something for wine and a willing woman.' I dropped my loose change into his soiled lap while his fingers scrabbled for something in the bottom of an almost empty begging basket. He was fingering a coin over and over. His sightless eyes turned full up at the sky in concentration.

Now he grabbed me again and held the coin out to me without letting go of it. 'Don't steal it from a brother-in-arms.'

'I wouldn't do that. Why do you show it to me?'

'Somebody said it's a *solidus*, but how would I know? It feels funny. Is it the real thing?'

'Looks like solid gold. Lucky day for you.'

I was going to move on when he clutched at my boot cuff. 'But I don't recognize the profile. Please, is the money good?'

I examined the coin closely now as it rotated between his grimy fingers. I saw the large eyes and strong curving chin, the sharp long nose and the curling hair of Magnentius.

'Yes, don't worry. The man's gone now, too fast and bold for our times.'

'But it *is* gold?'

'Yes, it's gold. The metal always survives the man and the Empire's gold is as good as ever.'

The End

—Q. V. HUNTER—

Connect with the author at:
eyesandears.editions@gmail.com.

Did you enjoy this book? Then please introduce Q. V.
Hunter to new readers with your comments on Library Thing
and Goodreads or the book distribution platform of your
preference—Amazon, Smashwords, iBookstore, Kobo, or
Barnes & Noble.

GLOSSARY AND PLACES

Actium—a promontory in Western Greece
Aginnum—Agen, France
Aquileia—Aquileia, France
the Alsa River—the Ansa River, France
Arelate—Arles, France
armillae—gold armbands awarded for bravery
Atrans—Trojane, Slovenia
Augusta—honorific for emperor's wife or close relative
Augustus—honorific for emperor
Augusta Raurica—near Kaiseraugst, Switzerland, east of Basel
Augusta Taurinorum—Turin, Italy
Augustodunum Haeduorum —Autun, France
Augustonetum—Clermont-Ferrand, France
Augustoritum—Limoges, France
Avaricum—Bourges, France
biarchus—mid-ranked *agens*
Bononia—Bologne, France
bulla—a child's amulet
Brigantium—Vorarlburg, Austria
Brundisium—Brindisi, Italy
Burdigala—Bordeaux, France
carnificina—work of a torturer or executioner
Carnuntum—Petronell-Carnuntum, Austria
Carthago—Carthage, North Africa
Castra Peregrina—headquarters in Rome of the *schola*, the
    agentes in rebus
Castrum Rauracense—a river fort attached to Augusta Raurica,
    east of Basel, Switzerland
cathedra—a wide-seated armchair
Celeia—Celje, Slovenia

centenionalis—a large bronze coin introduced by Constans and Constantius to replace the *follis*, worth 40 *nummi*

Cibalis—Vinkovci, Croatia

circitor—one rank above *eques* in the five ranks of *agentes*

cisium—a small cart for a rider and minimum baggage, pulled by two horses

Chi Rho—the two first Greek letters of Jesus Christ's name, painted on his soldiers' shield by Constantine before his decisive victory at the Milvian Bridge, and later on coins issued during the Constantinian era

codex, codices—paged books bound to a spine, as opposed to scrolls

Colapsis River—Kupa River, Croatia

comitatus—suite of *comes* or counts, around the emperor

Comum—Como, Italy

conciliarum—councilor

consistorium—imperial council

contubernalis—tent-mate

contus—lance of four meters' length, requiring expertise

Cularo—Grenoble, France

cornicen—army signaler playing a brass horn, the *cornu*

cubicularius, cubicularii—bedchamber attendant

curiosus, curiosi—nickname slurring imperial agents

Cursus Publicus—the imperial state highway and postal system

dispensator—majordomo

Decetia—Decize, France

Divodurum Mediomatricum—Metz, France

draco, dracones—flying dragon, wind pennant

Emona—Ljubljana, Slovenia

eques—the lowest rank of *agentes in rebus*

fauces—small foyer or passage leading to Roman atrium

fibula—a large pin to fix tunics at the shoulder

evectio—a license to use the Cursus Publicus network

garum—fermented fish sauce

Gallia—the Roman province of Gaul, part of modern France

Garona—the Garonne River in southwest France, and northern Catalonia, Spain

Gates of Trajan—the Succi or Ihtiman Pass, Bulgaria
Hasta Pura—Arrow without a Head, a silver spear battle award
Hispanic Tarraconensis—north, central, east Spain
Horreum Margi—Ćuprijai, Serbia
imperator—emperor
imperatrix—empress
insulae—five- to six-story apartment blocks
labrum—washtub, basin, bath
latrunculi—two-player board game similar to Checkers
Londinium—London, England
Lugdunum—Lyon, France
Lutetia—Paris, France
magister equitum—Master of the Horse, a title revived in the
    Late Roman Empire, when Constantine I established it
    as one of the supreme military ranks
magister militum—Master of the Infantry, previously *magister
    peditum* under Constantine I, eventually amalgamated
    with *magister equitum* in the Late Roman Empire
magister officiorum—a senior imperial office created under
    Constantine (306-337) to limit the power of the
    praetorian prefect, until then the emperor's chief
    administrative aide
manceps—shopkeeper, contractor, also used for franchise
    holder managing a state
mansio, mansiones—Cursus Publicus relay station, or village
    providing services and horses
Mediolanum—Milan, Italy
Moesia—parts of Serbia, Macedonia and Bulgaria
Mursa—Osijek, Croatia
Naissus—Niš, Serbia
Nisibus—Nusaybin, Turkey
Oriculum—Olricoli, Umbria, Italy
ostiarius—gateman, porter, janitor
Pannonia—Bosnia and northern Serbia
Peninsula of Haemus—Balkan Peninsula, named after King
    Haemus of Thrace
petanus—peacetime riding helmet

phalerae—gold, silver, or bronze disks worn on the breastplate
Pisae—Pisa, Italy
popina—restaurant
praepositus—foremost (officer)
pugio—a short dagger
retiarius—gladiator fighting with a weighted net, dagger and
    trident
the Rhenus River—the Rhine River
the Rhodanus River—the Rhône River
Roma—Rome, Italy
the Sava—the Sava River in Croatia
Samarobriva—Amiens, France
Sardica—Sophia, Bulgaria
Servitum—Gradiška, Bosnia and Herzegovina
Singidunum—Belgrade, Serbia
Sirmium—Sremska-Mitrovica, Serbia
Siscia—Sisak, Croatia
spatha—a double-bladed Late Roman sword
taberna—tavern or shop
tablinum—study
thermae—public baths
the Tiberis River—the Tiber River
Ticinum—Pavia, Italy
tiro, tirones—recruits
Tolosa—Toulouse, France
torc—gold neckpiece awarded for heroism
Tomi—an ancient Greek colony, now Constanta, Romania
triclinium—dining space, either enclosed or under a trellis
tubincen—horn used for attack and retreat signals
turma—Late Roman cavalry unit of thirty men
Upper Sea—the *Adriaticum* or Adriatic
Vicus Helena—Elne, France
Viminacium—(near) Kostolac, Serbia
Vindabona, Noricum—Vienna, Austria
vir, viri—man, men
volo, voluntarius—a slave earning manumission through
    military service

vitulinum—vellum, expensive writing material from animal skin

HISTORICAL NOTES

Whereas the available records informing *The Veiled Assassin*, (the first volume of the *Embers of Empire* series) fall short on dates and biographical details, the source materials for *Usurpers* suffer from almost too much rich detail. One conspiracy after another surrounds the imperial clan. It's small wonder that the foremost contemporary historian, Ammianus Marcellinus, wrote so much about the dramatic rivalries of the post-Constantine I courts. His almost modern eye for the telling detail, such as the purple cloak discarded by the fleeing Emperor Constans, brings this turbulent period to life.

Some scholars dispute Ammianus' reporting as biased by his years of military service under General Ursicinus, but we have historians Zozimus and Zonaras weighing in with vivid accounts of their own, not to mention the clearly prejudiced description of Mursa from none other than that last Constantine ruler, Julian the Apostate.

The year 350 AD tossed up no fewer than three claimants for the western half of the Roman Empire—Magnentius, Vetranio and Nepotianus—at a dizzy pace. The uncharacteristic clemency shown to Vetranio by Constantius II, who murdered so many of his own family for merely *existing* as contenders for power, stands out. The loyal old soldier, renowned for his dogged pursuit of literacy into middle age, retired to Bithynia where he lived another six years after his public resignation—although how or why he died then is left to the reader's suspicions.

There are different dates set for the formal promotion of Magnentius' brother Decentius to Caesar. Some accounts time it before the June 350 declaration of Nepotianus in Rome, while others cite a promotion as late as mid-351 as a response to the elevation of Gallus.

Many supporting characters, including the warriors General Claudius Silvanus and Gaiso, (sometimes recorded as Gaison or Gaisco,) as well as the Treasury Secretary Marcellinus, are all historical figures that make their fleeting mark in the pages of history. They leave as many questions as answers in their wake. For example, I searched in vain for a fuller description of Gaiso's rank, full name, or military record. Despite his role in such a cataclysmic event, the full name of Marcellinus eludes history as well.

As for Paulus 'The Chain' Catena, his reputation is richly savaged by Ammianus who identifies him in Book XIV as a Spaniard and in Book XV as a Persian. Hence, I've made him a Spaniard with a trace of Persian in his ancestry, as it's unlikely a full-blooded Persian would have served in a Roman court of this era.

Other details about Catena are clear. He gained notoriety for his witchhunt across Roman Britannia for refugees from the defeated Magnentius camp. This campaign left a bitter aftertaste because he broadened his mandate into a vicious and indiscriminate purge of the elites of Roman British society. Catena then participated in the equally dramatic events surrounding the new Caesar Gallus, depicted in the third volume of the *Embers of Empire* series, *The Back Gate to Hell*.

Apodemius was also a historical figure, one of fewer than a dozen of Rome's powerful intelligence agents to find themselves 'outed' from the shadows by historians. His own role in the interrogations around the disastrous usurpation attempt by General Silvanus to come after this story, as well as the torture and arrest of Caesar Gallus was too noteworthy to elude Time's Pen.

The Manlius family was an actual old Roman clan, but both the Senator and his son Atticus are fictional attempts to bring readers closer to the dilemmas of aristocratic families coping with the 'usurpation' of new blood from both within and outside the family circle.

The eunuch Lord Chamberlain Eusebius lived and breathed. He drew particular venom from Ammianus

Marcellinus for both his backstage manipulation of Constantius II's mounting paranoia, and his ill-disguised greed for other people's real estate. The sarcastic Ammianus is the real-life source of Apodemius' quip in Chapter Five of *Usurpers* that the Emperor Constantius II has only '*some* influence' over the conniving eunuch.

The sadistic Constantia's individual travels before the years of her second marriage to her younger cousin Caesar Gallus are not well documented. However, her proclivities for torture and intrigue don't escape the master of juicy rumors. As Ammianus writes, 'Constantia's pride was swollen beyond measure. She was a Fury in mortal form, incessantly adding fuel to her husband's rage, and as thirsty for human blood as he.' (And if the author of '*The Decline and Fall of the Roman Empire*, Edward Gibbon, called Ammianus 'his faithful guide,' who are we to question such a poisonous portrait?)

In recreating events some 1700 years old, I tried not to be waylaid by minor contradictions. Primary sources differ on the location of Constantius' first days in conference with Vetranio, ending in Sardica. Some report the two men met in Naissus first and then moved to Sardica. I chose the simpler account.

I should also note that, to my knowledge, only Zonaras reports the appeasement sacrifice of a maid by Magnentius under the direction of a woman magician followed by the issuing of a blood-wine concoction to the troops. We'll never be sure of this episode, but Mater Magnentius' earlier career as a fortuneteller at Constantine the Great's court adds to the impression of an inherited family taste for the supernatural.

Like England's King Richard III, Magnentius was perhaps a victim of coloured propaganda written by his victorious enemies. They would be inclined to furnish evidence after his defeat that his barbarian nature made him unworthy to rule. One noted academic points out that it takes three generations of early historians to go from outright condemnation of Magnentius as a 'barbarian,' to less emotional and more factual details of his lineage and education as a descendant of barbarians.

—USURPERS—

It is hard to portray a man like Constantius II who presents us with a number of contradictions. Though ruthless enough to manipulate the army into killing off his family rivals for succession, he displays later efforts to restrain his vindictive side for the sake of maintaining the Empire's unity. Perhaps his overweening desire for concentrated, orderly resistance to outside threats explains all his actions.

Sadly, the best description of his person—Ammianus' sketch of an unmoving, unblinking visitor riding in taciturn glory on his first visit through the streets of Rome a few years after the Battle of Mursa—is not fertile material for fiction.

Perhaps the most intriguing to me of all the historical persons in this story is the virgin girl-woman Justina. She would survive to finish an extraordinary career as the powerful grandmother and doyen of the Valentinian dynasty nearly fifty years on. Her transitory role as the second recorded wife of Magnentius is an enticing hint at the charisma over others that she exercised to the full many years later. Her physical beauty stunned both male and female contemporaries a decade after the Magnentius episode and brought her to the attention of her sponsor's husband and her next suitor, Emperor Valentinian I.

She bore Valentinian four children and survived to act as regent during the reign of her son Valentinian II. She ruled over the Western Empire as a contemporary to the redoubtable Pulcheria who controlled the Eastern Empire as the regent of her little brother, Emperor Theodosius II.

I hope experts in Late Antiquity will forgive my ruthless compression of what was in fact a painful, drawn-out demise for Emperor Magnentius and his brother Decentius. For the sake of fictional pace, I've sped up the 'decline and fall' of one of the fourth century's most compelling and ambiguous figures. In reality, it took another year of mop-up battles, strategic harassments by Constantius II, and military defections for Magnentius to accept that his bid to reform the Empire was doomed. But fall on his sword he did, eventually. According to Julian the Apostate's *Orations*, he did so at the direct order of Constantius.

Roman ring-keys can be found in a number of museums. They vary in size and style. When writing of Laetitia, I pictured the kind of key that hinges over to curl into the palm, invisible to anyone looking at the ring band from the outer side of the hand. It would have been of the smallest scale typical of such items, both to fit on her finger and to be unobtrusive when secreted into a *bulla*.

Similarly, let no reader quibble with my description of the early 'Swiss army knife' Apodemius issues Marcus as he sets off to spy on Magnentius. One of these extraordinary all-purpose tools, complete with hinged spoon, is on display in the Antiquities Wing of Cambridge's Fitzwilliam Museum.

ACKNOWLEDGEMENTS

Adam, Alexander, *Roman Antiquities: An Account of the Manners and Customs of the Romans*, Collins and Hannay, New York, 1833

Banchich, Thomas, and Eugene Lane, *The History of Zonaras: From Alexander Severus to the Death of Theodosius the Great*, Routledge, New York, 2009

Barnes, Timothy D., *Athanasius and Constantius, Theology and Politics in the Constantinian Empire*, Harvard University Press, Boston, 2001

Brown, Peter, *The World of Late Antiquity*, Thames and Hudson, London, 1971

Bury, J. B., *The Cambridge Medieval History, Volume I*, M. Gwatkin, J. P. Whitney, ed. Cambridge University Press, 1936

Cameron, Averil, *The Cambridge Ancient History Volume XIII: The Late Empire, 337-425 AD*, Cambridge University Press, 1997

Cameron, Averil, *The Later Roman Empire*, Fontana History of the Ancient World, Fontana Press, 1993

De Tillemont, Lenain, *Histoire des Empereurs, Vol. IV Diocletian to Jovian*, Charles Robustel, Paris, 1704

Echard, Laurence, *The Roman History from the Removal of the Imperial Seat by Constantine the Great, to the Taking of Rome by Odoacer K. of the Heruli and the Ruin of the Empire in the West to its Restitution by Charlemagne, Vol. III*, Christ College, Cambridge, 1696

Flavius Claudius Julianus Augustus, *The Works of the Emperor Julian*, Vol. 1, William Cave Wright, transl., William Heinemann, London, 1913

Gibbon, Edward, *The History of the Decline and Fall of the Roman Empire*, J.B. Bury, ed. with an introduction by W. E. H. Lecky, Fred de Fau and Co., New York 1906, The Online Library of Liberty

—USURPERS—

Heather, Peter, *The Fall of the Roman Empire, A New History*, Macmillan, Oxford, 2005

Kelly, Christopher, *Ruling the Later Roman Empire*, Harvard University Press, Boston, 2006

Knapp, Robert C., *Invisible Romans: Prostitutes, Outlaws, Slaves, Gladiators, Ordinary Men and Women . . . the Romans that History Forgot*, Profile Books Ltd. London, 2013,

Goldsworthy, Adrian, *How Rome Fell, Death of a Superpower*, Yale University Press, New Haven, 2009

Goldsworthy, Adrian, *The Complete Roman Army*, Thames & Hudson, London, 2003

Marcellinus, Ammianus, *The Roman History of Ammianus Marcellinus during the Reigns of the Emperors Constantius, Julian, Jovianus, Valentinian and Valens*, Book I, translated by C.D. Yonge, Henry G. Bohn, London, 1862

MacDowall, Simon, *Late Roman Cavalryman AD 236-565*, Osprey Publishing, Botley, Oxford, 1995

Stambaugh, John E., *The Ancient Roman City*, The John Hopkins University Press, Baltimore, 1988

Wace, Henry, William C. Percy, ed., *Dictionary of Christian Biography and Literature to the End of the Sixth Century AD, with an Account of the Principal Sects and Heresies*, Hendrickson Publishers, Peabody, Massachusetts

Zosimus, *New History, Book II*, Green and Chaplin, ed., London, 1814

Also: deepest thanks to the online communities of:

Romanarmy.com, Jasper Oorthuys, Associate Webmaster, and Jenny Cline, Founder

LacusCurtius at the University of Chicago, webmaster Henry Thayer

ORBISvia at the Stanford University

Forum Ancient Coins and

Academia.edu

With special thanks to Macmillan Publishers, whose map was the basis for the map included herein.

About the Author

Q. V. Hunter's interest in Roman history began with four years of Latin study and university courses in ancient religions. A fascination with Late Antiquity deepened when Hunter moved to a two-hundred-year-old farmhouse in the vicinity of a former Roman colony.

Colonia Equestris Noviodunum was founded around 50 BCE as a retirement community for Julius Caesar's cavalry veterans. It was listed as the *civitas Equestrium id est Noviodunus* in the *Notitia Galliarum,* (the fourth-century directory listing all seventeen provinces of Roman Gaul.)

Noviodunum became Rome's most important colony along the Lake Leman—with a forum, baths, basilica and amphitheater. Its potable water came via an aqueduct running from present-day Divonne, France. It belonged to a network of Roman settlements radiating out from Lugdunum (Lyon, France) around the Rhône Valley. Caesar established these settlements to supervise the defeated Celtic Helvetii who were shifted there against their will after the Battle of Bibracte in 58 BC.

As a result of Alemannic invasions in 259-260 AD, much of Roman Noviodunum was razed but it flourishes again today as the Swiss town of Nyon.

Hunter is married to a self-proclaimed 'Ur-Swiss,' a descendant of Alemanni who settled farther north of Nyon in the Alpine lake region that gave birth to the three founding cantons of the Confederation Helvetica, i.e. Switzerland, in the thirteenth century.

They have three adult children.

Made in the USA
Middletown, DE
22 November 2017